An American Putsch

by

Matthew Legare

Copyright

www.matthewlegare.com

Black Mist Books
Paperback ISBN – 978-1-7323090-6-7
Ebook ISBN – 978-1-7323090-5-0

Cover Design by Caroline T. Johnson

Mailing List

Join my mailing list! You'll receive updates, deals, and the free prequel novella, *Conspiracy in Tokyo*! Just visit www.matthewlegare.com.

Thanks!

Author's Note & Acknowledgments

This novel is set in November 1934 and is written to reflect attitudes and mindsets that might be outdated. No offense is intended when using words that have fallen out of favor, instead it's merely to capture the zeitgeist of the Great Depression and people whose beliefs and morals might be different than us today.

As with all my novels, I am grateful to my friends and family, my readers, my cover designer, my editors, and my other half, Jenny.

November 1934

New York City

CHAPTER ONE

The night was cold and wet, filled with an evil dread. It was the same creeping fear that came just before going over the top, straight into the teeth of enemy fire. Mike Rafferty squeezed his eyes shut, reminding himself that this was Brooklyn, not France. However, the two men walking behind were members of his old platoon, blurring past and present even further.

He shook his head, but dark memories lingered. Rain also fell that November night in 1918, when Second Lieutenant Rafferty charged headfirst into a shell that gouged out his nose, leaving him a disfigured freak. The French had a name for unfortunates like him – *gueules cassées*, men with broken faces.

A prosthetic mask now hid his butchered flesh, but rain dribbled inside, itching terribly. Rafferty ignored it and focused on the mission ahead. He couldn't show weakness in front of his comrades. During the war, they'd slogged through hell for Lieutenant Rafferty and they'd do it again, loyal soldiers even out of uniform. They were about to fight another war, not for capitalist bosses, but for world revolution.

Sallow, gaunt, and with greasy blond hair, Eddie Gardner resembled a living ghost, eyes wide in a hollow, shellshocked gaze. A wool scarf couldn't hide a twisted scar where a German bullet sliced through his throat, silencing him forever.

Peter O'Hare was still intact, at least physically. A brute who brawled in Bowery pubs, O'Hare was simple-minded, but loyal to the core. All three comrades were Irish-Americans, veterans of the Fighting 69th Regiment, but only O'Hare had bright red hair and twinkling green eyes, highlighted by a ruddy complexion.

Misty rain swirled about and Rafferty pulled his flat cap down, sinking deeper into his leather coat. Silently, they walked deeper into Brooklyn's Canarsie neighborhood, to the very outskirts of New York City. Far from the glitz of Manhattan, Canarsie was dotted with warehouses, factories, and mills, half of which were abandoned husks thanks to the depression. The streets were also deserted, except for a pair of headlights, piercing the gloom. A truck lurched forward down Avenue N, trundling past them and back into the darkness. Rafferty checked his watch. Five till midnight.

On the corner of 80th Street, an imposing three-story warehouse spread out, its bottom windows alight in a pallid glow. It was the same address Colonel Lopez had given them, where he said the guns would be. Rafferty squinted through his glasses and surveyed the warehouse. Rain speckled the lenses, but it didn't matter. They were just for show anyway, meant only to hold up his prosthetic nose, creating a facade of normality, hiding the freak beneath.

Tactics and strategies drilled into him from officer training returned, revealing the best plan of attack. Storming the front door or the loading bay in back was suicidal, since they were only armed with pistols. However, according to Lopez, there was a small office on the third-story, making for a perfect entry point. Slinking through the shadows, Rafferty led his men around to the alleyway and underneath a fire escape.

Gardner and O'Hare hoisted Rafferty on their shoulders, allowing him to grasp the ladder. With one heave, he was on the platform, able to help Gardner and O'Hare up. They crept along the fire escape, slippery with rain, pausing in front of the third-story window.

Rafferty gripped his 1911 Colt automatic, the same pistol he'd used during the war. His pulse quickened, just as it always did before going over the top. He glanced back at O'Hare and Gardner, holding Colts of their own, ready for battle.

Rafferty rammed the butt of his pistol against the window, once, twice, and, on the third try, it shattered into tinkling glass. Smashing the opening clear, he crawled through, followed by O'Hare and Gardner, their wet shoes crunching the shards. The office was furnished with a desk, file cabinets, and two flags – one American, the other the standard of the National Crusaders, its fearsome bald eagle clutching a rifle and sword.

Footsteps pounded outside.

"Who's there?" a voice demanded.

The door creaked open and a soldier stepped forward, rifle at the ready. Rafferty squinted through his smudged glasses and saw a Doughboy, an American soldier from the World War, ready for action. Blinking through his daze, clarity soon returned.

The man wore the old-style Army uniform, a high-collar khaki tunic and "overseas" side cap but stripped of US insignia. In its place was a blue armband with a stylized eagle design, and three stripes on his sleeves. Not a soldier, just a Fascist gangster, a member of the National Crusaders, the Khaki Shirts.

Rafferty sprang up, pressing the pistol against the man's temple.

"Don't make a sound," he hissed in a whisper.

The Khaki Shirt nodded while O'Hare collected his rifle. Gardner leveled his rod at the Fascist's stomach, a gleam in his cold, shallow eyes.

"My friend there has an itchy trigger finger," Rafferty said. "But I'll restrain him if you answer a few questions."

"S-sure…"

"How many men are in the warehouse?"

"Five…another Khaki Shirt and three porters."

"Show us where the guns are."

The Khaki Shirt nodded, and Rafferty pushed him forward, keeping the pistol trained on his back. They traipsed out of the office and down to the second floor where a long catwalk extended over the main loading floor.

In the pale glow of overhead lights, another Khaki Shirt, rifle slung over his shoulder, watched three porters at work. The back gates were wide open, revealing the truck from earlier, parked in the loading dock. Using dollies, the porters brought large wooden crates out of the truck's bed, depositing them in the main bay.

Gardner covered the Khaki Shirt with his automatic, while Rafferty stooped over the guardrail. O'Hare crouched down beside him, the rifle steady in his thick hands.

Time to strike.

"Tell your friend to drop his gun," Rafferty ordered.

The Khaki Shirt glanced around, searching for some escape. A jab from Gardner's heater was enough to discourage him.

"Up here, Jones!" he called out, voice booming off the warehouse walls. The Khaki Shirt below jerked up, then fumbled with his rifle.

"Don't move if you want to live," Rafferty said. "My friend here was a sharpshooter in the war. Your head is practically a bullseye for him."

Still in position, O'Hare offered a mocking wave. The rifle slid off the Khaki Shirt's shoulders and clattered to the floor. All four men raised their hands in surrender. They knew the drill. Prohibition, and now the depression, had accustomed New Yorkers to stickups.

On the catwalk, O'Hare kept a bead on them, while Rafferty, followed by Gardner and the Khaki Shirt prisoner, traipsed down the stairs. Pocketing his Colt, Rafferty scooped up the discarded rifle and looked it over. A Springfield bolt action, standard issue for troops during the World War.

Lopez had been right about everything so far, but Rafferty needed to verify the most important detail. He heaved the rifle butt against one of the nearby crates, splintering the wood apart. More Springfield rifles were visible, nestled on a bed of straw, instruments of destruction destined for South America. The Merchants of Death – arms dealers and munition makers – were gorging themselves on that bloody war in the Gran Chaco, like vultures stripping a carcass clean. A veritable arsenal was stuffed inside these crates, just as Lopez said there'd be.

"Start loading these back on the truck," Rafferty said to the porters.

They stared back, dumbfounded. Were these fellow workers, proletarian comrades? By the look of their smudged, unshaven faces, they were overworked, underpaid, and desperate, but grateful for any job in this depression. They were to be pitied, even if they worked for one of the Merchants of Death. The Khaki Shirts, glowering in frustrated rage, were a different matter altogether. Just like their ilk in Germany and Italy, these Fascists were mercenaries of the boss class, hired to terrorize the proletariat.

Bloodlust rose within Rafferty but a sharp intake of breath cooled his anger. He remembered his first kill – a frightened German teenaged soldier in a muddy trench – and the empty, washed out feeling it left him with.

Instead, he gestured for Gardner to bind the two Khaki Shirts together. Misguided fools of the lumpen proletariat were to be pitied, not shot in cold blood. That punishment would be meted out to the Merchants of Death themselves.

"We don't want to kill fellow workers, so don't give us an excuse," Rafferty said, then gestured to the porters, "Now start loading those guns back onto the truck."

Another motion from the Springfield rifle spurred them along. Grabbing dollies, they loaded the truck bed back up, while the two Khaki Shirts fumed in impotent silence.

Fifty crates, some five thousand firearms – rifles, Thompson submachine guns, and pistols – stood in neat rows like building blocks as the porters snapped the truck door shut. Gardner went to work, binding them with leftover rope. Rifle slung over his shoulder, O'Hare drew closer with a dumb grin plastered across his simple face.

"Look, Lieutenant. Turkeys trussed up for Thanksgiving."

Rafferty didn't respond, keeping his rifle trained on the bound prisoners. A rasping grunt from Gardner announced they were good to go. Rafferty and O'Hare ditched the rifles, too cumbersome for the ride back, and they all hurried over to the truck. Gardner sat beside Rafferty while O'Hare took the wheel.

The engine sputtered to life, then shot forward into the night. Thick raindrops smacked against the front window, obscuring the barren streets of Canarsie to a murky haze. It didn't matter, since O'Hare, a laid off trucker, could drive these streets blindfolded. Rafferty allowed himself a triumphant smile. The mission was a complete success. Guns that would have been used on workers in South America would soon be turned on the bosses in a bloodletting that would dwarf the Red Terror in Russia.

For the first time in years, Mike Rafferty was glad he'd survived the war.

CHAPTER TWO

Few things were gloomier than Horn & Hardart on a rainy morning. Sandwiches, soups, and pies hid behind small glass doors, only a nickel each. For fifty cents, a man could eat like a king, even if he didn't have a castle. But despite the bargain rates, an automat was nobody's first choice for breakfast. Grim-faced patrons shuffled by like a funeral procession, wearing their worries like a second skin. The depression had added an extra five years to everyone, it seemed. Sounds of scraping silverware and drizzling rainfall outside filled the automat like a forlorn dirge.

A sad sight indeed, but for Max Dietrich, Horn & Hardart served as not only a restaurant, but also a meeting spot for clients too ashamed to enter his office.

"Sure you don't want anything?" he asked, before finishing the last bite of huckleberry pie, downed with a swig of coffee.

Across the table, the client shuffled in his seat, eyes sliding back and forth. Any member of the New York Republican Party would naturally be concerned about being seen with such an unsavory private detective.

"No, I'm fine. I'd like to discuss your work with us so far, Mr. Dietrich."

"Me too. Since the election is today, I'd like my final payment, please."

"They're predicting a Democratic sweep."

"You don't need to be a PI to see that. Dickstein is a shoo-in for reelection, even if his pockets are lined with graft."

The client tensed at the name, then lowered his voice. "The fact remains that you were hired to find some...*information* on him to aid our campaign but didn't deliver."

"Didn't deliver? Those written statements didn't count?"

"Dickstein accepting bribes as head of the Immigration Committee didn't help us in the polls," the client said through tight lips, "Besides, the 12th District is full of immigrants who bribed their way to citizenship, courtesy of Congressman Dickstein."

"That's not my problem. Maybe you should have run a better candidate. But after Herbert Hoover, a leper colony is more popular than the Republican Party."

"The average voter is a fool, Mr. Dietrich. They don't understand scandal unless someone is caught with their pants around their ankles. You promised *something* that would guarantee our victory."

"And you promised me another hundred once I delivered dirt. If accepting bribes to bypass the immigration quota isn't a scandal, then this country is even more crooked than I thought."

An irritated bristle, then, "Since the information you provided is worthless, we must renege on your final payment."

Anger tightened Max's throat, but he managed to say, "Is that so? And what if I decide to pay a visit to *The New York Times* and give an interview about our *agreement*?"

A sly smile. "We signed no formal contract. Given your reputation, Mr. Dietrich, we're not concerned about the press seeing you as credible."

Max sharpened his eyes into a razor stare. "One day, the shoe will be on the other foot. Someone will hire me to look into you and your friends. What skeletons are dangling in your closet?"

The client stood, then slammed a palmful of nickels onto the table. "We won't leave you empty-handed, Mr. Dietrich. Go buy yourself another cup of coffee and another slice of pie. Isn't that how that little ditty goes?"

An urge to toss the coins back in the bastard's face rose like bile, then slid back down. He'd need every cent he could get, since winter was just around the corner. Max's eyes followed the little worm as he slithered out, then took in the rest of the automat. People-watching always calmed him down.

At a nearby table, a woman sucked down a bowl of a ketchup in hot water – makeshift tomato soup. Still, she fared better than the man sitting at the table across from her. Bloodshot eyes and stubbled chin clashed with his suit, suggesting he was between odd jobs. Over endless cups of coffee, he pored through the classifieds in *The Times*. Him and every other schmoe in Midtown.

But even he wasn't as bad off as the down-and-outer near the entrance. Like a character from a Dickens novel, his emaciated frame hovered close to another customer enjoying a small feast -- ham and eggs, toast, baked beans, with a slice of pie, all for just twenty-five cents. Gaunt, shabby, and wretched, he was the epitome of a Forgotten Man, reduced to eating leftover scraps before the busboys cleaned up.

No matter how low you were on the food chain, there was always someone lower.

Max scooped the nickels into his pocket and walked out. A wave of misty rain hit him as he joined throngs of New Yorkers flowing south on Broadway. Shops were just opening up, those that still survived, dotted with posters of the blue eagle, symbol of the National Recovery Administration. Another one of President Roosevelt's New Deal schemes, the NRA attempted to prop up small businesses by implementing a labyrinth of confusing codes, discouraging cutthroat competition. Results were mixed at best, since unemployment remained north of 20%.

Still, Roosevelt continued to rely on a roster of egghead professors to guide the New Deal, his plan to lick the depression. Nicknamed the Brain Trust, they helped spawn even more alphabet soup organizations hoping to stimulate the economy. In addition to the NRA, there was the AAA, the Agricultural Adjustment Administration, the EBA, the Emergency Banking Act, and the CCC, the Civilian Conservation Corps, to name a few. Run by Army officers, the CCC was particularly popular, since it gave unemployed young men something to do, albeit build useless parks and bridges nobody asked for. Still, happy days weren't here yet, no matter what the rubes and boobs thought.

Pockmarking a few storefronts were posters proclaiming, "*Share the Wealth*," Senator Huey Long's campaign for some half-assed attempt at Bolshevism. Even fewer displayed a cracked bell, the symbol of the conservative Liberty League, surrounded by the slogan "*The New Deal is a Raw Deal.*" New York City had become the battleground of ideologies, a no-man's-land for morons.

On the corner of Broadway and 43rd, Max cut westward over to Seventh Avenue. Behind him, Times Square blazed with neon lights, clashing with the gray sky. Up ahead, the Paramount Theatre marquee twinkled, advertising Marlene Dietrich in *The Scarlet Empress*. For a moment, he wondered if the actress might be a distant cousin from the Fatherland. Maybe Fräulein Dietrich could float him a loan?

His office building loomed opposite the Paramount, somber and dull against the sea of lights. On the corner, a magazine kiosk overflowed with issues of *The New York Times*, *Daily News*, *TIME*, and *Photoplay*, but Max's eyes were drawn to the rows of pulps, each issue stamped with the NRA blue eagle. Even fiction was regulated these days. *Argosy*, *The Shadow*, *Doc Savage*, *Dime Western Magazine*, *Detective Fiction Weekly* – all offered escape for just ten cents each. But even these petty luxuries seemed wasteful nowadays.

Near the building's entrance, a hard-bitten bum hawked apples, five cents apiece. His clothes were damp tatters and thick stubble coated his sunken cheeks. His leathery face was haunted by a vacant stare, the type only a veteran could wear. If that weren't enough, a missing arm confirmed he'd left a good chunk of flesh behind in France. The Forgotten Man from earlier flashed in Max's brain. Scrounging leftovers at automats was bad, however, selling apples in the rain made even his cynical heart bleed. Every cent mattered now, but veterans *had* to look out for one another. Nobody else would.

Max tossed him a nickel and plucked up an apple, just as the drizzling rain thickened into a full shower. God always was quite the practical joker. If life had taught Maximillian Dietrich anything, it was that no good deed went unpunished.

CHAPTER THREE

Inside his office, Max set the apple on his desk, stripped off his soggy overcoat and fedora, then hung them on a coatrack. Dietrich Investigation Services was more a coffin than a business now, matching the rest of the fourth floor. Of the five total office spaces, only it and a collections agency remained.

When the stock market crashed in '29, Max had barely noticed it, having socked away enough coin to last years, with or without work. Reality hit hard in December 1930, when, during a bank run, his life savings went up in smoke, just like a magic trick. The depression followed soon after like some Biblical plague, leaving millions unemployed. Dietrich Investigation Services treaded water ever since, staying afloat by taking on any case, no matter how unsavory.

A small, outer office had held a secretary's desk, whom Max had laid off months ago, while the larger inner office housed him and what was left of his business. Now, only his own desk remained, accompanied by a few filing cabinets, two chairs, standing lamp, percolator, and a telephone, now cut off due to unpaid bills. Although barren, the office had all the necessary amenities – a small water closet and sink became a makeshift darkroom, and a leather davenport doubled as his bed.

You couldn't see clients in an apartment, so Max had broken his lease. All too late he cursed himself for renting a fourth-story office so close to Times Square. Rent was always cheaper below 14th Street. The money from that Dickstein job would have paid the bills till the end of February, but now he might be joining the army of the unemployed by Thanksgiving.

Perhaps he could take a stab at writing pulp stories in the meantime? Hell, he had plenty of cases he could rework for the detective rags. Standard rate was a penny a word, so after writing a few hundred stories, he might be able to pay this month's rent.

A longshot, but one thing was sure, he wouldn't head west like those dumb Oakies in the dustbowl, searching for a promised land that wasn't there. No, he'd stay and starve in New York City. There was no better city to die in. As the great New Yorker Al Smith once said – *'I'd rather be a lamppost on Park Row than the governor of California.'*

The rain beat against the window, reducing the view of the Paramount Theatre below to a wet smear, hazy with neon lights. Max gazed out, almost hypnotized by the dull glow, until a knock at the outer office door shook him out of his morning torpor.

"It's open."

A lean, broad-shouldered man entered with confident strides. His fedora and trench coat were damp, but that rugged, smiling face was instantly recognizable. Stern brown eyes matched a headful of chestnut hair. A strong nose sat above a squared jaw, while a cleft dug into his firm chin. Along with the muscular body of a sportsman, he was the spitting image of a real-life pulp hero; an actual Doc Savage, the Man of Bronze, made flesh.

Max stood, beaming. "Well, well, if it isn't Richard Osborn."

"Hello, Maxie."

They clasped hands, old comrades reunited. A spit and polish West Point graduate, Richard Osborn was an All-American hero – handsome and gallant. Especially when compared to Max Dietrich, the son of German immigrants, whose blond widow's peak, blue eyes, tall, lanky frame, and a pointed chin, sharper than a dagger, all resembled a stretched-out scarecrow. But their differences had faded away in the trenches, replaced by something akin to friendship.

"Hardly recognized you in civvies, Richard."

"It has been a long time, hasn't it?"

Osborn took a seat across from Max's desk, his brown eyes taking in the paltry office – a doodle rather than a painting. No doubt an Army officer squirmed at such haphazard furnishings, but Richard Osborn always made exceptions for Max Dietrich.

"Too long," Max said. "1929, if I remember correctly. Right after I set up shop here. Weren't you a captain back then?"

"I *was*."

"Well, you must be a major by now."

"Actually, I resigned my commission, Maxie, for something more important." Osborn revealed a gleaming wedding band.

"Congratulations, then. Who's the lucky Mrs. Osborn?"

"Cornelia Haskell."

The name echoed familiarity.

"Haskell…the arms dealer, right?"

"His daughter."

"That's why you resigned?"

Osborn chuckled. "There isn't much room for promotion in the Army these days. It's a skeleton force now. Hell, Romania has a bigger military than America."

"I'm sure the munitions industry pays better anyway."

"Always the cynic, Maxie! Still a bachelor?"

Max shrugged. "I prefer transactional relationships when it comes to women."

Osborn chuckled again, more genuine this time. "You're right, there *is* money in guns. Speaking of which, my father-in-law might have a job for you."

"What does an arms dealer need a shamus for?"

"I'll let him tell you." Leaning back, Osborn gave a knowing grin. "Don't play coy, Maxie. I know you need the work."

"What makes you say that?"

"I tried calling, but the phone's disconnected."

"A regular Sherlock Holmes. But you're right, Richard. Business has been slow. In fact, a client just stiffed me."

"Who?"

"The New York Republican State Committee."

Contempt twisted Osborn's handsome face. "Republicans, Democrats…Hoover, Roosevelt…all filth from the same manure pile."

"You noticed that too, huh?"

"This depression calls for men of action, not bloated politicians who blather on while our people starve. Congress is a vacillating mishmash of crooks, squawking about high ideals with little substance." Osborn held his head high. "That's why I created the National Crusaders."

"The Khaki Shirts?"

Osborn smiled. "Our nickname."

"I read an article about your boys roughing up some Communists. Didn't know my old lieutenant was such a big shot in that outfit."

"I try to keep out of the limelight. No interviews given to the lying press."

"*The Times* called you boys the 'American Nazis.'"

Osborn's features darkened, more menacing than the storm outside. "Filthy libel. The Nazi Party is run by degenerate homosexual perverts and Jew baiters. The National Crusaders is a respectable organization, modeled after Mussolini's Black Shirts."

A tense silence followed, punctured only by the steady drumbeat of raindrops. This wasn't the same cool-headed second lieutenant Max had served under. But the offense was understandable. While Adolf Hitler was viewed as a vulgar Hun, Benito Mussolini was the toast of American high society. Hell, even the *Saturday Evening Post* had translated his autobiography. Just last year, New York welcomed Italo Balbo, an Italian Fascist aviator, with a ticker tape parade. No German could expect such a warm reception. Max knew that from personal experience.

The distinction was clear. While German National Socialism was viewed a rebranded Prussian militarism, Italian Fascism was seen a legitimate political movement by many respectable citizens, one that might work wonders in the United States. More than a few Americans wished for their very own Mussolini to straighten out this wretched depression.

Still, Richard Osborn seemed like the last person to enter politics. A career soldier, apolitical to his core, dedicated to nothing except the US Army. And while the depression had birthed a variety of American Fascist parties, they were pale imitations compared to the absolute dictatorships in Europe, circus clowns striving to become ringmasters.

This sudden burst of political action, along with marrying a millionaire's daughter, reeked of a money-making con. While Fascism was far more odious than most politics – letters from relatives still in Germany convinced Max of that – he could always respect good graft.

"So, Richard, what's this job about?"

"All I can say is that it pays well but requires discretion," Osborn said, standing up. His posture remained firm and rigid, as if on the parade ground. "No contracts, no receipts, and definitely no cops. Do you have any qualms about taking a job from a Merchant of Death?"

Given all Max had seen in the trenches, he'd have preferred an offer from Count Dracula. Even if they survived that mess, a lot of decent Yank, Limey, Frog, and Kraut boys lost eyes, limbs, and faces just so men like Elias Haskell could earn a tidy dividend. But high-minded ideals were a luxury Max couldn't afford these days. Instead, he stood and slid back into his damp overcoat and fedora.

"Let's not keep Mr. Haskell waiting then."

CHAPTER FOUR

Elias Haskell lived on the Upper East Side, specifically on Fifth Avenue, the boulevard of New York's elite. Max sat beside Osborn in the backseat of a taxi, watching Central Park whiz by in a streaming blur. Last year, an enormous Hooverville – shantytowns named after Herbert Hoover – had consumed the site like a monstrous tumor, until the city cracked down and demolished it. A clear contrast to the elegant condominiums on its right, a demarcation between the winners and losers of life.

The taxi pulled up to a sleek, twenty story building, complete with an awning and garishly uniformed doorman. The rainstorm had thankfully thinned into a drizzle. After paying, Osborn led Max inside. The lobby was decorated in a series of black and gold triangles, zigzags, and chevrons, forming a modern art aesthetic. They strolled to the elevator, leaving damp footprints behind, quickly mopped up by an attendant.

"Fancy," Max said. "But why aren't we meeting Haskell at his office?"

"Mr. Haskell prefers to work directly out of his penthouse."

Possibly, or perhaps he couldn't afford the office space? The elevator dinged and they shuffled inside, greeted by a teenage operator, who brightened at their sight.

"Good morning, Mr. Osborn," he chirped, before shooting them up to the twentieth floor. They exited into a smaller lobby, then made their way to the penthouse's sitting room, decorated in the same dazzling designs. A sleek divan and glass coffee table, along with a grandfather clock made up the chic furnishings.

A butler appeared and took their hats and coats, allowing Max to inspect Osborn's charcoal gray Glen Plaid suit. A

Brooks Brothers item, no doubt, but one aspect in particular drew Max's attention. A red silk tie, matched together with a red handkerchief, made for a bold choice. Much more than Max's own blue herringbone blazer, which had seen better days.

As the butler retreated, another patter of footsteps drew closer. A woman approached, around thirty years old – tall, pretty, and smug. She strutted toward them with a swishing stride and clacking high heels. A yellow, frilly dress hung off her thin frame, and her brunette hair was fastened in a permanent Marcel wave. Eyeshadow and lipstick accented her already gorgeous face and gray eyes, molded into a coy indifference. No jewelry aside from a diamond wedding ring with a gold band accented her outfit, but it glittered brighter than Times Square.

"Cornelia, darling," Osborn said, taking her into his arms for a deep, passionate kiss, dragging on for several moments. Cornelia flashed a smile so brilliant it dimmed her sparkling ring, then finally acknowledged Max.

"Oh, is this your detective friend?"

"Maximillian Dietrich, the finest private eye in New York. Maxie, my wife, Cornelia Osborn."

"Richard exaggerates. I'm the only PI he knows."

Cornelia's smile seemed to harden. "Pardon me, Mr. Dietrich, but you don't look like a private detective. A librarian, perhaps..."

"In my business, Mrs. Osborn, it pays to blend in, not stand out. And I assure you, the only books I read are the pulps."

That pulled a laugh from her, haughty and condescending, but it was something. "Please, call me Cornelia, Mr. Dietrich."

"It's Max, but not Maxie, since that seems to be your husband's preferred method of torturing me."

"Well, Max, I hope you're as good as my husband says you are." Her smile dropped. "We can't afford to be wrong."

A flustered cough from Osborn. "Cornelia darling, perhaps Maxie should hear this from your father? How is the old man anyway?"

Shaking her head, Cornelia said, "Hasn't slept a wink since last night's call."

"Don't worry about a thing, darling. Maxie and I will take care of everything."

Cornelia nodded, but flashed a skeptical frown before sauntering over to the divan. Well, what had he expected? Old money types were all alike, concerned that some shamus would nickel and dime them on expenses but fail to keep skeletons inside their closets. Not that Max could blame her. Everyone, rich or poor, had something to hide.

Osborn gestured for him to follow, walking out of the sitting room and toward a pair of thick, oak doors, resplendent with ivory handles. Without knocking, they entered a spacious office, its massive windows overlooking Central Park. There was no modern art here, the atmosphere firmly rooted in the 19th century – maplewood floors and walls, high bookshelves, a stocked bar cabinet, and an enormous oil canvas depicting a battle from the Civil War, dramatizing Union bluecoats storming a Confederate position.

The other side held a portrait – a stern-looking man with thick sideburns and decked out in a frockcoat, one of the old Robber Barons from the Gilded Age. Below it was a golden plaque labeled "*Lucius Haskell, Founder.*" Apart from paranoia, vanity typified these American aristocrats. Next to the windows was a heavy wooden structure, resembling a miniature fort more than a desk, with two leather upholstered chairs in front. A glass stock ticker and mounted globe sat atop the desk, flanking a stooping figure, silhouetted in the morning sunlight.

"Mr. Haskell," Osborn said, "This is Max Dietrich, the man I told you about."

Stepping forward allowed Max a better view of Elias Haskell. Wiry eyebrows hung over cold gray eyes that sunk into deep sockets. High cheekbones sat above a slash-like mouth and jutting chin. Haskell's hair was a gleaming silver, but his sallow skin was scarred by mazes of wrinkles. A double-breasted black suit hung off his lank frame, a skeleton outfitted for his own funeral.

Osborn stepped around the desk, helping the old man to his feet, or rather, his foot, since one leg was an obvious prosthetic. Gripping a metal cane – solid steel, by the look of it – Haskell hobbled over and extended a shriveled hand. Max took it with a gentle shake, hoping Haskell's bones wouldn't crumble to dust. But despite a fake leg and gaunt body, this old-timer seemed animated with boundless energy and seething anger.

"Greetings, Mr. Dietrich," he rasped like a hissing snake. "Richard here has told me quite a bit about you." Something resembling a smile twisted Haskell's face. "Sit down, Mr. Dietrich. We have much to discuss."

CHAPTER FIVE

Max and Osborn took their seats while Haskell hobbled back behind the desk, a king returning to his castle.

"Care for something to drink? I have liquor dating before Prohibition." He gestured to a drink cabinet stocked with everything from Scotch from Glasgow to moonshine from West Virginia. All that was missing was a bottle of green absinthe.

"Maxie doesn't drink or smoke. But a devious mind hides behind that Boy Scout exterior."

Haskell heaved a brittle laugh. "That's right. Richard told me you were a Prohibition agent, right? Still on duty?"

"Something I learned as a Prohi was that alcohol reveals secrets best kept private," Max said.

"I'll bet you busted a lot of bootleggers?"

Max scrutinized Haskell's withered face for hints of duplicity. Clients tended to overestimate their cleverness, laying bait for traps. But as long as you knew what they wanted, they were easy to avoid. People hired Max Dietrich because they wanted a PI willing to snoop around in the dirt, not a discount Dick Tracy. Right now, honesty would work best.

"Provided I was being paid by other bootleggers. I only raided speakeasies when they got stingy with bribes."

"It sounds like the entire Prohibition Bureau was nothing more than a criminal racket," Haskell snorted.

"Well, we couldn't all join the Untouchables."

"Is that why you joined? For the graft?"

Max shrugged. "I read too many *Nick Carter* dime novels and *The Bradys* mysteries when I was a kid. Filled my head with fantasies of being some great detective, but when I came back from the war, there was a hell of a slump going on. The Police Department wasn't hiring, but my family had connections with Tammany Hall, so I got fixed up as a Prohi, the poor man's detective."

"Then why did you become a *private* detective?"

"The writing was on the wall. By '29, I knew Prohibition was on its way out. So, pocketing what bribes I could, I resigned and set up Dietrich Investigation Services. Richard was one of my first clients."

"Oh yes, you did a job for him, didn't you?"

"It was technically for Richard's commanding officer, Major-General Nathaniel Norris."

"Go on…"

"You see, Norris commanded our regiment during the war, the 358th. But afterward, he got kicked upstairs to the War Department and Richard here became his adjutant. President Hoover had just taken office was a real stickler for 'balanced budgets.' Apparently, General Norris was worried that a pacifist group, the War Resisters League, was pressuring Hoover to cut military spending."

"Oh yes, they think I'm the devil incarnate." Malevolent pride glinted in Haskell's eyes.

"I might be a close second," Max said. "You see, Norris hired me to snoop around on its members, to find any dirt."

"And what *did* you find, Mr. Dietrich?"

"Most were just grieving mothers and widows, but others were Bolshies, soaks, pansies, and slackers during the war. After promising not to air their dirty laundry, they backed off and Hoover agreed to a *slightly* bigger budget for 1930."

"Unfortunately, the Hoover administration cut military spending a few years later," Osborn said, voice laced with bitterness.

"You can blame *that* on the depression," Max said.

"Tell me Mr. Dietrich, what is your opinion of the Peace Movement?" Haskell asked.

Max considered his answer. He'd been one of those rubes who marched off to war, believing that idiotic slogan, "The world must be made safe for democracy." He'd prove that despite his German heritage, Max Dietrich was pure

American. Instead, he found himself crawling through mud and slime, dodging bullets from scared German boys, while men like Elias Haskell gorged themselves with profits. War was great graft, Max conceded, but in today's cutthroat market, he couldn't be choosy with clients. Always tell your mark what they wanted to hear, even if it burned your throat on the way up.

"Men have been killing each other since Cain and Abel, so I don't think any group or treaty will change that."

"You're referring to the Kellogg-Briand Pact?"

"What else? High-minded boobs thinking they could outlaw war? If Prohibition taught me anything, the more you ban something, the more people want it. Human beings love killing each other over slogans and flags."

"And the armaments industry? What is your opinion about men like me?"

"You mean the Merchants of Death?"

Max softened his comment with another wide smile, concealing his own bitterness. Few creatures made his skin crawl more than arms dealers. Gallons of blood and flesh had paid for Haskell's fancy penthouse and chic furniture. Especially galling was the way Uncle Sam tossed aside veterans who were too broken or bugsy to work anymore. But, Max reminded himself, the war was over. All that mattered was surviving this depression.

"You weren't very popular among Doughboys, I'll admit. Sure, machine guns and heavy artillery make it easier, but men can slaughter each other with kitchen knives and toenail clippers."

Haskell nodded, his worldview validated.

"Too true, Mr. Dietrich. Mankind has a bloodthirst that can never be slaked. That's what my father—" he pointed to the portrait labeled "*Lucius Haskell*," "—knew when he founded this company. During the War Between the States, he supplied the Federal Army with rifles, pistols, and cannons. Sherman's men marched from Atlanta to the sea with Haskell-made guns! But the newspapers called him a coward, just for sending a substitute."

"A substitute?"

"Back then you could send a man off to war in your stead, providing you paid him enough. But Haskell men are no cowards. We love this country and will sacrifice our blood for it." Swinging his feet out from behind the desk, he slapped his right leg with a hollow thud. "During the war with Spain, I volunteered and fought in Cuba. A bullet tore through my kneecap and took my leg, but it was a small price to restore our family honor. My son…my son solidified it…"

"Your son?"

Haskell choked back a flood of emotion. "Francis was a proud Haskell man. He served with the Lost Battalion and made…the ultimate sacrifice."

Max offered a sympathetic nod. During the Battle of the Argonne Forest, a unit of American troops had been cut off in German territory. Completely surrounded, they held their position for six days, beating back waves of German assaults. They were eventually rescued, but suffered grueling casualties. Dubbed the Lost Battalion, they were lauded as heroes, even though their shellshocked commander eventually killed himself out of grief.

Osborn sensed the welling sorrow and interjected. "Sir, perhaps it's time to share why we asked Maxie here."

The words brought Haskell back to reality, sharp and alert.

"Forgive me, Mr. Dietrich, but I have many enemies. Even though Richard vouched for your character, I must be cautious. Many private investigators are veterans, and many veterans despise arms dealers." Haskell leaned back, an ominous look spreading across his face. "Last night, five thousand guns, *my* guns, were stolen. And you must find them before it's too late."

CHAPTER SIX

Max took out a notepad and pen and started jotting notes.

"Don't you think it'd be better if there was no record of this?" Haskell asked, an order disguised as a suggestion.

Secrecy was one thing, but this was like reading a magazine in the dark.

"We know you can keep your mouth shut, Maxie," Osborn said. "Your past work proved that. It's why I recommended you for this job in the first place. But we can't afford any records getting back to the law."

"Aw shucks, that's the only reason? And I almost believed that crack about me being the 'finest detective in New York.'"

"Richard told me that you have connections with New York's underworld who might know something about last night's robbery," Haskell said. "These are useful contacts that more…upstanding private detectives might lack."

"It always pays to know a few crooks." Max grinned and shut the notebook. "Can I at least know who purchased the guns?"

Haskell leaned forward, his shriveled hands reaching around the desk globe. Twirling it around, a claw-like finger landed over South America, between the landlocked countries of Paraguay and Bolivia.

"Are you familiar with the war in the Gran Chaco?"

Roosevelt's New Deal and the economic depression dominated daily headlines, while foreign affairs were reduced to a distant second. However, tucked in between the back pages of the newspapers were reports of a brutal conflict in South America, the details of which were hazy at best. If the Great War had taught America one thing, it was that the world's affairs were none of her business. Besides, the average Yank didn't know the difference between the Gran Chaco and Timbuktu.

"Only in passing," Max offered.

"The Gran Chaco," Haskell began, "is an arid region of forests and fields that runs between Bolivia and Paraguay, a contested area for both countries. Over two years ago, a series of border skirmishes escalated into full-scale war, which has remained a stalemate ever since."

A concise explanation, but Max remembered a few editorials hinted at motives other than national honor.

"All this fuss over a wasteland? Surely there has to be more."

A smile stretched Haskell's taut, sallow skin. "You're more informed than you let on, Mr. Dietrich. Yes, it is speculated that there's oil in the Gran Chaco. As a result, Standard Oil has lent its support to Bolivia, while Royal Dutch Shell stands behind Paraguay."

"Ah, that makes more sense. And let me guess, you sell weapons to both sides?"

The strained smile drooped. "Haskell Munitions only sells armaments to Bolivia. We have a contract and I'm a man of my word."

"Sounds like a good racket."

"No, a good racket was the Orient some ten years ago. There were hundreds of warlords tromping across China, each wanting his soldiers armed to the teeth. Happy times for this company."

"Not like today, I assume?"

"No, not like today. Ever since Chiang Kai-shek cleaned up the warlords, Haskell Munitions lost its best market."

"And Bolivia is your latest customer?"

Haskell bristled. "You're quite blunt, Mr. Dietrich, but you're correct. To be perfectly honest, the depression has hit Haskell Munitions hard. Without this order, we'll collapse."

The posh penthouse, the fancy liquors, the dapper clothes – all just makeup on a corpse.

"Mr. Haskell, perhaps this would be a good time to renege on that contract and start selling to Paraguay."

"Unfortunately, we couldn't even if we wanted to, Mr. Dietrich. You see, my company is among the lower-tier armaments makers. At the top, you have the powerhouses. Vickers-Armstrongs, Krupp, and Schneider-Creusot."

"Pardon my ignorance, but you do make guns, right?"

A bitter sigh hissed through Haskell's cracked lips. "The depression has taken that from us too. Our Long Island factory went under two years ago."

"May I ask why?"

"On Memorial Day, 1932, a gang of Reds staged a protest out in front of it, convincing the workers to strike. They were arrested, but the damage was done, forcing the plant's closure soon thereafter." Haskell shook his head. "The smell of blood attracted sharks. Vickers-Armstrongs offered to buy me out, but I'd rather be dead than sell my father's company to a gang of Limey swindlers. Luckily, the Chaco War began soon after and Richard negotiated a contract with the Bolivian government. Although Vickers supplies most of Bolivia's weaponry, they come to us when they want a supply of cheap guns quickly. We can deliver five thousand rifles to them in under a week, whereas those Limeys take far longer. Usually, our guns are used to reinforce their outpost garrisons or for training purposes."

"Even though you don't actually make guns anymore?"

"That was only part of our business, Mr. Dietrich. Our factories used to manufacture weapons, some of our own designs but mostly contracted orders. But since 1918, my company has been the largest purchaser of second-hand and decommissioned weaponry. Our agents—" the gray eyes slid over to Osborn "—purchase surplus weapons from all over the world and store them at a warehouse upstate."

"How much of your inventory was stolen last night?"

"Nearly all of it. You see, this recent order was our biggest yet and cleaned out our entire supply. The payment we're owed will save the company from ruin."

"I see. And the guns were stolen from your warehouse upstate?"

"Not exactly. Whenever we receive an order, we transport the guns from upstate to another, much smaller warehouse in Canarsie. A sort of staging area, if you will. From there, it's loaded onto one of our speed runners."

"Speed runners?"

"Discretion is important, Mr. Dietrich. Crates of our weapons are smuggled out of the warehouse and onto speed boats. Then, after dark, they're whisked out to sea and loaded onto friendly vessels, away from prying eyes."

"Ah yes, bootleggers used the same trick. But why not drive them straight to the docks?"

Haskell frowned. "You're very inquisitive, Mr. Dietrich, but I should expect that. The Manhattan and Brooklyn ports are off limits, lest we alert the authorities. Therefore, we must store them in Canarsie until speed runners off Coney Island and Rockaway Beach are readied."

"Mr. Haskell, what's with all the cloak-and-dagger theater?"

"Congress passed an embargo in May, blocking all armaments sales to both Bolivia and Paraguay. Anyone who violates it faces a ten thousand dollar fine and two years in prison," Haskell sneered, like a skull twisting its mouth. "There was a similar embargo when all those Chinese warlords were killing each other, but we used intermediaries as salesmen, mostly Italians. Besides, back then, there wasn't this ridiculous hysteria around the arms industry like today. Now do you understand my need for secrecy, Mr. Dietrich?"

Max nodded, considering the implications. Well, this was no time to get cold feet, not unless he wanted to start a new career as a Forgotten Man.

"Do you have any idea who stole your guns?"

"My workers got a good look at the bandits, but I surmise they're nothing but hired muscle."

"And the brains? Perhaps Vickers?"

"Doubtful. We've kept our contract with Bolivia a tight secret. But I do have a prime suspect…"

Haskell rummaged through his desk, withdrew a slick magazine, and slid it across. Its cover showed an undersea diver scouring the wreckage of a sunken ship and was titled – *Fortune, March 1934*. The magazine of old money.

"Turn to page fifty-three."

Max flipped it open and read the title: "Arms and the Men."

"That damnable article is the source of all my woes. It's what inspired Senator Nye to start his self-righteous committee against us so-called Merchants of Death."

Just this year, Senator Gerald Nye, a country bumpkin from North Dakota, had launched himself to national fame by railing against the private munitions industry. Although America had emerged on the winning side in 1918, the lack of anything to show for it soured many Yanks toward their victory. A bitter resentment grew, along with rumors that America had been duped into sending her boys over there to satiate the imperial goals of Britain and France, and to reap profits for greedy bankers and arms makers.

Then along came Senator Nye with bombastic speeches, claiming that the Merchants of Death had masterminded America's entry into the war to enrich themselves, confirming cynical suspicions that had festered for years. He'd even set up a Congressional committee to investigate the arms industry. Max almost sympathized with Nye's crusade, but politicians were just as dirty as arms dealers in his book.

"That buffoon wants to nationalize the entire arms industry," Haskell hissed, ready to bare fangs. "We're his boogeyman, a cause he can ride to political power. I'd wager he's behind this. You see, Nye subpoenaed me to testify before his ridiculous committee next week."

Despite his age, Elias Haskell seemed animated and inflamed by hate and greed, the perfect cocktail for longevity.

"Why would a sitting senator hire yeggs to sabotage you?" Max asked.

"Nye is a publicity hound, Mr. Dietrich. Just like Elliot Ness held press conferences at Capone's stills, I imagine Nye will 'discover' my weapons in front of reporters. Then, I'll be fined ten grand for violating the arms embargo, and Nye will have bagged a Merchant of Death. Sharks like Vickers and Krupp are too big to catch, but Haskell Munitions is the perfect fish to show off."

"Do you know if the guns are still in the city?"

Osborn's thick voice cut in. "We've had no sightings of that truck they stole. My Khaki Shirts have been monitoring all the roads."

"But if Nye is behind this, they'll eventually head for Washington."

"Then you don't have much time, Mr. Dietrich."

"All right, but first let's talk money—"

"What are your rates?"

"Fifteen dollars a day, plus expenses."

"You'll get twenty a day, plus expenses, and a thousand once the job is done. Providing that you never speak of this assignment again."

"You'll get twenty a day, plus expenses, and a thousand once the job is done. Providing that you never speak of this assignment again."

Suddenly, that mask of wrinkles was the most beautiful face Max had ever seen. He fought off an urge to kiss the old man then and there, giving a grateful nod instead.

"Mr. Haskell, for that kind of dough, I'll trek into hell itself for your guns."

"That won't be necessary, Mr. Haskell, so long as you bring them back by the eleventh."

"Armistice Day? That's five days from now." Delivering a stockpile of weapons on the day the World War ended was just another of God's sick jokes. Max almost laughed, but bit back his amusement.

"That's how long I was able to stall the Bolivians. But beyond that, the deal's off and my company dies. We're all counting on you, Mr. Dietrich."

That didn't just mean the old man, Richard Osborn, and the pampered princess in the next room. It might be a bloody industry, but hundreds worked for companies like Haskell Munitions, people who couldn't quit jobs just because of Gerald Nye's lofty crusade. Besides, for that much dough, Max could swallow his distaste for the Merchants of Death.

He tapped the issue of *Fortune*. "Mind if I borrow this?"

Haskell waved a dismissive hand. "Just burn it once you're done reading it.

CHAPTER SEVEN

Max stuffed the magazine into his blazer, then followed Osborn out of the office and back into the foyer. Cornelia lounged on the divan reading *I, Claudius*, the latest darling of the literary world. Max couldn't help but wonder if the novel was an intentional slight at his own tastes. But then again, for society girls, snobbery was second nature.

"Cornelia, would you mind entertaining Maxie? I need to change before we head out to Canarsie."

Well, the matching tie and handkerchief were a bit obvious.

Cornelia tossed the book aside, smiling. "Of course, darling. I can't wait to pick his brain about the case."

Chuckling, Osborn strode away to a private room, followed by the butler.

"In over your head?" she asked.

"Don't worry, I can swim."

"Richard told me you were a joker."

"Only on the outside. Inside, I'm crying."

Giggling, she reached for a silver cigarette case and fixed a smoke between her lips. Max struck up a match and leaned closer. Her scrutinizing gray eyes ran over him.

"Still skeptical?" he asked, waving the match out.

She took a long drag. "Forgive me, but I've learned not to be too trusting, especially of private detectives. They're always looking to swindle you. Besides, Richard may like you, but I'm suspicious of anyone who doesn't drink or smoke yet still carries a matchbook."

"Richard mostly likes me because I saved his life."

"That's right." Cornelia blew out a puff of smoke. "During the war. The Battle of Saint-Mitchell or something?"

"Saint-Mihiel. A major victory for the AEF."

"The what?"

"The American Expeditionary Force. Just a punchy name for all the Yanks sent over there."

"Oh yes, that was a fun little ditty, wasn't it?" She whistled a few bars of "Over There."

"And as for the matches, they give these away at Horn & Hardart."

Cornelia gave a blank look and took another puff.

"You know, the automat…"

"What's an automat?"

"Where commoners eat slop."

She laughed out a cloud of smoke. "Just pulling your leg. Even *I'm* not that clueless. So, have you solved the case yet?"

"As usual, the butler probably did it."

"Somehow, I doubt that." Leaning back on the divan, Cornelia drew again from her cigarette. "My father is blaming Senator Nye again, isn't he?"

"What makes you say that?"

"Because he thinks Nye is out to ruin him."

"Hasn't the good Senator declared war against war profiteers?"

"True, but he has a committee to do that. Why on earth would a senator hire thugs to steal guns?"

Max shrugged. "Who knows? But I can tell you one thing about politicians…the corrupt ones are bad enough, but the sincere ones are much worse."

"And you believe Nye is sincere?"

"Maybe. The point is, he's a potential suspect. Unless you want to stop this charade and share your own theory?"

"Isn't it obvious?" Cornelia paused, blue smoke trailing from her cigarette throughout the foyer in long tendrils. "The Paraguayans. Tell me, how much do you know about the Gran Chaco?"

"I'm learning a lot lately."

"The long and the short of it is this. Paraguay's winning the war. Word is that they're preparing a major offensive.

Bolivia needs all the firepower it can get, hence their recent order from us."

"What about a rival munitions company getting rid of the competition?"

Dragging on her cigarette, Cornelia gave the idea some thought. "It's possible, but doubtful, even if they discovered our Bolivian contract. You'd be surprised how chummy the arms industry is."

"Do tell..."

"We're a sort of salesman for the big boys," she said, smoke pouring through her teeth. "We sell their used weaponry in China and South America to whet appetites, then our customers go to Vickers and Schneider-Creusot for the newest models."

"Very symbiotic."

"Yes, it is rather like a living organism."

"So that's what Richard is? A door-to-door gun salesman?"

She stubbed her cigarette out. "He *was*. Now he leads the National Crusaders."

"Right. I've read a few stories of his Khaki Shirts fighting with Communists but never knew he was their leader."

"I think it's wonderful! Cut all the Bolsheviks open and see if they're red on the inside!" She clapped her hands, then flushed with shame. "Sorry. You're not a *fellow traveler*, are you?"

"A business owner rooting for the Bolshies? That's a bit like turkeys eager for Thanksgiving. So, when did your husband set this outfit up, anyway?"

Cornelia thought for a moment. "June 1933. Shortly after we returned from our honeymoon in Europe."

"And that's when he quit being your father's salesman?"

Her pretty features hardened. "What Richard does now is far more important."

"Tell me, how did you two meet?"

"He didn't tell you?" Her gray eyes rolled. "Men. We met at a reception thrown by the Army, in January 1932. Richard was so striking in his uniform and swept me right off my heels." She let out a satisfied sigh, full of dreamy memories. "I lived in New York, he was in Washington…it was difficult. But Richard resigned his commission, and we were engaged within a month. How's that for a fairy tale?"

She practically melted into the divan with a contented smile.

"Quite romantic."

"So, as you can tell—" she spread her arms around the lounge "– I'm accustomed to the good life. Please solve this case. I wouldn't last a day in some Hooverville!"

"Or worse, eating at an automat."

Cornelia flashed a helpless smile, the very model of a damsel in distress. Max Dietrich wasn't much of a Prince Charming, more like a dragon who'd sell his services to the highest bidder. But Richard Osborn, strutting back into the foyer in a crisp military uniform, was a 20th century knight in shining armor.

Brown leather jackboots gleamed as he walked, but more impressive was the khaki tunic, held up by a Sam Browne cross belt. Gloved hands clutched a riding crop, adding even more authority to his attire. Completing the outfit, a side cap – nicknamed the "overseas cap" – covered Osborn's chestnut-brown hair, the same style they'd both worn in France. In fact, the whole outfit was the spitting image of a Doughboy – the American soldier of the World War. Except for one distinct difference.

All US Army insignia had been stripped, replaced with new regalia. Silver badges depicting a proud bald eagle, clutching a rifle and sword, adorned Osborn's stiff, high "choker" collar, epaulettes, and side cap. A final touch on his left sleeve was a blue armband emblazoned with a stylized red-and-white bald eagle, like the NRA thunderbird only more menacing. Head to toe, Richard Osborn was an All-American Fascist.

He presented himself at attention, insignia twinkling on his broad shoulders. The uniform was more a tunic than a shirt, but the "Khaki Tunics" didn't have the same ring to it.

"Very smart, Richard. Those are US Army duds, right?"

A small smile cracked Osborn's rigid composure. "They were. This model has been discontinued in favor of a new design with an open collar and white shirt. Haskell Munitions doesn't just buy used weapons, but also surplus uniforms."

"Better than leaving them for the moths, I suppose."

The smile dropped, his riding crop tapping against his boot. Apparently, Richard Osborn had thin skin when it came to his own *Fascisti.* He marched over to Cornelia and whisked her up in his arms. After another elaborate kiss, Osborn plopped her back down on the divan, next to *I, Claudius*, spread wide open. Then, clicking his heels, Osborn's arm shot out in a Roman-style salute that would have made Mussolini proud.

Cornelia raised her chin high, her slender arm returning the salute in a display of Fascist romance. Max's own warning replayed in his mind. Corrupt politicians were bad enough, but the sincere ones were much, much worse.

CHAPTER EIGHT

Osborn drove Elias Haskell's private Packard over to Canarsie, parking across the street from a looming three-story warehouse. The ride over had been a trip down memory lane, reminiscing about the war. Specifically, the Battle of Saint-Mihiel, where they'd netted fifty prisoners, thanks to Max's fluent German.

They hopped out of the Packard and Osborn marched into the warehouse, Max trailing behind. His former lieutenant always led from the front. Inside, they were greeted by a dozen Khaki Shirts, arms raised.

"Salute the Chief!"

Osborn returned the gesture. "At ease, Crusaders."

The Khaki Shirts resumed their duties. Max leaned closer to Osborn and whispered, "Chief?"

Osborn's handsome face glowed. "Italians follow a duce, Germans a führer. Americans are led by a chief!"

"Ah, so that's what that little bird on your collar stands for."

Osborn nodded. "Our privates are named crusaders," he said, pointing to a Khaki Shirt with a single stripe on his sleeve. He indicated another wearing two stripes – "Crusader second class" – and one wearing three – "and crusader first class."

"And officers?"

"Squad leaders wear a gold rifle crossed with a sword, and function as subaltern. Troop leaders wear silver versions and command field offices."

Field offices? How many Khaki Shirts were there? Max dismissed the thought and focused on the matter at hand.

"So, this is where it happened? Who saw the suspects?"

Osborn snapped his fingers, beckoning a Khaki Shirt officer in a Sam Browne belt with thin lips, beaked nose, and eyes like lumps of coal. Gold rifle and sword badges on his side cap, collar, and shoulders twinkled in the pale overhead lights like little constellations.

"Squad Leader, this is Max Dietrich, a private investigator in our employ. Maxie, this is Squad Leader Grant Kilmer, one of my most trusted officers. His squad forms my personal bodyguard detachment."

Max whistled. His old CO had become quite the big shot. Hitler had his SS and the *Moschettieri del Duce* guarded Mussolini with their lives. Why shouldn't the Khaki Shirt Chief have his own Praetorian Guard? After all, politics these days was akin to gang warfare.

Osborn waved his hand and ordered Kilmer to, "bring the witnesses."

Kilmer saluted, then swaggered across the warehouse grounds, soon returning with three men in workman coveralls. Porters, no doubt, followed by two dejected-looking Khaki Shirts.

"We found them tied up this morning, Chief."

"Disgraceful. You let bandits rob us! I should have you all flogged."

The crew traded nervous glances, suggesting that it wasn't an idle threat.

"You three" – Osborn's riding crop rose to the porters with a hiss – "get out and don't breathe a word of this to anyone. You'll be interned at the Long Island camp until we need you again." He turned to one of the Khaki Shirts. "Crusader Jones, you will escort them along with Squad Leader Kilmer."

A nod dismissed them, and following Kilmer, they marched back across the warehouse, out of sight. Only one Khaki Shirt remained, a thickset figure with wide shoulders, with a weathered face in a perpetual snarl. Sharp blue eyes above a bristly mustache, flitted back and forth between the Chief and Max. A typical bully boy, drawn to this type of rough politics.

"Crusader First Class Bill Compton," Osborn said, jerking the Khaki Shirt to attention, "This is Max Dietrich, a private investigator. You will relay every detail from last night to him."

Compton's frame eased a little. "Y'see, it started a little after midnight. The truck from upstate had just arrived when I heard some ruckus upstairs. When I went to inspect, three intruders ambushed me."

"All carrying guns?"

"Yeah, Colt automatics."

"Sounds like they knew how to handle weapons. Think they were vets?"

Compton shrugged. "Probably. Two of 'em looked chewed up."

"Describe them."

Compton's snarl grew more vicious. "One looked like a big, dumb Mick. Typical Paddy, red hair and all. The other was some kind of mute. Pale and scrawny. Couldn't even talk on account of his throat. Looked like he took a bullet in the pipes."

"And the third?"

A contemptuous growl. "Some sort of freak. Had one of those masks with glasses and a phony nose. They're easy to spot."

"A prosthetic?"

Compton offered a blank look.

"Never mind. Anything else?"

"Mentioned somethin' about 'fellow workers' like some kinda Bolshie."

Max assembled the details into a coherent narrative. They could be hired henchmen, but the fact that they'd stolen from Elias Haskell, a hated war profiteer, and that crack about "fellow workers" suggested an ideological dimension. The Merchants of Death had many enemies, but hadn't Haskell mentioned factory strike back in May '32?

"What happened then?" Max asked.

Humiliation burned through Compton. "They tied us up and ordered all the guns loaded back onto the truck, then left."

"What's the vehicle's make, model, and license plate?"

Compton answered with a blank stare.

"A green Mack truck, Model AC. Tag number is 534-765," Osborn cut in. "We can continue the discussion in the upstairs office."

"Thanks, but I'd like to look around here first."

"Go right ahead, Maxie."

The warehouse was empty, save for a few pallets and crates. Most were sealed shut, but a few had been pried open, revealing stocks of canned foods and reserve rations. It was the same chow all Doughboys ate during the war, as if the Khaki Shirts were planning for a field campaign. Other than that, there was nothing, and Max followed Osborn upstairs.

CHAPTER NINE

They entered a small side office overlooking the entire warehouse. The chill from outside hissed in through a shattered window, while shards of glass glittered in the afternoon sun. Crude, but effective. The rest of the office remained untouched.

An eye-catching poster dominated the room, showing a Khaki Shirt, arm stretched out in a Fascist salute, guided by the spirits of Washington and Lincoln. Below, a bold font proclaimed, "*The National Crusaders Stand For 100% Americanism!*" In the corner, the Stars and Stripes hung alongside the Khaki Shirt flag – a blue standard bearing the National Crusader eagle.

"I half-expected a portrait of Mussolini," Max kidded, getting a frown from Osborn.

"Fascism is for Italy, whereas National Socialism is tailored to the German soul. The fasces and the swastika are foreign to the American eye, and therefore unsuitable for the National Crusaders." He swept his hand toward the eagle flag. "Our people demand native symbols to salute. The bald eagle, the Stars and Stripes, Washington and Lincoln...these are the icons for our movement."

"Star-spangled Fascism?"

Another, even deeper frown. "Our movement is not a mere facsimile of Fascism, but a new form of Americanism, designed to invigorate the country and propel it into the future."

Americanism – the peppy slogan that meant just about whatever you wanted it to mean. It'd been on everyone's lips during the World War, a backlash against "hyphenated Americans" and possible foreign allegiances. Instead, it emphasized an extreme loyalty to the United States above race, creed, and heritage. A lovely fairy tale, one Max Dietrich had bought hook, line, and sinker.

But that was the past. Now, Max just nodded and slid his gaze toward a map hanging just above Osborn's desk. It showcased the entire Eastern Seaboard, highlighting regional Khaki Shirt field offices in New York, Philadelphia, Baltimore, and Washington DC. A private army had sprung up in Uncle Sam's backyard.

"How many men are under your command?"

Osborn shifted, then glowered at the impertinence.

"Come now, Richard. I need to know these things."

"Five thousand in New York, and five thousand along the East Coast. We don't have any office out west…yet."

Ten thousand nationwide? Nothing to sneeze at, but perhaps *army* was a bit of a stretch. Osborn would need a hundred thousand more if he was going to become the American Mussolini. Max surveyed the office. On top of the desk was a rotary telephone, along with neatly stacked paperwork – membership applications, uniform guides, and field office communiqués.

"Anything missing?"

"Thankfully, no. They were here for the guns. Think the Communist Party is behind it?"

"Perhaps. Where's the order invoice?"

A hush fell across the room. "Unfortunately, I'm not at liberty to share private company documents."

"Richard, this only works if I have access to all pertinent information."

"Mr. Haskell's orders. No papers, no receipts, no records. Sorry, Maxie."

"Fine then. So those two bruisers were the only ones on guard duty?"

"Yes."

"Something bothers me about that. Only three intruders broke in? How did they know they wouldn't be mowed down by an army of trigger-happy Khaki Shirts?"

Osborn's eyes narrowed. "What are you implying?"

"That they had an inside man who tipped them off that security was light."

"Impossible." Osborn swished the crop through the air. "Compton and Jones are stupid but loyal to the core."

"And the porters?"

"Unlikely. They're housed upstate and didn't know of the Bolivians' order until the last minute. A short time to coordinate a robbery."

"Why were only two men on guard duty?"

"Most National Crusaders are stationed out in Long Island. We have a camp there for training, on the grounds of Haskell's old factory."

"Training for what?"

"Politics, marching, street fighting. Our members are all veterans, but they've grown soft potbellies. We retrain them out there."

"That must cost a lot of dough. How much are your Khaki Shirts paying in dues?"

Osborn's face went cold. "I don't charge my men fees. Their loyalty is payment enough."

"Then, who's funding all this?"

"Mr. Haskell, of course."

Max nodded, but doubt crept in. Quite a lot of money to spend when your company was near death.

"What are they training for? Another war?"

A darkness swept over Osborn. "We are already at war, Maxie. The Communists are rallying, just like they did in Russia, ready to overthrow this rotten system. If the cops are incapable of holding back this Red menace, then the National Crusaders will fight them in the streets, in the fields, and in the sewers if need be."

Max nodded along. Since the depression began, political violence had been on the rise, pitting Communists against a cavalcade of far-right groups. During Prohibition, the Ku Klux Klan had claimed millions of members, but now its white hoods and secret rituals seemed old hat compared to modern Fascist parties, parading around in colored shirts.

The Silver Legion of America – the Silver Shirts – down in North Carolina screamed about Jewish blood libel, while the New York-based Friends of the New Germany promoted a friendly portrait of Adolf Hitler.

There was also Senator Huey Long – the Kingfish – that loudmouth from Louisiana whom some considered a Fascist and others insisted was a card-carrying Communist. Now Richard Osborn and his National Crusaders were on the march. The winds were blowing away from democracy and toward the lunatic fringe.

"Mind if I use your phone?"

"For what?"

"I have an old pal in the Police Department who might be able to help us out. Works in records now."

Osborn slapped the riding crop against the desk. "No! You heard Mr. Haskell. If this gets back to Senator Nye—"

Max held up placating hands. "He won't hear anything, I swear. Trust me, this guy is more yegg than cop. We worked together during Prohibition. Helps me out all the time and keeps his mouth shut. For a price, of course."

A few moments of hesitation passed, before Osborn gave a reluctant nod. Max plucked up the phone and asked the operator for Police Headquarters in downtown Manhattan.

"Sergeant Frank Burks please."

Minutes elapsed before a gravelly voice came through.

"Burks here."

"Hiya, Burksy."

"That you, Dietrich?" The gruff voice lightened a little.

"Who else? Listen, I got a favor to ask."

"Let me guess. Arrest records on some politician?"

"Close. I need some information about a radical. The Red Squad might have something."

"Gonna need more details than that."

"Wears glasses and a veteran, so he must be in his thirties or early forties. Has one of those prosthetic masks with a fake nose. He's what the French called a…" Max fumbled for the term.

"*Gueules cassées*," Osborn chimed in.

"Right, *gueules cassées*. A man with a broken face should be easy to spot."

"Could take time, Max. Lotta pictures to go through."

Max glanced over to Osborn, impatient and scrutinizing. Time wasn't on their side. He'd need to zero in on the likeliest time period this man might have been arrested. All signs pointed to one date.

"Limit your search to any Bolshie arrested between May and June, 1932. Snag whatever photographs meet that description and I'll have someone ID them."

"Meet ya at McSorley's?"

Of course Burks wouldn't turn down an opportunity to drink himself stupid at his favorite tavern. Which meant Max would foot the bill.

"Sure, at half-past five."

He hung up and turned back to Osborn, straining the crop in his hands.

"You'd better be right, Maxie. We can't afford any mistakes."

Jekyll had suddenly become Hyde, and the change was frightening. If there was one thing Max had learned in dealing with Prohibition mobsters, it was that ingratiating yourself was key to survival.

"You can count on me, Richard. But I'm going to need to grease a few palms."

Osborn opened a pocket on his tunic and handed over a thick envelope of cash. Max flipped through rows of tens and twenties adding up to over two hundred clams.

"Very generous."

"Mr. Haskell said to spare no expense. Like I said Maxie, this is the most important case you'll ever work. Don't let me down."

Max tucked the envelope into his overcoat, next to the issue of *Fortune* magazine.

"I'd like to borrow Compton for a few hours. Mind giving us a ride to McSorley's?"

Osborn nodded, then began rummaging through the desk. He pulled out a thin blue book titled *100% Americanism, a political manifesto, by Richard Osborn, Chief of the National Crusaders.*

"Something to read," he said, handing it over. "Maxie, I know you're disillusioned with America. Hell, you have every right to be. So was I. This country is drowning in corruption, graft, and weakness."

"You noticed that too, huh?"

Osborn ignored the joke, too enraptured by his own words. He straightened, riding crop tucked under his arm, a commander ready to bark orders. "What happened in Italy is possible here. Just read that book and you'll see. Behind your cynical facade lies the soul of a patriot."

Max pocketed the manifesto and nodded. Perhaps he'd ingratiated himself a little too much.

CHAPTER TEN

McSorley's Old Ale House was an Irish saloon on 7th Street in the Lower East Side. Dating back to the Civil War, it was one of the few bars that survived Prohibition by selling watered down piss called "near beer." But in 1933 McSorley's returned to its roots, boasting the slogan "*Good Ale, Raw Onions, and No Ladies*" since only men were allowed inside.

The interior décor was stuffed with knick-knacks, old newspapers, sawdust floors, and a fastened pair of handcuffs on the bar rail, left behind by Harry Houdini himself. Years ago, Max had his last beer here, just before shipping off to France. Wishbones hung off an overhead lamp, left behind by Doughboys as a sign of good luck.

After Osborn dropped Max and Compton off, they took a table near the back. The Khaki Shirt chief claimed he had other business to attend to, but most likely he didn't want to set foot in such a dive. Besides, a 100% American would balk at the Irish atmosphere, accompanied by an entirely Irish staff. All that was missing was a Paddy belting out "Danny Boy."

Most of the clientele consisted of unemployed riff-raff and day laborers, hunched over half-drained beers. A waiter plopped down an entire tray of dark ale – McSorley's always served half pints – along with raw onions and cheese. Compton downed a beer in large gulps, spilling a little on his lapels. Before leaving Canarsie, Compton had changed into a threadbare suit so as not to attract attention, reducing this fearsome Khaki Shirt into just another Forgotten Man.

"Ain't you gonna have any?" Compton asked with foamy lips.

"No, but save some for my pal, okay?"

"So, you think it was some Bolshie with a rap sheet?"

Max swallowed some cheese, then shrugged. "Just a hunch. If these guys are robbing entire gun shipments, chances are they have records."

"Goddamn Reds," Compton spat out the word with a bit of onion. "We'll pay 'em back real soon."

"How long have you been with the National Crusaders, Mr. Compton?"

"Over a year now. Got laid off from my job at the meat packing plant and was floppin' in a Hooverville. Chief Osborn came through one day on a recruiting drive, looking for vets."

"Just veterans?"

Compton sipped another beer. "Didn't have to fight in the war s'long as you had military service. The Chief is looking for soldiers, not eggheads."

A good point, especially if they were going to conquer the Communists in the streets. But a creeping uncertainty left Max wondering *who* was behind this. Elias Haskell was on the verge of bankruptcy, or so he'd said.

"Tell me, Mr. Compton, are you and the other Khaki Shirts paid?"

After a large swig of ale, Compton said, "Only squad leaders and above earn any dough. Enlisted men like myself get free lodging at the Long Island barracks and three squares a day."

"I see. And you don't pay dues?"

"Nope. Mr. Haskell takes care of all that."

"I see. What does Haskell get out of this?"

"We moonlight as strikebreakers." Compton smacked his fist into an open palm. "Cracked a few Bolshie skulls with my bare hands."

Max took a mouthful of cheese, letting his mind wander. Funding a ten-thousand-man army would bleed anyone dry. What was the angle? Sure, Elias Haskell retained a loyal army of strikebreakers, but the return on investment seemed paltry. Unless he monetized them.

"Only for Mr. Haskell?"

"Nah. We busted heads for Standard Oil, Bethlehem Steel, Du Pont, and a few others. All in civvies, of course. The Chief doesn't want bad publicity."

"Of course."

Well, that made more sense. Perhaps Haskell was renting out his Khaki Shirts as Strikebreakers Inc. to cover business losses? The front door opened, tearing Max out of his theories. A thickset police officer strutted across the bar and straight toward them. His eight-point cap shadowed a round, ruddy face while a paunchy gut strained against his long blue "horse blanket" overcoat. But the gold chevrons on his sleeves granted Sergeant Frank Burks some degree of authority, even though he'd spent the last few years fattening up behind a desk in the Records Department.

He and Max had made a good team during Prohibition, shaking down bootleggers and speakeasies. Those days were long gone, but they'd remained friends ever since, comrades in graft.

"How're ya, Dietrich?" Burks said after a rough handshake.

"Always happier when I see you, Burksy."

The Sergeant pulled up a chair and gave Compton a pleasant smile.

"Your new assistant?" Burks asked, already slurping down a half-pint.

"No, part of a case I'm working. Speaking of which…"

Burks wiped his mouth, then fumbled inside his horse blanket coat, whipping out five mugshots, fastened together with a safety pin. Max took the photos, then slid them over to Compton. The Khaki Shirt flipped through them and within seconds, his eyes flared.

"That's him. The fourth one."

Max glanced at the photo. A haunting ghost glared back behind glasses, underneath a mop of brown hair. A firm slit passed for a mouth, while a prosthetic mask, attached to the glasses, reconstructed his nose, hiding whatever horrors lurked beneath.

Burks set his beer down and pulled out a small notepad. "Let's see…number four…ah, Michael Rafferty. Graduated from Columbia University in 1917 and served as a second lieutenant in the 69th Regiment. Say, wasn't that a Paddy unit?"

Max nodded. "The Fighting Irish of the Fighting 69th."

"Not much about Comrade Rafferty until Memorial Day 1932, when he was arrested for causing a riot. Led a strike at the Haskell Munitions factory. Got ugly real fast. Lots of arrests that day."

"So I heard," Max said, letting the information simmer in his mind. First, Rafferty ruins Haskell's factory, then steals the old man's guns. Another political stunt? Or something more personal? "Where's this guy now, Burksy?"

"Last known address was in Harlem."

"Harlem? Guess Reds and jigaboos go together," Compton cut in, between sips of beer.

"That's everything you have on Rafferty?" Max asked.

"Everything that was in his file. Speaking of which, this peep show ain't free."

Max slid fifty bucks over. Burks stuffed the bills and photos into his horse blanket coat, then threw back another pint.

"Have a few more on me," Max said, sliding over another fiver, along with his notebook and pencil. "Just give me Rafferty's address."

Burks shrugged, palmed the five, then scribbled down an address. Max returned the notebook to his overcoat pocket, then stood up. Compton bolted to his feet, a vicious gleam in his bleary eyes.

"We're going Red hunting?"

"No, you're going to stay here and drink yourself stupid. The last thing I need is a lynch mob behind me," Max said.

"But I—"

"Keep an eye on him, Burksy. See that he finds his way back to Canarsie."

Compton slumped back into his chair.

"Don't worry, Dietrich. We'll have a great time."

Max headed toward the door. There was no time to waste. Mike Rafferty was waiting.

CHAPTER ELEVEN

The room was dilapidated, but Rafferty had seen worse. New York tenements were infamous for filth. Although he had lost his ability to smell long ago, Rafferty sensed a musty odor hanging in the air. Cracked walls, dim lighting, and cramped quarters aside, this flophouse was a suitable hideout. Its squalidness served a purpose, since the rickety floorboards were easy to remove.

Gardner pulled up a loose plank, revealing a large pit below. Rafferty placed two full-sized Thompson submachine guns inside, along with five extra drums of bullets. A little bonus for all their hard work.

A knock rattled the door. Rafferty glanced at his wristwatch – six o'clock sharp. Military men were always punctual. Gardner set the planks back down and covered them with a dingy rug. Rafferty walked across the room and answered. Despite a soggy trench coat and drenched fedora, Colonel Juan Lopez stood stiff and imperious. His round face and dark eyes were impassive, but a twitch in his waxed mustache betrayed annoyance.

Rafferty welcomed him in and locked the door. A faint disgust curled Lopez's plump lips. Was it his face? No, the mask held firm, hiding the mass of shredded skin.

"What do you have to report?" Lopez asked, his Latin accent lacing every word.

Rafferty beamed in triumph. "The mission was a complete success."

"And the guns?"

"They're being held at the Liberty Warehouse in Red Hook. Unit 20. Just across the East River. O'Hare is guarding them."

Lopez's mustache relaxed as his head bobbed up and down. "Good! My superiors will be pleased."

Gardner let out an irritated hiss.

"What does he want?" Lopez asked.

"Our payment," Rafferty answered.

"Are you Communists or businessmen? What would your Comrade Stalin say about such devotion to money?"

"We follow Trotsky, Colonel, not that Red Fascist in Moscow. The two grand you promised, please."

"Do you not support Paraguay's struggle against the aggressor?"

An insulting statement. The entire Left knew that the Gran Chaco was Paraguay's rightful territory, but this bloody masquerade had been concocted by oil companies and the arms industry. Both Paraguay and Bolivia could benefit from revolution, killing a few thousand of their own bourgeoisie. For now, Mike Rafferty would concern himself with his own country.

"That's not our business, Colonel. Besides, we have plenty of enemies here. Capitalists on Wall Street. The Fascistic Khaki Shirts. And Stalinists who run the Communist Party USA like slave drivers for Moscow."

"My superiors do not care about your infighting. You three were chosen because we felt you were sympathetic to Paraguay's struggle."

"And not because I led the strike against Elias Haskell?"

The mustache twitched again before a sly smile spread underneath it. "Amigos, let us not bicker. Of course, you shall receive your money. I simply needed to confirm that the guns were secure."

"We can take you there if you'd like."

Lopez held his hands up. "No need, Señor Rafferty. I trust you completely. And I also trust that you and your comrades can fulfill one last mission."

"Which is?"

The dark eyes narrowed. "Get rid of the guns."

"What do you mean? Doesn't Paraguay need them?"

"The important thing is that Bolivia does not acquire them. Since we are unable to secure transport out of New York, it is better to simply deprive the enemy of them."

The dank room suddenly felt even smaller. Nothing galled Mike Rafferty more than being duped. Whether it was the US government claiming to "make the world safe for democracy," Stalinists using him and other veterans as propaganda pawns, or a Paraguayan Army officer with ulterior motives, Mike Rafferty was nobody's rube any longer.

Gardner seemed to sense the anger, his hand sliding toward the pistol in his pocket. Reason flooded back into Rafferty and he shook his head. Gardner relaxed and leaned against the wall. Perhaps there was a silver lining to this after all.

"Of course, Colonel. They'll all be at the bottom of the East River by tomorrow night."

"Excellent. I shall return tomorrow at noon with your payment. Until then, amigos."

Lopez saw himself out, leaving a strange silence lingering in the little room. Gardner piped up with a scratchy whine. Rafferty patted his shoulder and smiled.

"Don't worry, Eddie. I have big plans for those guns."

Gardner jabbered again, gesturing to the ratty rug that hid a small arsenal beneath the floorboards.

"Those too. The future of this country will be written in blood and bullets."

CHAPTER TWELVE

The depression hit Harlem worse than most neighborhoods in New York. A decade prior, it had been the epicenter of the Jazz Age but now, almost half of Harlem's residents were unemployed. No matter how bad things were, the Negro always had it worse. The result was evident as Max walked down 125th Street – shuttered storefronts, dilapidated buildings, and ragged men, shivering in alleyways.

During Prohibition, he'd frequented the Cotton Club, Harlem's premier jazz club owned by white gangsters who allowed only white patrons. After collecting his take, Max would submerge himself in a symphony of soul courtesy of Duke Ellington's orchestra. That decade of decadence was gone forever now, like some ethereal fantasy. All that mattered now was keeping his head above water, and that meant solving this case.

Max stopped in front of a brownstone – the address on Burks's notes. Despite the late hour, a young boy lingered on the stoop, entranced by a game of jacks.

"Hey, son," Max called out.

The boy glanced up with widened eyes. White men weren't a common sight here, especially after dark. Max gave a small grin to soften the intrusion.

"Y-yeah, mister?"

"Where's the super?"

The boy jumped to his feet, scattering the jacks. "He's my daddy. I'll go get 'im!" He scurried inside and returned leading a middle-aged man. Pot-bellied, stooping, and marred with a perpetual scowl, he resembled all building superintendents, regardless of color.

"You police?" the super asked with a suspicious glare.

It was always good to play into people's assumptions, especially if they lent you authority.

"I'm a detective," Max answered. "Looking for Mike Rafferty. Know him?"

"That white boy? Yeah, I know him. But he doesn't live here anymore."

"Why not?"

"Turned out to be some kinda Bolshevik. Not too many white tenants rent in this neighborhood, but we looked the other way for that Mick on account of his face. Veterans gotta watch out for each other, you hear me?"

"Amen to that. I served in the 358th."

"Was with the Harlem Hellfighters myself. But my tolerance has a limit, you know? That white boy stirred up trouble, spoutin' off about how the Communist Party was the Negro's best friend, and how landlords would be lined up against a firing squad. Got so bad I threw his ass out."

"When was this?"

"Oh, about six months ago."

"Know where he is now?"

"Dunno. Maybe he moved to Moscow."

"Thanks for your time."

Max turned back toward the subway station, several blocks away, reviewing the facts as he walked. Sending a Red Mick to recruit the Negro working class showed how desperate the Bolshies were. Most likely, Rafferty had been reassigned elsewhere to rouse the rabble. Thankfully though, Max still had a contact in that nest of vipers calling itself the Communist Party USA.

*****

Back at his office, Max checked his mail, finding only an overdue phone bill and a pamphlet from the American Liberty League. Underneath a caricature of President Roosevelt – sitting on an opulent throne with a garish crown – were the words, "*Help us defeat King Franklin the First!*"

Well, he could always use more scratch paper around the office. Max tossed the mail onto his desk and after hanging his coat up, settled on the couch with the issue of *Fortune* magazine.

The article "Arms and the Men" opened dramatically enough, declaring that it "cost about $25,000 to kill a soldier during the World War." Well, most Doughboys would be surprised they were worth that much. From there, the article spotlighted a veritable rogues gallery of international gangsters - the Merchants of Death.

America had Bethlehem Steel, who despite claiming not to produce arms, still offered aircraft carriers, battleships, and submarines in their official catalogue. There was Krupp in Germany, Schneider-Creusot in France, Skoda in Czechoslovakia, all far worse than Al Capone or John Dillinger. These munition makers, according to the article, prolonged the war by years, ensuring that the entire industry made a handsome profit. Even worse, the article alleged, French arms dealers donated generously to Adolf Hitler's campaign, who now rattled sabers about another war.

The point was to keep the world in a constant state of tension, always preparing for the next conflict. Special attention was paid to Sir Basil Zaharoff, the Greek-born salesman for Vickers-Armstrongs, who'd traveled the world, instigating war scares, then sold weapons to the dupes who fell for them. Now, Zaharoff was retired and wheelchair-bound, but Vickers still made its blood money. Nicknamed the "Stepmother of Parliament" due to its chummy relations with the British government, the company was a master of intrigue and its tentacles stretched into Italy, Spain, Canada, and even Japan. Hell, even American arms dealers, the article stated, were an "open book compared to *any* European big business."

Quite a yarn, even more thrilling than the pulps. Max could see why some high-minded boob like Senator Gerald Nye would be moved by these scribblings, since the article wasn't subtle about its desire to see the entire armaments industry nationalized. Unfortunately, it was mostly irrelevant to this case. But there was one brief line that piqued Max's interest – the massive chemical company Du Pont, which had made a fortune during the war, had recently purchased a controlling stock in Haskell Munitions Incorporated. According to Compton, that was one of the companies the Khaki Shirts broke strikes for.

Max tossed aside the issue of *Fortune* and digested the information, but fog swirled around his brain, preventing any coherent theory from forming. Instead, he reached into his coat and pulled out Osborn's manifesto – *100% Americanism.* Although fatigue gnawed at his muscles, Max couldn't resist. It was a slim book, less than a hundred pages, but each paragraph packed enough dynamite to level a city block.

The depression, Osborn argued, revealed the greatest weakness in America – corrupt leadership. Congress was owned by Wall Street, which had swindled and speculated its way to power. Twenty percent of the workforce was still unemployed, driving millions into the abyss of poverty. When honorable veterans attempted to secure financial help from the Federal Government during the so-called Bonus March, they were driven out of Washington at bayonet point by the US Army. As a result of this political and economic catastrophe, the Communists were gaining support. The country inched closer to a godless revolution.

Only under the rule of a strong leader and a mass-based patriotic party, could America survive. The National Crusaders, Osborn went on, would beat back this Red threat just as Mussolini had in Italy. The Italian Fascists had much to admire, he insisted, such as their emphasis on national rebirth, overthrowing corrupt elites, and purifying society of decadent rot.

However, Osborn countered, his own political ideology was not a mere copy of Fascism. Inspired by the best parts of Mussolini's movement, Richard Osborn had created a new form of Americanism, the patriotism of the future.

Which sounded a lot like another name for Fascism, Max thought. He kept reading anyway.

Once the National Crusaders came to power, America would be reorganized according to the so-called Corporate State, as exemplified in Italy. Not a business corporation, but a new type of body politic, with industries structured into corporations, like organs forming a healthy national body. Taken from the Latin word for body – *corpus* – these corporations would harmonize labor and capital for the good of the nation, eliminating class conflict by agreeing upon wages, prices, and employment conditions, all under the firm guidance of the State. Osborn quoted Mussolini, "*Everything in the State, nothing outside the State, nothing against the State.*"

To Max, it sounded like an even more labyrinthian version of Roosevelt's NRA, trying to regulate the economy with its busybody "fair codes."

To rescue America from depression, Osborn declared, the Corporate State would embark on massive public works campaigns – repairing roads, building bridges, constructing dams, but above all, strengthening America's defenses. That meant a new army, a new navy, and an independent air force, one that would make the country strong again. And what would Chief Osborn do with all these soldiers? He quoted Mussolini again, writing, "*The growth of empire, that is to say the expansion of the nation, is an essential manifestation of vitality, and its opposite a sign of decadence.*"

War loomed large in America's salvation.

Far from espousing the "master race" fantasies of Hitler, Osborn insisted that men of all ethnicities would be allowed to don the khaki shirt. Provided they were white, of course. Negroes would maintain their natural "servile" role, and Jews would be allowed to remain in the country, provided they harbored no Communistic thoughts. Quite tolerant for American Fascists. But then again Benito Mussolini – unlike Adolf Hitler –

never had it out for the Jews, so maybe Osborn was just following suit.

The National Crusaders, Osborn insisted, would defend and uphold the Constitution by crushing its enemies.

Dangerous radicals and degenerates – anarchists, Communists, homosexuals, and liberal intelligentsia – would simply be deported to Russia. Let Stalin deal with that dreck.

Congress and Wall Street would be reformed, not for selfish gain but to make America prosperous for all, not just the ruling class. Only then, could *true* democracy prevail. Under the guidance of the National Crusaders, the citizenry would be remolded into a new type of American – stoic, frugal, and shorn of the disease of liberalism.

The realization struck Max that this wasn't some elaborate swindle. The spit and polish West Point officer was now a sincere Fascist, a man who believed what he was selling. Still, Max reminded himself, Fascist or not, Osborn was a paying customer.

He closed the book and let sleep swallow him.

CHAPTER THIRTEEN

Early the next morning, Max paid his overdue bill, and, after ensuring his telephone was reconnected, headed down to Union Square. The sky was still gloomy under a blanket of thick, gray clouds, threatening another rainstorm. Every November 7th, the Communist Party USA held a rally at Union Square to commemorate the Bolshevik Revolution of 1917. Partly because of the open space and partly because its official headquarters was just a block away on 14th Street.

Stepping into the park, Max guessed there were about three hundred onlookers. A thin line of uniformed cops stood around the perimeter, not enough to handle a crowd this size. The relationship between the New York Police Department and the Communist Party had always been acrimonious, but recent events had strained it to a breaking point.

During a strike five years ago, some Red named Steve Katovis was shot dead by a trigger-happy policeman. The Party threw him a lavish funeral attended by fifty-thousand onlookers, creating a martyr for the revolution. Now, each side viewed the other as a mortal threat.

Ever since the depression began, hundreds of Forgotten Men came to gawk at these homegrown Bolsheviks, and more than a few signed up. In just a few years, membership ballooned from five thousand to twenty-six thousand, as more and more men were enticed by stories of full employment in Russia and promises of revenge against Wall Street.

A small stage was set up near the equestrian statue of George Washington, now obscured by rows of fluttering Red flags. Several in the crowd carried placards of Joseph Stalin and Vladimir Lenin, an unsubtle hint where their true loyalties lay. The Bolshies had even set up a small kiosk, hawking issues of the *Daily Worker*, *Labor Defender*, and *New Masses*, the Communist magazine known for satirical cartoons sharper than those in *The New Yorker*. Max could admire the hustle.

Up on stage, a crimson banner hung high, emblazoned with the words, "*Workers Unite for a Soviet America!*" The Party bosses sat beneath it, American Lenins waiting for their turn to blow hot air. Earl Browder, the Party's general-secretary and number one Stalin sycophant, reviewed his notes. James W. Ford, the nation's most prominent black Bolshevik sat next to William Z. Foster, the Party's chairman. However, rumors swirled that Foster's health was in decline, and many usurpers were eager to take his throne.

At the podium stood the person Max had come to see – Comrade Susan Partridge.

Despite a face creased with age and tension, she exuded an icy attractiveness. Tightly done up auburn hair, wide blue eyes behind glasses, and a tweed coat with pleated skirt, combined to create a sort of commissar-next-door look. An unlikely employer, but Max owed several past jobs to her. As head of the Membership Office, Susan Partridge hired Max to spy on ex-members, dissidents, informants, and anyone else who went against the Party line.

"As we celebrate the 17th anniversary of the historic proletariat revolution in Russia," she shouted, "we, in America, are reminded that the past is prologue. An economic crisis strangles the working class of this country, while the Soviet Union abounds with steel, milk, and grain."

Some in the vast throng nodded along, their fantasies validated. Unshaven, ashen faces sparkled with hope, gullible rubes captivated by this Bolshevik Scheherazade's fantasies about a worker's paradise in Russia. Then again, America itself was a fairy tale, a childish dream too many still believed.

Party workers fanned out throughout the crowd, passing out pamphlets. Max accepted one and read through it. The blue thunderbird, logo of the National Recovery

Administration, was at its center, marred with an ominous swastika. "*The NRA is the 'National Retrogression Act.' Don't be fooled by Social Fascism!*" it warned.

Max pocketed the pamphlet and scanned the crowd for Mike Rafferty. Most were men, hard-bitten workers who'd been laid off from factories, the docks, and the subway. None resembled the bookish bandit from the mugshot.

"What about all them starving Ukrainians?" a voice called out.

Behind the podium, Susan Partridge's eyes flashed with rage. Rumors of a horrific famine in the Ukraine had soiled Stalin's boasts of a workers' paradise.

"Lies!" Partridge hissed with more venom than a cobra. "All lies! There is no such famine! The Union of Soviet Socialist Republics has plenty to eat. But those in glass houses shouldn't throw stones! How many of you would have starved without soup kitchens? How many of you sleep on park benches? How many of you truly believe that *happy days are here again*?"

More murmurs of approval from the throng, but the heckler continued, this time shouting about forced labor camps in Siberia. Two Party workers made a beeline toward him, shoving him out of the crowd with brass knuckles, a taste of what dissenters would get in a Soviet America.

Susan Partridge concluded her speech to a smattering of applause, then descended offstage. It was the men's turn to speak, after all. Ladies – even Communist ones – were just a warmup act. Max stepped toward her, and, after a glare of recognition, she gestured for him to follow. They made their way behind the statue of George Washington, just as Earl Browder stepped up to the microphone.

"Lovely stories," Max said. "I'm surprised you didn't tell them the Kremlin was made of gumdrops."

"What do you want?" Partridge asked with folded arms. "We don't have any work for you right now."

"I'm not looking for a job, just one of your members." Max paused, then added, "Mike Rafferty. Remember him?"

Her blue eyes widened. "Rafferty's very popular as of late."

"What do you mean by that?"

"A few months ago, some other snooper asked a bunch of questions about him."

"Who?"

"Don't know. Don't really care either."

"What nationality was this private eye? Paraguayan? Bolivian?"

"No, very American. He did have the decency to know that money talks in all languages."

"What's the matter, Comrade Partridge? Running out of dough? I thought this whole melodrama was funded by Joe Stalin."

Anger tightened her lips. "That's none of your business."

"Oh, I see. It's not the Party asking, just you. Skimming the top off those membership dues doesn't cut it these days?"

A furious scowl warped her face. "If you've come to insult my character—"

Max shut her up by shoving a ten-dollar bill into her palm. She glanced around, then stuffed it into her tweed coat. The scowl evaporated, replaced by a smug superiority.

"All right, Mr. Dietrich. You've got yourself a deal."

CHAPTER FOURTEEN

The clouds above Union Square rumbled as Earl Browder blathered on and on. Max looked up and felt a single droplet of rain smack his forehead. He'd have to make this quick.

"Tell me everything you know about Mike Rafferty."

Partridge smirked. "For starters, he's no longer a comrade of ours. He's been expelled."

That wasn't surprising. The only thing Communists hated more than social democrats, capitalists, and Fascists, were other Communists.

"What is he? A Lovestoneite?"

The Communist Party USA was notorious for its factional infighting, in particular the group led by Jay Lovestone, who made up the "Right Opposition" to Stalin.

"No, not a Lovestoneite," Partridge sneered. "Rafferty is a Trotskyist."

Max let out a whistle. Even worse than Lovestoneites, Trotskyists – or the "Left Opposition" – were the ultimate evil. To the Party line, Leon Trotsky was Judas, Brutus, and Satan rolled up into one man. Their hatred officially stemmed from differing ideologies. Stalin proclaimed the policy of "Socialism in One Country," whereas Trotsky advocated permanent worldwide revolution. But as far as Max could tell, they were just two big fish fighting over the same pond.

"Why can't you Bolshies just kiss and make up already?"

Anger flashed in her face. "There will be no reconciliation with the enemies of the people, Mr. Dietrich. You might want to remember that when our time comes."

A hollow threat, since a Communist couldn't get himself elected dog catcher, much less president.

"Why'd you kick him out?"

Partridge's anger gave way to contempt. "He started bringing up the Ukrainian famine at meetings. Even had the gall to accuse Comrade Stalin of deliberately starving the people. Doesn't that fool realize the Soviet Union is struggling against landowners, wreckers, and spies? Omelets require many broken eggs…"

"I thought you just said there wasn't any famine."

She caught herself. "Of course there isn't! Even liberal rags like *The New York Times* say so. However, we can't have Party members repeating such counterrevolutionary propaganda. The nerve of that…that gargoyle!"

"So, when did you and Rafferty have this little spat?"

"About six months ago."

"Really? I'm surprised you didn't hire me to tail him."

"Not necessary. He was a low-level functionary, a man whose desires were greater than his abilities. We posted him up in Harlem to recruit more Negroes into the Party, but he failed miserably. Guess his ugly mug scared people off."

"Don't need a crystal ball to predict that. Why'd you send a Paddy up there?"

"Unfortunately, we don't have many colored comrades…"

"No wonder. Does Rafferty have any friends, I mean, *comrades*?"

"Yes. Two men who were in his platoon during the war. Those fools would follow Rafferty anywhere, even into the sewer of Trotskyism."

"Their names?"

She thought for a moment. "Eddie Gardner and Peter O'Hare," then added, "All three were anti-social reprobates with bourgeois and homosexual tendences. We published a full denouncement in the *Daily Worker*."

"*Bourgeois*" and "*homosexual*" were favored slurs leveled against ex-Party members, despite there usually not being a lick of truth to any of it. Max had spied on enough wayward Reds to know the lengths the Party went to smear anyone who crossed it.

"Where is he now?"

Susan Partridge offered a shrug. "How should I know? Like I said, we kicked him out months ago."

"Comrade Partridge…the Party never lets its enemies out of its sight. Let me guess, you have your own spy network now? That's why you haven't been needing my services as of late…"

She flashed a wide grin, like a hungry animal. "It saves us money to use our own members, Mr. Dietrich. But we learned a lot from your methods."

Max shook his head. Even the Reds had hit hard times. Onstage, Browder's speech reached fever pitch.

"We here in America should be so lucky to have a Stalin guide us through this depression. Instead, we have Roosevelt, a pampered aristocrat, a creature of Wall Street, a Fascist wolf in liberal wool! Never let your guard down against Social Democracy, a mask that hides its true face – Social Fascism! This 'National Recovery Act' is nothing more than a watered-down version of Mussolini's Corporate State! Furthermore…"

"You Reds are all wet if you think spitting on the New Deal is the way to go," Max said. "The rubes and boobs love FDR."

"Unfortunately, you're right," she said. "This current strategy has failed. Comrade Browder is traveling to Moscow soon to argue for a people's front against Fascism. Our numbers are paltry, and we must resort to allying with Lovestonites, social democrats, and…*liberals*." She almost vomited the word.

"But not Trotskyists?"

"Never." Partridge was as immovable as the Rock of Gibraltar.

"So where is Rafferty now? Don't worry, I won't tell him about the 'gargoyle' crack…"

Her lips compressed tight and her frame tensed. Another ten bucks loosened her up.

"His last known residence was a flophouse in the Bowery."

Max handed her a notepad and she wrote the address. Another smattering of rain sprinkled down, but Max's attention was gripped by the khaki mass advancing toward Union Square like a brown tidal wave. The National Crusaders were on their way. The thin line of cops parted, letting them advance straight into the park without any resistance. Well, the Khaki Shirts doubled as strikebreakers, so maybe the Police Department also let them run wild on Reds too. A nice setup. Any deaths would be blamed on the Khaki Shirts, sparing the cops more headaches like Steve Katovis.

"The National Crusaders," Partridge sneered.

"Yeah, I heard you and them don't see eye to eye."

"These bastards have lured some of our comrades away with empty slogans and uniforms."

"Birds of a feather. You Bolshies are your own worst enemy."

Partridge opened her mouth to respond but shut it just as quick, her blue eyes bugging in fear. Across the park, the Khaki Shirts broke through the pitiful defensive line, surging forward, waving everything from baseball bats to blackjacks. Max counted at least forty before giving up. At its head he recognized the officer from yesterday, Squad Leader Kilmer. And here he was, an island of neutrality in the coming war.

They smashed through the crowd, splitting it asunder. Most gawkers were uninterested in actually fighting a class war and fled pell-mell. A few diehards dropped their leaflets and rushed toward the khaki wall. They swung brass knuckles and a few pocketknives, but the Reds were hopelessly outmatched in weaponry. Baseball bats broke bones, blackjacks split kneecaps, and batons cracked noses.

Within seconds, the Red defenses collapsed and Squad Leader Kilmer pressed his advance. Browder, Ford, Foster, and the other Party bigwigs shambled off the stage and made a break for it, Susan Partridge following close behind. They bolted down 14th Street, back to the relative safety of their nearby headquarters, an inglorious retreat for American Communism.

The Khaki Shirts kept coming, sharks aroused by blood. Their baseball bats splintered the magazine kiosk, sending copies of *Daily Worker* and *New Masses* whipping about in the damp wind. All too late Max realized his mistake and began running, only to be cut off by a pair of Khaki Shirts, both swinging batons.

"Where ya goin', ya Red rat?" one asked between sadistic giggles. "Back to the sewer?"

"I'm…I'm not with them," Max said, his voice brittle as glass.

The other Khaki Shirt slammed his baton into Max's gut, sending air whooshing out of his lungs. Doubling over, he sank to the ground, gasping for breath as pain knifed through his body. Looking up, his sight was obscured by the two Khaki Shirts, peering down at him like giant lizards sizing up a mouse.

CHAPTER FIFTEEN

Rain splattered down as Max gasped for air, words choking his throat. A mention of Chief Richard Osborn would tame these dumb bruisers, but his tongue locked up, just as the baton rose for the killing blow.

"Stop!" a voice cried.

Crusader First Class Compton tromped over. The other Khaki Shirts snapped to attention, arms up in rigid salutes.

"This one's no Red," Compton said, "I'll vouch for him. Go clean up over there."

He jerked a thumb over the rest of Union Square, now a churning sea of khaki and blue uniforms. The cops swept in to restore order, but only the Reds had cuffs snapped on them. Gusts of wind scattered their propaganda leaflets throughout the park and down 14th Street, a final mockery. Out of the chaos, Squad Leader Kilmer strode toward Max, jackboots squelching in the wet soil.

"Ah, Dietrich," he said, a grin crinkling his cheeks. "You're in a bad way, old boy!"

Max sucked in a lungful of chilly air and heaved himself to his feet. "Thanks…to your gorillas…"

"Not their fault, old boy. They thought you were a Red!"

Max ignored him. The pain in his gut subsided with each breath and he didn't want to send these brutes into another brawl. The fighting was over, the last of the Communists hauled off, leaving the Khaki Shirts to lick their wounds and bask in a victory salute. The lead cop – a lieutenant with gold bars fastened to his collar – broke off from his men and headed over to Kilmer.

"Lieutenant," Kilmer said, "I wish to give a statement. My men and I were peacefully protesting this Red rabble when one hauled off and attacked us."

A knowing twinkle shimmered in the Lieutenant's eye. "Of course, I saw the whole thing. A cut-and-dry case of self-defense."

They exchanged salutes, satisfied with the ruse they'd crafted. A nice little arrangement. The Khaki Shirts cut their teeth in street fighting and the cops got to throw a few Reds in jail. The Lieutenant walked away, leaving Max alone with his Fascist rescuers. Raindrops continued to fall, dotting their khaki tunics and side caps. Still, they stood tall, proud warriors yearning for another battle.

"Tell me, Squad Leader," Max said. "Is someone paying you to provoke the Reds?"

"No, we do that free of charge. Does that bother you, Dietrich? Are you a little pink on the inside?"

"Not at all. Just figured if you're out here roughing up Reds in the rain, you might as well get paid for it."

"The cops look the other way when it comes to Communists."

"Speaking of which, sir," Compton cut in, "Browder and the others escaped."

Kilmer laughed. "Let them run. It's only a matter of time." He turned to Max. "So why are you here, Dietrich? Let me guess, the warehouse thieves must have been Bolshies, right?"

"Brilliant deduction. Guess that's why they made you squad leader."

Kilmer sneered, and Compton stepped forward.

"Sir, I say we storm their headquarters right now! It's just down the street! That Red, Rafferty, must've stashed the guns in there—"

"Down, boy," Max said. "Rafferty isn't even a member of the Party now. Had too many wrong opinions so they kicked him out."

Face flushed with anger, Compton balled his fists like a firecracker ready to burst. The war had created thousands of Comptons, angry men thirsting for blood, bullies who found strength in uniforms and groups. The last thing Max wanted was to be the outlet for such fury.

"Don't worry, I'll find Rafferty and Haskell's guns," he said, holding up placating hands. "Then you can do whatever you want to him. But I need you Khaki Shirts to keep a low profile for the time being. I don't want Rafferty to get word I'm on his trail and take a powder out of the city."

Kilmer and Compton traded glances, then the Squad Leader gave an approving nod.

"Chief Osborn trusts you," Kilmer said, "and that's good enough for me."

A cynical thought crept into Max's mind. Rafferty and his gang must have had insider knowledge of where the guns would be stored, but from whom? Perhaps this entire scheme had been concocted by Richard Osborn to arm his Khaki Shirts on the sly?

Across Union Square, the Khaki Shirts lined up as if on parade. The few onlookers who lingered cheered them with Fascist salutes and cries of "America for Americans!" They looked like clowns, but even clowns could be dangerous. The rain began beating down harder, another signal it was time to go.

Max turned toward the subway station. "Thanks for the show. I usually have to go to Coney Island for a carnival." He started walking but could almost feel the angry glares from Kilmer and Compton burning on his back.

*****

A short trip on the subway took Max to the Bowery, the southernmost neighborhood in Manhattan. Once filled with the opulent mansions of New York's elite, the Bowery had devolved into a seedy pit, worsened by the depression. Unemployed "Bowery Bums" took shelter from the rain underneath the Third Avenue Elevated Rail. Sailors on shore leave staggered from saloon to brothel, trailed by pickpockets. Some Forgotten Men thronged around a Salvation Army kitchen, awaiting their midday bowl of soup.

Endless rows of flophouses offered single rooms for rent, none more than a dollar per night. A perfect hideout for Rafferty and his gang. Max sized up the three-story tenement building across the street from the elevated train. It was the same address Partridge had given him, a perfect hideout for someone as desperate as Rafferty. He entered the vestibule, shook his coat and fedora free of water, then knocked until a little landlady answered. Her face was a maze of wrinkles, ravaged by time, and her silver hair was tied in a bun so tight her skin looked stretched back.

"Vhat do you vant?" she croaked in an Eastern European accent, thicker than syrup.

"Good morning, ma'am. I'm looking for a man named Mike Rafferty. We believe he's flopping here."

For emphasis, he flashed his old Prohi badge – long enough that she knew it was official, quick enough that she couldn't read anything on it. After all, even during Prohibition those badges hadn't commanded much respect.

She babbled a stream in another language, then switched back to English. "My vord…are you vith the Police?"

"I'm a detective." A half-truth was always better than a full lie.

"I…I don't ask for names…"

Max sighed. "Rafferty wears glasses and a fake nose. Probably rooming with another man with a sliced up throat, and a large Irishman with bright red hair."

The woman's shriveled head bobbed up and down, wracking her foggy brain. "I…I think they are in 310 still…you must understand, people come in and out so often…"

"310? All right, I'll check. Now ma'am, he might be armed and dangerous."

"Should you call for backup?" she asked with widened eyes.

"Not yet. But if I'm not back down here in ten minutes or so, then call for help…"

Nodding, the old woman slunk back into her room. Max walked up the empty stairs to the third floor, taking in the details. Each floor had one shared bathroom, a luxury, since some flophouses had only one toilet per building. In fact, despite noticeable cracks and scurrying cockroaches, this was one of the nicer dumps he'd seen. And that hinted that Rafferty and his gang had come into some money recently.

Reaching room 310, he paused and gathered his thoughts. Mike Rafferty might be on the other side, but he needed to be sure. If Rafferty did answer, Max could always play dumb, act like he had the wrong room, then he'd slip out and phone Osborn.

Drawing a deep breath, he knocked and waited. Inside, hushed murmurs and padded footsteps stirred. Seconds later, the door swung open, revealing a gaunt man lurching forward. His skin was tight and sallow, interrupted by deep pink scars that gouged his throat, lips marred in a sneer. Max slid his gaze downward and found a Colt automatic in the man's grip, aimed straight at his heart.

CHAPTER SIXTEEN

Max had stared down enough guns to know when escape was impossible. He didn't resist as the man jerked him inside the dank room. Three tattered mattresses, blotted with stains, and two rickety chairs, were the only furniture. Max's gaze roamed around the room until settling on Mike Rafferty, leaning against the corner.

He looked the same as his mug shot – an eerie, cold face interrupted by an artificial nose. But an intelligent disposition flickered behind his glasses. Phony specs holding up prosthetic masks were a common way to hide disfigurement, and Max wondered what sort of monster lurked beneath.

Both Rafferty and the other man wore dark leather waistcoats, crinkled from the rain, and gray flat caps – the unofficial uniform of the working class. But despite Rafferty's mangled flesh, the rest of his spindly frame befitted an intellectual dilettante playing dress-up as the proletariat. The most work this man's hands had done was writing articles for *New Masses*. Still, times like this were like walking across a minefield blindfolded. The only hope of survival was ingratiation, then escape.

Rafferty stepped forward and frisked Max, snatching out his old Prohi badge and the Communist Party pamphlet. The Reds seemed relaxed now, probably because this intruder was unarmed. Max thanked his lucky stars. Not only had he left his PI license back at the office, he'd also pawned his old pistol months ago for a few extra clams. Carrying either now would be a ticket to a makeshift firing squad.

Across the room, the gunman stepped forward and swung his automatic toward the chair, gesturing for Max to sit. Rafferty and the man began chatting – or at least, that's what it sounded like. The gunman choked out gurgling noises while Rafferty nodded along.

"My comrade says he recognized you through the peephole," Rafferty said.

Max divided glances between the two. "You understood him?"

Rafferty grinned. "Enough to get the gist. His name's Eddie Gardner. Said he's seen you at Party meetings but can't recall who you are…"

Openings like this didn't come often and Max dove right in.

"He's right. I *was* a Party member."

"Well, that explains this," Rafferty said, crumpling up the pamphlet and tossing it on the floor, then handed the badge back to Max. "But what about that?"

"Bought it at a pawn shop," Max answered, tucking it inside his coat. "Ain't no more Prohis but their badges fool chumps just the same. Gets me into a lot of places."

Rafferty laughed and gave a side glance over to Gardner, who hissed out some more gibberish.

"What's your name?"

Max used the first alias that popped into his mind. "Harry Vincent."

"Mr. Vincent," Rafferty said aloud, rubbing his chin. "Sounds familiar…"

It was the name of one of *The Shadow's* most trusted agents, but a college boy like Mike Rafferty had probably never read a pulp magazine in his life.

"Maybe from Party meetings?"

"Perhaps..." Rafferty pulled up the other chair and sat across from Max. "Why are you here, Mr. Vincent?"

"You're Mike Rafferty, ain't ya? The one who led that strike against the Haskell factory?"

"The very same. Did Partridge send you?"

"Hell no. I ain't no snooper for that bitch. In fact, I quit the Party today. That's why I came looking for you guys."

A gleam shimmered behind Rafferty's glasses. "Is that so, Mr. Vincent?"

"Yeah, Trotsky was square all along. I'm sick of taking orders from Joe Stalin. He's no better than the old Tsar was!"

"Worse than the Tsar! Stalin's so-called 'Socialism in One Country' is just Red Fascism!" Rafferty's fists tightened, bulged his eyes, blazing like a preacher spouting fire and brimstone. "While Communists slit each other's throats, the Fascist beast grows stronger every day."

"You mean Hitler?"

"Yes, but this country has many little Hitlers of its own. That lunatic Pelley, down in North Carolina, for instance. Right here in New York, there's Richard Osborn, the so-called *chief* of the Khaki Shirts."

"Sounds familiar..."

"A vainglorious militarist. Eddie and I had many scrapes with his Khaki Shirts in the past. Fascism means war, Mr. Vincent, a new war that will consume all humanity in the conflagration. True Communists like us must strike back, or else the moneyed classes and their Fascist hirelings will plunge the world into another senseless slaughter!"

Gardner laid a hand on Rafferty's shoulder, soothing the palpable rage. After a few deep breaths, he calmed down and fixed Max with a scrutinizing stare.

Gardner laid a hand on Rafferty's shoulder, soothing the palpable rage. After a few deep breaths, he calmed down and fixed Max with a scrutinizing stare.

"Mr. Vincent, please understand that we have many enemies in this city. How did you find us?"

"Partridge hired bloodhounds to sniff you out. I came down here to warn you and join up."

"Unsurprising," Rafferty sneered. "But we have another hideout."

"That sounds like you're planning something…"

"Perhaps…but let's talk about you, Mr. Vincent."

"What do you want to know?"

"Convince me *you're* not one of Partridge's bloodhounds."

Max searched his memory for every detail about Communist infighting – Lenin's last will and testament naming Trotsky as his true successor, collectivization, Stalin's Five-Year Plan, but the famine ravaging the Ukraine stood out.

"It's like I said, I'm through with Stalin. After what happened in the Ukraine, I can't trust anything that comes outta Moscow."

Rafferty leaned forward. "What do you know about the Ukraine?"

"Enough to know what they print in *The Times* and *New Masses* is hogwash. But when I brought it up at Party meetings, Comrade Partridge said I was parroting 'counterrevolutionary claptrap.'"

"She said the same to me." Rafferty shook his head. "But I know the truth now. It was a year ago, right after Roosevelt recognized the Soviet Union and a few thousand Ukrainians protested outside the Soviet Consulate here."

A grimness spread through Rafferty's face, harder than that mask he wore.

"Partridge ordered me to organize a counterprotest. We could only muster about a hundred comrades, but we fought dirty. We spat at them, emptied garbage cans over their heads, called them liars and Fascist dupes."

Rafferty shook his head, then continued. "But they remained steadfast, never wavering in their cause. Doubt crept in, and I soon spoke to some Ukrainians who'd escaped. They told me tales worse than any horror story. Bodies piled up like logs. Human beings turned into walking skeletons from hunger. Parents eating their own children."

"However bad you have it, someone else always has it worse…" Max muttered.

"True, Mr. Vincent, but it confirmed a suspicion that had been growing inside. I was being used by Stalin to attack fellow workers."

"Oh, I agree, that's why Stalin's gotta go. Trotsky had it right when he wrote, '*The completion of the Socialist Revolution within national limits is unthinkable.*' The whole world must be liberated or nobody is…"

Rafferty brightened at the quote. Ideologues loved having their opinions validated, no matter how banal the platitudes were.

"Are you a veteran, Mr. Vincent?"

Max nodded. "Served in the 358th Infantry Regiment."

"Eddie and I were with the 69th."

"The Fighting 69th?" Max widened his eyes in forced amazement.

Rafferty took a deep breath. "Once that name invoked pride within me. But after this—"

He unhooked his glasses, pulling the prosthetic mask off with it, revealing a hideous, scarred gash, punctured by two small slits, the last vestiges of his nose. Even more grotesque, was that a good chunk of his flesh had been scooped out, his face dented in. A horrible sight, but Max had seen even worse heaps of flesh rotting in the trenches.

"You didn't flinch," Rafferty said, smiling. "If only my wife was as stoic."

"Your wife?"

Rafferty shrugged, then hooked the mask and glasses back on. "We were married right after I graduated from Columbia. Just before my son was born, America entered the war. Like millions of other dupes, I joined up, and was commissioned a lieutenant."

He sighed, full of regrets, forlorn, and a nameless dread that Max understood too well.

"While I was in France, my wife sent me endless love letters, saying how deeply she missed me. But when I returned, she took one look at me and started screaming. Can't blame her, I guess. After all, her husband was dead and a monster had taken his place." He blew out a bitter laugh. "She took off the next day with my son and I haven't seen them since."

Max could sympathize. Before shipping out, he'd proposed to a local girl in the neighborhood, swearing to marry her when he returned with a chestful of medals. Just before the war ended, he received a letter, explaining how she'd fallen in love with someone else, a slacker – one of the cowards who'd shirked the draft – as if she wanted to rub salt into the wound.

Rafferty drew a deep breath and continued. "Now I realize that us Doughboys were nothing more than hired mercenaries for Wall Street and the arms industry. Men like Eddie and I were turned into mindless weapons to murder fellow workers in different uniforms." Rafferty shook his head, bitterness carved deep into his face. "But they'll all get theirs soon enough."

"You mean bump off a few Merchants of Death?" Max chuckled. "Where do I sign up?"

"Your zeal is admirable." Rafferty leaned back in his chair, running his eyes over Max. "But I don't know if we can trust you just yet."

"You want references?"

"Perhaps…but for now, you'll be kept on ice until we can verify who you really are. Until then—"

A knock pounded at the door and silence smothered the drab little room. Too early for the landlady since it couldn't have been more than five minutes. The mute trotted over to the peephole, then rasped a gargled word to Rafferty.

"Let him in."

Opening the door, Gardner ushered in a swarthy man, dressed in a sopping-wet trench coat and fedora. Somehow though, his handlebar mustache remained upright. His plump cheeks and thick eyebrows tightened as he fixed Max with a conspiratorial glare. Cornelia Osborn's words reappeared in his mind.

'Isn't it obvious? The Paraguayans.'

CHAPTER SEVENTEEN

Rafferty greeted the newcomer with a handshake. "Come in, Colonel Lopez."

"Who's this?" Lopez nodded over at Max, scrutinizing him up and down.

"He claims to be a comrade," Rafferty said. "But we'll find out."

The words seemed to shake Lopez, his stern authority melting away. "What does he know about our arrangement?"

"Nothing yet."

Lopez frowned, withdrawing his eyes from Max. The Colonel's accent was thick and undoubtably genuine, but as a native New Yorker, Max couldn't tell if he hailed from Paraguay, Bolivia, or anywhere else in South America. Lopez withdrew a thick envelope from his trench coat and handed it over to Rafferty. The Red thumbed through rows and rows of bills, then pocketed it. Payment for last night's job, no doubt.

Lopez drew himself up, his authority returning. "Our business is concluded, Mr. Rafferty. Providing you got rid of the goods?"

"They'll be gone soon enough."

Lopez nodded to each man, turned, and stalked out of the room, leaving a trail of wet footsteps behind. Alarm flashed through Max. Were they talking about the guns? If so, did that mean they were being shipped to South America? Or something else?

His thoughts were interrupted by Gardner stooping closer, eyes screwed up in a suspicious gaze. Hopefully, this mute wasn't privy to Max's dirty jobs for Partridge. The air seemed even colder now, and Max shivered underneath his damp coat.

"Nervous?" Rafferty taunted, sitting back down.

"Just cold. So, what're ya gonna do with all that dough?"

"This isn't for us, Mr. Vincent, but for our future plans. The Stalinists and Lovestonites dominate Communist politics in America. We'll need proper funding to compete with them."

"So, is Colonel Lopez a comrade?"

"No." The word echoed like a gunshot. "We did a job for him. That's all."

The opening to fish for more information was small and dangerous. Ask just enough to get Rafferty talking without revealing anything that might prove fatal.

"He sounded Spanish…is he from South America?"

Rafferty and Gardner exchanged glances, cautious men planning their next move. After a sigh, Rafferty relaxed. And why wouldn't he? In this squalid little box, he was the master of life and death.

"He's the Paraguayan military attaché."

"In New York? I thought they were only at embassies in Washington…"

A frown sagged Rafferty's mouth. "Some attachés are stationed at consulates."

"Ah, so you've been to the Paraguayan Consulate?"

"No, too risky. Colonel Lopez has always contacted us directly."

The words hung in the chilly air. Something seemed off about this whole setup. A cynicism deep inside Max whispered another theory. Perhaps the Bolivians, wanting to save a little money, simply hired Rafferty as an unwitting dupe? Few Americans could tell a Bolivian accent from a Paraguayan one, and Colonel Lopez could play the role easily enough. Conjecture filled Max's brain until Rafferty cut through again.

"But enough about Lopez…let's talk about you, Mr. Vincent."

"What do you want to know?"

"More about your politics, for one."

Max glanced at his wristwatch – he'd been sitting in this dump for almost ten minutes and if that landlady pulled through, he'd have some distraction. But then what? Well, he'd cross that bridge when the time came. The important thing was to keep Rafferty talking, which wouldn't be hard. Idealogues were natural speechifiers. Now was as good a time as any to bring up Haskell.

"Well, closing down that munitions factory left a big impact on me. The Party big shots are all talk, but you took action."

Rafferty smiled, enraptured by his past deeds. "Few creatures are more vile than war profiteers."

"Why Haskell? Aren't there bigger fish to fry?"

Another shrug. "No reason. His factory was the closest, that's all."

Off to the side, Gardner kept gawking as if they were at the Bronx Zoo and Max was the main attraction. If only that landlady would hurry. He needed to keep this blowhard talking.

"So, will you be donating that dough to the League?"

Rafferty and Gardner perked up at the name. The Communist League of America was the biggest Trotskyist party, but it hadn't even topped five hundred members. Susan Partridge had hired Max to spy on their leaders and discovered them to be more blundering incompetents than bomb-throwing revolutionaries.

"No, we have other plans," Rafferty said, sitting opposite of Max.

"Which are?"

A gleam of light caught Rafferty's glasses.

"The only way this system, this American system of racial and economic exploitation will end, is if a bullet pierces its heart. Capitalism is rotting from within and the American people know it. Look at the way they cheered outlaws like Dillinger."

"You guys gonna rob banks like a gang of Red Dillingers?"

"John Dillinger was a common crook, his crimes a product of capitalism. But he was on to something. Bankers, capitalists, and politicians are the true public enemies and should be washed away in a storm of bullets."

On its face, the plan reeked of stupidity. After all, this wasn't Japan where they assassinated their leaders every other week. But the depression left a lot of law-abiding Americans eager for radical change. Even a Bolshie Dillinger gang didn't sound too far-fetched these days. How many Forgotten Men would sympathize if Rafferty gunned down a banker or two? And how many would join him?

A strangled hiss from Gardner yanked Max out of his thoughts. His eyes brightened and his scarred throat throbbed. He stomped over to the crumpled pamphlet and scribbled something across it. Handing it to Rafferty, the mute sank a hateful glare into Max so sharp, he felt a stabbing pain.

"Well, well, Mr. Vincent. Looks like Eddie remembered who you really are."

Rafferty showed him the pamphlet, scrawled with an accusation – *"THAT'S MAX DIETRICH, A SHAMUS!"*

CHAPTER EIGHTEEN

Gardner whipped out his automatic, blocking any escape. Fear squirmed inside Max's gut, but he fought it back and searched for a plan. He leaned against the flimsy chair, filling the frigid room with a loud creak. The rickety piece of junk might be ready to break apart, but it could make a good bludgeon. Providing that old lady showed up.

"So, Mr. Dietrich," Rafferty said, "looks like you're one of Partridge's bloodhounds after all."

There was no point in lying about his name now. At least they didn't suspect anything about Haskell's guns. Let these idiots think he still worked for Partridge.

"All right, you got me. What do you want to know?"

"Why'd Partridge send you?"

"Isn't it obvious?"

"No."

Max shrugged again, stretching the time out more. "Well, like you said, she wanted to keep tabs on you."

A grimace twisted Rafferty's scarred face. "I already know that. But *why*?"

"To see if you were going to start a new party that might siphon members away. And since you're not, I'll be on my way."

Max jumped to his feet, but Gardner's pistol followed him.

"I don't think so, Mr. Dietrich. Not after everything you've heard."

Eyeing the automatic, Max said, "A gunshot would draw attention, even in this neighborhood."

"True, but luckily, I learned how to strangle men during trench raids without making a sound."

Rafferty rose, his face growing harder than his prosthetic nose. He no longer resembled some bookish intellectual, but the Grim Reaper made flesh. Max tensed, his muscles tightening into firm knots. He wouldn't go down without a fight. A sudden knock sounded at the door like a bombshell. Rafferty and Gardner spun around, leaving themselves wide open.

Max grabbed the rickety chair and, with one swift heave, smashed it over Rafferty's head. It splintered apart, sending the Red sprawling to the floor in a twisted, unconscious heap. A chair leg remained in Max's hand like a wooden missile waiting to be fired. He hurled it across the room, smacking Gardner in the face with a loud thwack. The mute staggered to his knees, pistol clattering to the floor.

For a brief moment, Max considered diving for the gun, but Gardner, wincing in pain, reached out, and seized the weapon. Dazed, he jerked the pistol upward and squeezed out a shot. It went wild cracking the window, sending a torrent of rainy wind swirling inside. Max took off toward the door and swung it open, just as another gunshot cracked, ripping a chunk of wood from the frame.

The landlady stood on the other side, gawking, then shuffled out of the way. Living in the Bowery trained people how to save their own skin. Max bounded down the stairs with slapping footsteps. He pushed his way through the vestibule, then heard heavy steps pounding behind him. Gardner was closing in.

Out on the street, Max looked up at the Third Avenue station as a train trundled south, meaning a north-bound train was just minutes away. The rain had subsided into a drizzle, soaking the enormous throng outside the Salvation Army kitchen. It was lunchtime, and a mass of unemployed Forgotten Men lined up for a free bowl of soup, a real feast these days.

As Max approached, the Bowery Bums didn't bat an eye, too fixated on their own misery to pay him any mind. That wouldn't do. A distraction would put some distance between him and Gardner. He glanced back. The mute stumbled out onto the street, still wobbly from his headwound, the automatic swishing around for a clear shot.

"Look out!" Max shouted, grabbing the nearest Forgotten Man. "That nut is gonna kill us all! Run for your lives!"

Fear rippled through the line. One Bowery Bum broke and ran, followed by another, then another. Within seconds, the entire throng devolved into a panicked mass, darting every which way, spilling out into the wet streets, rushing down the sidewalk, slick with rain, desperate to escape.

Elbowing through the crowd, Max ran closer toward the Third Avenue station. Mechanical clatter screeched up above, announcing the arrival of a northbound train. He looked back and saw Gardner pushing forward, the Bowery Bums clearing a path for this insane gunman.

Max rushed up the stairs toward the train, its doors flung wide open. In a quick bound, he hopped the turnstile, landing feet first and stumbling inside the waiting car. Grasping a leather strap, he straightened himself up, just as the doors whooshed shut.

A few deep breaths calmed him as rainwater dripped from his clothes, collecting in a puddle on the floor. A few passengers met him with annoyed stares, but kept quiet. Through the windows, he saw Gardner standing on the platform, the automatic impotent at his side.

The train lurched out of the station and began trundling uptown. Through the windows, Max waved farewell at Gardner, fuming in hateful silence.

*****

Rough hands shook Rafferty back to consciousness. He ignored the pain searing through his head and struggled to focus, the room a fuzzy blur. Nearby, an angry, accented voice screamed babbles of insults. Dazed, he looked up. The landlady's blurry face warped in terror before she stumbled toward the door, shrieking for help. Pawing his face, Rafferty felt only scarred, mutilated flesh. Where was his mask?

After a few moments, his vision focused, and Rafferty saw a pile of smashed splinters, the remnants of the shattered chair. Fumbling at his forehead, he felt no blood thankfully. Across the room was his prosthetic mask, knocked clean off by the blow.

Eddie Gardner tromped in, scooped up the mask, and handed it over. Rafferty hooked it back on and struggled to his feet, his senses regained.

"What happened?" Rafferty asked, grateful his words weren't slurred, a telltale sign of a concussion.

Gardner mumbled out a hissing stream, mostly incoherent, but the phrase "Dietrich escaped" came through the gibberish. No time to waste. Rafferty glanced over at the spot where the Tommy guns hid underneath loose floorboards.

Outside, the landlady said, "I call Police! They come soon! Lock you both up!"

The hell with the choppers. All that mattered now was escape. They weren't even needed now. Rafferty patted his coat, ensuring the envelope full of dough was still there, then stormed out of the room, Gardner trailing close behind. Pushing the landlady out of the way, they thumped down the stairs and out onto the street. Dozens of Bowery Bums milled about in the rain, palpable terror lingering in the air.

"Dietrich's work?"

Gardner nodded with a disgusted snarl.

"We need to get back to O'Hare. Now."

They took off in a run northward, toward the Brooklyn Bridge. Let Dietrich have his victory. There were many more guns waiting for them.

CHAPTER NINETEEN

The train rocked back and forth as Max sank into his thoughts, reviewing each theory. This entire heist could have been orchestrated by someone on the inside. Elias Haskell? Why would he want to sabotage his own company? Insurance, perhaps. No, this wasn't the corner grocery collecting an arson check. His pampered daughter? Possible, but why would Cornelia jeopardize her privileged lifestyle? Richard Osborn had motive to arm his Khaki Shirts for a bloody street war with the Communists. But why couldn't he just ask his father-in-law for some heavy artillery?

Perhaps Mike Rafferty had contacts inside Haskell Munitions' upstate warehouse, or the Khaki Shirts themselves. But that didn't square with what Max had just witnessed – bumbling, would-be revolutionaries slumming in a flophouse. Regardless, Colonel Lopez was the key to all this, and if Max was going to find him, time was of the essence. Although Rafferty admitted they didn't ever contact him at the Paraguayan Consulate, they might phone ahead to warn him.

If he was Paraguayan.

The pestering thought that Lopez was Bolivian refused to die. Money was the angle for most crimes, even among nations. Saving a few grand in this depression might be a matter of national security, especially when fighting a war.

Either way, he'd find out soon.

*****

Foreign consulates dotted the city, but New York's Midtown neighborhood, specifically the eastern half, between 35th and 53rd, held the most. The Bolivian Consulate was located on the corner of 42nd Street and 2nd Avenue, directly opposite the Paraguayan Consulate on the other side. An irony that proved God had a sense of humor.

A directory listed the Bolivian Consulate was listed on the fourth floor, and Max took the stairs. Its office was marked by a simple plaque reading, "*Consulado General de Bolivia en Nueva York*." Max knocked and braced himself, assuming the role of a New York City detective. If Colonel Lopez was indeed here, then he'd better project some authority.

A few moments later, a middle-aged man in a baggy suit answered.

"May I help you?" he asked, his accent thick and heavy.

Max flashed his badge, then pocketed it just as quick.

"Detective Vincent. I'm here to see Colonel Lopez."

The Bolivian gaped back in confusion. "I'm sorry, señor, there is no one here by that name."

Perhaps Lopez was just an alias?

"Is the military attaché on duty?"

The man nodded and invited him in, but Max hesitated. He'd walked into enough lion's dens for the day.

"Have him meet me out in the hall," he ordered with all the authority of a New York bull.

The Bolivian went back inside and after a few minutes, a tall, distinguished-looking man stepped out. From his dark eyes, which held Max in an icy glare, to his chiseled, stony face, he was the epitome of a South American military officer. Most impressive was his steel-gray tunic, with a high collar and epaulettes, reminiscent of the German Army's *feldgrau* uniforms that Max had seen close up.

"Captain Hugo Morales," he said, clicking his heels, "at your service."

"Detective Vincent," Max said. "Captain, I'm looking for a man named Colonel Lopez. White, medium build, round cheeks with a waxed mustache. We believe he is attached to the Bolivian Consulate."

"I don't know who you're speaking of, Detective. The only colonel on our staff is the chief military attaché down in Washington."

"Oh? And that makes you…?"

The Captain clicked his heels again. "An assistant military attaché."

Max fought back disappointment. Every detective hated seeing their pet theory die, but perhaps Colonel Lopez was actually who he said he was.

"Captain, could this officer, this Colonel Lopez, be attached to the Paraguayan Consulate?"

Morales grunted a laugh. "Not a chance, señor. Paraguay only has one military attaché in your country, stationed in Washington at their embassy. And his name is definitely not Lopez, nor does he have a mustache."

"Perhaps this Colonel Lopez could be a spy working undercover?"

Another grunt, more contemptuous this time. "Unlikely. We keep track of the Paraguayans here, señor. They're not sending officers to their consulates, not when they're desperately needed at the front. Our two countries are at war, you know."

"So I've heard. Tell me, Captain, why are you stationed here? I didn't realize the Bolivian Army needed so many attachés."

Morales's face remained rigid, but a brief tremor on his lip betrayed his fear. "My government simply wants to foster better relations with your country. Anything more detailed is classified, I'm afraid."

That included procuring weapons from Elias Haskell, but there was no need to embarrass him.

"Thank you for your cooperation, Captain."

They exchanged handshakes and Morales walked him back to the stairs. "By the way, Detective, what is this in reference to?"

Max gave a smile. "Sorry, Captain. That's classified."

CHAPTER TWENTY

The Paraguayan Consul General was a jocular little man named Juan Ortiz, plump as a pumpkin, who welcomed Max into his office with open arms. Unsurprising, since Max had now assumed the identity of a *New York Times* reporter, eager to get Ortiz's comments on the Chaco War. Flattered that an American newspaperman showed any interest in his country's struggle, the Consul General showed Max around the office without even asking for credentials. Paraguay's consulate ran on a skeleton crew, five people in total, none of whom resembled Colonel Lopez.

"I'll be happy to share my thoughts, Señor Vincent," Ortiz said, sitting behind his desk.

Max took a seat and glanced up at two imposing portraits on the wall. One civilian – labeled "*Eusebio Ayala, Presidente*," and one military man, "*General José Félix Estigarribia, Comandante en Jefe*."

"But first, let's have a drink," Ortiz insisted, grabbing a bottle of Jack Daniels from a nearby bar cart. "To Paraguay's inevitable victory!"

There was no need to bring up Colonel Lopez just yet. This man was a talker, and with a little booze, he'd spill everything.

"Sorry, Consul. Our editor doesn't allow us to drink on the clock, but don't let me stop you."

Ortiz frowned, but poured a glass anyway, then threw back the whiskey with a satisfied sigh, a man confident in victory.

"Tell me, Consul, is there any truth to the rumor that a new Paraguayan offensive is about to begin?"

Ortiz looked ready to spit up his drink. "Where did you hear that?"

"All reporters have sources…"

Setting the glass aside, Ortiz said, "Señor Vincent, you know I can't discuss military strategy with the press. But rest assured, Paraguay will defeat Bolivia's mercenary army soon."

"Of course," Max said, jotting in his notepad. "What do you say to those who claim this a war for oil? It's common knowledge that Standard supports Bolivia and Shell aids Paraguay."

"It's true that Standard Oil is the puppet master behind this criminal war. Your illustrious Senator Huey Long called them 'rapacious thieves and robbers' who purchased Bolivia's government." A dreamy smile spread over his face. "Ah, a great man of the people! You know we named a fort after him?"

"Fort Long?"

"A fitting title, don't you think? It is an incontestable fact that the Gran Chaco belongs to Paraguay! There is potentially a limitless supply of oil there, enough to develop our economy, stricken with poverty. Why should we not accept the assistance of Royal Dutch Shell to benefit our nation?"

Max couldn't fault the logic, since all wars boiled down to money.

"That brings me to a matter I'd like to discuss, Señor Vincent." Ortiz paused for effect. "The involvement of American industrialists in this war."

Max played ignorant, hoping Haskell's name would be left out. "Oh? Didn't the Roosevelt Administration declare an arms embargo?"

"Yes, and Paraguay has scrupulously upheld it. But the Bolivian bandits still buy weapons and supplies from arms dealers.'"

"Please, go on…"

"Mostly from Vickers, but also from some American companies, most notably Haskell Munitions. Have you heard of them?"

"I'm familiar."

"And it's not just guns. Bolivian soldiers were caught wearing American-made uniforms just a few months ago. We even lodged a complaint with Senator Nye."

Max let his surprise show.

"It was in *The Times*," Ortiz said. "Nye even promised to investigate."

"I must have missed that issue. But our coverage of the Chaco War *has* been lacking in the past. That's why I'm here. We want to provide our readers with a comprehensive overview of the conflict."

A pleased look flooded Ortiz's plump face. Now was as good a time as any to bring up Lopez.

"Consul Ortiz, are you familiar with an officer named Colonel Lopez?"

"No. Should I be?"

Selecting his words carefully, Max continued, "Some of our sources claim that a Paraguayan Army officer is secretly sabotaging arms deals, right here in New York."

"A fantasy! My government does not resort to such intrigue! No doubt this 'Colonel Lopez' is a Bolivian agent sent to sow confusion."

"I considered that..."

"Believe me, Señor Vincent, we would never sabotage any arms deals that Bolivia makes."

"Why's that?"

Leaning forward, Ortiz whispered, "It's how we supply our troops."

"Oh?"

"Most of the guns that our soldiers are now fighting with were captured from the Bolivians. Under the leadership of General Estigarribia—" Ortiz gestured at the portrait of the man in a glittering uniform "—our forces have captured enough arms to last for the next forty years. All while Bolivia foots the bill! Quite a bargain, eh?"

Max conceded that. After all, why interrupt your best supply of weapons with cloak-and-dagger theater? Still, the thought that Colonel Lopez was part of a Bolivian plot refused to lift from Max's brain.

"Well, Consul, perhaps this 'Colonel Lopez' is acting on behalf of the Bolivian government."

"Perhaps…" Ortiz rubbed his flabby chin. "Your 'Colonel Lopez' might be the alter ego of that brute across the street, Captain Morales!"

"They're two very different people, Consul. Even if Morales had a mustache, they'd look nothing alike."

"A mustache you say? Describe him…"

"White skin, medium height, with a round face, thick eyebrows, thicker lips, and a waxed, handlebar mustache."

Recognition struck Ortiz. "A man bearing that description came to see me about a month ago. He claimed to be researching a part for a play."

"What was his name?"

"Unfortunately, I don't remember. He spoke Spanish with an accent I couldn't place, but I'd wager it was Cuban. I do remember his ridiculous mustache. He looked like Don Quixote, but I kept that to myself. The Cubans are a very theatrical people."

"What was the play?"

"Some satire on the arms industry and its role in the Chaco War. Supposedly, this man was going to play a Paraguayan Army officer. He claimed he wanted to give an authentic performance. You know how actors can be. Asked me countless questions about my country, our history, our culture, and our army."

Max jotted everything down, nodding for Ortiz to continue.

"We are a small, landlocked nation, Mr. Vincent, surrounded by ravenous wolves. I explained our tragic past to this actor, particularly the War of the Triple Alliance."

"The War of the Triple Alliance?"

A schoolteacher twinkle came to Ortiz's eyes.

"Back in 1864, when your civil war was almost finished, my country went to war against the combined might of

Brazil, Argentina, and Uruguay. Our troops fought valiantly, but Paraguay was occupied. Even though ninety percent of the country's population died in this war, they continued to resist the invader under the leadership of our president, Francisco Solano Lopez."

"Lopez?" Max circled the name on his notepad. "Do you think this actor just took the name?"

Ortiz's chubby cheeks drooped, suggesting he *hadn't* thought of that.

"Perhaps, but Lopez is a very common name in South America."

True, but laziness was a commonality among all nations. Clues and facts were more disjointed now, blurring any coherent narrative, but Max sensed he was close to the truth.

"Did this actor say where he performs?"

Ortiz sank into ponderous thought, then snapped his fingers. "Oh yes, the Alvin Theatre. I saw *Mary of Scotland* there. A lovely play."

Max flipped his notebook shut. He'd squeezed everything he could out of this windbag.

"Thank you, Consul. I believe I have enough."

"But the interview just began…"

"It'll be supplemented by reports from our South American correspondents. I just wanted to have a few quotes from the Consul himself."

Ortiz lurched to his feet and walked Max over to the door. "How about this? 'Paraguay stands firm in its just cause.'"

"Perfect. Consul Ortiz, you've been a bigger help than you realize."

CHAPTER TWENTY-ONE

It was raining hard again when Max left the Paraguayan Consulate, so he hailed a taxi across town to the Alvin Theatre on 52nd Street. He hadn't been to a Broadway show in years, but during Prohibition, tickets were given out to Prohis as soft bribes. Even today he could still whistle the tunes from the *Ziegfeld Follies*, *The Cocoanuts*, and *A Connecticut Yankee* by heart. Outside the theater hung a fiery red poster with the words *Coming Soon – Anything Goes.*

Broadway theaters usually shut down for months so the cast could practice new dance and song routines, but luckily, the door was unlocked. Max made his way to the orchestra seating, where two men sat in the back row, watching a live performance. Cast members, costumed in sailor suits, danced and pranced in front of a nautical backdrop. A woman took center stage, dressed in a sleeveless, black shirt and billowing white pants. Max recognized her long, prominent nose and booming voice as Ethel Merman's, the First Lady of Broadway.

She bawled out a catchy ditty, steeped in blue humor, turning the Alvin Theatre into a tawdry nightclub. For a few minutes, one could forget the world was going to hell, and drift away on waves of frivolity. But reality rushed back when Ethel Merman stumbled over a few words, then snapped her fingers.

"Aw, shit! I always fuck up the lyrics in the third verse."

The two men in the orchestra traded glances, before one – a dark-haired, big-eyed dandy – spoke up.

"The line isn't 'If Mae West undressed you like,' dear."

"Christ, I know that, Cole! Goddamn it, why do you have to write so many fuckin' tongue twisters?"

It made sense now. Cole Porter, the maestro of musicals and America's preeminent songwriter, was the brains behind

Anything Goes. Watching from the side, Max resisted the urge to ask for an autograph. Cole Porter fell silent as the other man, burly, with a thick mustache under his bulbous nose, interjected.

"Ethel dear, why don't we take it from the top again?"

"Aw, stick it up your ass, Howard! My pipes are drier than the fuckin' Sahara. I'm taking five," she bellowed, striding offstage.

The extras in sailor suits stood there like lost children, until Cole Porter flicked his wrist, dismissing them. As the stage emptied, Max stepped out from the sidelines and made a beeline for the men.

"Good afternoon, gentlemen. May I have a word with the director?"

Cole Porter flashed an annoyed glance. "He's all yours, Howard. Pay him whatever he wants, but just get rid of him."

Porter stood and stalked off, a contemptuous stink trailing behind him. After a handshake, Max took a seat beside his friend.

"Howard Lindsay," the man said, every syllable sharpened with perfect affectation. "I direct this little circus. Quite sorry you had to see that outburst."

"Not at all. It made my day."

Lindsay grunted. "And what agency are you with, Mister…?"

There was no point in playing dress up in a houseful of actors. Besides, these two already sized him up as a shamus.

"Dietrich. Max Dietrich. I'm sort of a one-man operation."

"Yes, well, how much do you want?"

"For what?"

"You're here about Mr. Porter, aren't you?"

A sudden realization gripped Max. He'd identified Cole Porter as queer just by observing certain mannerisms, lost to most laymen. Hell, plenty of previous jobs were spent trailing men to pansy bars, sent by jealous wives, suspicious employers, and unscrupulous rivals. Many Broadway actors, Wall Street brokers, and city politicians led double lives as "Twilight Men." A veritable moneybags like Cole Porter must have legions of private eyes peeping into his bedroom.

"Mr. Porter's private life is no interest to me."

Lindsay relaxed a little, but suspicion still hung in his expression. "Then *why* are you here, Mr. Dietrich? Or rather, *who* sent you?"

Haskell's stipulation of strict secrecy would get him nowhere on Broadway. Men like Howard Lindsay and the theater elite responded only to clout.

"Elias Haskell, the munitions maker."

The name sent a thunderbolt through Lindsay, who sat stiff in his seat. "Mr. Haskell, you say? Why didn't you say so?" He stuttered a hapless chuckle. "What do you want to know?"

"I'm looking for a cast member of yours. Round face. Handlebar mustache. Medium build. Probably Cuban. Ring any bells?"

"Loud and clear. I'll remember that ridiculous mustache until the day I die," Lindsay said, disgust settling on his face. "Yago Garcia. We cast him as one of the shipmates, in the background, but it came to light he had a criminal past."

"What kind of past?"

"He was a bootlegger during Prohibition. Smuggled rum from Cuba. But then he went straight and joined Broadway. Not too many roles open for his type though. Not with that accent anyway."

"When did you fire him?"

Lindsay rubbed his own mustache, thinking. "Oh, around two months ago. Right about when rehearsals began. Some of our cast remembered him from the old speakeasies."

"Sounds like you were looking for a reason to can him."

"Well, money's been tight around here, Mr. Dietrich. Even with the support of some affluent donors, we've had to cut the fat, so to speak."

Max couldn't blame him, especially not after laying off his own staff. "Know where Señor Garcia flops?"

"If I did, you and Mr. Haskell would be the first to know."

Lindsay's tone and cadence indicated he was telling the truth. At least now Max had a name, a real name, and a time frame that lined up perfectly with "Colonel Lopez's" visit to the Paraguayan Consulate about a month earlier. Thankfully, Haskell's name carried some weight around the theater crowd. But why?

"Thanks, Mr. Lindsay. Just one of more question."

"Ask away."

"Have you met Mr. Haskell?"

Lindsay's mustache swished back and forth in confused irritation. "No, but I'm acquainted with his lovely daughter."

"Cornelia Osborn?"

"Why yes. She's one of the Alvin Theatre's most generous donors."

CHAPTER TWENTY-TWO

After leaving the Alvin Theatre, a growling hunger guided Max down to Horn & Hardart on Broadway, between 46th and 47th Streets. Hot coffee sounded like heaven in this greasy rain. But before entering, he ducked into a nearby phonebooth, plugged in a nickel, and rang up Sergeant Burks.

"Burks here."

"Need another favor, Burksy."

A hoarse laugh crackled through the line. "On Rafferty or someone new?"

"Yago Garcia. A Cuban bootlegger. Should have a record. Tell me everything you have on him."

"Sure, but it'll cost you more than the going rate. Brass is crackin' down on any leaks these days."

Max doubted the wisdom of speaking over a potentially tapped phoneline, but if Burks wasn't worried, neither was he. "I'll pay you double *and* treat you to another round at McSorley's."

"Deal. I'll have somethin' for you by the end of my shift."

That meant Burks would call around five. Max checked his wristwatch – 2:40. "Sure. Ring me at my office."

"Finally paid the phone bill, eh?"

Broadway proved infectious, prompting Max to sing, "I'm in the money, Burksy," before hanging up.

*****

After satiating himself with corned beef, baked beans, cherry pie, and coffee, Max returned to his office a few minutes before five. The ceaseless rain had soaked through his clothes, leaving him feeling pruned and slimy. Thankfully, a broom closet doubled as a wardrobe, and Max changed into a fresh suit and socks, then began drying his overcoat next to a buzzing Waage electric heater. It was one of the few personal items he hadn't pawned off yet, and soon, thanks to Haskell's paycheck, he'd have enough dough to refurnish this glorified cave. But a troubling detail nagged him – the connection between Yago Garcia and Cornelia Osborn.

Could it just be an innocent coincidence? The more Max ran it over in his mind, the more absurd that sounded. Why would an actor impersonate a Paraguayan Army officer and orchestrate the heist of some five thousand submachine guns, rifles, and pistols? Because he was hired to, of course. But what was Cornelia Osborn's angle in all this?

The desk phone gave a shrill ring, jerking Max out of his thoughts. He answered and Burks's gravelly voice came through.

"Your boy has a record as long as my arm. Mostly chicken shit offenses, but Garcia was a rumrunner for Arnold Rothstein's gang. Surprised you two never met."

"My bribes came from the yeggs in charge, not the muscle." Max grabbed his notepad. "But I already know about Garcia's past exploits. Where does he live now?"

"Last known address is a flat in the Lower East Side. The German section, to be precise."

Max jotted down the details. "Ah, my old haunt."

"That's right, you grew up in Kraut Town, right?"

"We called it Little Germany, Sergeant. I'll pay up next week, Burksy. Just put it on my tab."

Before Burks could protest, Max hung up then considered his next move. Once they found Garcia, the guns wouldn't be far behind. But unanswered questions prickled his brain. What was Cornelia Osborn's involvement in all this? Was Richard Osborn setting him up? What were these guns really meant for?

Something told him he didn't want to know.

*****

Max took a cab over to Haskell's penthouse, where he was greeted by the stone-faced butler. He glanced around for Cornelia or Richard Osborn, but the sitting room was empty.

After handing over his sodden overcoat and fedora, Max asked, "Are Mr. Haskell and Mr. Osborn in?"

The butler ignored the question until he'd hung up Max's clothes, then replied, "They're in a meeting and do not wish to be disturbed."

"They'll want to see me."

The butler's lips drew back against his teeth. "And why is that?"

"Just tell Mr. Haskell it's urgent."

A frown soured the butler's already sour puss, but he went into Haskell's office anyway. Left alone, Max half-expected Cornelia Osborn to be listening from afar. He considered confronting her, but this was enemy territory, and only conjecture backed up his theory, not hard evidence. Maybe something more concrete could be gathered from inside her private room and–

The office door creaked open and the butler beckoned Max inside. He entered and found Elias Haskell sitting behind his desk, observing him like a vulture eyeing fresh carrion. Underneath the Civil War painting stood Richard Osborn, decked out in khaki slacks and a fancy blue blazer.

But Max's attention was pulled to a third man, sitting across from Haskell, who also turned to face Max. His features were strangely familiar. Although dressed in a charcoal doubled-breasted worsted suit, a military uniform would have been more fitting.

Recognition hit him. This was Major-General Nathaniel Norris – Richard Osborn's former commander and the man who'd hired Max all those years ago. The General had changed very little since then. Wide shoulders held up a large, clean shaven face, ruled by a Roman nose just above full lips and a sharp jawline. Flecks of gray ran through his close-cropped brown hair. His big, blue eyes were set apart, and held Max in a commanding glare.

He was still the same flinty officer who led them to victory at Saint-Mihiel, back when he was just a colonel commanding the 358th Infantry Regiment. But somehow, Norris's stern face had developed an even harsher disposition, as if his skin had tightened into a leathery hide.

"Welcome, Mr. Dietrich," Haskell said. "We've been expecting you."

CHAPTER TWENTY-THREE

"Expecting me?" Max said, closing the door as the butler left. "I'm ashamed to be so predictable."

Haskell's crackling laughter poured out. "Richard told me how quickly you get results."

Osborn greeted Max with a handshake. "That's right. No secret is safe from Maxie here. He could dig up dirt on Shirley Temple if need be."

Max shrugged. "Everyone has something to hide. Especially the innocent."

"'Where the light is brightest, the shadows are deepest.' Goethe," Norris said, unable to hide a faint midwestern drawl. He stood up, revealing his full statute. At six foot, he stood around Max's height, but instead of lanky and stretched out, the General was broad-shouldered, barrel-chested, and every inch a soldier's soldier. Despite being well past sixty, this was a man who could make short work of men half his age.

"Maxie, you remember Major-General Nathaniel Norris, right? General, this is Maximillian Dietrich. We hired him for that War Resisters League job, back in '29, remember?"

Norris nodded, but not approvingly. Nevertheless, he gave Max a tepid handshake, like a man grasping a slimy eel. Someone as distinguished as Major-General Norris wouldn't associate with reprobates like Max Dietrich any more than lions mingled with jackals.

"Yes, I remember. That information was...*useful.* Too bad Hoover eventually cut our budget though."

"Richard tells me Roosevelt isn't much better."

Disgust curled Norris's lip. "No, he's far worse. Army officers are now commanding his Civilian Conservation Corps like some third-rate Boy Scout troop. The US Army is nothing but a force of chocolate soldiers now. If any foe wished to attack America, now would be the time, and that man in the White House would be to blame."

"That man in the White House" was a favored epithet for Roosevelt-haters, when they were too disgusted to even utter his name. Max glanced over Norris's impeccable suit and tie, as if Osborn had personally dressed him.

"Traded in your uniform for civvies, General?"

"Washington was bad for my health, so I retired last year."

"General Norris has been down in Bolivia," Haskell broke in, reasserting his dominance, "working as a military adviser. Just returned to America this week."

Norris and Max took seats across from the old man, while Osborn lingered off to the side. Apparently, Haskell and Norris were already well-acquainted with each other, despite him playing coy earlier. How many other secrets was this old vulture hiding?

"The Bolivians owe you a lot, Mr. Haskell," Max said. "First guns, now military advisers."

"Well, Norris came highly recommended by Richard," Haskell said. "He was the General's adjutant, you know."

Osborn and Norris shared a glance, full of secrets. Garcia's whereabouts could wait for a few minutes, Max decided, while he probed for more details.

"How is the war going, General?"

Norris's suspicious eyes searched the office until Haskell and Osborn gave reassuring nods.

"Maxie's a friend, General. One you can trust."

That loosened Norris a little.

"This war is a dreadful affair. The Gran Chaco is called 'the Green Hell' for a reason. Troops fight in scorching heat, plagued by swarms of stinging insects, while being pounded with heavy artillery and rifle fire. But worse for us, despite superior numbers and equipment, the Bolivians have lost battle after battle." The General shook his head. "They're too beholden to German strategy."

"Germans? In Bolivia?"

"An infestation," Norris sneered. "Some of the Kaiser's old officers were cashiered out of the new German Army, and they wound up in South America, selling their services to anyone gullible enough. Up until last year, a Kraut named Hans Kundt even commanded the entire Bolivian Army. I was the only American military adviser in Bolivia. You'd think there'd be Yanks down there, since we actually won the war!"

Max remembered Captain Morales's uniform, an imitation of German *feldgrau.*

"Any advice I gave was discarded in favor of some Prussian son of a bitch with a 'von' in front of his name. You know what the Bolivian president said to me about his generals?" Norris asked aloud. "'I gave them everything they asked for – weapons, trucks, whatever they wanted. The one and only thing I could not give them was *brains.*'"

"An honest politician," Max said.

That pulled a laugh from the General. "President Salamanca's honesty will get him killed. Mark my words, his generals will overthrow him by the end of the month. Those South Americans have coups at least once a year. Or a *putsch*, as the Krauts call it."

"Do they now?" Max laughed. "Well, I guess the generals need someone to pin their failures on."

"Too true, Mr. Dietrich. But the fewer politicians in this world, the better."

"Couldn't agree more, General."

Hate warped Norris's stony features. "Especially that Jew in the White House."

Max paused for a moment. "You mean Roosevelt?"

"Rosenfeld," Norris drawled. "That's his real name. 'Roosevelt' is just a mask to fool the gentiles with. FDR is actually descended from a lineage of Dutch Hebrews, but the Jew York Times won't report that."

"Mr. Dietrich," Haskell cut in, irritation in his raspy voice, "if you came to deliver a progress report, please do so."

Max glanced over at Norris, then back to Haskell. "Should we speak privately?"

"The General already knows of our *problem*. So please, don't beat around the bush."

For someone who'd just returned from South America, Nathaniel Norris was surprisingly well-informed.

"I think I found who stole your guns."

Haskell's gray eyes gleamed. "Go on…"

Best to leave Cornelia's name out of it until Max had more than just a hunch.

"An out-of-work actor named Yago Garcia. Former Cuban bootlegger. Apparently, he posed as a Paraguayan Army officer named 'Colonel Lopez' and hired some Red named Mike Rafferty and his friends as muscle. You remember Rafferty, right?"

"The Bolshevik who closed down my factory," Haskell snarled, his cane cracking against his desk. "That bastard Nye…he's the brains behind this!" The wrinkled skin convulsed with hatred. "Don't you see? When I go down to Washington and testify before his ridiculous committee, he'll show off all my guns before the press, proving I violated the arms embargo."

The logic still didn't follow and Max couldn't bite his tongue. "You think a sitting senator would hire Communists for an armed robbery?"

Sneering, Haskell waved a frail hand. "These self-righteous types will stoop to any trickery so long as it justifies their cause. Senator Nye fancies himself a knight and me a dragon to be slain."

Max gave the theory some thought. Perhaps Haskell was onto something, but if Gerald Nye was the mastermind, then what was Cornelia Osborn's role in all this?

"This man, Garcia," Osborn spoke up, "where is he now?"

"The Lower East Side," Max said, pulling out his notebook.

"You can give me the directions on the way there. I want you by my side again, Maxie, just like during the war." Drawing closer, Osborn laid a hand on his shoulder. "Besides, there are some things I need to discuss with you."

Standing up, Max followed Osborn to the door. Glancing back, Haskell and Norris had already resumed conversation, men of destiny plotting their next move. Max suddenly understood how pawns on a chessboard must feel.

CHAPTER TWENTY-FOUR

Max followed Osborn into a nearby study, furnished with a rotary telephone atop a polished, wooden cupboard. Rain slapped against the window, but a glowing fireplace crackled with heat. Cornelia Osborn lounged on a chair, buried deep in *I, Claudius*, looking comfortable in a long-sleeved, white button up shirt tucked into a pair of wide-legged, charcoal-colored trousers.

A daring ensemble, since most women wore pants only when horseback riding or, like Ethel Merman, performing. But this was a woman whose lifestyle, fashion included, was always on the cusp. Cornelia greeted them both with a welcoming smile, but Osborn embraced her with a tempestuous kiss.

"Darling, can you please keep Maxie company while I change? It'll only be a few minutes."

"Of course, Richard," she said, tossing *I, Claudius* aside. "He can save me from this drivel."

"That bad?" Max asked.

"At risk of sounding like a philistine, it's more potent than chloroform. But my book club says it's destined to be a classic."

"Well, you know what they say. Classic literature are books everyone agrees are great, but nobody wants to read."

Cornelia gave a little laugh. "Maybe I'll read some of the pulp magazines you like, Max."

"I'll loan you a few of my favorites. You can use them as birdcage liners after you're done with them."

After a gracious chuckle, Osborn left, and Max made his way over to the fireplace, soaking in the cozy warmth. Several photographs adorned the mantel. Elias Haskell as a young man, his beaked face still recognizable. Another showed the entire Haskell family, Elias, his wife, little

Cornelia and her big brother, what was his name? Oh yes, Francis.

Next to that was a photo of a bookish-looking man in owlish glasses – Francis Haskell, Max presumed – all grown up and in an Army officer's uniform, ready to ship out to Europe and meet his death in the trenches. Next to that was a photograph of Cornelia in an elaborate wedding gown and Richard Osborn in a ritzy tux and top hat, the epitome of two happy newlyweds. Max moved on to a rather odd picture – a much younger Cornelia, robed in a medieval gown, against the backdrop of a stage.

"Your ancestor?" Max asked with a grin.

"Very funny. That was from when I played Juliet, about six years ago."

"On Broadway?"

Cornelia chuckled. "Oh, God no, some local production. But I've had an affinity for the theater ever since."

"Is that so? Are you a patron?"

"Of course. It's the favorite pastime of the idle rich, you know."

Max decided to press his luck. "Oh? What theaters?"

"Take your pick. There's Haskell money floating up and down Broadway." She joined him near the fireplace. "But you know, Francis was the real expert in art."

"Your brother, right?" Max asked, gesturing to the photo of the young man in uniform.

Cornelia nodded. "He was the biggest bookworm I knew. Read all the classics to his kid sister. *Treasure Island*, *Huckleberry Finn*, *The Time Machine*. And the theater? Let me tell you, my big brother could quote Shakespeare in his sleep!"

Max looked back at Francis's picture, his gawky, studious face out of place in a US Army uniform.

"Yes, your father told me he was in the Lost Battalion."

She blinked away a film of tears. "Francis didn't belong there. He's too sensitive. He isn't warlike at all. He should have become a writer or a theater critic." A melancholy sigh escaped her pouty lips. "But you remember the spirit of 1917, right? Every American had to go 'make the world safe for democracy.'"

Max dug deep for a joke, anything to lighten the mood. "It *was* a catchy slogan. Not as memorable as those Burma-Shave jingles though."

That got a giggle from her, just as Richard Osborn returned to the study. He'd changed out of his playboy lounge clothes and back into the uniform of the National Crusaders – his high-collared khaki tunic starched, side cap rakish, blue armband fastened, leather Sam Browne belt and boots gleaming in the light of the fireplace. A riding crop tapped against his side, but Max's interest was diverted to a side holster, filled with a Colt 1911 automatic pistol.

"Let me see that address, Maxie."

Max handed over the notepad with Yago Garcia's whereabouts. Osborn examined it with a stern, unblinking gaze before asking, "Think Rafferty is flopping with Garcia?"

"Doubtful, since he doesn't even know his true identity. Garcia *might* have a rod on him though."

"Then we'd best be prepared."

Osborn strode over to the rotary phone, dialed a number, then said, "Squad Leader Kilmer? Assemble your men. I have a mission for you." He repeated the address in the Lower East Side. "Be there in forty-five minutes."

Osborn clanged the phone down, then turned to Max. "Are you armed?"

Admitting to pawning off his gun wouldn't go over well with these bluebloods, so he answered with a half-truth.

"Not today."

Osborn walked across the study, opened a cupboard, and retrieved a small revolver. Max recognized it as a Colt snubnosed, nicknamed the Detective Special, designed for concealment. Nowhere near as powerful as the cannon in Osborn's holster, but deadly nonetheless.

"Thanks, Richard," Max said, pocketing the snubnosed. "Does every nook and cranny in this place have a gun stashed?"

"This *is* a Haskell household, Max," Cornelia said. "Now just where the devil are you boys off to?"

"Maxie has a lead on the thieves."

Cornelia lit up. "You found Daddy's guns? That's wonderful news!"

Max looked her over. Well, she did know how to lay it on thick. Apparently, Juliet hadn't forgotten her acting lessons.

"Darling, please," Osborn said, "we'll tell you all about it afterward. Nothing to concern yourself with now."

Cornelia covered her mouth, then sauntered back to the chair and returned to *I, Claudius*.

Facing Max again, Osborn asked, "Ready Sergeant?"

"Ready…Lieutenant."

Osborn spun on his heel and marched out of the study, Max following close behind. He didn't look back at Cornelia. He didn't need to. For all his faults, Richard Osborn was as innocent as a newborn babe. The true mastermind, Cornelia's partner, had been revealed. Now, he just had to prove it.

CHAPTER TWENTY-FIVE

The sun had set by the time Rafferty and Gardner reached Brooklyn's Red Hook neighborhood. No trains ran here, and, after crossing the Brooklyn Bridge, they had to slog through the drizzling rain on foot. The neighborhood was a melting pot full of Negroes, Jews, and Italians who worked the docks alongside each other with a grudging acceptance. Many found employment at the Liberty Warehouse, a sprawling complex on Pier 41 overlooking the East River.

A massive Hooverville had blighted Red Hook up until just last month, when Mayor La Guardia cleaned it out. A shame, too, since Hoovervilles were fertile recruiting grounds, full of angry men ready to smash this corrupt system. But for now, Rafferty and Gardner skirted the main five-story warehouse. An elongated two-story structure jutted out from the main building, extending into the East River. With Colonel Lopez's money, they'd rented a small garage at the far end.

When they reached unit 20, Rafferty banged on the massive door and cried, "It's us, O'Hare! Open up!" Minutes passed until the large metal door screeched open, allowing Rafferty and Gardner to slip in underneath. The Mack truck lay parked in the middle of the unit, its bed packed with an immense arsenal.

At the entrance, O'Hare fumbled with the chains, lowering the door shut. Light was scarce inside, but traces of the setting sun broke through a window, illuminating a Tommy gun leaning off to the side, next to a small, alcohol stove. A dozen or so cans of food lay scattered about near an empty coffee mug.

"Look what the cat dragged in," O'Hare said with a giggle. "You two look like hell. Want some joe?"

They nodded and O'Hare scooped coffee grounds into the mug, heated up some water, and within a few minutes, handed Rafferty a steaming cup. Rafferty took a deep sip and sighed. It was G. Washington's Prepared Coffee, the same instant, caffeinated sludge all Doughboys drank in the trenches, but in this wet weather, it was heaven in a cup. He handed the mug to Gardner, who slurped down as much as his scarred throat allowed.

"Why're you here, Lieutenant?" O'Hare asked.

"Some shamus came snooping around the flophouse."

"Who?"

"Max Dietrich. Probably working for Partridge, so we took a powder. Even left our choppers behind." Rafferty flashed the envelope full of cash. "We barely escaped with this."

"Hell, we can always buy more gats with that much dough."

"We won't need to. Colonel Lopez ordered us to get rid of Haskell's stash."

A dumbfounded look swept over O'Hare's pasty face. "Gee, Lieutenant, I guess we can just dump 'em in the East River…"

"Don't be stupid. Think of the possibilities this private arsenal opens up. We have Lopez's two grand, and we can double that if we sell half of these weapons to any two-bit public enemy in the Middle West. Then we can really start cooking."

"Yeah?" O'Hare brightened. "Then what happens?"

"Then the American Red Terror begins. We'll hit every Hooverville from here to Chicago, gunning down members of the boss class along the way. Not just capitalists, but Fascists gangsters, and Comrade Partridge will all get a bullet too. Make another cup, Eddie. We need to be alert when we leave tonight."

Another dumbfounded look overtook O'Hare. "Tonight, Lieutenant?"

"Yes, at midnight sharp. I don't want Partridge or Haskell to find us here, so we need to make tracks soon. We'll slip out of the city under the cover of darkness and head upstate to plan our next move." Rafferty leaned against the truck bed. "We have many enemies, comrades, but thankfully, there's a bullet for each one."

*****

The Packard headed south, threading through rain-soaked streets. Sitting in the passenger seat, Max eyed Osborn. The Chief's gloved hands gripped the steering wheel so tightly it looked ready to break. Thankfully, he'd donned a beige trench coat before they left, hiding most of that flashy uniform. Stealth would be needed for what was coming, though New Yorkers were accustomed to minding their own business. However, for men like Richard Osborn, everything was theater.

"You sure you want to wear those duds?" Max asked.

Staring ahead, Osborn said, "I want this rat to know who he stole from. The National Crusaders do not forgive."

Max almost felt sorry for Yago Garcia, but thoughts of Haskell's payment dismissed any sympathies.

"You said you wanted to talk to me about something?"

"Yes…do you remember the BEF?"

That brought back some memories. In 1932, seventeen thousand unemployed veterans had congregated in Washington DC to demand payment of a cash bonus they'd been promised after the World War. The only problem was that the bonuses weren't available until 1945. But these vets, penniless, hungry, and angry, couldn't wait that long.

They dubbed themselves the BEF – the Bonus Expeditionary Force – a play on the American Expeditionary Force, and the whole movement became known as the Bonus March. Led by a former sergeant named Walter W. Waters, they set up an enormous Hooverville in Washington and demanded their bonuses right then and there.

"Who could forget the Bonus March?"

Osborn flashed a grin. "Well said, Maxie. But did you support it?"

"Of course. What veteran wouldn't?"

"General MacArthur."

Max almost balked at the name. Although an arrogant prick, Douglas MacArthur had been a competent officer during the war, the most important trait of any commander. He'd even earned a reputation as a general who led from the front, disdaining shells, bullets, and mustard gas. That said, the General was an arch-conservative, a man who thought any government assistance was veiled Communism.

"Well, MacArthur's an exception. Shame how he treated those BEF boys," Max said, with more bitterness than he'd expected.

"Yeah," Osborn growled. "A real shame."

Thick silence filled the car, punctured only by the drumbeat of rain and squeaking windshield wipers. The Packard rolled past Union Square, now a soggy marsh. Did Squad Leader Kilmer tell his chief all about this morning's brawl? No need to bring it up now, since Richard Osborn looked ready to breathe fire.

"I was there during the summer of '32," Osborn finally said. "It was shortly after I left the Army and proposed to Cornelia. I didn't need the money, of course. It was the principal of the matter. These men fought for America, gave their flesh and blood for this country. A measly cash bonus was the very least Uncle Sam could give them."

"You went down to Washington? I can't picture Cornelia in a Hooverville."

"Women are soft, vapid creatures," Osborn sneered. "There's a reason we don't send them into combat. They can't understand the bond that soldiers, that *men*, share."

There was some truth to his words, Max admitted. Distinguished men like Richard Osborn didn't associate with reprobates like Max Dietrich under normal circumstances. But after they'd survived the fury of Saint-Mihiel and slogged through the mud and slime of the Argonne Forest, an unlikely connection had been forged between them. But something hinted that wasn't the type of bond Osborn meant.

"I vividly remember the elation when the House passed the Bonus Bill, and the bitter disappointment when the Senate killed it," Osborn went on. "I even met with General Norris at the War Department, to put political pressure on President Hoover. The General was sympathetic to the BEF, and I even convinced him to say a few words of encouragement to the marchers. In mufti, of course."

"I'm sure the brass didn't like that."

"They almost court-martialed him. Meanwhile, Hoover sent his hatchet man General MacArthur and the whole goddamned US Army into the BEF's encampment. Soldiers, armed to the teeth, marched in and cleared us out like we were a pack of filthy tramps."

Max remembered newsreels of troops bombarding the Bonus Marchers with tear gas, then charging them with fixed bayonets, tanks, and cavalry as if they were Red Indians on the plains. Despite such reckless aggression, casualties were light – some fifty injured, one veteran dead, along with an unfortunate infant who'd choked to death on tear gas. □ The whole sordid affair shattered Hoover's already unpopular administration and handed Roosevelt a landslide victory.

"Thousands of veterans were tossed out of the capital like trash," Osborn snarled, weaving the Packard in and out of steady traffic. "They even claimed we were Communists, plotting a revolution. After the smoke cleared, Walter Waters told reporters he planned to start a Khaki Shirt movement, but that blowhard was all talk. I took his dream and made it a reality."

The words seemed more of a threat than a boast. Another strained silence filled the car until Osborn spoke again, his voice booming like a thunderclap.

"Tell me, Maxie. If a government treats its veterans with such dishonor, does it even deserve to exist?"

CHAPTER TWENTY-SIX

Max considered the question. Was Osborn sincerely asking or simply baiting a trap? As with gangsters, survival among Fascists meant telling them what they wanted to hear. Did that make him a chameleon? Maybe. But those lizards changed colors for a reason.

"That's radical talk," Max said with a tight grin. "But so was 1776. And look how that turned out."

Osborn gave a satisfied nod, then rolled the car up to a nearby curb. Max peered out the window. Through the slashing rain, a familiar street was visible – Avenue B, the German Broadway. They were in *Kleindeutschland* – Little Germany – where he and thousands of other German-Americans had grown up.

The tenement buildings, Tompkins Square Park, and beer halls flooded him with warm memories, but they were soon extinguished by darker thoughts. The time when – while Max was fighting in France – his father had been beaten by a drunken thug, leaving him a drooling, braindead vegetable. Papa Dietrich's thick Bavarian accent was enough to brand him as a German spy. The judge even dismissed the attempted murder charge as a manifestation of patriotic fervor, and gave the brute a slap on the wrist. Luckily, the Spanish flu gave the old man a merciful death soon afterward.

"We're here," Osborn said, parking the car across from a four-story brownstone at the corner of 11th Street and Avenue B. Max eyed the entrance. Since the vestibule was most likely locked, they'd need to trail behind a resident. After some ten minutes, a middle-aged woman shrouded by an umbrella, shuffled up the stairs to the brownstone's front door.

Max patted the snubnosed revolver, ready to burn a hole in his coat pocket. They hopped out of the Packard, splashing through the floods of rainwater that gurgled into gutters. The woman fumbled with her umbrella, but graciously held the door for Max and Osborn, who went in after her. A quick inspection of the mailboxes showed that "Y. Garcia" resided in apartment 403. They bounded up the stairs but slowed their pace to stealthy steps when reaching the fourth floor, predators stalking prey.

"Garcia will recognize me through the peephole," Max whispered.

Osborn nodded, understanding the plan without words. Pressing himself against the wall, Max drew his pistol, while Osborn knocked at the door. The bait was good, and after some commotion inside the apartment, the door creaked open.

"Yes?" an accented voice drawled.

Osborn heaved his jackboot forward, tearing the door open with a firm kick. Max followed right behind, jerking the snubnosed revolver straight between Garcia's eyes. They hurried inside the room as Garcia raised his hands in timid surrender. The pompous Paraguayan Army officer was gone, replaced by a disheveled middle-aged man, shivering in a bathrobe and slippers. All that remained was that waxed mustache, twitching in stunned disbelief.

Osborn shut the door then decked Garcia right in the mouth. A grotesque crunching noise rang out as the Cuban sank to his knees, blood and chipped teeth dribbling onto the floorboards. Max averted his eyes and searched the apartment for any other accomplices but found only a one-room studio with a dingy bed, rusty stove, and ratty chair.

"Hello again, Colonel Lopez," Max said, plopping down on the bed. "Or should I say, Yago Garcia?"

Garcia's eyes bulged as color drained from his face. Blood flecked his mustache, now a tousled mess. He divided glances between Max, still covering him with the revolver, and Osborn, fists balled at his side.

"P-p-please," Garcia whined, "I just followed orders…"

"Who is your contact?" Max asked.

"Some woman…she had a funny accent…maybe British..."

"What did she look like?"

"Don't know! We always communicated by telephone."

"I don't see a phone here…" Osborn growled.

A pitiful whimper leaked from Garcia. "Th-there's one out in the hall. Everyone on the floor uses it."

"And you have no idea why this woman contacted you?"

"Sh-she knew I was an actor and wanted me to p-p-play a part. I had no choice! The theater fired me and I had b-bills due!"

"Yeah," Osborn said, his voice tight and cold. "A lot of guys can't make ends meet these days. Too many foreigners undercutting them for work..."

Garcia gave another choked cry, then looked to Max for mercy.

"Better fess up, sweetheart," Max said with a shrug.

"It's the truth!"

"So how did you get all that dough to pay off Rafferty and the others?" Max asked.

"At a locker in Grand Central Station. The m-m-money was always there…b-but I never saw her…"

"Enough of this," Osborn cut in. "Where are the guns?"

"I told R-r-rafferty to get rid of them."

Osborn's heavy jackboot lifted, then crashed against Garcia's cheek, sending him sprawling across the floor. Another burst of blood gushed from his lips along with an agonized cry.

"Calm down, Richard," Max said. "Rafferty has other plans. He and his gang are going to start their own little revolution, courtesy of Mr. Haskell."

Osborn's eyes flared, a beast aroused by blood. "You miserable spic. Tell me where you hid them!"

Garcia lifted his head again, smeared with blood. "At the Liberty warehouse...unit 20…"

Osborn summoned Max over to the window, overlooking Avenue B. The rain hadn't let up, but a pair of headlights were visible, pulling up behind the parked Packard, followed by two more sedans.

"Kilmer's right on time," Osborn said, glancing back over at Max. Garcia was now doubled over on the floor, blubbering in his own blood. Max couldn't hide a frown. He'd seen enough beatings to know they rarely produced reliable results. Besides, the stutter in Garcia's voice indicated he was likely as ignorant as he claimed. Then again, nobody could really trust an actor.

"This isn't the place for a private Spanish Inquisition, Richard. Besides, we'd better get a move on. Rafferty is spooked enough and could take a powder out of town any minute."

The rage inside Osborn seemed to subside and he nodded in agreement. Stepping over to Garcia, he heaved him up by the back of his neck, and hissed, "So, you're an actor, huh? Ever see that picture, *The Most Dangerous Game*?"

Quivering like jelly, Garcia managed to nod.

"You'd better pray the guns are still there…or else you'll reenact that movie…out in the woods, stripped naked, running for your life, while I hunt you for sport."

CHAPTER TWENTY-SEVEN

The Packard cruised deep into Red Hook. Kilmer and his squad followed behind in three sedans, only their headlights visible in the steady downpour. Max glanced over at Yago Garcia, beside him in the backseat, shivering in his soggy bathrobe and slippers, rainwater pooling on the floor. He almost felt sorry for the poor schmuck, but kept the Detective Special's hammer cocked and ready, just in case.

Osborn drove like a madman, weaving in and out of traffic, gunning the motor until, finally, the Liberty Warehouse spread out before them. A large five-story structure tapered off into an elongated row of units on a small peninsula, jutting out into the East River. The only guard was an iron gate that surrounded the main complex.

Storm clouds swallowed up any moonlight, but a few glowing streetlamps provided some illumination. Osborn pulled alongside the curb, killed the headlights, and cut the motor. Kilmer and his squad pulled in after, piled out, and mustered to attention. Max prodded Garcia out of the Packard and followed Osborn.

They all wore uniforms, but like their chief, trench coats gave them some degree of concealment and protection against the slashing rain. There were twelve in all, a few recognizable – Kilmer, Compton, and Jones. The others possessed the same brutish physique, tight-lipped snarl, and steel-eyed glower that were practically a second uniform.

They clustered around the main gate, locked with a paltry chain. Osborn drew his sidearm and a small black tube from his trench coat – a silencer. After screwing it on, he fired off a clean, quiet shot, breaking the chain. Osborn led the Khaki Shirts deeper into the main lot, Max and Garcia trailing behind. Units 1 through 20 were apparently on the other side, stretching out over the water.

"Garcia," Osborn snapped. "I have a mission for you."

The Cuban stepped forward, his slippered feet splashing through puddles. "Y-yes?"

"Go up to unit 20 and demand entry. Mr. Dietrich tells me they'll recognize you as a Paraguayan Army officer." Osborn jammed the silenced Colt into his gut. "Better make this your finest performance, 'Colonel Lopez.'"

Garcia's head bobbed up and down, supplicating and obedient. Osborn turned to the other squad members and nodded. They all drew pistols, augmented with silencers. Tonight's operation was to be surgical, precise, and silent. Just like a trench raid.

"Richard," Max said, holding up his snubnosed, "maybe I should stay behind. I left my silencer at home."

Osborn nodded, then gestured for the Khaki Shirts to follow. Garcia plodded alongside him but as they neared unit 20, Osborn and his men crouched down, blending with the shadows. Peering through the whirl of rain, Max saw Garcia amble toward unit 20's gate, draw himself up, and thunder out, "Comrades! Let me in! It's Colonel Lopez!"

*****

Raindrops pelted the grimy window, like the staccato blast of a machine gun. Though he had to squint, Rafferty could make out the time on his wristwatch. Two hours to midnight. Hopefully the weather reports were right and this soup would clear up soon. Driving a truck full of munitions in this muck would be like setting fireworks off at a gas station.

Rafferty polished off his fourth cup of coffee, yet a stubborn fatigue refused to lift. Once out of the city, he'd sleep for a week. Eddie Gardner stared out the window, his sallow face haggard and drawn. Only Peter O'Hare was alert, his face brighter than his ginger hair. He wolfed down a ration of canned spinach, while his Tommy gun sat inert off to the side.

A fresh wave of rain beat down atop the warehouse, almost burying a bellicose voice from outside.

"Comrades! Let me in! It's Colonel Lopez!"

They froze. Dumbfounded, Gardner and O'Hare looked over at Rafferty, soldiers waiting for orders from their lieutenant. Could it be a trap? Outside, another round of pleas erupted.

"Open up! It's an emergency!"

"Let him in," Rafferty ordered. "But be careful. If someone's with him, plug them all."

O'Hare nodded and headed toward the gate, but Rafferty called him back.

"Don't forget your chopper," he said, handing over the submachine gun.

"Thanks, Lieutenant."

O'Hare tromped off, then squeezed through the small opening between the truck and front gate. In the trace amount of light, Rafferty could see him fumbling with the gate, the Tommy gun slung over his shoulder. That idiot. He'd be a sitting duck if someone were to ambush him—

A hissing noise zinged through the air, exploding through O'Hare's eyeball and out the back of his skull. Gore geysered up as he stumbled backward, then thumped down to the floor, chopper clattering beside him. Rafferty recognized the buzzing whoosh of a silenced gunshot, a cold-blooded execution.

Through the small gap, Colonel Lopez was visible, almost tragicomic in bathrobe and slippers, his wet mustache drooping. Several figures rushed past him, wrapped in beige trench coats, wearing high choker collars and side caps – the Khaki Shirts!

There was no time to escape with the Mack truck. The entire unit would soon be overrun with these Fascists. Khaki Shirts took up defensive positions around the hood, probing their pistols for clear shots. Gardner gurgled out a strained whine, desperate for orders.

Drawing his Colt automatic, Rafferty pumped out a few shots straight into the back window. Glass shattered into glittering shards, offering their only chance of escape. Rafferty heaved himself up and through the small, jagged opening. He extended a hand and lifted his comrade out, just as the Khaki Shirts unleashed a volley of silenced, zipping bullets.

Outside, Rafferty and Gardner dashed over to the fence encasing the warehouse grounds. Fat raindrops plunked into the inky water, crashing up against the rocks. But the clouds had parted, allowing blotches of bright moonlight to spill out. The Statue of Liberty glowed a bright, hypnotic green in the harbor.

Guttural shouts echoed from inside the warehouse. The Khaki Shirts were closing in, sharks smelling blood. Rafferty and Gardner took the fence, then stumbled down the craggy rocks. The murky gloom of the East River opened up like a bottomless pit. In the near distance, Manhattan' skyline twinkled like a million glittering diamonds.

More commotion behind them, followed by the tromp of heavy boots. Rafferty patted his coat, ensuring the two grand was still there, then jumped. He sank deep into the water, its intense cold biting into his skin. He pushed down the pain, silently thanking himself for those swimming lessons he took at Columbia University.

Head above water, Rafferty began kicking toward shore, his fingers – numbed from the cold – never loosening around the pistol. Gardner splashed beside him, an awkward swimmer but staying afloat nonetheless. Rafferty glanced back in an act of defiance.

Behind the fence, a dozen Khaki Shirts glared back, fuming in hatred. In the pallid moonlight, he recognized a few faces from the other night. But they all paled in comparison to another man, tall, broad-shouldered, and imperious. Rafferty had seen him before in street fights – Richard Osborn, the Fascist playboy, Chief of the National Crusaders.

He'd pay for this, Rafferty swore. Osborn and all his Fascists.

Even if it killed him.

CHAPTER TWENTY-EIGHT

Osborn had made good on his threat. Well, half good. Garcia was stripped naked, but instead of being hunted like wild game, his hands were tied to a pillar while the Khaki Shirt Chief whipped him raw. Max had seen sadism in spades during the war and Prohibition, but this scene was something straight out of the horror pulps. It didn't help that flashlights provided the only illumination – careful not to draw unwanted attention – as if they were in a haunted house.

Max drew his eyes away and over to the corpse, sprawled out in a soup of his own brains. Gardner and Rafferty had escaped, so that meant Osborn's men had plugged Peter O'Hare. Poor sod never knew what hit him. Another sharp crack rang out, followed by Garcia's slobbering wail.

"Talk!" Osborn growled. "They must have a safehouse! Where is it?"

Squad Leader Kilmer and the other Khaki Shirts circled their chief like good little Indians, shining their flashlights on Garcia's quivering body.

Moments passed before the Cuban blubbered out, "The flophouse in the Bowery. That's all I know…I s-s-swear…"

"Even they're not stupid enough to return to that dung heap," Osborn mused aloud. He brought the riding crop down again, slicing open a long gash across Garcia's back. Blood gushed out like a gory waterfall. Sliding down against the pillar, Garcia sobbed a tortured scream, before another blow against his flayed skin cut him off. Osborn thrust the riding crop underneath Garcia's double chin, lolling his head back up.

"So, you were just going to pocket the money and leave town. Right?"

"Yes! I already b-b-bought a bus ticket to Hollywood!"

"And why should I believe that? You're an actor. All actors are liars."

The riding crop slashed once more, tearing off a chunk of Garcia's skin, along with half his handlebar mustache. Blood and hair sprinkled Osborn's boots. Garcia writhed in pain as blow after blow chopped him up like roast beef. Max winced again. A squirming sickness rumbled inside him, demanding to stop this freak show.

But before he could speak, a grotesque wail cut through the warehouse. Garcia vomited up a gargling screech as his bound hands slid against the pillar, twitching about in his own gore. Within seconds, his eyes glazed over and dimmed, and his body, now a maze of bloody gashes, went limp. Towering over the heap of flesh, Osborn steadied himself with long, hoarse gasps of air.

"Christ, Richard, that was a damn fool thing to do! He could have told us more and you just killed—"

Kilmer drew closer, a predatory gleam in his eye. Near the truck, the Khaki Shirts stiffened and fixed Max with cold stares, swishing their flashlights straight at him.

"Do not speak to our Chief like that."

Max glanced over at Osborn, still panting over Garcia's mashed up corpse. Old friends or not, Osborn was capable of anything in this state. He held up his hands and backed off. Osborn nodded to Kilmer, who led the other Khaki Shirts to the Mack truck. They began unloading crate after crate, schlepping them over to the sedans waiting outside. Max eyed the truck bed with a quick glance. Although dark, he made out the truck was now only half full, still loaded with crates of rifles, pistols, machine guns, and other goodies courtesy of Haskell Munitions.

Very queer.

"Chief," a Khaki Shirt bawled, tromping up to them. "Captain Morales is here."

The name jerked Osborn to attention. He straightened up, fixed his side cap, and handed the bloody riding crop to Kilmer, grabbing a flashlight instead.

"Bring him to me."

A Khaki Shirt escorted Captain Morales into the garage. The Bolivian officer had shed his *feldgrau* uniform and was now decked out in a beige trench coat, fedora, and foul expression.

"Captain Morales, thank you for coming so late."

"Mr. Osborn…this is most irregular."

"Yes, Captain, it is. But I have an unfortunate confession. Your guns were hijacked by—" Osborn swept a flashlight over to what remained of Garcia and O'Hare "—Communist scum."

Morales examined Garcia's bloodied remains, slumped against the pillar. "I've seen this man before. He visited the Paraguayan Consulate a few weeks ago." His head lifted toward Max, then lit up with recognition. "You!"

"Hi there, Captain," Max said with a little wave.

"Mr. Dietrich is a private investigator," Osborn cut in, "who found your guns."

The Bolivian officer stiffened, nodded his gratitude, then followed Osborn into the bed of the Mack truck. Minutes ticked by before they exited, the tension in Morales's face replaced by pleased triumph.

"All right, Mr. Osborn. The important thing is that the guns have been returned and the authorities were not involved. Please give Mr. Haskell my regards, and the gratitude of my country."

"Of course, Captain. We apologize for the inconvenience. My men will assist you."

Kilmer took the driver's seat, Captain Morales beside him, while eight other Khaki Shirts hopped into the bed of the truck. The engine rumbled to life and the truck shot out of the warehouse into the night.

"Where are they off to?" Max asked.

"We load up the guns on speedboats, then race them out to freighters. Just to avoid any prying eyes. Don't you remember what Mr. Haskell said?"

"Sorry, it's been a rough day."

"Not as rough as it was for those two." Osborn beamed a light at the twisted bodies.

Max forced a smile. An implacable curiosity rose within him. Just why had those Khaki Shirts emptied out half of the truck? Had Morales changed his order? If not, who were those weapons really for? Still, one glance at that whipped-up mincemeat stifled any questions.

"Well, at least Captain Morales is a satisfied customer."

"I was thinking, Maxie. Garcia mentioned a British woman. Think she was working for Vickers? They're a Limey company, after all, and always trying to one-up us in the South American market."

"Didn't Mr. Haskell say they were in the dark about his contract with Bolivia? That woman could have been anyone and her accent could have been put on. Lots of actors in this burgh."

Max had to admire Cornelia Osborn's talents. Throw on an English accent and pull off the perfect crime. For a moment, he considered sharing her role in this bloody misadventure. But he wasn't getting paid enough to step into that no man's land. Besides, he still had to unmask the real mastermind behind all this intrigue.

But for now, fatigue gnawed at every muscle demanding rest.

"I think I'm going to retire for the night, Richard."

"Of course, Maxie. Thank you for all your work." They shook hands.

"I'll swing by tomorrow for the rest of the payment."

Osborn shuffled in place. "Tomorrow will be quite busy. The day after, perhaps."

"I'll be there."

Osborn turned to the three Khaki Shirts left behind. "Crusader Compton, drive Mr. Dietrich back to his office. As for this filth—" he sneered down at O'Hare and Garcia "—throw them into the river with the rest of New York's garbage."

CHAPTER TWENTY-NINE

Rafferty kicked his legs harder as the Manhattan coastline came into sight. The swim across had been rough and choppy, but he and Gardner were almost there. Docks loomed before them, deserted at this late hour. Gardner heaved himself onto dry land first, then flung out a hand to help.

Bobbing in the choppy water, Rafferty gripped Gardner's hand and pulled himself up onto the dock. Minutes stretched out as they lay on their backs, sucking in gulps of cold air. Water dripped off their drenched clothes and pooled around them. It had stopped raining though, just one more cosmic joke played on fate's favorite sucker – Mike Rafferty. At least he'd saved the money.

Rafferty yanked the envelope from his coat pocket but found only a wet slop of green pulp. His fingers grasped for any undamaged bills, but the money squeezed through his fingers like unmolded clay. They'd escaped with their lives, but that swim had melted two grand to pea soup.

Numbness spread through his body, before his senses reignited with rage and despair. All that for nothing. Water trickled over his skin, seeping into the cavernous gash on his face. The mask – where was it? He spun around, eyes searching every which way. The phony glasses that held the prosthetic nose were also gone, both sinking to the bottom of the East River. Despair overwhelmed rage, bringing back bitter memories from the war, when the doctors removed his bandages and revealed the monster Mike Rafferty had become.

The same misery engulfed him now. Back then, he hadn't had access to a gun, but now he could end it all so easily. Rafferty rummaged inside his coat, but Gardner drew up beside him. A slow, trilling hiss leaked out, both a plea and a demand. He was right, Rafferty conceded. They couldn't die yet. There were many scores to settle. But for now, they needed shelter, food, and a change of clothes before succumbing to hypothermia.

Then they'd find Richard Osborn.

And Max Dietrich.

*****

It was half past one when Compton dropped Max off at his office. After stripping out of his wet clothes, he blasted the electric heater and sank onto his couch. He shut his eyes, but Garcia's bloodied corpse kept appearing. The same nightmares plagued him after the war, German ghosts haunting his dreams. For the first time in years, Max Dietrich wanted a drink. Thankfully, grogginess overtook him and closed his eyes.

*****

Max squeezed out the last dollop of Burma-Shave and lathered his face. His office bathroom was small, but it sufficed for basic amenities, although he still showered at the local YMCA. The razor nicked his cheeks and chin a few times, unsurprising, since it'd lasted for three months now. But with Haskell's payment, he'd treat himself to the sharpest razor money could buy.

After washing the shaving cream off, Max examined his reflection. A long, drawn-out face stared back. Underneath the blond widow's peak, worry lines creased his forehead, and tired blue eyes, rimmed with red, opened wide. He looked like hell, but what man wouldn't after these past two days?

None of that mattered though, since it'd be payday soon. But the unanswered questions from last night plagued him. What did Osborn want with those weapons? He considered the possibilities, but one person might know. Besides, he had plenty to ask Mrs. Cornelia Osborn. His detective's curiosity had been aroused.

A throbbing growl reminded Max he hadn't eaten in hours. It was almost noon, but before eating, he'd play his ace. Max grabbed the desk telephone and called Haskell's penthouse. After a few rings, the butler answered.

"Is Mrs. Osborn there?"

"One moment."

A few minutes ticked by before Cornelia bothered to answer.

"This is Cornelia Osborn."

"Hope I didn't tear you away from *I, Claudius*."

"Well, well, if it isn't Max Dietrich." She giggled. "I have to eat crow. Richard wasn't lying. You really are the finest detective in New York City."

"So, you got the news?"

"Yes, and I just want to say thank you for saving my father's company—"

"Is Richard there?"

"No, he and Daddy are out with General Norris, and—"

"Good. May I be frank?" Max continued without an answer. "I know you hired Yago Garcia, *Juliet*."

A tense silence followed, then, "W-what do you mean?"

"And I know all about your brother too."

"Who…told you?"

"Look, if you don't want hubby or Daddy Warbucks to discover your double dealings, meet me at the Port Arthur Restaurant in Chinatown. Be there in about an hour."

Another strained silence, then she snarled, "All right."

A sharp click ended the phone call.

CHAPTER THIRTY

The Port Arthur Restaurant served a mostly white clientele for lunch, Max included. The ornate decor – pristine tablecloths over mahogany tables, embedded with mother-of-pearl, and a baby grand piano – lent it a classier atmosphere than other chop suey joints littering Chinatown. Oriental aesthetics carved into the arches, along with a row of Chinese paintings depicting willow trees, singsong girls, and Chinese gods, evoked the feeling of Old Peking.

The waiter dropped off a plate of chow mein, and, after a few bites, Max relaxed over an issue of the *Daily News*. A real rag compared to his preferred paper, *The New York Times*, but it had a good selection of comic strips. Besides, he needed a little light reading after the past day.

As predicted, the mid-term elections were a Democratic sweep, and Congressman Dickstein had been reelected to New York's 12th District by a landslide. President Roosevelt now had a willing Congress and he promised even more New Deal legislation.

There was even better news for Samuel Dickstein. He, along with Congressman John McCormack, would continue to head the Special Committee on Un-American Activities, dedicated to unmasking the Nazi and Fascist menace inside America. Top target for Congressman Dickstein was the Friends of the New Germany, headquartered in New York.

A full exposé was given on Bruno Hauptmann, a German immigrant who'd been arrested back in September for kidnapping the Lindbergh baby. Apparently, he'd ransomed the boy off fifty thousand dollars, much of which had been paid in gold certificates. Unfortunately, the baby turned up dead just weeks later.

In the end, it was a simple gas station attendant who did Hauptmann in. Not the brightest yegg, Hauptmann paid with gold certificates, which had been withdrawn from circulation by orders of the Federal government. Suspicious, the attendant jotted down Hauptmann's license plate which led the bulls straight to his place in the Bronx. A quick search revealed that Hauptmann still had thousands of the same gold certificates Charles Lindbergh had paid to get his son back.

First the Kaiser, then Hitler, and now Bruno Hauptmann. No wonder America still held Germans in such low regard, Max conceded.

In Kelayres, Pennsylvania, three Democrats had been shot and killed outside the home of a local Republican boss – just for taunting him in the run-up to the elections. The United States was tearing apart at the seams, echoes of 1861.

An interview with Senator Gerald Nye demanded a full reading. In it, the Senator had some cutting words about General Douglas MacArthur, the Army Chief of Staff, who'd recently visited Turkey. Rumors alleged that he'd talked up the Turkish General Staff about the virtues of modern American military equipment.

"It looks to me that General MacArthur is pretty much a salesman," Nye was quoted. "It makes one begin to wonder if the Army and Navy is just a sales organization for private industry."

But Nye reserved his most bitter venom for, arms makers themselves. The Senator guaranteed that his Special Committee on Investigation of the Munitions Industry would unmask the intrigue and double-dealing that had swindled America into the World War. One line stood out – Nye referred to Elias Haskell specifically as an "American Zaharoff," likening him to the infamous munitions salesmen. He looked forward to, "questioning Mr. Haskell about his blood-soaked riches next week."

In Geneva, the World Disarmament Conference was scheduled to disband, thanks to numerous setbacks. Hitler leaving the League of Nations spooked France enough that it refused to disarm. Japan seizing Manchuria promised a future war in the Far East. Not to mention the bloodbath in the Gran Chaco. The Conference was a noble failure, but a failure, nonetheless.

The funnies sprinkled throughout offered a brief respite from all the world's troubles. Buck Rogers battled interplanetary evil in the 25th Century, while Dick Tracy matched wits against the sinister Doc Hump. Mickey Mouse searched for the Sacred Star of Zwoosh, and a new strip – *Terry and The Pirates* – saw adventures in far-flung China. Ridiculous stuff, but more entertaining than *I, Claudius.*

Max stared out onto Mott Street, Chinatown's main thoroughfare. A Blue Eagle poster was plastered on the window, announcing to everyone that Port Arthur abided by NRA codes. A red sedan – a sleek Daimler – parked on the other side of Mott. A woman stepped out, decked out in a beige trench coat, heels, white leather gloves, and a green handkerchief pulled around her brown hair. Despite the cloudy day, round sunglasses obscured her face in a paltry disguise. Cornelia Osborn was hard to miss.

She entered the restaurant with reluctant steps. Folding the newspaper up, Max waved her over to his table. Grimacing, Cornelia took a seat as if it were coated in thumbtacks. A Chinese waiter trotted up and greeted her with a wide grin.

"Anything to eat?" he asked, grin widening. "Any friend of Mr. Max eats on the house."

The chicken chow mein curled Cornelia's upper lip, and she waved the waiter off.

"You eat here for free?"

Max gave a shrug. "About a year ago, two punk teenagers from Little Italy held this joint up with switchblades. The cops here turn the other way when crime happens to the Chinese, especially if the criminals are white. I'm a regular here, so when I heard about it, I tracked the punks down myself, boxed their ears, and made them cough up the dough. Ever since, I eat all the chicken chow mein I want."

"I didn't know you took Chinamen on as clients."

"Yellow, black, white, Red Indian…so long as their money's green."

"Yes, well, since we're on the topic of money, how much do you want?"

Max took another bite. "What do you mean?"

"That's what you called me for, isn't it? Blackmail?" Her lip curled up even further. "Have you no honor?"

"Drop the Little Orphan Annie act. Listen, lady, right now, all I want is answers. I already know you hired those Communist Three Stooges. But why would a pampered princess want to sabotage Daddy Warbucks?"

Cornelia's white-gloved hands pulled the sunglasses off, probing him with those steely gray eyes of hers.

"Please Mr. Dietrich." She leaned closer, voice throbbing, lips pouting. "No more questions."

"Come off it, lady. That damsel in distress act doesn't suit you. Besides, I don't trust any woman I don't pay myself."

"You're disgusting." She drew back. "Fine then. Will three hundred work? Then we'll never mention this again."

Max polished off his chow mein and considered the offer. Three hundred bucks, plus what Haskell owed, would banish any financial woes. But recent memories flashed through his mind, demanding answers.

"Lady, in the past two days, I've had the wind knocked out of me by Fascist hatchet men, nearly greased by Communist gangsters, and watched your husband whip a man to death. A man, *you* hired. Right now, I want answers more than dough."

"All right, Mr. Dietrich, you allege that I orchestrated this entire affair. Who do you think Richard and my father will believe? Their little princess, or a money-hungry scoundrel, who lives in other people's dirty laundry?"

Max almost laughed. Juliet didn't know who she was dealing with.

"Okay, Mrs. Osborn…let's talk turkey."

CHAPTER THIRTY-ONE

As Max considered his next line of questioning, Cornelia Osborn withdrew a silver case and squeezed a cigarette between her lips, waiting for a light. He smiled, then tossed her a Horn & Hardart matchbook.

"Such a gentleman," she said, lighting up.

"Don't insult me. I can play just as dirty as you."

Cornelia blew out a cloud of smoke as her body relaxed, but those gray eyes firmed in defiance. "You didn't answer my question, Mr. Dietrich. How on earth will you prove all this?"

"Well, it's a bit of a yarn, so bear with me. First, I'd remind Daddy Warbucks and Richard that you are a very generous donor to the Alvin Theatre, where Yago Garcia was recently employed as an actor. You remember Garcia, right? The Cuban bootlegger who couldn't outrun his criminal past."

"Who?"

"Don't play dumb. That handlebar mustache is hard to forget. Anyway, after Howard Lindsay sent him packing, you rang up Garcia and hired him, using your finest British voice that you mastered back in your acting days. So your Limey alter ego entices Garcia into a job, promising him a big payday.

"What can he do? He's already a criminal with a long rap sheet. He can't go back to Cuba, since he's probably wanted for something even worse there. But with the money he gets from you, he can start a new life in Hollywood. So, he agrees. And like all good actors, he researches his role, a Paraguayan Army officer. Consul Ortiz remembered him very well."

She took a deep puff, fuming in silence.

"However, a dandy like Garcia wasn't the muscle you needed. New York City has unlimited thugs for hire, but that might get you involved with the Mob, and you're smart enough to avoid that. Besides, you want the heist to look political, so what do you do?"

Smoke poured from her nostrils like an angry Chinese dragon. "Do tell…"

"That's when you say, 'Ah ha!', and remember Daddy Warbucks had a run-in with some Bolshies back in 1932. An unfortunate veteran with a broken face, Mike Rafferty, had a grudge against the Merchants of Death, your father included. 'The perfect fall guy!' you say to yourself. So, you hire a private investigator to track him down."

"Oh, so I *also* hired a private eye?"

"My contact in the Communist Party told me some other shamus was poking around for Rafferty's whereabouts. Don't think I forgot that crack you made about private eyes 'always trying to swindle you.' We are, but that line tipped me off that you had previously hired one who screwed your pocketbook."

She scowled, sucking down another drag of cigarette smoke.

"Anyway, your plan almost worked, but luckily, I found the Rafferty Gang right before they lit a powder with all those Haskell guns. You wanted Rafferty to dump all of Daddy's guns in the East River, but he had other plans. But here's where I'm stumped, Cornelia, er, Mrs. Osborn. Why? Why would a little pampered princess want to ruin her meal ticket?"

"You're the detective. You tell me."

A snake-like trail of smoke coiled upward from Cornelia's cigarette while her gray eyes seemed to stare straight through Max. The smiling waiter returned, cleared the plate, presented a fresh ashtray, then trotted off.

"Well," Max began again, "that issue of *Fortune* magazine your father loaned me was chock full of information. Did you know that the Du Pont Corporation purchased a controlling interest in Haskell Munitions stock? That must have injected that dying company with just enough cash flow to keep it alive. But why, I wonder? Haskell's still selling arms to Bolivia, I saw that with my own eyes. But here's the queer thing…only half of that shipment is going to South America. You see, the Khaki Shirts took half those guns for themselves, and gave the rest to Captain Morales."

Cornelia's mouth parted.

"Don't know anything about that, do you?"

"No, I don't, and neither do you. All you have are theories, Mr. Dietrich." She took another drag and sent the smoke wafting across the restaurant.

"Very true. But let me share some. It involves a spoiled daughter throwing a tantrum. She hatches an elaborate scheme to ruin her father, a despicable Merchant of Death. Maybe she got religion, or someone else put her up to it."

Cornelia rested her chin atop her gloved hands, the cigarette smoldering. "Who?"

Max allowed a triumphant grin. "Your brother, Francis Haskell."

The gray eyes flared, then shrank back into pinpoints. "My brother died during the war."

"That's what your family wants people to think, but it's not true."

"Ridiculous." She dragged again and rolled her eyes in contempt. "Your theory is hogwash. Besides, Richard always gives me an allowance, so what would I need a partner for?"

"That may be, but you and I both know that Francis is alive."

Cornelia Osborn looked away, eyes wandering about, searching for escape. The cigarette continued to burn, sending blue threads of smoke sprawling up between them, until ash sank onto her white leather glove. She mashed it out, then lifted her gaze to meet Max, now calm and accepting.

"How…did you know?"

He shrugged. "A small mistake on your part. 'He's too sensitive. He isn't warlike at all.' You usually don't refer to the dead in present tense."

"Fine. Francis Haskell *is* alive. But he's not behind this. Not in the way you think."

"Either way, I'd like to speak to Francis myself."

"I don't think that's a good idea. Please, just name your price and let's forget all about this."

Max sighed, leaned forward, and lowered his voice.

"One more question, then." Without waiting for her response, he asked, "How long have you known your husband is a homosexual?"

CHAPTER THIRTY-TWO

Cornelia Osborn's pretty features crinkled in anger. But each passing moment seemed to cool her fury until a defeated smile bloomed across her lips.

"What gave it away?"

"The way you act around each other. Only teenagers kiss each other with that much passion. Besides, all marriages are scams for some reason or another."

"Your cynicism isn't nearly as charming as you think it is…"

Max laughed. "To be honest though, the signs were there. During the war, you couldn't drag us out of French brothels, but Lieutenant Osborn never set foot in there."

"He is a West Pointer, you know. French whores don't befit an officer and a gentleman."

"True, but when I saw him again in civilian clothes, he wore a matching handkerchief and necktie. A subtle signal for men of that persuasion. Added to that, there were all those lingering stares he gave General Norris."

"You sure know a lot about these…*men*…"

"A lot of past jobs involved exposing them for suspicious wives or jealous rivals."

Her defeated smile soured into a scowl.

"Look, lady, I never said I was a Boy Scout and I've made peace with how I earn a living. You've had money all your life, so you don't know what the world is really like. Unlike people, the only thing that won't fink on you, stab you in the back, or try and kill you is a dollar bill."

"Well, you're smarter than I was."

"Why don't you start at the beginning?"

"Fine. As I said, we met at a dinner party back in '32. Daddy always maintains strong connections with the Army and Navy, and we were invited to some officer's ball down in Washington. He always took me along to entertain those crusty old generals in the War Department. Anything for a lucrative contract."

Max tapped the copy of the *Daily News*. "Senator Nye called your father the 'American Zaharoff.'"

"He'd take it as a compliment." She paused. "But Zaharoff sold guns for Vickers, so perhaps not. Anyway, my father was chatting with Major-General Norris, who introduced us to his adjutant, Captain Richard Osborn. He was Prince Charming, Charles Lindbergh, and Rudolph Valentino rolled into one."

Max had heard more than a few rumors that Valentino had also swung that way but kept those to himself.

"Sounds like a Hollywood romance."

She expelled a wistful sigh.

"It was, in a way. He courted me, sent love letters, poems. Sappy, yes, but I swooned. You see, I despise the pretentious society snobs of New York's elite. I'd rather marry a jellyfish than one of them. But Richard was smart, sophisticated, and had been to war, unlike those pampered slackers. And he had such promise too. In ten years, he could have been a general himself! However, he was living in Washington and I in New York, complicating our budding romance. So, imagine my surprise when he resigned his commission and moved up here."

"He told me it was because there wasn't any room for promotions under Hoover."

Cornelia scoffed but didn't respond. The silver cigarette case flashed open again as she withdrew yet another smoke. She lit a match and puffed away for a few moments in sulking silence, the restaurant's piano serenading them both.

After several drags, she replied, "That's just Richard's cover story. He's very good at spinning a yarn, especially to gullible dimwits like me. The night he arrived, we went on a carriage ride around Central Park, where he popped the question. It was all very romantic."

"Every girl's dream."

"Unfortunately, my dream didn't last long. Daddy hired Richard as a salesman and, given his connections with the Army, he secured a few contracts, but nothing big. This was the summer of 1932, right when the Bonus March converged on Washington."

"Seems to have made an impression on him."

"It was all he could talk about for weeks. Barely got any work done. Eventually, he took a train down to Washington without even telling me. After all, he went down to meet his real lover. Even convinced General Norris to make a statement in support of the BEF. But then General MacArthur cleared the Bonus Army out of Washington like a roach nest. Richard was tear gassed and beaten, but that didn't bother him. Seeing all those unemployed veterans treated like a motley gang of tramps filled Richard with a seething hatred toward the government. One that he's never relinquished."

"Richard did mention that the BEF commander, Walter Waters, talked about starting a Khaki Shirt movement," Max said. "Guess that rubbed off."

"Possibly. But in name only. You see, soon after Richard returned to New York, the Chaco War broke out and he was able to secure a very lucrative contract with Bolivia. It saved Haskell Munitions from going belly up. We were married shortly after and ran off to Europe for our honeymoon. London, Paris, Rome…"

"And Richard was more interested in Mussolini than in you?"

"A good guess. He was also smitten with the Croix-de-Feu, that French veterans organization. Kept saying 'That's what the BEF should have been.' But Paris was just an appetizer. The main course was in Rome. When Richard saw all the black uniforms, the marching, the salutes, the flags, and Mussolini grandstanding like some 20th century Caesar, and he fell head over heels for Fascism."

"And unlike your marriage, that wasn't a sham."

For a moment, Cornelia looked ready to weep, but then her face broke into a wide grin. She took a final drag before extinguishing her cigarette. The pianist struck up a rendition of "Let's Do It," a charming ditty by Cole Porter, but given the circumstances, it sounded more like a mocking funeral dirge.

"You really know how to hurt a lady. But it's true. Well, when we got back from Europe, Richard tried to convince Daddy to fund a new movement based off the Black Shirts. At first, Daddy shot him down. Said the company was just beginning to recover and didn't have cash to fund his pet project."

"So, what changed?"

"I'm not sure exactly. But it was around the time Roosevelt went off the gold standard."

Max remembered that political earthquake like it was yesterday. Until just last year, every dollar spent had been worth a fixed amount in gold. After the stock market crashed and banks fell like dominoes all over America, people began exchanging their paper bills for solid gold and started hoarding like a nation of misers. But President Roosevelt needed fast cash to stimulate the economy and spend his way out of the depression.

In June 1933, FDR took America off the gold standard and could print as many dollars as needed for the New Deal. The wealthy predicted an end to Western civilization. But there was no collapse, nor was there a miraculous cure to the depression.

"At first, I thought the National Crusaders were going to a legitimate political party. Even Hitler ran for president," Cornelia said, almost choking on bitterness. "But there weren't any Khaki Shirt candidates in these midterm elections. So much money is poured into their uniforms, training, and that barracks out on Long Island. My father's business is on quicksand, and he's investing in this political theater."

Highlights from that *Fortune* magazine article along with Compton's boasts reentered Max's mind.

"The Khaki Shirts were set up in June 1933, right? Was this also around the time Du Pont purchased a controlling interest in Haskell stock?"

"Yes."

"It sounds like Du Pont's money gave Daddy Warbucks enough dough to turn the Khaki Shirts into a private strikebreaking army."

"Yes, that's all they are. Hired thugs and muscle. I suppose my father pockets some of the money renting them out to scare workers. Many business magnates in the Liberty League use them. Secretly, of course."

"The Liberty League?" Max chuckled. "I keep getting their pamphlets in the mail. How much do you know about them?"

"Not much, other than its membership is a veritable Who's Who in big business, my father included. Richard and my father don't tell me anything. After all, what does a woman know about politics?"

"Speaking of Richard, how did you discover his double life?"

"Little things tipped me off. He'd claim he was out with a potential client and didn't think I noticed the bite marks on his neck. Even though there was no lipstick, I was convinced there was another woman. In a fit of jealously, I hired a private investigator."

"The same shamus who overcharged you?"

She nodded. "He followed Richard to a place in Greenwich Village called Polly's."

"The pansy joint? Tailed a lot of marks there..."

Her lip curled again in disgust, far worse than seeing a plate of chicken chow mein.

"Yes, well, it turned out that General Norris was in town and Polly's is their favorite meeting spot. After a few drinks they went uptown to Everard...and..."

She didn't have to finish. Everard was the most popular Turkish bathhouse in the city, a favored spot for the homosexual community, earning the nickname "Everhard."

"The PI did some more digging and found the truth about why Richard resigned his commission. Turns out, his love letters to General Norris were discovered by other Army officers. Richard took the fall for both of them and claimed it was 'unrequited love' so Norris could keep his commission. But he was given a choice. Resignation or a blue discharge."

Max couldn't fault Osborn for choosing the former. Blue discharges were the preferred method of purging homosexuals from the US Army. Its stain was enough to ruin a man, following him around like an evil curse.

"Why didn't you confront Richard?"

"I showed my father the evidence, but—" she bit her lip, squeezed her eyes shut "—he didn't care. If it wasn't for Richard, his company would have failed. He told me to keep quiet or I'd be written out of the will. I realized that Haskell Munitions was his real child. Francis and I were just possessions."

"So, what did you hope to accomplish by throwing Daddy's guns into the East River?"

"I don't know…pay him back for ignoring his only daughter? I mean…what would you do in my circumstances? There aren't a lot of options for me without a man's money to live off of."

"Exactly. That's why I'm a little skeptical of your story. Why ruin your only chance at a kept life?" His eyes narrowed, the accusation sharp and direct. "Perhaps if you'd let me talk to your brother Francis, then maybe I'd believe your story."

Cornelia squirmed in her seat, gazing out the window. Finally, she said, "All right…but fair warning. You aren't going to like what you see."

CHAPTER THIRTY-THREE

Max followed Cornelia out of Port Arthur, pausing to let a tourist bus lurch down Mott Street. Out of towners gawked around from the open top, as a bus barker narrated through a microphone.

"And now, ladies and gentlemen, we are passing through Chinatown. Beneath these streets lurk countless opium dens and sing-song girls. Yes, there are many hidden worlds here in mysterious Chinatown!"

The tourists gasped at the Yellow Peril in their midst, as the bus rolled down Mott and out of Chinatown. Cornelia led the way to her Daimler across the street, opening the passenger door for Max. He settled into the upholstered seat, feeling the snubnosed revolver inside his coat pocket. It'd be easy to grab on the off chance Cornelia was leading him into a trap.

They took off across the Brooklyn Bridge, and the Daimler wove through dense, snarled traffic. Only when they reached the furthest reaches of Brooklyn, leading out to the spacious expanse of Long Island, did Max puncture the silence.

"So, Francis lives out here? Let me guess, a mansion in the Hamptons?"

"In a way," Cornelia answered, eyes set on the road ahead.

More vague riddles. Perhaps with some gentle prodding, she'd allow more secrets to flow.

"Has Richard ever talked about the war?"

"Only in a general sense," she said. "He mentioned some battles and that he received a medal from Norris." Her gray eyes flashed over to him. "And that you saved his life."

Now it was Max's turn to fall silent. Memories of the war conjured up an unsettling feeling of dread, as if it had never really ended and peace was a dream. The details were still clear. President Woodrow Wilson declaring war against Germany in 1917, stating that "the world must be made safe for democracy."

A noble goal, but it was smothered in a tidal wave of anti-German hate. Wagnerian operas were banned. Dachshunds were kicked to death in the streets. Sauerkraut was renamed "Liberty Cabbage."

But Max Dietrich was going to show Uncle Sam he was just as patriotic as any American. Without waiting to be drafted, he marched to the local recruiting station and joined the Army, winding up in the 358th Infantry Regiment.

Soon, Max found himself training in Iowa with a gaggle of hick farm boys who laughed at his fast-talking New York accent and scrawny physique. Almost all of the 358th Regiment were from rural areas, men who'd never even seen a general store, let alone the Statue of Liberty. Only in Max's platoon commander, Second Lieutenant Osborn from Baltimore, did he find a kindred spirit. Two city boys in a sea of country bumpkins. The unit shipped out to France in 1918, taking part in the first big American offensive of the war – the Battle of Saint-Mihiel.

Max looked out the window. Rows and rows of endless, sparsely populated fields flitted by. Although soggy from the recent storms, they were nothing compared to the thick quagmires of mud in France. The incessant drumbeat of rain on that September morning was still fresh in Max's mind, along with the palpable tension that seized his throat like a vise. The 358th Regiment spearheaded the assault at the crack of dawn. Savage fighting followed and in the thick of combat, Max spotted Lieutenant Osborn, struggling for his life against a German bayonet, inches away from his throat.

Unable to get a clear shot, Max screamed in fluent German to surrender. The Kraut obeyed, a side effect from endless drilling by Prussian officers, and dropped his rifle. A chain reaction followed, with what remained of the German company surrendering en masse. Their platoon netted fifty prisoners that day, and Max, one of the only German speakers in the entire regiment, interrogated them all. Osborn promoted Max to sergeant and thanked him personally.

"Your husband…is a decent man," Max said, until Garcia's bloodied corpse reentered his mind. "Or was, at least."

"What makes you say that?"

"You don't understand. You've never been to war. It changes people. Like seeing the world in color, and now you can only see black and white."

"I know all about what war does to people, Mr. Dietrich. I think the depression changed Richard more. The war provided an enemy abroad to fight and kill. But now, the enemy is the government."

Max nodded and stared out the window, until a series of haunting structures loomed in the distance, like foreboding mountains. Brown, neoclassical buildings formed a massive complex, but their dark facades and tinged windows looked like something out of *Dracula*.

"We're here," Cornelia said, with an air of finality.

At last, Max realized where they were – Kings Park State Hospital for the Mentally Insane.

CHAPTER THIRTY-FOUR

The waiting room was more pleasant, decorated with portraits of Governor Lehman and President Roosevelt, giving the facade of a post office rather than an insane asylum. Max sat beside Cornelia in silence, his mind spinning with conjecture, but unable to voice anything. Francis Haskell hadn't died in the war, but his mind had. He wasn't the only one who'd gone mad over there. Thousands of men had been reduced to babbling, shell-shocked husks, unable to dress, feed, or bathe themselves. Now they were locked away in nuthouses, unpleasant memories best forgotten.

A middle-aged nurse in a starched white uniform approached.

"Mrs. Smith," she said to Cornelia. "I'm so glad you came. Francis has been so lonely."

Cornelia didn't respond, but glanced at Max, a hint to keep quiet. He shrugged. It was no skin off his nose if the Haskells used aliases. The nurse led them up the stairs to the third story. Weird howls boomed throughout the hallways, anguished cries belonging to men past the point of no return.

They paused in front of a cell labeled "Smith, Francis," and the nurse fixed Max with a hesitant stare.

"I've never seen you before, sir."

"He's a…family friend," Cornelia answered.

"Is he…aware of your brother's condition?"

"More or less."

"Please," the nurse said, almost teary-eyed, "try not to stare."

The door creaked open, and Max followed Cornelia inside to a padded cell, shrouded in shadows. Small traces of sunlight seeped through a barred window, allowing Max to see a crouching figure, lurking in the corner. The door clanged shut behind them, sending a chill through Max. His hand drifted toward the snubnosed revolver inside his pocket, but he fought off the urge. The dark silhouette shuffled around like some giant crab but remained hidden.

Cornelia bent down and whispered in a soft voice, "Francis, it's me, Cornelia. You remember your little sister, right?"

The figure emerged from the darkness on all fours, a wild animal sniffing out intruders in its lair. Its thin, gaunt body was clad in white hospital pajamas, and the little visible skin had dulled to a deathly pallor. It lurched forward until the trickles of sunlight lit up its face – what was left of it.

Max had seen plenty of grisly sights during the war. Machine guns sawing men in half. Soldiers bloated like balloons after a gas attack. Heavy artillery pounding human bodies to pulverized stumps of meat. But the horror that crawled toward him now was in a different league.

Any human features had been shaved off, leaving behind a jigsaw puzzle of snarled skin and twisted flesh. The nose, like Mike Rafferty's, was torn clean off, leaving behind a flaring, pulsating cavity, like an agape mouth eternally screaming. Worse still was the lower half, which had been completely obliterated. No jawbone remained, and the mouth was reduced to a small, puckered hole oozing long trails of saliva, like an asshole dribbling shit.

The legs were now just chopped-off stumps, but a pair of withered arms propelled the rest of this fleshy husk around the cell. Deep scars crisscrossed every inch of skin, remnants of countless past surgeries. Gnarled nubs stood where ears had been, and a ratty nest of blond hair covered its scalp. One eye was completely missing, showing only a dark, cavernous socket. But the other eye, colored a Haskell steel gray, held Max in a paralyzing grip.

"Poor Francis," she said, stroking the creature's filthy hair. Faint, strangled whimpers poured out of what was left of Francis's mouth, a lost dog reuniting with its master.

Max swallowed his disgust and said, "You…you proved your point. Does…does your father know about this?"

"Of course. This was all his idea…" Cornelia gave a deep sigh, full of bitter melancholy. "Let me start at the beginning. As I'm sure my father told you, he volunteered to go fight in Cuba, and even lost a leg there. Well, he expected the same from Francis. Of course, my brother should have been a college professor, not a soldier, but ever since my grandfather paid a substitute during the Civil War, the Haskell name has been tarnished by cowardice."

"So, Daddy Warbucks didn't want his son to be a slacker? Can't say I blame him…" Max left out his fiancée running off with a draft dodger. Any past grievances seemed insignificant compared to this freak show.

"No, he didn't, and Francis was pressured to join. My father arranged for him to receive a commission as a second lieutenant in the 308th Infantry Regiment, and off to war he went."

"He said Francis was killed in action with the Lost Battalion."

"Yes, it's a gallant story, but only half-true. Francis *did* serve in the Lost Battalion, cut off from the rest of the regiment, surrounded by the entire German Army. But then he disobeyed direct orders to hold their position, attempting to lead his platoon in a breakout. Whether it was cowardice or genuine concern for his men, it doesn't matter, since they didn't get very far. Artillery opened up, blasting them all to pieces. Only one soldier escaped, who reported their noble deaths."

"How'd your family take the news?"

"My mother was devastated. Father was too, but publicly, he was proud that a Haskell man died for the country. He's harder than steel, that man. 'Steel doesn't break,' he says. 'A true Haskell has steel in their veins.'"

"A good motto for a businessman."

"But lousy for a father." Cornelia drew her hand from Francis and stood, wrapping herself in a full embrace. "The newspapers celebrated our family's sacrifice, but there was one problem. A German patrol found Francis, somehow still alive by the grace of God. And it turns out that the shells that landed on my brother were from *American* artillery batteries. Guess their aim was off that day."

Max glanced back over at Francis, scurrying on all fours, slobber dripping behind him. What kind of God would let a man live in that state? Then again, the Almighty was one hell of a practical joker. Cornelia went on.

"Even in that state, an American officer was a valuable prize. So, the Krauts took my brother prisoner and sewed him up, just enough to keep him alive. His dog tags had been lost in the shelling, so Francis Haskell became an unknown soldier. But the Germans figured they could interrogate him and have him write his answers down. Unfortunately, poor Francis had completely lost his mind, unable to communicate in any way. I think going crazy was the only sane response. Don't you?"

Max just nodded.

"My brother languished in a German hospital until after the war, when they identified him through fingerprints and contacted our family."

"Let me guess…it wasn't a happy reunion."

"To say the least. My mother fainted after seeing what became of her darling boy. Hell, I vomited all over my new dress. But my father just stared, his eyes harder than steel. Father's money kept this whole horrid affair out of the papers, and we took Francis back to America, checking him in here under a false name."

"Aren't there plastic surgeries available? Prosthetic masks? Something to hide…all that…"

A gurgling whimper squeezed out from what was left of Francis's mouth, like an offended protest. But the one bulging gray eye drooped, showing his fatigue. Francis Haskell crawled back to the shadowed corner like an enormous cockroach scurrying back to its crevice.

"The doctors said he'd never recover his sanity. So, according to my father, it'd be a waste of money to patch him up. 'Why put a mask on a madman?' he said. Dead, Francis Haskell was a hero, but alive, he was a slobbering freak, a monster, a family shame. So, we locked him away here, all alone. He slurps down soup through a straw, wallows in his own filth, and waits for death. And my father has forgotten about his only son."

Osborn edged into Max's mind. "And gotten a new one."

Cornelia almost giggled. "Richard is everything my father wanted from a son. Strong, virile, and in one piece. A worthy heir. Who cares if he's a fairy?"

"How'd your mother take it?"

"She couldn't. She'd wake up in the middle of the night, screaming that Francis was there in the room, judging her. A few years ago, she took a long bath and poisoned herself."

"Why are you telling me all this?"

"Because Francis Haskell is the future." She paused, then turned to Francis, curled up in the safety of darkness. "Goodbye, big brother. I'll see you again soon."

Max followed Cornelia out of the cell and into the hallway, away from this bottomless pit of nightmares.

CHAPTER THIRTY-FIVE

They left Kings State Hospital in silence, but Max let his mind wander far and wide, Cornelia's words ringing in his mind – '*Francis Haskell is the future.*' How many new Francis Haskells were being created every day in the Gran Chaco? Still, that war might as well have been on Mars, as far as Americans were concerned. The average Yank didn't give a good goddamn about foreign adventures these days. Or so they said. With a peppy slogan and a new enemy, courtesy of the Merchants of Death, Max bet a new generation of Yanks would make the world safe for democracy again.

Max waited until they were back inside the Daimler and on the road before speaking.

"What are you hoping to accomplish with all this? If Daddy Warbucks goes down, so do you."

Cornelia didn't answer right away, instead kicking the Daimler up a gear. The bland Long Island landscape whirled by in an amorphous blur. She bit her lip, choking back a little sob.

"It'll be a small price to pay to avenge my brother."

For once in his life, Max considered whether he'd been *too* cynical. Had he misjudged this pampered princess? But that didn't answer a more troubling question. Where had Richard Osborn taken those guns? One possibility lit up in the afternoon haze. He'd ignored it for too long, but now it forced itself from his throat.

"They're planning a putsch," then added, "A coup d'é tat."

"Who?" Cornelia asked, eyes set on the road.

"Your father and your husband."

Max found himself diving deeper, back into Osborn's manifesto with its endless praise of war. A putsch was insane, but the depression made America a little crazy. And if, against all odds, Osborn took power, a new war loomed in the future. Try as he might, Max could never forget the old war, with its fields of corpses, shattered landscapes, and broken dreams. He didn't have many ideals left but saving a new generation from that slaughter was one of them. Cornelia's voice yanked him out of those brooding thoughts.

"A coup? Mr. Dietrich, like you said, the Khaki Shirts are just glorified strikebreakers! What chance would they stand against the US Army?"

"Those missing guns might help even the odds."

"Regardless, there's no more than ten thousand Khaki Shirts nationwide. And even with those guns, the Army has tanks, poison gas, and airplanes. It'd be a massacre."

"Don't the Khaki Shirts have a barracks in Long Island?"

"About twenty minutes west of here."

"How about we drop by?"

She gave a snide laugh. "Do you have a death wish?"

"Aren't you the Chief's wife? Can't you stroll up for an inspection?"

"I'm nothing but an ornament. Why would a dimwitted socialite be sneaking around there? Besides, they just teach pot-bellied veterans how to street fight with the Bolshies."

"Look, how about we just swing by? If the Khaki Shirts are busy earning their merit badges for marksmanship, then you owe me an egg cream."

"Fine," she sighed.

The Daimler turned and headed west. A few gas stations whooshed by, but much of Long Island was deserted. The mansions of New York's elite were usually hidden off the beaten path. Cornelia jerked the steering wheel onto a series of bumpy backroads, far away from prying eyes. Minutes passed before the Daimler pulled off the road, crawling over soft ground, still moist from the recent rain.

Max peered out the front window into the sparse forest ahead. On the horizon, a two-story factory loomed, its smokestacks still and inert. But there was activity inside, evidenced by several silhouetted figures passing in front of the many windows. A dozen or so small, wooden structures and tents surrounded the factory like a series of forts. The Civilian Conservation Corps operated similar barracks, but this was no CCC camp. Dozens, no, hundreds of Khaki Shirts, in full uniform, marched along the field as if on parade.

"This is all Haskell land. Used to house a few hundred workers. But once the factory closed down, my father laid them all off and planned to convert it into another warehouse."

"Until Richard convinced him to turn it into a Fascist boot camp?"

"Good guess."

Max focused on the horizon. Details were impossible to make out, but the National Crusaders performed the same drills every soldier did – low crawling, double time, falling in, falling out, and about face. Max stepped out onto the soggy ground. The air was cool and crisp, banishing any lingering stupor from the asylum and snapping him to full attention.

"What are you doing?" Cornelia gasped. "They'll see you!"

He didn't respond, taking plodding steps closer. A few trees provided cover as he scoped out a suitable vantage point. Cornelia also exited the Daimler, her high heels squelching through the moist grass, wobbling to keep her upright.

"Get back to the car before—"

Max slid a hand over Cornelia's mouth, shushing her, just as a loud crack boomed – the volley of rifle fire. Somewhere, on the other side of the barracks, squads of Khaki Shirts must be at target practice. The hundreds of visible Khaki Shirts appeared to be unarmed, but several sentries posted at the barracks gates brandished Tommy guns, ready to rake the field with bullets.

One National Crusader drew Max's attention. Strutting through the field, decked out in full uniform and side cap, was Chief Richard Osborn, lording over the compound as if it were his own private fiefdom. A civilian walked alongside him, and though his face was obscured, that worsted suit and broad shoulders were enough to identify General Norris. Elias Haskell hobbled alongside them, lurching atop his silver cane. Well, no wonder Osborn couldn't meet today. Preparing for a putsch was time consuming, after all.

Over the staccato blast of rifles, a chorus of voices rose from the camp. Max recognized the song as the "Battle Hymn of the Republic," but growled with more menace than a war chant.

He pulled his hand off Cornelia's mouth, allowing her to gasp deep breaths. They stumbled back to the Daimler, stomped the mud from their shoes, slid inside, then pulled back on to the main road. The Daimler sped westward, back toward New York City, as they sat in strained silence. Few things were more satisfying than having one's theory proved correct, but now all Max could feel was a smothering sense of hopelessness.

"Looks like I owe you an egg cream," Cornelia said, her pretty face suffused with a coy grin.

"I'll take a rain check."

"What should we do? Go to the Police?"

"And report them for what? America's natural resources are guns and the lunatic fringe. Besides, I saw just how chummy New York cops are with the Khaki Shirts."

"Well, this is Long Island."

"You know what I mean. I don't think the hick cops out here will care about the National Crusaders playing soldiers in the dirt. No, we'll have to go higher."

"You mean G-Men?"

"Not G-Men. Just a New York congressman."

"Who?"

There was one New Yorker whose personal mission was to slay the Fascist dragon in America. But just thinking his name knotted Max's stomach and tightened his throat.

"Samuel Dickstein."

CHAPTER THIRTY-SIX

The office for New York's 12th Congressional District was located on the Upper East Side, a few blocks from Central Park and Elias Haskell's penthouse. Congress had recessed in August, meaning there was a good chance Samuel Dickstein was now lurking around New York. No doubt a career conman like Dickstein fattened himself up with bribes in Washington, but graft was plenty in the Big Apple. Rats didn't stray too far from their food sources.

Inside, the directory said Congressman Dickstein's office was in Suite 311, but Max felt paralyzed.

"What's wrong?" Cornelia asked.

"There's a good chance Dickstein'll slug me."

"Why?"

"I was hired to dig up dirt on him."

"You have a lot of enemies, don't you?"

"Yes, but in my line of work, having the right enemies connects you to the right friends."

She shook her head, that Fifth Avenue snobbery returning. "I thought money was your only friend."

"*Best* friend. Not *only*."

"Why did we even come here then?"

"Because I hope Dickstein hates Nazis more than me."

"My husband is not a Nazi." She sounded almost offended.

Max shrugged. "Close enough. You saw him and Norris out there. They sure as hell weren't preparing for the Macy's Thanksgiving parade. Dickstein is co-head of a congressional committee set up to investigate Fascist activities."

"Co-head?"

"Congressman McCormack is the other, but I'm not traveling to Massachusetts. The tricky thing is even getting to see Dickstein. My name might get the cops called."

Concern wrinkled Cornelia's face as she dug into her handbag, pushing away tubes of lipstick, eyeshadow, and that fancy cigarette case, until she retrieved an embossed business card – "Richard Osborn, Lead Salesman – Haskell Munitions Incorporated."

"Who carries around their husband's business cards?"

She giggled like a child sharing a dirty secret. "A vindictive wife. I sprinkle these around at fairy clubs, just for fun. Anything to make him squirm."

"You want me to play Richard Osborn?" Max tapped his sharp chin. "I don't have the right jawline."

Cornelia soured, then said, "Just to get in to see Dickstein. Then we can drop the masquerade."

Max pocketed the business card and considered his options, which weren't many. He'd made a career out of bluffing, so why stop now? They strode up to the third floor, Suite 311, then knocked.

A feminine voice called out, "Come in!"

Inside was a small office, furnished with a small couch, along with portraits of President Roosevelt and the honorable Samuel Dickstein.

"May I help you?" a dowdy secretary called out from behind her desk. Stacks of files, receipts, and paperwork looked ready to swallow her up.

Max switched on the charm with an ingratiating smile. "Well, I certainly hope so. We're looking for Mr. Dickstein."

"Oh, I'm sorry, but Congressman Dickstein has stepped out for the day."

"That *is* a shame." Max presented the business card. "Would you please tell the Congressman that Richard Osborn would like to speak with him?"

The secretary squinted at the card. "Osborn…Osborn…where have I heard that name before?"

"I'm the Chief of the National Crusaders." The secretary still looked confused, so Max added, "The Khaki Shirts."

"Oh. I see." A dark cloud swept over her face as she turned to Cornelia. "And you are?"

"Mrs. Osborn."

The secretary squinted again, but her recognition was more benign now. "Oh yes, I've seen you in the papers."

"Don't believe those society rags," Cornelia said with a drawling laugh.

"What did you want to speak to Congressman Dickstein about?"

Max and Cornelia traded confused glances. Maybe they should have rehearsed this.

"Just tell him I have some information that will be of use to his committee," Max answered.

The secretary pursed her lips as she scanned a nearby desk calendar, then said, "Congressman Dickstein is available tomorrow in the afternoon. Around five?"

"Works for me."

She jotted down the appointment time on the back of one of Dickstein's own business cards, then handed it over. Max beamed another warm smile before tucking it into his pocket. After a round of pleasantries, they left the office, descended the stairs in silence, and walked out into the sullen afternoon.

"Now what?" Cornelia asked as they entered the parked Daimler.

"Now, we wait."

Cornelia replied with a frown, then, "I doubt my father and Richard are the top."

"That's why we're going to talk to Dickstein. He has more authority than we do."

The murky sky opened up with a pitter-patter of rain. Just a light drizzle for now, but every splat on the windshield echoed the crashing rifle volley from earlier.

"No, that won't do," Cornelia stated, her face hard and ashen. "You said it yourself. Dickstein can be bought. We should have a backup plan."

"Such as?"

A lighter flared as she lit up a cigarette, the day's tension evaporating from her stiff frame. "Every time General

Norris comes to town, he and my husband have a little date. They tell me they're off to some gentlemen's club, but in reality, they frolic off to that ritzy pansy bar I told you about."

"Polly's?"

"Yeah." She blew out a puff of smoke and started the engine. "You mentioned spying on a few fairies there?"

Max shrugged. "It's owned by the Mob, so they have all sorts of secret passageways, trap doors, and thin walls left over from Prohibition. It's easy to eavesdrop there."

"Good." Gears clanged and the Daimler sped up, merging with the traffic on Third Avenue. "They mentioned going out tonight, which means they'll end up there."

"Lady, I've had a hell of a day. We'll tell Dickstein all about it tomorrow."

She gave a sneering laugh. "You're a piece of work, Mr. Dietrich. You float a theory about my husband planning a coup, and now that it looks to be true, you want out."

"I know where the missing guns went and who hired Mike Rafferty. I'd say my curiosity has been satiated."

Her gray eyes flashed him a mocking glare. "Has it?"

No, it hadn't. While Elias Haskell and Richard Osborn were most likely the executors of this putsch, they probably had the backing of men with even deeper pockets. An inner voice urged him to turn back now, hand this entire affair over to Dickstein and forget about it. But like Eve and every other curious idiot, Max had to taste that forbidden fruit.

"No," was all he could mutter. "But I don't work for free."

At the intersection of Third Avenue and 59th Street, a traffic cop in a rain slicker halted them. The Daimler slowed to a stop, allowing Cornelia to rummage through her handbag. She handed over a wad of bills, three hundred bucks in total, then hit the gas as the cop waved them through.

"You Haskells always have money to burn…"

"I told you, my husband gives me an allowance. I only spend it on Broadway theaters and private dicks."

"A bad investment. But it's your money, so that means you're the boss."

"Wonderful. Next stop, Polly's."

"No," he said, tucking the money away. "I'll need a change of clothes first."

CHAPTER THIRTY-SEVEN

Back in his office, Max changed into a crisp Brooks Brothers gray suit, topped off with a red tie and matching crimson handkerchief, then freshened himself up with a quick shave in the bathroom. Opening the bathroom door, he found Cornelia Osborn taking tepid steps around the davenport, his desk, and coat rack, as if surveying an open sewer.

"It's no Fifth Avenue, huh?" Max said.

"How do you live like this?"

"Believe it or not, princess, I have it better than most of the Forgotten Men out there," Max said, applying the rest of his disguise in front of the bathroom mirror. Pulp magazines were full of flawless masks, elaborate makeup, and perfect wigs that created perfect doppelgängers. But all Max could muster today was a fake beard, some bronzer, and phony glasses. A feeble attempt, but it'd have to suffice. He stepped out and presented himself to Cornelia.

"How do I look?"

She glanced up. "Like Groucho Marx with a beard."

"All I need is a cigar." He rummaged through his desk until he found a stethoscope, an essential tool for eavesdropping. He donned his overcoat and stuffed the instrument inside a pocket, while Cornelia occupied herself with his mail.

"Are you a member?" she asked, tapping a pamphlet on his desk, atop the crinkled issue of *Fortune* magazine. It was the Liberty League's logo, the Liberty Bell, emblazoned with the slogan "*The Old Bell Is Still Ringing*" along with a plea for America to "*Return to a Sound Dollar.*"

"No, but since your father is, I'd wager they have something to do with all this."

"Why?"

Max shrugged. "That much old money gathered in one place isn't some glorified country club. Besides, isn't it their entire mission to defeat Roosevelt?"

"Through elections, not a coup. Can't they just buy a new president in '36?"

"Buying politicians is as American as apple pie, but if the recent Democratic sweep was any hint, FDR isn't going anywhere next election. If I were a Liberty Leaguer, I'd just pay to oust him outright. It's funny how much they hate him, given the silver spoon he was born sucking on."

"He's a traitor to his class," Cornelia said. "The New Deal, specifically the NRA, is restructuring the economy to benefit the entire nation, not just our modern-day Robber Barons. Any loss of power is an affront to these types. Believe me, I grew up around them." Her gray eyes went cold. "I'm a patriot, first and foremost and this plot reeks of treason. My country will not be ruled by some puppet of Wall Street."

Max considered the possibility of foreign involvement. Perhaps Benito Mussolini and his Black Shirts were bankrolling this entire scheme? Doubtful, but after today, he was ready to believe anything. Even so, one thing was certain.

"As you said, there's still the US Army," Max said. "Your husband might have followers and guns, but no tanks, poison gas, or airplanes. Any competent general would make short work of the Khaki Shirts."

"Then we need hard facts to present to Dickstein. Names, dates, and details he can't just dismiss or take a bribe for. I'll poke around my father's office for anything. I'll telephone you later…say, around midnight?"

"It's a date."

*****

The alleyway was dark, and Mike Rafferty yearned to disappear into its shadows forever. Without a mask, the world now gawked at his naked hideousness, like a zoo creature out of its cage. After their narrow escape, he and Eddie Gardner had taken refuge at the Bowery's Salvation Army station. There, they'd gotten a change of clothes, a hot meal and much needed sleep. Although the staff was pleasant and welcoming, their stares betrayed a deep disgust.

Not that he could blame them. What was Mike Rafferty other than shattered flesh, a walking corpse? But now, his soul was dead too. Suicide still whispered evil thoughts into his mind, but even though he'd lost his faith years ago, a strict Catholic upbringing had left its mark. Besides, he couldn't kill himself just yet. Not when there were many people to blame for the miserable state he'd been reduced to.

Susan Partridge. Richard Osborn. And Max Dietrich, who seemed to be the weakest target. A quick search in the Salvation Army's phonebook revealed that Dietrich Investigation Services rented an office on 43rd and Seventh Avenue. But he needed to be sure.

Nearby, the Paramount Theatre pulsated with pallid lights, piercing the dusky gloom of twilight. But the alleyway remained deserted, covering Rafferty and Gardner with a murky shroud. Still, Rafferty felt exposed as he watched and waited. The scarf Gardner had lent him was tied around the bottom half of his face, covering his wounds but now he looked like some ridiculous Wild West bandit. No matter. He'd make sure to show his true face soon. It'd be the last thing Max Dietrich ever saw.

A chorus of high-pitched hisses erupted from Gardner as he pointed at the building. Rafferty peered through the darkness and saw two figures emerge. One, a fancy-dressed woman, some sort of rich socialite, was trailed by a tall, lanky figure sporting thick glasses and a beard. The gray overcoat and fedora were neither special nor familiar, but a long, slim frame and pointed chin were enough to identify that two-faced shamus.

Even disguised, there was no place on earth Max Dietrich could hide from revolutionary justice. The Colt automatic, stuffed inside Rafferty's waistband, yearned to escape. The two entered a Daimler and drove off, allowing Rafferty and Gardner to emerge from the alleyway's mouth unseen. Who was that woman? Why was Dietrich wearing that getup? More questions piled up as Rafferty led the way into the office building.

They'd have all the time in the world to ask Dietrich when he returned.

CHAPTER THIRTY-EIGHT

Greenwich Village had long been home to Bohemians, artists, and misfits who didn't belong anywhere else. Rich kids from Fifth Avenue slummed down here, rubbing elbows with swindlers, slackers, and radicals. However, in the past decade a new community had made the Village their home. Previously, most homosexuals had been confined to sleazy alleyways and underneath train tracks of the Bowery while the more erudite mingled in fancy clubs on the Upper East Side.

But during Prohibition, speakeasies sprang up like weeds all throughout New York, and the epicenter was Greenwich Village. Always attracting a fanciful crowd, many speakeasies simply went queer, kicking off the so-called "Pansy Craze" in 1930. Even posh uptown socialites came down to the Village to watch drag queens imitate the latest Broadway show. But as the depression worsened, attitudes hardened and forced these men back into the shadows.

Cornelia dropped Max off at the intersection of Seventh Avenue and West 4th Street, dead center in fairy land. Streets zigzagged and curved into winding mazes, as if you needed a map to find your way out.

To his left loomed Stewart's Cafeteria, attracting enough pansies to double as a drag ball. Out-of-towners peered through the cafeteria's windows, gawking at men in makeup and women in suits. But the whole neighborhood was now honeycombed with queer bars, far more secretive than the old speakeasies.

Polly's was one of the most popular haunts here, but it attracted a specific type of clientele – masculine and wealthy. Located just above a drug store on Seventh Avenue, the bar was unmarked and concealed from prying eyes. Max entered through the front door, where a sour-faced clerk greeted him. He nodded, but headed toward a backdoor, labeled "*Private*" tucked away behind a magazine rack.

He walked into a tight hallway with a metal staircase leading up to another door, unchanged since Prohibition. Max knocked and waited until a small rectangle frame slid open, revealing a pair of scrutinizing blue eyes.

"Password?"

"Open sesame."

"Very funny, fairy."

"Open up," he said, flashing a five-dollar bill. "It's Max Dietrich."

"No shit! Sorry, didn't recognize you in that getup!"

The door flung open, revealing a beefy bouncer, crammed into a three-piece suit. He sat on a stool, meaty hands gripping a crinkled pulp magazine – *Strange Tales of Mystery and Terror.* Its cover showed a voluptuous redhead, wearing nothing but a nightie, huddled beside two snarling wolves.

"*Wolves of Darkness,*" Max said. "A classic. How are you liking it?"

"A real hoot, Mr. Dietrich. Better than the pictures!"

"Buy yourself some more downstairs," Max said, tucking the five in between the pulp's pages. Polly's changed the password for entry, far more often than Max cared to remember. But by donating his old pulp magazines, along with a regular bribe, the bouncer allowed Max to come and go as he pleased.

Max made his way to another door – unlocked this time – that led into the main lounge of Polly's. Here was a veritable shadow world just beneath the veneer of normality. Most importantly, it was hidden from the cops. Just this year, the New York State Liquor Authority stopped issuing licenses to any bar deemed "morally degenerate." The Mob swooped in, and now, all fairy bars were run by organized crime.

A medium-size bar sat off to the side, adjacent to a dimly-lit lounge, seating around forty dapper men, two per table. A drag queen occupied the stage, a dead-ringer for Ginger Rogers. Fitting, since she serenaded them with a flawless rendition of "We're in the Money."

Max used to despise these Twilight Men, an affront to everything deemed "natural." But now hatred had turned to pity. Shunned by society, they were forced to wear masks just to survive. Max wondered how many lives he'd ruined just for a paycheck but pushed it out of his mind. Morality was for the rich these days.

Next to the bar was a hallway, leading to five separate private rooms, used for private events and backdoor screwing. Even here, these men had to keep it discreet. Max looked over the audience, decked with matching ties, handkerchiefs, and boutonnieres, drinking up the drag queen with dreamy stares. This was the one place they could afford a soft touch or a sly kiss without risking their lives.

Max continued reviewing the tables, Most men were too enraptured by the performance to even turn around, but Richard Osborn's chestnut brown hair and strong jaw were unmistakable. He shared a table with another man of similar build whose gray-flecked hair and broad shoulders betrayed him as Nathaniel Norris.

For a brief moment, Osborn looked around, a man accustomed to observing danger everywhere. Max tensed, but Osborn's anxious eyes passed over him without stopping, indicating the disguise was good enough. Still, Max retreated to the bar for safety.

"What can I get you?"

"Your boss," Max said, sliding another five across. The bartender palmed the bill and trotted off to the hallway. After a few minutes, he returned with a greasy man in a double-breasted pinstripe suit and slicked back hair – Mob connections oozing from every pore. Few of these bars had any visible gangster presence, but Polly's was a cut above the rest, and the clientele expected a high degree of security.

Thankfully, Max's old contacts with the Mob ran thick, and for the right price, any rule could be broken.

"What's the rumpus, buster?" the gangster asked.

"I'm here on a job."

"That you, Dietrich?" After a nasally giggle, the gangster said, "Hell's bells, we got a regular Lon Chaney here."

After shushing him, Max pulled the gangster into the mouth of the hallway. "See those two?" Max jerked a quick thumb over at Norris and Osborn. "I need you to get them into one of your private love nests."

"So you can spy on them? Gee, I dunno Dietrich. These queers appreciate their privacy."

Max slipped a twenty into the gangster's pocket. "I just need to eavesdrop a little."

"No photos, all right? And this is the last time. It ain't like the old days no more. The boss wants these fairies spending dough without having to worry whether or not some slippery shamus is gonna rat 'em out to their wives."

"Didn't even bring my camera."

"All right then. Pop into room four. I'll send your boyfriends there in about ten minutes."

Max stalked down the hallway, ignoring the hushed conversations, whimpers, and groans from behind closed doors. He entered room four, the largest private den, complete with a davenport, coffee table, decorative Persian rug, and lacy pillows.

He'd been here plenty of times before, and by instinct, he yanked up the Persian rug, revealing a trapdoor, a relic from Prohibition. Tunnels that used to haul bootleg liquor into Polly's led out to the side entrance of the drugstore downstairs. He descended a small wooden staircase and pulled the Persian back over the top, snapping the trapdoor shut in one quick motion.

Submerged in the subterranean gloom, Max pulled the stethoscope from his coat pocket, plugged it into his ears, and placed the diaphragm along the wooden trapdoor. Crude but effective, since the walls in Polly's were paper-thin. Now all he had to do was wait.

CHAPTER THIRTY-NINE

Alone in the darkness, Max heard the shuffle of footsteps cross the floor. Through the stethoscope, he could make out distinct voices, directly above him now.

"Sorry again, gentlemen," the gangster said. "But we're expecting a large party who'd like an exclusive show with our own 'Ginger Rogers.'"

"This is most irregular." There was a sharp edge in Osborn's voice.

"My apologies. Please, make yourselves at home here. I'll send up a bottle of wine for you two. Free of charge, of course."

"White," Osborn said.

"White, of course, of course."

The door slammed shut, followed by some rustling noises, and the groan of springs as they sank into the davenport. An irritated sigh blew out before Osborn spoke again.

"Well, at least we can talk in private."

"I don't know if that's a good idea," Norris said, his thick voice booming like a gunshot. "Can't we discuss the details at my hotel room?"

"I need an answer now, Nate. Haskell is getting impatient."

"Oh, don't be that way, Dick. You know the odds are against us."

Nate? Dick? Max shook his mind clear and tried to focus.

"You saw my men today. Despite their wrinkles and potbellies, they still know how to handle a rifle. And what's more, they're loyal to the core."

"They are impressive, I'll admit. But why do you want me to join? *You're* their chief, after all."

"Unfortunately, the National Crusaders number ten thousand men, at most. Richard Osborn's voice carries only so far, but General Nathaniel Norris roars like thunder. If you donned a khaki shirt, veterans would flock to our banner by the thousand."

"You exaggerate, Dick."

"Nate, you were the one officer to come out in support of the Bonus March. What's more, you said it while you were still on active duty, career be damned."

A gravelly laugh erupted. "And my career was damned after that."

"That's not the point. Those men worshipped you. I saw it myself at BEF headquarters. Few men inspire adulation like that. I have a plan to swell our ranks tenfold. But it requires your support."

"How? You're forgetting the US Army and that ruthless son of a bitch, General MacArthur. You saw what he did to those unarmed Bonus Marchers!"

"I'll never forget," Osborn said, the anger palpable even from this distance. "But just leave that to me and my father-in-law."

"I still can't believe you married into that family and all their blood money."

"I had few options after I took the fall for both of us, Nate. After all, I needed a job, and Haskell was hiring," Osborn said with a bitter snarl. "While I despise that greedy bitch, the old man and his money are still useful. But all our planning will be for naught if we don't have your support."

Ponderous silence stretched out. Max fought off fatigue gnawing at his arm and kept the stethoscope pressed against the trap door. At last, Norris spoke again.

"I…I don't know, Dick."

"You've read my manifesto. The Corporate State is the only hope for America now. Anything else is a bandage on a fatal wound," Osborn said, words firing off like a machine gun. "Look at what wonders Mussolini has done for Italy! Organizing each industry into separate corporate entities has harmonized society for the good of the nation and neutralized the Communist threat forever."

"Of course, I agree. While I despise that man in the White House, the fact is that his National Recovery Administration is the closest thing this country has to the Corporate State, albeit contaminated with Jewish perversions. We must have a nation built on Christian economics, purged of Hebrew usury."

"Now, now, Nate. We can't scare the Yids just yet. It might arouse suspicion. Once we take power, we'll sort out the Jews. I suspect 99% will be deported back to Russia, but we might need to keep a few around."

"Better to shoot all the kikes and let Christ Almighty sort them out. America can't become a truly Christian nation while the Jewish serpent strangles our banking system. Their plan is all laid out in the *Protocols*, Dick!"

Max wasn't surprised that *The Protocols of the Elders of Zion* was Norris's real Bible. Supposedly a record of the secret Jewish plot to rule the world, the *Protocols* had been exposed as a forgery, the perverted fever dreams of anti-Semitic crackpots, but that didn't stop the lunatic fringe from believing it.

"Nate..."

"My point is that the NRA is the very thing that Haskell and his rich friends want to abolish. That's what this plot is all about, right?"

Osborn gave a knowing chuckle, full of secrets.

"The NRA won't be going anywhere...but it will be *improved.* Only patriots like you and I can return America to its former glory. Let those old money snobs think Richard Osborn and Nathaniel Norris are callow mercenaries for capitalism." A contemptuous scoff. "The look on their faces when we line them up before a firing squad will be even sweeter."

"Dick, these are some of the top businessmen in the entire country. Lots of Jewish money is behind them. You really think we can outfox this cabal of Shylocks?"

"We'll have the guns, won't we? Big business got in line after Mussolini and Hitler took power. Those stuffed shirts will be given two options. If they go along with us, all will be dandy. Profits for them, prosperity for America. But if they go against the Corporate State, then we'll have our very own Saint Valentine's Day Massacre for Wall Street."

Another chuckle, far more menacing this time. Even Norris joined in.

"I'd love to see these godless East Coast snobs mowed down. But won't we need them for the future?"

"Unfortunately, yes. But luckily, I've got Elias Haskell wrapped around my finger. That old man views me as a replacement for his son."

"It's an outlandish plot, you have to admit that."

"These are outlandish times, Nate. The Communists are mobilizing their forces, just like Russia in '17. We must strike first."

"My…my wife is getting suspicious…of us, Dick. And there's my son. He's still in the Army. What do I tell him if it fails?"

"All the more reason we must succeed. Then we won't have to explain anything to anyone. Look, just come with us to the Liberty League tomorrow. We'll lay out all the details then."

"Tomorrow?"

"Yes, at noon. You're the key to whether this entire mission succeeds or fails. America needs you." Then, in almost a whisper, "*I* need you, Nate."

Another elongated silence filled the stethoscope. Max could almost see the battle raging on Norris's stony face. To coup, or not to coup? Such plots were abhorrent to the American system. That sort of intrigue happened in Europe. George Washington had declined to become king, after all. But Americans had overthrown plenty of other governments in the past – from Hawaii, to Nicaragua, to Haiti. It was only a matter of time before some wise guy decided to try it out here.

"All right, Dick. I'll do it. For America," Norris said, an imperious tone infecting every syllable. "And…for you."

The door creaked open, and a new set of footsteps padded across the floor, then traipsed back out. The wine had been delivered, just in time for these two superpatriots to toast their little plot. Glasses clinked, and Osborn cheered, "To victory!"

Their conversation lapsed into grunts, an indication of inflamed passions. Max pocketed the stethoscope and stretched his stiff muscles. It was time to go. He'd gotten all he could out of the lovebirds for now. Climbing down the steps, he flared a Horn & Hardart match, then plodded through the tunnel toward the back exit.

*****

It was half-past eleven when Max returned to his office, fatigue gnawing at every nerve. His body ached for sleep, but he still had that late-night call with Cornelia Osborn. He had quite a lot to share. Even if those two idiots failed, their incompetence could result in a second civil war. And this time, it wouldn't be north against south. Max didn't believe in much, but he felt a duty to today's youth not to be suckered by sappy slogans and fake ideals, like he had been.

Max removed his disguise just before reaching his office, lest someone mistake him for a late-night prowler, but dread creeped over him. Gripping the office doorknob, a few splinters of wood broke off and drifted to the floor. Evidence that it had been jimmied open. The door swung open and Max peered into the smothering darkness, broken only by the Paramount's neon glow in the distance. Everything appeared normal, but in the inner office, a faint silhouette, the outline of a man, was sitting behind the desk. A burglar searching for valuables? A Forgotten Man just wanting to warm himself up? Or something worse?

Max whipped out the snubnosed revolver and took soft steps forward. Opening the door to the inner office, he made his move and jerked the pistol into position.

"Hands up! Don't move!"

The Paramount's flickering lights provided just enough illumination to make out Mike Rafferty glaring back at him, his mutilated face beaming with a triumphant smirk. All too late, Max noticed a second silhouette step out of the corner, a pistol barrel gleaming in his peripheral. A drawn-out hiss was Eddie Gardner's way of saying, "*Gotcha.*"

"Welcome back, Dietrich," Rafferty said. "We've been waiting for you."

CHAPTER FORTY

Max considered his options. Any attempt to use his gun would earn a bullet in his brain after the first shot rang out. Or he could just surrender and wait for execution. Both were lousy options, but the second was especially galling.

"I wouldn't try anything," Rafferty said, smug with victory. "Before he was wounded, Eddie Gardner managed to shoot five German soldiers, still in their trenches."

They must want something from him, Max thought; or else he'd be dead already. That meant there was still a way to outsmart these Red dopes in one masterful bluff. His fingers relaxed, and the revolver clunked to the floor. Gardner emerged from the shadows, scooped up the snubnosed, and returned to the corner. Max completed his surrender by lifting his hands up.

"Good choice," Rafferty said.

"What happened to your mask, handsome?"

Rafferty's self-satisfied grin dropped. "Very cute. You know I lost it running from your pals."

Ignorance was not only bliss, it was Max's best chance at coming out of this alive. After all, there was no direct link between him and Richard Osborn. At least none that Rafferty knew about. He silently thanked himself for staying behind during that raid at Liberty Warehouse.

"My pals?"

"Cut the act, Dietrich. At first, I thought you were one of Susan Partridge's bloodhounds. But now, after seeing this—" Rafferty held up the Liberty League pamphlet, then slammed it back down – "I think you were hired by that Merchant of Death – Elias Haskell."

"Who?"

"Don't play dumb. How else would Richard Osborn and the Khaki Shirts know where we stashed Haskell's guns?"

Max let his hands drop and shrugged. "If I found your flophouse, it wouldn't be too hard for other snoopers to sniff you out."

Confusion strained Rafferty's scarred features. "Then who was that ritzy dame you were with earlier? And what's with the disguise?"

"You caught me. I'm a modern-day Bluebeard seducing lonely New York heiresses."

Rafferty leapt to his feet and lashed out a fist, slamming it into Max's gut, doubling him over. The Red sneered, twisting his face into an even uglier mass of mangled flesh. How could a man still live with wounds like that? But then again, compared to poor Francis Haskell, Mike Rafferty looked like Clark Gable.

"Enough jokes," Rafferty sneered, coming around the desk to tower over Max, squirming on the floor. "Talk!"

A sharp kick dug into Max's stomach again, squeezing any remaining air out of his lungs. He looked around the office for some way to escape, but everywhere ended with a bullet square between the eyes. Agony seared through his muscles, blurring his thoughts. One thing was certain though. Despite his bluster, Rafferty still appeared to be in the dark about everything, which offered some opportunity.

The full truth would earn Max a bullet, but he couldn't play dumb for much longer. After all, he *had* tracked them down to that Bowery flophouse. Perhaps he could claim he was working for someone else? Someone these Trotskyists respected?

Rafferty lifted his foot and brought it crashing down against Max's side. A pitiful moan burst out his throat, but he fought back the pain and focused. His gaze swept around the office again, not for escape, but for some placating excuse. He could see the top of his desk, strewn with bills, that Liberty League pamphlet, and the crinkled issue of *Fortune* magazine. That stupid rag had started this whole mess, but also offered a way out.

Gerald Nye might be part of the bourgeois establishment, but he and Rafferty shared a common enemy. Taking a steadying gulp of air, Max choked out, "Idiots! I'm working for Senator Nye!"

Even in the darkness, Max could see their confusion. Rafferty and Gardner exchanged looks, unsure of what to do next. Air pumped in and out of Max's lungs as he used the brief interval to rehearse a new story in his mind. One that would save his neck.

"The senator who runs that munitions committee?"

Twisting on the floor, Max heaved himself to his knees, and took another panting breath. He fought back his rage, swallowed his fear, and said, "The very same. Nye hired me to investigate Elias Haskell."

Rafferty glanced back at Gardner, who gurgled a perplexed whine.

"You said it, Eddie. Why would the esteemed Senator Nye hire a two-bit shamus like Max Dietrich?"

Sucking down another breath, Max lifted himself to his feet, ignoring the pain throbbing across his torso. Instead, he straightened his tie and overcoat, smoothed his fedora. He only had one shot at this performance.

"For that very reason. I've been gathering dirt on all these bigwigs for years now. I'm where Washington and Wall Street go when they want secrets."

Rafferty pursed his lips, then said, "And what did you find out, Dietrich?"

The truth would work better now. With a sigh, Max said, "It's a long story."

"We've got all night." Rafferty went back behind the desk, then plopped down in Max's leather chair. "Eddie, if you think he's lying, feel free to blast away. Now…start talking Dietrich."

CHAPTER FORTY-ONE

Max rubbed his side, but a dull soreness lingered. Biting his lip, he sucked down the pain and planned his next move. This Bolshie egghead was book smart, he'd give him that. Anyone who could read through all of Karl Marx's and Leon Trotsky's scribblings without falling asleep had to have some brains. But there was a certain naivete and gullibility inherent in all the lunatic fringe, preferring simplistic myths to complicated truths.

"Well," Max began, "Senator Nye has long suspected Elias Haskell of violating the arms embargo and shipping weapons down to Bolivia in secret. He didn't want to get G-Men involved in something that was only a hunch. The local cops can't be trusted, since they make Sodom and Gomorrah look like a tent revival. So Nye hired me."

"A swindler like you?"

"I don't swindle my clients."

Rafferty clammed up, then motioned for Max to continue.

"Haskell has been funding the National Crusaders, but I'm sure you already know that. What you don't know is that only half of Haskell's stockpile of munitions were sold to Bolivia."

"And the other half?"

"They're shipped out to the Khaki Shirt camp in Long Island. I saw it with my own eyes. Hundreds of men, marching in formation, armed to the teeth. But when your gang swiped that last shipment of guns, it complicated their plans."

"How do you know all this, Dietrich?"

Yes, how did he know all this? Without a connection to Richard Osborn, was he clairvoyant?

"Through an informant in the National Crusaders."

"Who?"

He felt himself sinking further into a swamp, but the chance to kill two birds with one stone presented itself. "That woman you saw me with."

"What's her name?"

Revealing Cornelia Osborn's identity would complicate matters. An alias right out of the pulps would suffice.

"Some bored heiress named Nita Van Sloan. Last summer, she vacationed in Naples and became enamored with Mussolini. You know these old money types, they all need to have a cause. Hers was supporting local Fascists, but she's since had a change of heart."

Rafferty nodded, tasting the name in his mouth. Nita Van Sloan was the love interest and longtime fiancée of the Spider, a pulp hero meant to cash in on the Shadow's popularity. Even the name sounded aristocratic enough.

"What changed her mind?"

Max shrugged. "Women are fickle creatures. One day they're Fascists, next they're New Dealers in love with Roosevelt. Give them enough time and they'll be Bolshies."

"So, this Nita Van Sloan told you that we stole Haskell's guns? How did she know?"

"She heard from Osborn himself that you were the prime suspect, and passed it along to me. After all, they remembered the strike you led."

"Did she know we were hired by Paraguayan Army Intelligence to swipe those guns?"

Max shook his head. No reason to burst Rafferty's bubble and reveal Colonel Lopez was nothing more than a two-bit Broadway actor. Nothing galled a rube more than learning he'd been had.

"So, let me get this straight, Dietrich. Nye hired you to investigate Haskell's violations of the arms embargo. But through this Nita Van Sloan, you learn that we swiped the guns, and that's how you tracked us down in the Bowery?"

The story was shakier than a house of straw, but it was the best Max could come up with on the fly. He nodded anyway.

"I don't suppose you have a contract between you and Senator Nye, do you? Something to confirm you actually are working for him?"

"Given my reputation, most clients stay off the record."

"Very convenient. Why should we believe you, Dietrich? After all, you lied to us before, claiming to be a comrade."

"That was only to find Haskell's guns—"

Rafferty held up a stifling hand as Gardner drew closer, pistol in hand. There was no way to prove that he and Nye were connected, but there was another guardian angel, whose business card rested inside his pocket.

"There's no contract, but Senator Nye did put me in contact with Congressman Samuel Dickstein—"

The name stirred up a palpable anger. "Dickstein? He's a liberal Red-baiter who stokes fears of the Communist boogeyman. Bastard even tried to outlaw the Communist Party."

Perhaps Max had chosen the wrong guardian angel. Still, a skilled player could work with whatever card they'd been dealt.

"That may be, but he hates Fascists more. Even has a committee to investigate them. He's the one who introduced me to Nita Van Sloan."

"Why is Nye working with Dickstein? One investigates the arms industry and the other investigates Fascism?"

"Think, man, don't you see why they'd work together?" A blank stare from Rafferty said he did not. "It's because Osborn and Haskell are planning a coup d'é tat."

Alarm flashed through Rafferty, and he leaned closer, eyes narrowed. "First, you're working for Nye, now with Dickstein. I don't suppose you have any proof of this arrangement either?"

Max slowly eased into his pocket, gripped Dickstein's business card, and tossed it on the desk.

Rafferty examined it, then shot back a quizzical look. "You're meeting with him tomorrow?"

"To report what I've discovered."

"And that is?"

Max took a deep breath. Now was time for the truth, the full truth. "Like I said, Haskell has been arming the Khaki Shirts, who will be the Stormtroopers to carry out this coup."

"Won't the Army fight back?"

Max shrugged. "I don't know how exactly they're going to pull their little scheme off, but I do know it has deep pockets. Bought and paid for by the American Liberty League."

The name soured Rafferty's confused expression into a hateful glare. "Go on."

Another opportunity presented itself, too good to pass up. "You see, that's why I was wearing that getup. I was playing a rich stockbroker. Ms. Van Sloan and I had dinner with some important Liberty Leaguers tonight. They invited me to a meeting at noon tomorrow."

Rafferty leaned back in the leather chair. "So, Haskell and Osborn are plotting to overthrow Roosevelt?"

"They're just the front men, but dollars to doughnuts it goes much higher." Time to throw a bone to this hungry Communist. "Don't you see? The elite of American capitalism are planning to install a Fascist dictatorship."

But Rafferty just nodded along, his mind somewhere else. Maybe an appeal to patriotism would work?

"Look, maybe I'm all wet asking a couple of Reds to think of their country, but just picture America under Fascist rule. They'll come down hard on Reds and liberals alike. Maybe both of you have given up on Uncle Sam, but I'm not handing my country over without a fight."

The words were sappy and trite, but meaningless slogans like that had galvanized an entire generation of men to go "Over There," himself included. A tense silence fell between him and Rafferty, who sat staring at Dickstein's card. The gears were turning in this radical's head, no doubt wondering if he was somebody's dupe yet again.

"You're wrong, Dietrich. I loved this country once. Hell, even gave half my face for it." Rafferty looked up, brown eyes rimmed with tears. "You were in the war, right? Where'd you see battle?"

"Saint-Mihiel and the Meuse-Argonne Offensive."

"The 69th didn't see much action at Saint-Mihiel, but we caught hell at the Meuse. My platoon was ordered into battle on November 7th, just a few days before the war ended. Our regiment was tasked with securing a vital position from the Germans. Hill 252." Rafferty let the name hover in the air, like a phantom from a previous life. "You remember what it was like, right Dietrich? Slashing rain and mud pits that would swallow a man whole. And the endless gunfire, enough to deafen you."

"I'll never forget."

"Early in the morning, I led my platoon into battle, but the Germans were dug in. Half my men were killed or wounded within minutes. Eddie here caught a bullet in the throat and almost died in the mud. As their lieutenant, I rallied the remaining men for a final charge, but as we started out across no man's land, that's when I heard it."

He didn't have to say the word "shell." No Doughboy could ever forget that horrible, otherworldly screech that drove men mad under constant bombardment.

"I ran into a blinding flash, then fell face first into the mud, bleeding out before slipping into unconsciousness. When I awoke, my nose had been torn off, and my perfect life crumbled into dust. My wife ran out on me with the baby, I still don't know where they are. No law firm would hire a disfigured freak, despite my chestful of medals. The only job I could find was as a bookkeeper, hidden away in a musty office. Eventually, a prosthetic mask helped stave off some of the disgusted stares, but it didn't keep the nightmares at bay."

Slumping in the leather chair, Mike Rafferty looked like a weeping gargoyle.

"What was it all for, Dietrich?" he asked, drying his eyes.

Max offered a cynical laugh. "To make the world safe for democracy, of course."

Rafferty laughed too, then wheezed a depressed sigh. "We all bought that bill of goods, didn't we? Only after I read *The Daily Worker* and *New Masses* did I learn the truth! American banks had loaned millions to Britain and France. If Germany won, they wouldn't be paid back one single dollar. Merchants of Death like Elias Haskell sold weapons to both sides, prolonging the bloodbath for years. For what? To feed the maw of capitalist greed!"

Explanations from Communist rags presented just as simplistic an explanation as "making the world safe for democracy," but Max kept that to himself. Let Mike Rafferty remain in his fantasy world of heroes and villains, of victimizers and victims.

"America is nothing but a lie," Rafferty sneered. "Our so-called revolution was a coup by wealthy landowners, using the lower classes for cannon fodder. And for what? Freedom? Is Canada any less 'free' than us? And they didn't send their sons to die in a rich man's war!"

"If Osborn has *his* coup, you can bet your ass there'll be another war," Max said. "Only this time, America will be on Germany's side."

Rafferty fell into another tense silence and squeezed the remaining tears from his eyes. Gardner traipsed across the room, patted Rafferty's shoulder, then offered a soothing noise, like a mother cooing to her child. Comrades till the end.

Rafferty looked up, eyes puffy but dry now. "All right, Dietrich. You made your point."

CHAPTER FORTY-TWO

Max felt the remaining tension drain from his body as Gardner pocketed his automatic.

"Glad you trust me, Rafferty…"

"Oh, I don't. But I do believe your story. Or rather, the part about a coup." He shook his head, full of bitterness. "Trotsky has long warned of the dangers of Fascism, which is nothing more than the final stage of capitalism. Once the bourgeoise feel their power is threatened by the proletariat, they hire gangsters to install a dictatorship, dispensing with the facade of liberal democracy."

Max couldn't stifle a groan. "If this is going to turn into another political rant, just have your man go ahead and shoot me."

A scowl creased Rafferty's lips. "My point is that capitalism is a hydra, and Fascism is but one of its many heads. These economic royalists in the Liberty League will stop at nothing to crush the American worker. But the idiots who run the Communist Party USA are too busy purging themselves of Trotskyists and social democrats to see the Fascist wolf right outside their door."

"Meaning?"

"Meaning that we'll ally with you and those liberal hacks Nye and Dickstein for the time being. Until Richard Osborn is liquidated."

"Liquidated? Don't you want him on trial for treason?"

A contemptuous scoff. "Hitler was put on trial for treason after his failed Beer Hall Putsch. Ten years later, he was chancellor of Germany. That mistake won't be repeated here. I'll put a bullet in Osborn's brain myself rather than let the bourgeois courts coddle this Fascist snake."

For a moment, a desire to defend Osborn welled up inside Max, but he fought it back down. Whatever friendship they'd once had no longer mattered. Not with so much on the line now.

"Fine and dandy, but I still need to work within the system."

"Do what you have to, Dietrich." Rafferty rose and, along with Gardner, strutted toward the office door. "We'll contact you soon enough."

"Why don't you just leave your number? Tomorrow's going to be a long day."

Rafferty grinned, then wrapped a scarf around his shattered face, looking like a character straight out of the pulps – the Shadow in the flesh. "So the cops can track us down? Like I said, Dietrich, I don't trust you. Yet. We'll see what you have to say later."

"Can I at least have my gun back?"

Rafferty motioned to Gardner, who pulled the revolver out, whipped open the chamber, and let the bullets clatter to the floor. With a strangled giggle, the mute plopped the snubnosed Detective Special on the desk, and followed Rafferty out the door.

"Sweet dreams, Dietrich."

*****

Alone in his office, Max thumbed the bullets back into the revolver, then glanced at his watch. It was almost midnight and Cornelia would be calling any minute. Exhaustion returned with full force as he sank into his leather chair, eyelids drooping. A melee of thoughts swirled in his groggy brain until a sudden, shrill ring cut through them all.

"Yeah?" he answered.

"It's me," Cornelia's voice said, her voice echoey.

"Where are you?"

"In a phone booth. I didn't want Richard listening in, so I went to one of those automats. Horn & Whatsat?"

"Horn & Hardart."

"That's the one. So, what did you find out?"

"A lot. I overheard your husband and his boyfriend discussing their putsch. *Dick* requested *Nate's* collaboration and got it."

"Were you discovered?"

"Lady, I'm a professional. Richard is none the wiser. But there's a few things I still don't know."

"Like what?"

"Well, they discussed the plot in broad strokes, but concrete details were sparse."

"Well, as you said, Dickstein is going to want something meatier or else we'll look like Chicken Little."

"My thoughts exactly. Osborn and Norris are attending a Liberty League gathering tomorrow. Figured I could scrounge up something there."

"Yes, my father mentioned something about that. Unfortunately, I can't help you there."

"Why not?"

"What would I know about the Liberty League? I'm just some bubble-headed heiress, remember?"

"Good point." Max sighed again and tried to concoct a plan, but his mind was too fogged by fatigue to think straight. The mangled face of Francis Haskell penetrated his thoughts like an invading nightmare. "Since your father's involved…that means one thing."

"What?"

"War. Your husband writes about the need for a war in his manifesto."

"I've never read it."

"You should sometime. He quotes Mussolini saying '*War is to men what maternity is to women.*' Why else would they need the assistance of a former general like Norris?"

A mocking chuckle poured from the receiver. "You're something else, Max Dietrich. Now you're a pacifist? Didn't you spy on the War Resisters League?"

"I hate warmongers but I love money more. Besides, Norris and Richard weren't thinking of starting a war back then. They just wanted to keep their little brown suits and cushy jobs at the War Department. But now, your husband's head has been pumped full of Fascist fairy tales, he sees a new war as America's destiny."

"But against who?"

"Wish I knew…"

Max let out a yawn, loud and long.

"Are you okay? You sound exhausted."

"It's been a long night. Plus, I had a run-in with one of your former employees. Mike Rafferty."

The line went quiet, but Max could almost hear the chill running down Cornelia's spine.

"Rafferty? What'd he want?"

"To kill me at first, but we talked things out, so we're pals now. Had to spin one hell of a yarn, but he thinks I'm working for Nye and Dickstein. That guy really has it out for your husband. Fancies himself a Jack the Fascist Killer."

"We might be able to use him, you know? Men can be so gullible. Just tell them what they want to hear."

Words to live by. After all, they'd saved his own neck a dozen times over. And perhaps, it could get him in to see the inner sanctum of the Liberty League tomorrow. Max opened his desk and pulled out Osborn's manifesto – *100% Americanism*. Like any preacher, he was always on the lookout for new converts. Max Dietrich could play many roles, but a diehard Fascist would be a bit of a stretch. Regardless, he was running short on ideas.

"I just had an idea," he said.

"Oh?"

"Can't say just yet, but I'm going to sleep on it. I'll let you know in the morning if it's any good."

He hung up and plopped the book back on the desk, next to the issue of *Fortune*. He'd brush up on it again soon, but now his body ached for sleep. Max lifted himself off the chair, but within moments, slid back into it and fell into a dreamless slumber far away from Communists, Fascists, and all their plots.

CHAPTER FORTY-THREE

A steady drizzle pattered against Max's fedora and overcoat, but darkening skies threatened something heavier. The only sign of morning were traces of sunlight, poking through a curtain of clouds hovering above Manhattan. By the time he reached Haskell's penthouse, a growl of thunder cracked out, accompanied by a sudden downpour. The first thing to buy with Haskell's paycheck would be a sturdy umbrella, he decided.

Inside, the butler accepted Max's damp fedora and coat while Cornelia sauntered in to greet him. Even at this hour, she was decked out in click-clacking heels and a swishing green dress, offset by a frilly white collar. Although her brunette hair remained sculpted into a rigid Marcel wave, her eyes wouldn't sit still, darting back and forth like gray marbles.

They retreated into the lounge, warmed by the dull glow in the fireplace. From the mantel, Francis Haskell's face, young and handsome, beamed out from a photo.

"So, what's your plan?" Cornelia asked, dropping her voice.

"Simple. I'm going to ask to join their putsch."

Her mouth dropped, then, "What do you mean?"

"I'll say 'please.'"

"You're mad!"

Max shushed her, then said, "Look, when I was a Prohibition agent, there were two ways to fleece bootleggers. The first was just shaking them down as if I were a common crook. Plenty of Prohis did, and eventually they got a bullet in their backs."

"And the other?"

"I'd say, 'Hello, Mr. Gangster, I used to believe in Prohibition, but now I see what you boys are doing is a public service. Let me help. For a small cut, I'll protect your racket from rivals.'"

"That worked?"

"Like a charm. As long as people think you're on their side, they'll throw caution to the wind."

"Well, Richard may adore you, but my father can be rather skeptical about everyone who isn't family."

"Then I'll just have to play the perfect Fascist."

"It's a role I play all the time." She smirked. "Get out there and break a leg."

Max went back out to the sitting room and approached Elias Haskell's private office. Loud murmurs of conversations seeped through the door, but he knocked anyway, silencing them.

"Come in," Haskell said.

Inside, rain pelted against the windows from a sky darker than midnight. The office was bathed in pallid electric lamps, allowing Max to see every wrinkle on Haskell's gaunt face, stooping behind his desk. As always, a dapper suit – a charcoal three-piece – hung off his frail frame. But his clothes paled in comparison to Richard Osborn and Nathaniel Norris, clad in National Crusader uniforms and gleaming Sam Browne belts.

Despite his age, Norris filled out the khaki tunic well, as if not a day had passed since the war. The only minor alterations were that blue armband with the Crusader Eagle, and new insignia on his shoulders, high collar, and side cap – a silver sword crossed with a rifle.

Richard Osborn stood beside him, tapping his riding crop against his jackboot. Just the other day, that whip had been encrusted with Yago Garcia's blood and gore. But it was spotless now, ready for another victim. In the pale lights, Osborn's own bald eagle insignia twinkled on his shoulders and side cap, a subtle reminder he now outranked the former general.

"Hello, Maxie."

Max flashed Osborn a grin, then said, "I see you've got a new recruit."

The Khaki Shirts traded prideful looks, like a Fascist father and son.

"I'm pleased to announce that Nathaniel Norris has been commissioned into the National Crusaders with the rank of troop leader."

"That's pretty high up, right?"

"They usually command field offices, but Troop Leader Norris will serve a very special role as our head recruiting agent."

Behind his desk, Haskell broke in. "What brings you here today, Mr. Dietrich?"

"Well, I hate to be so forward, but there's the little matter of my payment. Cash please, no checks."

"Don't trust the banks, eh?"

"Losing everything in a run will do that."

"Banks?" Norris scoffed. "Nothing more than Jewish vice dens."

Haskell ignored that and rummaged through a desk drawer. He retrieved an envelope, bloated with cash, and slid it over to Max. "It behooves me to keep this off the books anyway. As we agreed, twenty an hour for your time, and a thousand dollar bonus."

Max scooped it up and tucked it inside his jacket. Counting it would only insult these old money types. With this much dough, and Cornelia's extra payments, Dietrich Investigation Services was saved. An inner selfishness urged him to turn around and head home, but too much had changed in the past twenty-four hours.

"Many thanks, Mr. Haskell."

The old man's smile stretched wider. "No, thank *you*, Mr. Dietrich. Admittedly, I had doubts concerning you, but Richard was right. You were the perfect man for this job."

That just meant Max was unscrupulous enough to not ask questions. It was a small opening, but one he'd have to take.

"Happy to help, gents. With that much firepower, I'll bet even those incompetent Bolivians can win the war now, right Gener— I mean, Troop Leader?"

Norris chuckled. "Let's hope so, Mr. Dietrich. But somehow, I doubt it."

"Even after they get rid of that weakling in charge?"

Norris let his surprise show. "You mean, President Salamanca?"

"That's the one. You mentioned his generals were planning a putsch. Remember?"

"Just a hunch I had. The writing was on the wall."

"Oh, come now, Troop Leader. You of all people have to agree that the military should run a war, not spineless politicians."

That seemed to warm Norris a little, who nodded along.

"Maxie here distrusts politicians almost as much as we do," Osborn said with a laugh.

Time for the clincher. Max withdrew *100% Americanism* from his pocket and placed it on Haskell's desk, next to the standing globe.

"You lay out a good case for getting rid of all those grafting rats," he said.

Osborn fixed him with an amused smirk. "Ah, you *did* read it. Tell me, Maxie, what was your favorite part?"

"Mostly your economic ideas. The National Recovery Administration just doesn't go far enough. Besides, it's too cumbersome, and only hurts the average American with all its confusing codes. But Mussolini's Corporate State has whipped Italy into shape, right quick!"

Osborn's smirk blossomed into a warm smile. Haskell though, barked a derisive laugh, bleeding into a burst of thunder from outside.

"Why the sudden change of heart, Mr. Dietrich? What happened to that money-hungry scoundrel we hired?"

"Well, that's just it, Mr. Haskell," Max said. "This country is going down in flames and the only people benefiting are the Communists. I saw them the other day at Union Square.

They're planning something big. People think the NRA codes are bad? Hell, once America goes Red, it'll be hard for a private eye, or anyone else, to make a buck."

Haskell leaned back, a sneer curling his dry lips. "Which is why we must defeat that man in the White House. His New Deal is watered down Socialism, an anthesis of everything America stands for."

"You mean, the Jew Deal," Max muttered, the words leaving behind a bitter aftertaste.

Haskell and Osborn exchanged looks, but Norris lit up like the Fourth of July.

"Too true, Dietrich!"

"General Norris…" Haskell hissed.

"But the lad's got a point," Norris said. "Jewish banksters caused the Wall Street crash and now they're getting even richer off President Rosenfeld's swindle."

The opening widened, allowing Max to waltz right through. "Excellent point, Troop Leader. You know, I still have some relatives over in Germany. They tell me the new government really turned things around there once they kicked the Jews out of business and politics."

"Hear, hear," Norris cried, his frame growing even taller. "Dietrich, permit me to speak candidly."

"We're all friends here, aren't we?"

A somber look spread over Norris. "I must admit, the Germans aren't my favorite people."

"You haven't had streusel, then."

Norris feigned a chuckle. "I realize you're a loyal American, despite your heritage. Richard told me all about your deeds in France, so your patriotism is not in question. But we fought a war against the Hun, and I'm not one to forgive and forget that easily. Besides, the arrogance of those Kraut advisers I saw in Bolivia was galling." He sucked in a deep breath, relaxing a little. "Although his 'master race' theory is a lot of bunk, Adolf Hitler is an inspiration for unmasking this insidious Jewish threat."

"Couldn't agree more, Troop Leader."

Off to the side, Osborn looked less than thrilled, whereas Haskell's crinkled face drooped in a dour frown. Rain continued smacking against the window, casting a sullen gloom throughout the pallid office.

"Sorry, Richard. I know you're not swell on *der Führer.* Mussolini's tops and all, but the Nazis have the right idea when it comes to the Jews."

"No, it's not that. Maxie, why are you sharing all this with us?" An eagerness flashed across Osborn. "Are you joining our cause?"

"In a way…"

It was now or never, do or die, kill or be killed. The appetizer was well-served, but would they devour the main course?

"You see, I know all about your plot. And I want to help."

CHAPTER FORTY-FOUR

Minutes dragged by in strained silence, amplifying the rainfall like the chatter of bullets. Cornelia's words from earlier echoed like a grim warning. '*We Haskells have guns hidden everywhere.*' No doubt Elias Haskell slept with a few heaters under his pillow. But other than a few wide eyes, there was no reaction.

Finally, the old man spoke. "And what plot is that, Mr. Dietrich?"

Max offered a grin, then, "The one to overthrow Roosevelt, of course."

Nobody stirred, but air seemed to drain from the office until Haskell rattled out a laugh.

"That's quite a claim. Can you back it up?"

"Sure, it's one hell of a plan."

A nod from Haskell prompted him to continue. Osborn and Norris stood silent but hung on every word. There was no reason to expose their romance or bring Cornelia into any of this. Just share enough to let this old buzzard know their little scheme had been figured out.

"Back in 1932, thanks to a Red protest and strike, your Long Island factory went belly-up. However, it still had a massive warehouse upstate, chock full of secondhand weaponry. But who to sell it to? Luckily, Mr. Haskell, you landed a standup salesman in the form of your son-in-law. He negotiated a very lucrative arms contract soon after the Chaco War started. How am I doing?"

A sharp laugh trilled from Osborn. "Go on, Maxie. This is quite riveting."

"Glad you like it, Richard. Well, after you saved the company, you had another brainstorm. Some countries in Europe had figured out how to stave off the depression and discipline striking workers. Italy's Black Shirts, for instance.

This company has firsthand contact with Italians, selling guns to Chinese warlords, so they probably shared all sorts of heroic tales about Il Duce. It's little wonder why Rome was on Richard's honeymoon tour of Europe.

"And when Richard returned back to America, he thought, 'aha, what if we have our very own Fascist Party here?' At first, Mr. Haskell, you wrote it off as nonsense. But then, when Roosevelt went off the gold standard, you and your rich friends got spooked. You all wanted to protect your fortunes from inflation, and your businesses from uppity workers talking about unions and strikes. Buoyed with cash from Du Pont purchasing stock in your company, you give Richard here the go ahead and the National Crusaders were born."

Osborn didn't reply, but his smile was telling.

"Not only did the Khaki Shirts rough up Communists, they were also rented out as strikebreakers for Standard Oil, Bethlehem Steel, and Du Pont."

"Well, well, Maxie," Osborn chimed in. "Someone's been doing a little snooping."

"It's in my nature, Richard. But in the future, you might want to tell Crusader First Class Compton to keep his trap shut."

"Oh, I will," Osborn said. Leather crackled as the riding crop strained in his hands.

"It was a nice little arrangement," Max continued. "The Khaki Shirts get to crack all the Bolshie skulls they want, and big business has its own private strikebreaking outfit. Not run-of-the mill thugs, mind you. The Khaki Shirts are organized like a military unit, tough and dependable."

Osborn beamed with pride.

"I imagine you eventually wanted the Khaki Shirts to intimidate FDR into going back on the gold standard, but something happened that demanded immediate action, Mr. Haskell. This June, Congress passed the arms embargo. Now your company risked being fined into bankruptcy. Even worse, that self-righteous Senator Nye launched a smear campaign against the arms industry and you in particular. So, what do you do?"

"Yes, Mr. Dietrich," the old man said, leaning back. "What do I do?"

Max listened to the drumbeat of rain, preparing his next move. He couldn't mention seeing them at the Long Island camp yesterday, nor anything to do with Francis Haskell still being alive. Did this dried-up death dealer even remember that his son – what was left of him, anyway – was still alive?

"Well, you already have a private army that's been in an unofficial war with the Communists. Why not sic them on a new enemy – the government?" Max shrugged. "I reckon that ever since June, you've been quietly sending stockpiles of your entire inventory down to the city. You can't just ship it out all at once, after all."

"Oh? And why's that, Mr. Dietrich?"

Max shrugged. "Too many bells would go off. After all, you're already violating the law by even selling arms to Bolivia. But I bet nobody in your company gives a damn about that. They're just happy to be employed, and Americans know more about the Land of Oz than they do about the Gran Chaco. But shipping a huge stockpile of weapons to equip a Fascist Party, even a Star-spangled-American-as-apple-pie Fascist Party, well, that might ruffle a few feathers. A concerned citizen might rat you out to the G-Men or Congressman Dickstein."

"A good guess, Mr. Dietrich." Haskell sounded amused, almost playful.

"Thanks, I try. So, the way I figure it is, whenever an order for the Bolivian Army is filled, you add in a few extra guns to skim off the top. So, when the shipment arrives in the Canarsie warehouse, Captain Morales arrives, takes the guns he ordered, and the rest are driven out to your Long Island camp."

Another laugh from Osborn, but Haskell and Norris kept still and quiet, like glowering statues.

"Don't tell me Compton spilled the beans on that too, Maxie?"

"No, I used my noodle to figure that out. So go easy on the poor schlub."

"Please continue, Mr. Dietrich," Haskell said. "What do I have planned with all of these guns?"

Time to lay it all out. Drawing in a deep breath, Max said, "My money's on the best Khaki Shirt marksman gets to take a shot at Roosevelt, probably when he's making a speech. The same way that Italian nut, Zangara, tried to kill him last year."

"His only crime was that he missed," Haskell growled. "Then what, Mr. Dietrich? I thought we were planning a coup d'é tat, not an assassination."

"Well, that's only step one. Step two is once FDR is kaput, the National Crusaders, armed to the teeth, rise up and occupy key cities. New York, Philadelphia, Washington…I saw a map in Richard's office. The Khaki Shirts have men up and down the Eastern Seaboard."

Another silence filled the room as Haskell, Osborn, and Norris – sized each other up. An entire conversation was happening through glances, raised eyebrows, and facial tics, one that Max wasn't invited to. Without a word, Haskell's bony hand eased to his desk and yanked open a drawer. A small automatic flashed in his spindly fingers – a Baby Browning, by the looks of it. But the make was indecipherable right now, since the pistol was leveled straight between Max's eyes.

"Well, Mr. Dietrich, if everything you say is true, why shouldn't I pull the trigger right now?"

CHAPTER FORTY-FIVE

Max had stared down many guns over the years. But more people had threatened to kill him in the past two days than during his entire stint as a Prohi. He looked over to Osborn and Norris for some sign of support. Osborn stared back with a relaxed grin, as if watching a Broadway show. Norris though, remained rigid and blank-faced.

"For one, Mr. Haskell," Max said, "my brains would splatter all over your father's nice portrait."

That pulled another laugh from Osborn. "Always with the jokes, Maxie."

"I'm glad you're laughing, Richard. I'm crying on the inside."

Even Haskell laughed this time, and the automatic sank a little. Now to hit the old man with some phony sincerity.

"Gentlemen, democracy is a sinking ship. It was never a very sturdy vessel, manned by boobs and rubes. What voice should your average yokel on a farm or some bonehead in the Bowery have in the government? Appealing to the lowest common denominator got America into this mess."

Osborn nodded along, and while Haskell looked intrigued, the gun kept still. Time to bring in reinforcements.

"American democracy is just a smokescreen behind which Jewish financiers operate. Thanks to some Shylock intriguers on Wall Street, my life's savings were wiped out in a bank run. Our elections are just pantomime theater, and if there's any way I can close the curtain on it, I'll wager everything I have left."

The words animated Norris like a wind-up toy soldier.

"The lad has a point, Mr. Haskell. I saw it myself in Washington. Jew technocrats swarming the White House like cockroaches. Good Christian men are being pushed aside for Yid professors and kike intellectuals. That miserable cripple is nothing but a puppet to the so-called 'Brain Trust.'" Norris scoffed. "A benign name for the Jewish serpent, coiling itself around the nation."

Finally, Haskell set the automatic aside – the Browning label now clearly visible – and let out an exasperated groan.

"General, please tone down the Jew-baiting," he said. "My colleagues admire Mussolini, but anything that reminds them of Hitler will stir only derision. Besides, we don't want to alarm Samuel Dickstein and his insufferable committee."

"That may be, but I will only hold my tongue until we take power," Norris snapped.

American Fascists – from the Silver Legion to the Friends of the New Germany – were almost to a man anti-Semitic. But officially, the National Crusaders were strangely ambivalent toward Jews, like most of the American populace. An old *Fortune* magazine article once said that a third of the American people were anti-Semitic, a third were pro-semitic, and another third couldn't care less.

But now it all made sense. The National Crusader policy toward Jews avoided attention from Dickstein's snooping un-American Committee and kept any potential Wall Street financiers happy. It was just good business, after all. But how long could they keep a rabid dog like Nathaniel Norris leashed?

"Ah, so my hunch was right," Max said. "You gentlemen are planning a putsch."

A crack rang out as Osborn slapped the whip against his boot again. "Didn't I say that Maxie here was the finest detective in all New York? We could use his talents, you know."

Max flashed a thankful smile but Haskell still frowned with skepticism.

"Only half-right, Mr. Dietrich. Your theory regarding the execution of our plot is downright vulgar. I'd never condone an assassination like some common gangster. And trying to seize New York and Philadelphia!" Haskell scoffed. "It'd only result in a civil war, and one the National Crusaders would lose."

"So I'm all wet on that part. How do you plan on pulling it off then?"

A bony finger wagged back and forth. "You're prying into matters that are none of your concern, Mr. Dietrich. Our business is concluded and you've been paid for your services."

Back at square one again. So close, yet so far. However, another bluff might sway this withered vulture.

"Mr. Haskell, you mentioned your 'colleagues,'" Max said. "That wouldn't happen to be the American Liberty League, would it?"

The gray eyes flared, then tightened. "You're well-informed, Mr. Dietrich. It is not just Richard and I who want to rid America of that man in the White House. Many patriotic citizens feel the same way and are ready to spend their very last penny to do so."

"Like the Du Ponts?"

The gray eyes screwed even tighter. "Among others."

"Dietrich, my lad," Norris cut in, "I am no fan of Wall Street. But thanks to the Liberty League, gentile money is funding a war against Jewish capitalism and Jewish Bolshevism."

Max wasn't sure how Jewish capitalists worked with Jewish Bolsheviks, but political contradictions and nonsense was par for the course among the lunatic fringe. He nodded anyway.

"Mr. Dietrich, you've proven yourself to be a reliable bloodhound, for a price," Haskell said. "But these are matters of politics, and I'm not convinced of your sincerity."

"That's just it, Mr. Haskell. I know all about politicians from snooping on their dirty laundry. Can you blame me for being so cynical? But Richard and the General here, hell, they're the first honest men in politics since Lincoln."

The two Khaki Shirts beamed brightly, but the old man remained aloof.

"I know many secrets, Mr. Haskell. Secrets that might help you after taking power."

"Oh?" The gray eyebrows lifted. "Such as?"

"Such as Dickstein's long history of graft. I have plenty of proof if you're interested."

Haskell perked up. "Anything regarding Senator Nye?"

"I'm sure I can scrounge something up."

The old man rubbed his chin, but the skeptical look lingered. "It won't make any difference soon…"

Osborn stepped forward. "Maxie has a lot of flaws, I'll be the first to admit that. But he's one hell of a detective, one whose talents I'd prefer to have working for us."

Max thanked him with a smile.

"What's more, he saved my life. And I intend to pay it back now." The crop slapped against Osborn's thigh, punctuating his statement. "I want him at my side."

"Hear, hear!" Norris chimed in.

Their words were more of an ultimatum than anything else. There could be no putsch without Osborn and Norris, since Elias Haskell had about as much charisma as a can of corned beef. A pang of guilt squirmed inside Max. His old friend had stuck his neck out for him again, unaware of the knife that would soon be plunged into his back.

"You raise a good point, Richard," Haskell declared. "Having Mr. Dietrich as an ally is preferable than having him as an enemy." He craned his head toward Max. "Under normal circumstances, I wouldn't extend this much trust toward a stranger. But Richard vouches for your character. Don't disappoint me."

Max grinned, but a problem remained. Dickstein would want to know exactly who was financing this plot and the exact details of how it'd occur.

"I never disappoint," he said. "But, since my 'gun down FDR' theory was all wet, I assume the real plan is being cooked up with the Liberty League? If that's the case, then I have a few tips on how to deal with swine like Congressman Dickstein."

"Maxie's got a point. He should attend today's meeting."

The defiance fled from Haskell's withered puss, an old man unable to sustain the vigor of younger men. He blew out a sigh, then said, "All right, Mr. Dietrich. The meeting's today at noon. Do you know where the Union League Club is?"

Max nodded as Osborn cut in.

"There's one condition though, Maxie."

"And that is?"

"I want a firm commitment from you. Join our ranks. Become a Khaki Shirt and believe in America once again."

Well, always give the audience what they want. Max clicked his heels and shot out his arm in a Fascist salute, reciprocated by Chief Osborn and Troop Leader Norris.

"I also have a condition, Mr. Dietrich," Haskell said. "Take your payment and run over to Brooks Brothers. Please, buy yourself a decent suit."

CHAPTER FORTY-SIX

The Union League Club was located on 37th Street and Park Avenue, a few blocks from the Empire State Building, looming over the city like an enormous tombstone. Thanks to the depression, businesses were still hesitant to enter into that oversized ghost town, now nicknamed the Empty State Building. However, the Union League Club regularly hosted New York's elite since the Civil War, although its current location had been built only a few years ago.

Max stood outside the entrance, rain plopping hard against his umbrella. He'd only partly taken Haskell's advice. Returning to his office, he'd changed into a black, three-piece suit, a "gift" during Prohibition days. But he had swung by a nearby Brooks Brothers, since their umbrellas were the only ones worth a damn against New York's biblical rain.

A limousine splashed through the wet streets, pulling up alongside the curb. A chauffeur hopped out with a voluminous umbrella of his own, then yanked open the passenger door. Elias Haskell heaved himself out, balancing on that steel cane of his. The prosthetic leg held firm as he shambled forward, the chauffeur keeping pace with the umbrella. Decked out in a black frock coat and top hat, Haskell resembled a Communist caricature of a capitalist plutocrat, like a cartoon straight out of *New Masses.*

Osborn and Norris followed, both wearing National Crusader uniforms. Disdaining umbrellas of their own, they walked quickly toward the entrance before rain turned their crisp tunics into mushy rags. A uniformed doorman came to attention and opened the door for the three of them, Max following close behind. The doorman shot him a skeptical glare but didn't protest.

Inside the lobby, dapper attendants took their hats, coats, and umbrellas. They soon led the four up a twin spiraling staircase to the second floor, where a portrait of Abraham Lincoln greeted them. Fitting, since the club had been formed in 1863 to support the Union cause. Inside was the talk of myths and rumors, since only New York's high society saw a glimpse. From what Max had heard, the building's nine stories hosted billiard halls, libraries, and over sixty bedrooms. However, the second floor was the farthest they ascended.

Beside a pair of open doors hung a poster, stamped with the Liberty League's logo – the cracked Liberty Bell – accompanied by the slogan "*The Old Bell Is Still Ringing*." They followed Haskell into a spacious dining hall. A glittering chandelier illuminated the amenities – leather chairs and an elongated table, serving hors d'oeuvres from every continent.

A pianist serenaded the room with Chopin, but the real entertainment was with the occupants. About fifty or so men – clad in silk ties, and glittering cufflinks, and suits that made Max's getup look like hand-me-downs from the Salvation Army – chatted in groups, drank champagne and coffee, snacked on sweetmeats, and lounged in upholstered thrones. Several faces were instantly recognizable from their mugshots in the daily papers.

Immersed in conversation with two other men was Irénée Du Pont, former president of the entire Du Pont Corporation, now head of the American Liberty League. Bland features – receding gray hair, half-lidded eyes behind spectacles, and a thin mouth just above a weak chin – were deceptive tricks, disguising a man who wielded far more power than most politicians.

Du Pont chewed a pipe, nodding along while two other men spoke. One, a gangling, horse-faced man with a high forehead, Max placed as John Jakob Raskob. A Du Pont financial official, Raskob had also once held the prestigious position of chairman of the Democratic Party. Beside them was another well-dressed gentleman, whose wide, lumpy face was just as disarming as Irénée Du Pont's. But Grayson Mallet-Prevost Murphy was a veritable wizard of Wall Street, who owned a brokerage firm closely associated with the House of JP Morgan.

Others were less recognizable, but an aura of old money hung in the air along with wafts of smoke curling out of cigarette holders, immaculate pipes, and fat cigars. Max followed behind Haskell and the others further into the room. A distinguished-looking man with hard features and stern eyes approached them with an open palm.

"Elias Haskell," he said, taking the death dealer's withered claw in a hearty handshake. "Good to see you, old boy."

"Hello, Teagle. I didn't know you were a Liberty Leaguer."

A gracious chuckle, then, "There's a lot of Standard Oil money flowing through this little club, so I figured I'd drop by and rub elbows a little. How's the munitions business?"

"Bed bugs are more popular than us, courtesy of Senator Nye."

"Well, thank you for taking the heat off of Standard. That loudmouth imbecile Huey Long rails against us as if we were the devil himself."

An amused grin curled Haskell's dry lips. "Why does the Kingfish have it out for Standard, anyway?"

Teagle shrugged. "Years ago, Long invested in a Louisiana well that struck oil, but we refused to drill there. He lost a mint, from what I hear. That arrogant blowhard is more crooked than Boss Tweed ever was. He only ran Manhattan, but the Kingfish controls an entire state."

Max stifled a laugh. Huey Long's self-righteous crusade against the oil empire was nothing more than a petty vendetta. Still, Max could admire the con. Rubes and boobs lapped up that whole "man of the people" masquerade. Just blame everything on the elites, and you could swindle the American people out of everything they owned.

"How *is* the oil business these days?" Haskell asked.

"Lousy. Hopefully, you can fix that." Teagle's stern eyes drifted over to the rest of them, hovering beside the old man.

"My apologies." Haskell gestured to the two National Crusaders, towering over both of them. "Permit me to introduce my son-in-law, Richard Osborn, the Chief of the Khaki Shirts. And General Nathaniel Norris, who has just returned from Bolivia as a military adviser. This is Walter Teagle, head of Standard Oil of New Jersey."

Max didn't get an introduction, but it didn't matter. His thoughts swirled with schoolboy lessons of Teddy Roosevelt's war against John D. Rockefeller's trust, which resulted in the monolithic Standard Oil Company being broken up into multiple smaller corporations, less powerful but still voracious. While the big shots talked, Max withdrew to a nearby table and munched on hors d'oeuvres, still within comfortable earshot.

"Ah, yes," Teagle mused, "the National Crusaders. You Khaki Shirts have been most useful."

Osborn clicked his heels. "Happy to help, Mr. Teagle."

"Plenty of union troublemakers have learned to shut their mouths after your boys paid them a visit. If any more Standard workers come down with the Red fever, I know just who to call." Teagle turned to Norris and asked, "Tell me, General, what is your opinion of the Chaco War?"

Brow furrowed, Norris said, "Not good. Bolivian incompetence is losing the war."

A deep frown creased Teagle's face. "Is there any hope?"

Haskell chimed in, "An intervention would even the score. One brigade of American Marines would mop up the Paraguayan Army."

"A lovely idea, but Roosevelt's Good Neighbor Policy makes that a moot point."

"Of course," Haskell said, but his tone hinted otherwise.

"I must say, Haskell, old boy, that is upsetting news. I feel like Standard bet on the wrong horse. It'll be salt in the wound if those Dutch bastards at Shell get first drilling rights in the Gran Chaco."

"Well, don't be too discouraged, Mr. Teagle," Osborn cut in.

"Oh, I'm not. I had a rather encouraging talk with representatives from Vickers."

"Vickers?" Haskell's gray eyes sparked with fury.

"Their report was more optimistic. Of course, it required Bolivia purchasing another large order from them." Teagle flashed a mocking grin. "They lay the blame on you, Haskell, old boy, for the state of the war. Turns out they uncovered your secret contract with the Bolivian government."

Haskell soured even further. "How?"

"Don't blame me, old boy, I didn't spill the beans. But Vickers claims that your company is underselling them. After all, the Bolivian government only has so much money to spend, even after our Wall Street friends float them some loans. Sure, Bolivia buys a lot of Vickers munitions, but Vickers says they'd be able to sell even more if your company wasn't supplying them with outdated weapons."

Snacking on a deviled egg, Max observed this odd pair – the Oil Baron and the Merchant of Death, the true rulers of the world. Here he was, a mere mortal watching the gods bicker on Mount Olympus.

When Haskell didn't respond, Teagle spoke for him. "It doesn't matter which guns the Bolivians use to win the war, so long as they win it. We're all in this together, old boy."

"Of course…"

After a customary handshake, Teagle departed and joined another group of dapper gentlemen, leaving Haskell stewing. Osborn and Norris kept their poise, but Max could almost feel the rage emanating from Haskell's skeletal frame like radio waves. Max averted his eyes to the center of the room, where a tall, familiar-looking man now stood. His beefy frame was crammed into a double-breasted, pinstripe brown suit, punctuated with a bright red bow tie. His bulbous nose and ruddy features, split with a jovial grin, combined to form the face of Al Smith – the former governor of New York.

CHAPTER FORTY-SEVEN

Politicians were a dime a dozen, but Al Smith was one of a kind. A loudmouthed New Yorker, he lauded the values of the big city, a place most Americans viewed as a den of decadence, crime, and unwashed immigrants. Despite being part of the Tammany Hall political machine, Smith's corruption was mild in comparison. He was one of the few politicians to admit Prohibition was a failure, demanding its full repeal.

After serving as New York's governor, Smith had been the Democratic nominee for president in 1928, going up against the stodgy Republican Herbert Hoover. It was a showdown between America's two halves – big city decadence versus small town sanctimony. Despite being a Prohi, Max admired Smith's straight talk and voted for him, but it wasn't enough. Hoover won by a landslide, and Max hadn't voted in an election since.

But Al Smith seemed in better spirits than ever, beaming as he addressed this room of stuffed shirts.

"Gentlemen, thanks for coming. When the American Liberty League was foist founded, just three short months ago," Smith drawled, his New York accent dripping off every word, "our patriotism moved us to spend our own hard-earned money to save America. Our foist challenge was these midterm elections and…" Smith's toothy smile grew even wider. "Well, we sure took one helluva drubbin', didn't we?"

Laughter rippled through the room. Even Max joined in. Al Smith was still a straight talker.

"It pains me, a loyal Democrat, to see my party taken over by a buncha smug eggheads who admire Lenin more than Washington." Smith blew out a frustrated sigh. "But we can't argue with reality, gentlemen. Roosevelt now has a solid

Democratic Congress, who'll rubber stamp whatever organization he wants to create next, the Constitution be damned! NRA, CCC, AAA…hell, the government is submoiged in a bowl of alphabet soup!"

Another smattering of laughter before Smith continued.

"But let's appreciate the successes we had. Thanks to our friend, William Randolph Hearst, and his newspapers, California rejected that atheistic socialist, Upton Sinclair, for governor. Guess God still has a sense of humor, eh?"

Apart from Nathaniel Norris, the only God this crowd worshipped was money. Elias Haskell seemed like the type who'd bribed the Almighty to let him hang on just a few years more. Richard Osborn though, probably prayed to the altar of Mussolini.

"Now, I've hoid a lotta defeatist tawk. Some say that the Liberty League should concentrate its efforts on winning the 1936 election. That's a lotta hooey! We have a duty to the Forgotten Man who's being swindled by King Franklin the Foist!"

That got a few heads nodding, Haskell's included. Across the room, Du Pont, Raskob, and Murphy slunk away to a private room under a blue veil of tobacco smoke.

"All Americans suffer under the NRA, the National Regimentation Act," Smith went on, gesticulating with every word, "which is watered-down Bolshevism, sucking the spirit of free enterprise from this here country. Whenever a storefront has to hang that damnable blue eagle, that Roosevelt buzzard, I see it for what it truly is—" he slammed a fist into his meaty hand – "a hammer and sickle!"

"Too true, Governor," Haskell called out.

"Instead of innovation and rugged individualism, Americans have to navigate these ridiculous NRA codes for 'fair play.' Well, every boy who played stick ball knows that life's not fair! But these codes stifle the entrepreneurial spirit of America. Bakers have a system of business codes. Cobblers have their own codes. Hell, even the burlesque shows have a set of codes that limit the amount of time the girlies can drop their drawers."

Laughter filled the smoke-choked room until Smith's broad grin sank into a furious scowl.

"That wasn't a joke. Next, brothels will get an NRA code for how many johns they can admit by the hour. The Brain Trust boys down in Washington think they can regulate every aspect of American life!" Smith shook his head until some joviality returned. Wagging a thick, cigar-like finger, his speech reached a crescendo. "Gentlemen, this is why we founded the Liberty League. Not for us, not for our wealth, but to uphold that sacred document, the United States Constitution! Liars in the press say the Liberty League supports Fascism. Phooey! The only *ism* we support is Americanism!"

Applause followed and Al Smith beamed an even bigger smile. He looked ready to speak again, when Raskob appeared from a side door, gesturing for him to follow. Smith gave a slight bow, then lumbered off into the same private room where Du Pont and the others had disappeared. The pianist struck up some more Chopin, and the Liberty Leaguers lapsed back into conversation.

Brimming with questions, Max half-turned to Osborn, but kept quiet as a tall, stately-looking gentleman approached. Attired in a dark green suit, blue tie splattered with red polka dots, and a high, starched collar, he upheld a stiff, military bearing, only outdone by General Norris. Below a high forehead, his long face was decorated with pince-nez glasses, balanced on a sharp nose, above a pursed mouth.

"Elias," the man said, gripping Haskell's hand.

"Ah, Sterling. I thought you'd moved to France."

"I did. But I wouldn't miss this meeting for the world."

Haskell's lips peeled back in a wide smile, looking like a grinning skeleton. "You remember General Norris and my son-in-law, Richard?"

"I should hope so, old man, since I'm the one who introduced you to the General!"

They shared a laugh as the man rolled his eyes over to Max, holding him in a scrutinizing gaze.

"This is Max Dietrich," Haskell chimed in, "an associate of Richard's. Mr. Dietrich, this is Robert Sterling Clark."

The name set off waves of recognition. That's right, Robert Sterling Clark, heir to the vast Singer sewing machine fortune. Mama Dietrich had spent her best years hunched over one of those contraptions, working long hours in the garment district.

"Call me, Sterling," he said, after a handshake, glancing over at Osborn.

Osborn responded with a laugh, then, "Maxie and I served together in France. Just like you and General Norris served together in China."

Max couldn't hide his surprise. "In China?"

Norris and Clark shared a triumphant look.

"Years ago, during the Boxer Rebellion," Clark elaborated. "Fighting the Yellow Peril in all its infamy."

"We nicknamed Sterling 'the Millionaire Lieutenant,'" Norris said.

Clark's stiff shoulders lifted up and down. "Being the idle rich suited me more, so I resigned my commission."

"You were a fine soldier," Norris insisted. "But a brigade of Yanks could whip a million Chinamen any day."

"What about the Paraguayan Army?" Haskell asked.

"Oh, a regiment would suffice," Clark answered, pulling out a gleaming pocket watch. "Our guest should be ready now."

"What kept him?" Haskell snorted.

"He traveled up to New York in mufti but after arriving here, the pompous ass insisted upon donning his uniform." Clark sighed. "Military men love their costumes, I suppose. So vainglorious…"

Osborn and Norris chuckled, but couldn't hide the flush in their faces. Clark glanced over at Max, then muttered, "Does he know?"

"He knows," Osborn spoke up. Haskell and Norris nodded their agreement, securing Max's ticket to a front row seat. Clark led the way through the smoky room, buzzing with hushed conversations. Another speaker took Smith's place, far less grandiose than the former governor, but that was a tough act to follow.

Max and the others entered a side door, where a small office opened up, dominated by a rectangular table. The room had no windows, lending it a tomb-like atmosphere, but a portrait of George Washington gazed downward. A strange irony, since he'd rejected a plot to overthrow Congress, so many years ago. Overhead, pallid lightbulbs glowed, revealing the occupants. Irénée Du Pont sat at the head of the table, flanked by Murphy and Raskob. Al Smith crammed himself into a seat beside them. Three other chairs were unoccupied.

But Max's eyes were drawn to a tall, imperious Army officer, standing next to a side door. Although Max had only seen that face in newsreels and newspapers, General Douglas MacArthur – US Army Chief of Staff – was unmistakable.

CHAPTER FORTY-EIGHT

General MacArthur's uniform outshone every other outfit in the room, especially Max's. A crisp brown tunic sparkled with medals and ribbons, boasting every award from the Purple Heart to the Croix de Guerre. A Sam Browne cross belt held the ensemble up, while a white shirt and black tie were offset by two "US" insignia pinned on the brown lapels. Khaki jodhpurs were tucked into stiff brown riding boots, polished to a mirror sheen. Four silver stars gleamed on his shoulders, slumping a little compared to Nathaniel Norris's rigid stance, but MacArthur's jutting chin, hawk nose, and razor-sharp blue eyes were more than impressive. A peaked service cap with a brown leather visor, ornamented with the American eagle, completed the uniform, the personification of the United States Army.

The demarcation between MacArthur's modern-style uniform, with its open collar and white shirt, compared to the outdated tunics Osborn and Norris wore, stiff and high-collared, was like the past and future colliding. A deep hatred gathered in Richard Osborn's handsome face, glowering at the man who'd crushed the Bonus March two years before. Was he also the same officer who discovered Osborn's forbidden love letters? But despite his personal feelings, the Khaki Shirt Chief kept still and silent. After all, he was a minnow in this pool of sharks. Max withdrew deeper into a corner, hoping to blend in like a quiet chameleon.

Lurching forward on his cane, Elias Haskell shook General MacArthur's hand with a warm smile.

"Welcome, General. Thank you for coming all the way from Washington on such short notice."

"Good to see you again, Haskell."

"You remember Nathaniel Norris, right?"

Norris stepped forward, offering a firm handshake.

"Of course I remember Major-General Norris," MacArthur said. "The Army hasn't been whole without him."

Norris cracked a smile, then gestured over to Osborn and Max. "My former adjutant, Richard Osborn, and Max Dietrich."

MacArthur acknowledged Max with the faintest of nods, before focusing on Osborn.

"Ah, yes…Captain Osborn," MacArthur said, blue eyes narrowing. "Your passion for the Bonus March was indeed admirable. I would like to clear the air about what happened that tragic July day." The General assumed a speechifying pose. "President Hoover misled me. False rumors circulated that the BEF was infiltrated with Communists and had become a mob animated by the essence of revolution. But, as a soldier, I am obliged to obey orders, regardless of my personal feeling."

The performance put Broadway to shame, and Max almost applauded. But newspaper exposés told a different story, one where General MacArthur ignored orders from President Hoover to simply clear the BEF from Capitol grounds. Instead, MacArthur pursued them across to their main camp in Anacostia, bombarding them with tear gas and a bayonet charge. But Hoover got most of the blame, one of many failures that cost him reelection.

"The past is the past," Osborn choked out, his features taut. "We must look forward to the future."

"Hear, hear!" Norris said.

Haskell took a seat next to Sterling Clark, Norris sat beside Al Smith, and General MacArthur ensconced himself at the far end, directly opposite Irénée Du Pont. He set his peaked cap aside, the metallic bald eagle twinkling in the overhead light.

"Thank you all for coming today," Du Pont began, setting his pipe aside. Staring straight at MacArthur, he said, "General, this August, we founded the American Liberty League with one simple purpose – to uphold that most sacred of documents, the United States Constitution. Real Democrats—" his eyes flashed over to Al Smith "—are being replaced by New Deal technocrats, who plan the economy with guidance from Moscow. Tuesday's election results remove any doubt that America is headed down the road of Socialism."

A few concerned murmurs rumbled through the room before Du Pont spoke again.

"But while we poured money into these doomed midterm elections, Elias Haskell was busy formulating a contingency plan. All he asked from us was a little extra financing, which we have provided. Would you please elaborate, Elias?"

The *Fortune* article appeared again in Max's mind. Du Pont had purchased a controlling interest in Haskell stock, and the presence of Grayson Murphy suggested that the funds had been loaned through his brokerage firm.

"Gentlemen," Haskell began, "we gather here from very different backgrounds and beliefs but united in common opposition to the New Deal. Like all Americans, I had high hopes when Roosevelt took office, but it's clear he's not up to the task of ending this depression. Instead, as Governor Smith so eloquently said, his NRA is a confusing maze of codes, strangling the entrepreneurial spirit of our people."

"Hear, hear, Mr. Haskell," Norris cut in. "But Roosevelt is a mere placeholder, an American Kerensky, ready to be overthrown by godless radicals in the Communist Party or Huey Long. We must act now or lose America forever."

Max forced back a laugh, remembering the vaudevillian retreat of Susan Partridge and her comrades the other day. Those clowns couldn't overthrow a court jester.

"Well said, General," Haskell continued, "and the Reds could take it without firing a shot, since that man in the White House has gutted our national defense. Even worse is what he's planned for the budget. General, please share your most recent meeting with the President…"

MacArthur drew himself up in his seat. "Several months ago, I was summoned to the White House to discuss budget matters for 1935. Roosevelt suggested cutting 51% of the Army's funding. I was shocked to my very core. Myopic politicians see our oceans as a suitable defense. To them, the Navy comprises the armed forces, whereas the Army is a glorified militia."

Max couldn't disagree. America distrusted large, standing armies, so whenever a war broke out, the US Army had to be rebuilt every time. The Navy though, received the hefty budgets for their battleships and airplanes, along with the public's affection. Even Hollywood wasn't subtle about their preference. James Cagney starred in *Here Comes the Navy*, but there was no *Here Comes the Army*.

"I saw a grim future unfold. Because of politics, the Army would be defeated, utterly routed in a future conflict. Unable to suppress my emotions, I let the President know my true thoughts." MacArthur's blue eyes blazed. "I said, 'When we lose the next war, and an American boy, lying in the mud with an enemy bayonet through his belly and an enemy foot on his dying throat spat out his last curse, I want it not to be MacArthur, but Roosevelt!'"

A stunned silence spread out, leaving these distinguished Liberty Leaguers wide-eyed. MacArthur let the shock linger before continuing.

"Tempers flared, and he thundered back, 'You must not talk that way to the President!' I offered to resign, but we came to a tense agreement. The budget would not be cut so dramatically, but over three thousand officers are now running Roosevelt's CCC camps like babysitters. Training has come to a halt. What little money we are afforded goes to retaining officers, so our arsenals have become derelict. My term as chief of staff is set to expire this month, and while I've done my best to fight for the US Army against scheming politicians, its best days are behind it."

Somber nods followed, then Haskell said, "Added to our troubles is that vainglorious braggart, Gerald Nye. I make no secret of my personal disdain but his vindictive Arms Committee impacts us all. Have you read the papers lately, General? He mentions you by name, citing your visit to Turkey as nothing but an armaments sale."

Resting on the table, MacArthur's knuckles tensed. "Yes, I saw that."

"However, Senator Nye is but one of Roosevelt's fangs. If we rid ourselves of that sanctimonious bumpkin, another will take his place." Haskell's gnarled hands tightened into fists. "No, we must cut off the snake's head."

Another silence fell over them, eerie and unsettling, as if some blasphemy had been uttered. MacArthur's gravelly voice soon broke the tension like a gunshot.

"What do you suggest, Haskell?"

On cue, Osborn stepped forward, clicked his heels, and took command.

"Gentlemen, in order to save America, we must look to Italy. In 1922, Benito Mussolini and his Fascist Party marched on Rome, demanding they be given power, or else they'd seize it by force! When the Italian King gazed upon a sea of Black Shirts flooding the capital, he couldn't oppose the national revolution. Instead, he appointed Mussolini prime minister, and Italy was saved from Communism."

Any previous bitterness toward MacArthur had vanished. Fiery passion now inflamed Osborn's chiseled face. Fascism aroused such intense fervor within him that everything else – money, romance, sex – must have paled in comparison. A coy grin spread his lips.

"But it was all just a bluff. Mussolini had no more than sixteen thousand Black Shirts in the entire country. The Italian Army could have crushed them with little more than a division. But their daring gambit paid off. Mussolini's sympathizers within the Army and the monarchy, convinced the King of Italy to give in. Gentlemen, the March on Rome shows us the way to victory!"

The Liberty Leaguers hung on every word, enraptured by this Fascist mythmaking. Even MacArthur let a dreamy expression cross his pompous face.

"Our plan is simple," Osborn went on. "For months now, my National Crusaders have been training with rifles, pistols, and machine guns – all provided by Mr. Haskell. And thanks to the generous donations from the gentlemen in this room, my Khaki Shirts are well-lodged and well-fed out in Long Island. They will march on Washington the moment I tell them to!"

A stern glare returned to MacArthur. "The King of Italy might have been fooled, but Roosevelt is a different matter. He'll order me to swat your Khaki Shirts like buzzing flies."

"An excellent point, General," Osborn said. "But the National Crusaders will only be the spear tip. There are five thousand Khaki Shirts in New York, five more along the Eastern Seaboard. They will join us as we march, out of the city into New Jersey, through Delaware and Maryland. But my ten thousand National Crusaders will only be the spear tip of a vast superorganization. Any Hoovervilles we pass offer many potential followers, but most of our new recruits will come from the many Civilian Conservation Corps camps along the way to Washington."

"CCC camps?" MacArthur snorted.

"Twelve in all, with the final stop being a camp in Elkridge, Maryland, a mere thirty miles from Washington. The CCC is mostly comprised of young men, but a good many are veterans of the World War, and many of them are former Bonus Marchers. They remember the speech General Norris gave to their encampment! And they admire how he resigned in protest after President Roosevelt refused to pay the bonus. The veterans at those camps will follow General Norris to hell and back."

MacArthur nodded, squirming a little. He was, after all, persona non grata with the BEF and most veterans around the country. But Nathaniel Norris had stood by them and sacrificed his own career on their behalf. So what if he was part of the lunatic fringe now? America was getting bugsier by the day.

"And the youngsters?" MacArthur asked. "Do you think they'll abandon their obligation to the government?"

Osborn smirked. "This depression has ravaged the youth of this country, just like a war. Young men are disillusioned with democracy. They crave a strong man to come galloping in on a white horse…a man like General Norris. After one of his speeches and a promise to end this depression, they'll consider it their patriotic duty to abandon their posts. And when this giant superorganization of veterans, youngsters, and Khaki Shirts reach Elkridge," Osborn took in a deep breath, almost euphoric, "several Mack trucks will be waiting there to arm them with Haskell rifles, Haskell pistols, and Haskell machine guns. Then we march on Washington DC!"

"Just how many men do you plan to recruit?" Du Pont asked, chewing on his pipe.

"We estimate ninety thousand."

"With your Khaki Shirts, that puts it at just a hundred thousand," Du Pont said, almost frowning. "We were hoping you'd amass five hundred thousand for this 'superorganization.'"

"We have friends in radio and print, don't we? If we say there's half a million men on the march, then there is."

Du Pont chuckled, pipe between his teeth. "A good point. Can you arm them all?"

"We've accumulated enough weapons to equip over half. Of course, my National Crusaders will handle the heavy stuff – machine guns and Thompsons. They've already been drilling out in Long Island. It doesn't matter if the other half is unarmed, since perception is more important. If our newspaper friends say they outgun the US Army garrison in Washington, then they do."

Pleased murmurs filled the office as the Liberty Leaguers gave Elias Haskell respectful nods.

Osborn spun back to MacArthur. "And remember, General, that a mere seventeen thousand veterans in the

BEF was enough to panic the White House. And they were all unarmed. What will Roosevelt do when this superorganization shows up at his doorstep, armed to the teeth? Sending in the US Army won't be so easy this time."

MacArthur's fist slammed on the desk. "I will not sacrifice a single American soldier!"

Osborn's coy grin morphed into a knowing smile. "Nor would we ask you to, General. The guns are just a bluff. But on paper, this superorganization will be more than a match for the truncated Army garrison in Washington. You, General, will simply tell Roosevelt, 'Mr. President, if we fight this force, it'll be civil war. One we might not win.' He'll have no choice but to meet our demands."

MacArthur raised an eyebrow. "And those are?"

"First and foremost, there will be the creation of a new cabinet position – the secretary of general affairs," Osborn circled the table, like a bomber closing in on its target. "Americans are averse to coups, but we have some newspapers on our side. They'll convince the people that Roosevelt is sick, tired, needing rest. The general affairs secretary will be granted broad, sweeping executive powers to save America from this depression. What's more, he'll take over the day-to-day duties of state, while the President steps back to a more ceremonial role. And the first secretary of general affairs will be none other than that great American patriot" – Osborn pointed straight at his secret lover – "General Nathaniel Norris!"

It was a better scheme than seizing cities through violent insurrection, Max conceded. That type of putsch was strictly for the pulps. But a bloodless coup would be swallowed by John Q. Public hook, line, and sinker. Americans prided themselves on being the freest people on earth, so long as the newspapers told them it was so.

"But General MacArthur, your cooperation is essential," Osborn said, his frame drawing up to a martial pose. "Will you join us to save America?"

MacArthur's blue eyes sank into deep thought. Committing treason was enough to leave anyone speechless, even him. The Liberty Leaguers remained rigid, awaiting an answer. Would they call the putsch off if he declined? This entire plot was akin to a piece of heavy machinery, a single malfunctioning part would ruin everything. After a few moments, MacArthur lifted his gaze, clouded with uncertainty.

"Gentlemen, it is true that I fear for our nation's future and firmly oppose the Roosevelt administration," he said, voice heavy with emotion. "But I do not share Mr. Osborn's affinity for certain European ideologies, nor General Norris's distaste toward the Jewish people. Furthermore, I took an oath to defend the Constitution from enemies, both foreign and domestic."

Air seemed sucked out of the room, until Al Smith's throaty voice bawled, "We're *upholding* the Constitution from a man who wishes to subvert it!"

Max almost laughed. At least Hitler and Mussolini were honest about their hatred for democracy.

"You all may have the best of intentions," MacArthur said, "but others might not see it that way. My adjutant, for example, Major Eisenhower. A good officer, if a bit too liberal. I had to conceal my trip from him, in case word leaked. He fails to see the danger America is in. Please, permit me a few days to consider this. Such actions should not be decided lightly."

Osborn stepped forward, teeth clenched. "We do not have a few days! The operation already has a set date – November 11th. Armistice Day is the zero hour! Besides, your term as chief of staff is set to expire this month. We must act now!"

"There is still a chance that the President will have me remain at my post," MacArthur said, almost smug.

"Are you placing your career before the nation?" Osborn growled. "If we postpone the march, Mr. Haskell will have to appear before Senator Nye's committee next week. Details about this plot will leak during questioning—"

Haskell held up a scrawny, silencing hand. "General, I understand your concern. Please, take a day to consider the implications." A crooked smile contorted his skeletal face. "But while you're in New York, please enjoy a Broadway show or a movie. We have the best theaters in the country. Perhaps that Shirley Temple picture…what's its name?"

"*Baby Take a Bow*," Smith answered. "Adorable little tyke."

"Indeed. She reminds me of my Cornelia when she was a little girl. Shirley Temple has the cutest dimples, don't you agree, General?" Haskell's smile turned mocking. "I even hear that's her nickname. Dimples."

CHAPTER FORTY-NINE

MacArthur's face went taut, color draining from his skin. A nervous twitch jerked his eyebrow as he withdrew a cigarette case and lit one up. Trembling fingers held the cigarette up to his lips as he drew in a deep drag. Tobacco seemed to calm him a little, but conjecture raced through Max's brain. What the hell was Haskell getting at? Somehow, he doubted it had anything to do with Shirley Temple. But that bit about "Dimples" turned this rock-hard soldier into brittle glass.

"A soldier has little time for pleasure," MacArthur said, taking another puff. "But you gentlemen make a fair point. My personal beliefs are of little consequence. What matters is America. You shall have my support."

"Hear, hear," Norris said, slapping the table. Osborn allowed a triumphant smirk, but the Liberty Leaguers remained subdued, like businessmen discussing the latest earnings report.

"Excellent, General," Du Pont said, lighting up his pipe. "To be quite blunt, there were many here who wanted *you* to lead this superorganization."

"Me?" MacArthur asked, growing paler.

"Yes, but as Mr. Osborn said, General Norris resonates with the veterans. Besides, your official post as chief of staff is far more useful." Du Pont clapped his hands and said, "Gentlemen, we have much to discuss."

Hushed murmurs erupted, but MacArthur fell silent, staring at his smoldering cigarette with a sullen glare.

"First," Haskell spoke up, "is the matter of the Chaco War."

Smith blubbered out a laugh. "What's a war in South America gotta do with us?"

"Quite a lot, Governor," Haskell said. "Both my company and Standard Oil have invested heavily in Bolivia's victory there, which is in jeopardy. We'd like to see a return on investment."

"Standard Oil?" Smith snorted. "Why, Teagle isn't even involved in any of this—"

"No, but if Bolivia loses, then Standard won't receive any drilling right to the Gran Chaco. The company will take another financial blow which will ripple throughout the country. Mr. Murphy—" Haskell's gaze slid to the banker "—if my company falls and Standard suffers, then your brokerage firm and the House of Morgan will be stuck with a plethora of loans that cannot be repaid. We'll have another Wall Street crash, far worse than 1929!"

"Quite right," Murphy said, nodding. "That sordid affair should be brought to an end as quickly as possible."

"Once their army overthrows President Salamanca," Norris said, "Bolivia will be more friendly to direct American assistance."

"So long as we end Roosevelt's damnable 'Good Neighbor Policy,'" Sterling Clark hissed. "It's an affront to the Monroe Doctrine."

"I don't like sending American boys to die," Norris continued, "but the Chaco War does impact us. A brigade of Marines should settle that fuss in a month or so."

They've done more in less time, Max thought. Cuba, Haiti, and Nicaragua had all been invaded at one time or another by the United States Marine Corps. Unofficial wars fought on behalf of the United Fruit Company, Standard Oil, and Wall Street.

Clark laughed. "A whole month? Why, the Devil Dogs will march into Asunción within a week!"

Max didn't know what Asunción was, but guessed it was the capital of Paraguay. Norris smiled, then turned to MacArthur.

"Any objections, General?"

MacArthur's eyes lifted from the smoking cigarette. "I'm an Army officer, Norris. However the Navy decides to deploy their troops makes little difference to me. But won't the admirals object to this entire...*affair*?"

"You, General, will ensure they do not become involved," Norris said. "Any disturbance in Washington will strictly be an Army matter. Besides, the Navy will get its share of the pie too. It won't just be the Army that receives a budget increase. New battleships, submarines, and aircraft carriers will placate the admirals. As general affairs secretary, I'll render any arms limitation treaty America has signed null and void."

MacArthur nodded and returned to his cigarette.

"Excellent," Du Pont said. "The next order of business?"

"There is still the matter of Senator Nye," Haskell answered.

"A firing squad would sort him out," Norris said.

"Unfortunately, such measures would alert the public. More subtle methods should be used before we consolidate power," Osborn said, turning in Max's direction. "Maximillian Dietrich is a private investigator in our employ, one who knows all the dirty little secrets of the political elite."

All eyes shifted toward Max, except MacArthur's, transfixed by his wisping cigarette smoke.

"Uh, yes," Max said, stepping out of the corner. "I have entire files on the grafters, dipsos, and whoremongers who make up our esteemed Congress."

"If Senator Nye continues with his little crusade," Osborn said, head held high, "we'll sic Maxie here on them. If he doesn't want his dirty laundry aired, then he'll shut up. The same for any squawking politician. Americans might cry foul if we throw Congressmen in jail, but they'll lap up scandals like pigs at a trough."

"And what if Nye has no dirty laundry?" Du Pont asked, pipe clenched between his teeth.

"Everybody has something to hide," Osborn said. "Right, Maxie?"

Max nodded as the Liberty Leaguers sized him up, another weapon they'd purchased. Perhaps his bluff had worked a little too well. Now, the scandals and corruption he'd dug up would be used to legalize a dictatorship.

Osborn continued, "With a little persuading, Congress will grant General Affairs Secretary Norris near unlimited executive authority. Then, the truly great work of rebuilding America can begin. Again, we must look to Italy and its Corporate State. Imagine it gentlemen, each industry organized into their own organ, cooperating for the benefit of the United States."

A dour gloom spread across the Liberty Leaguers, hinting that they couldn't imagine it. After a few moments, Haskell came to the rescue.

"What Richard means, gentlemen, is that we will have a disciplined workforce and lush profits. Mussolini crushed the labor unions, and Norris will do the same here."

Du Pont and the others nodded, their fears placated. The chemical kingpin said, "But to save America, we must save the economy."

Murphy agreed. "And that means returning to the gold standard. Any responsible economist says the same. Remember Germany's inflation? Without hard currency, American society will collapse."

"Hear, hear," Norris bellowed. "That is what I said to Roosevelt before resigning. The bonuses must be paid out to our veterans, not with scraps of paper, but with gold!"

"Of course," Murphy said. "Our boys deserve real money, not glorified confetti."

"Damn right," Sterling Clark said. "I'll gladly spend half my inheritance just to make sure the other half isn't worthless."

"Returning to the gold standard is imperative," Haskell said, his withered frame inflamed with passion. "The sound American dollar will be used to rebuild our depleted Army and Navy. Rifles, artillery, and machine guns are still important, but chemicals will be what nations rise and fall on."

Across the table, Irénée Du Pont puffed away on his pipe with an amused smile.

"My company has been in talks with the factories of Du Pont," Haskell elaborated, "to create an arsenal of gases that will make America an unstoppable force. Gases that fill lungs with blood, blind instantly, degenerate brain tissue, and eat away at flesh. These gases will win the next war."

And net Haskell Munitions Incorporated one hell of a dividend. The Geneva Convention had outlawed poison gas in war, but what was a scrap of paper compared to progress and profits? Even now, the mention of gas sent a shiver down Max's spine. No veteran could ever forget the sheer terror that mustard gas evoked, creeping toward the trenches like some vaporous Grim Reaper harvesting souls.

MacArthur's voice rose in a sullen groan, "The next war?"

"A real war, gentlemen," Haskell said, almost glowing. "Not some sideshow in the Gran Chaco. This war will unite America, harden our people, and grease the wheels of industry, banishing this depression forever!"

Who was going to tell those Bolivians and Paraguayans they'd died in a sideshow? But the old vulture had a point. What was more profitable than war? Of course, Haskell and his ilk would make the weapons, but there would be uniforms to sew, food to manufacture, bonds to be bought.

"A group of rich men plotting a war?" Du Pont chuckled, puffing away on his pipe. "Why, it sounds like one of Senator Nye's dastardly fantasies."

Haskell frowned. "Nye fails to see that war is a necessary evil. And without a strong munitions industry, we will be easy prey for stronger, more virile nations. How else will America overcome this crippling depression? A war is our only chance to stave off ruin."

"Against who?" MacArthur asked, dragging on his cigarette.

Again, Osborn had the answer. "Germany is one candidate. We've already fought a war with the Hun. Russia is another, and we can galvanize every patriotic American in a crusade against Bolshevism. The Yellow Peril is also a potential enemy. Japan's saber rattling threatens the white man's status in Asia. But men like Senator Nye have instilled a cynicism about sending our troops 'over there.' No, the next war must be fought in our own backyard."

"Where?" MacArthur's eyes narrowed.

"Mexico is the ideal enemy. Their presidents are nothing but puppets of that political boss, Calles, who's tantamount to a Bolshevik. They even joke about a 'Soviet Mexico.' Christians are persecuted by their atheistic government."

"Osborn speaks the truth," Norris said. "I'm sure General MacArthur remembers how we were almost drawn into their so-called Cristero War."

Stubbing out the cigarette, MacArthur said, "Only by the skin of our teeth did Hoover spare us involvement."

Osborn clicked his heels again. "Well, General, a new wave of persecutions might break out, angering America's Christian populace. Violence might overflow across the Rio Grande, and our national honor may be besmirched. Then, we will have no choice but to fight and America will be reborn in blood and fire."

Renewed vigor spread across MacArthur's drawn face, a glimmer of hope for the future. After all, he'd be the one to lead this new war. Max glanced around the room. The Liberty Leaguers smiled like American Caesars ready to cross the Rubicon. This hydra had many heads. Al Smith represented politics, who'd no doubt run the Democrats like a party boss. Du Pont and Haskell embodied the arms industry, Merchants of Death ready for another feast. Murphy and Wall Street would be rejuvenated after the 1929 crash. And Sterling Clark? As he said, he was the idle rich, content their inheritance would soon be returned to the gold standard. Nathaniel Norris, a man used to barking orders, would soon command the entire nation.

But what about Richard Osborn? Despite amounting to little more than hired muscle, he blazed with a fiery zeal that put George Washington – his portrait gazing down like some forgotten deity – to shame. However, Norris would become dictator, not him. Sure, his lover would be the most powerful man in America, but that wasn't grand enough for a man so enraptured by Benito Mussolini. What was his angle in all this? Max didn't know, and if he had to bet, neither did the Liberty League.

CHAPTER FIFTY

General MacArthur left as secretly as he came, and Du Pont led the others back into the main reception hall. Ice tinkling inside cocktail glasses mingled with the drone of conversation, accompanied by the notes of Chopin. The chemical kingpin soon left, followed by Raskob and Murphy, their business here concluded. Osborn, Norris, Clark, and Haskell congregated in a corner, sipping champagne, a toast to their imminent victory. Max though, stuffed himself with hors d'oeuvres and miniature cream puffs, washed down with coffee.

"How'd you like the show, Maxie?" Osborn asked.

"I have more questions than answers now."

"Oh?"

"Why is General MacArthur so afraid of Shirley Temple?"

Osborn and the others shared a laugh. "Well, Maxie, don't take this the wrong way, but a few months ago, we hired a shamus."

"I feel betrayed. Another New York snooper?" Max said, slurping his coffee. Was this the same private detective who tracked Norris and Osborn down to their love nest?

"No, Mr. Dietrich, this detective works down in Washington," Haskell said, swirling his cocktail glass. "We hired him to look into MacArthur's…affairs. Turns out the General has a mistress from the Philippines, half his age."

"Whose nickname is 'Dimples,'" Osborn snickered.

"Disgusting," Norris sneered. "Race-mixing is a sin against his nation and God. At least he's not some sodomite."

They laughed again, downing their champagne. General MacArthur was already despised by half of the country, but revealing his young mistress, especially one who had a different skin color, would throw the other half into a tizzy.

"But don't fret, Mr. Dietrich," Haskell said. "We'll have plenty of work for you."

"You mean, Nye?"

"Yes, *him*. I want you to look under every rock to find something. A secret that will make him my personal slave until the day he dies." Haskell's bony hand tightened around his cane, anticipating his vengeance.

Across the room, Al Smith's thick voice rang out like a gong, silencing the pianist.

"All right, gents, I gotta real treat for you all! Not for nothing, but I'm an old-school Tammany Hall Democrat, nothing like these New Deal technocrats! The dailies called us Tammany Tigers, but it's a badge of honor, I tell ya! Speaking of which, another gen-yoo-ine Tammany Hall Tiger just arrived to make a speech."

The front doors flung open and two attendants wheeled in an iron cage that imprisoned a snarling tiger, bigger than anything at the Bronx Zoo. Pacing back and forth, the beast flicked its green eyes side to side while its whiskers twitched up and down. Loud gasps gave way to amused chuckling.

"Now, this here Tammany Tiger wants to join the Liberty League. Let's find out if he's a true Democrat or some New Deal jackass." Smith waddled over to the cage, a broad grin stretching over his ruddy cheeks. "Tell me, son, what's your opinion of Franklin Delano Roosevelt?"

The tiger let out a throaty roar, bouncing off the walls.

"Speak up, my boy! What was that about Roosevelt?"

At the sound of the name, the animal bellowed again, its fangs stretching wide, ready for the kill. The crowd laughed and Smith lapped it up. Only a vindictive SOB would train a tiger to roar at the mention of Roosevelt.

More laughter, good-natured this time. Despite their politics of reaction and fear, the vast majority of these Liberty Leaguers appeared to be in the dark about the plot being cooked up right under their noses. Even this crowd of old money and powerbrokers had its share of rubes and boobs.

The pianist struck up an upbeat ditty – "The Sidewalks of New York." A fitting tune, since it had been Al Smith's official campaign song, but it reminded Max of long summer days growing up in the Lower East Side, Manhattan's 12th District—of course! He'd almost forgotten. Max checked his wristwatch – half past four. He'd need to huff it to keep his appointment with Congressman Dickstein.

Turning to Osborn, he said, "My apologies, Richard, but I have a few business matters to attend to."

Osborn nodded, but Haskell replied with a grimace.

"Your business is here, Mr. Dietrich."

Polishing off his coffee, Max conjured up a suitable lie. "A prospective client wants to meet. I'll have to decline since I'll be…rather busy this Monday. It's just good business."

The story placated Haskell, who slumped a little on his cane.

"Understood, Maxie. But we'll drop by bright and early tomorrow."

"Tomorrow?"

"To deliver your uniform. You're a National Crusader now, so you'll need to dress the part."

Well, he might as well act the part too. Clicking his heels, Max raised his arm in a salute like a good Fascist. Norris and Osborn returned the gesture, while Clark and Haskell stared ahead at Smith, leading these stuffy Liberty Leaguers in song.

*****

Raindrops struck Max's umbrella like bombs, but it kept him dry enough as he entered Dickstein's building on the Upper East Side. It was a little after five, but he took his time, leaving behind little puddles as he traipsed up the stairs to the third floor. Inside, Suite 311 appeared empty, Roosevelt's portrait the only face gazing back at him.

"Anyone here?"

The interior office door opened, and a figure emerged wearing a suspicious scowl. Samuel Dickstein was a small man but accompanied by a large presence. His three-piece blue suit, gleaming Rolex watch, twinkling diamond tiepin, and polished wingtips were impressive, though trophies of graft. Thinning gray hair sat above an angry, pinched face.

"Hello, Congressman," Max said, tucking the umbrella beneath his arm. "Sorry, I'm late."

"Good evening, Mr. Osborn," Dickstein said. "My secretary told me you made an appointment. Well, I sent her home early so a lady won't hear the things I'm about to say. It's beyond me why the leader of the National Crusaders wants to speak with a Jew—" The Congressman stopped, squeezing his eyes into a perplexed stare. "Wait a minute…you're not Richard Osborn."

"What gave it away? The chin?"

"I've compiled a file on Osborn. Who are you really?"

Max sucked in a deep breath and held it. Time for the truth. Dickstein was his only shot now, and there was no room for lies.

With a weary sigh, he answered, "You might not know me, but my name is Max Dietrich. A private detective."

Confusion warped Dickstein's tight features before sudden recognition inflamed them into a hateful snarl. The Congressman strode closer, snorted from the back of his throat, and spat straight into Max's face.

CHAPTER FIFTY-ONE

Saliva oozed down Max's nose and dripped to the floor in little plops. Anger bubbled inside him, demanding retaliation. His hand gripped the umbrella, still moist from rain, and he considered smacking it right across this grafting weasel's arrogant kisser. But there wasn't time for that. Instead, Max wiped the spit on his coat sleeve, and offered a disarming grin as a peace offering.

"Guess you *do* know who I am."

"Yeah, I know all about you," Dickstein hissed. "My campaign discovered that you were digging into my past. Never thought the GOP would stoop to hiring some two-bit dick."

Two-bit? Max bit his tongue, but the words poured out. "You're the one who swindled bribes out of poor huddled masses, yearning to breathe free. Even for a Tammany Tiger, you're crooked. But relax, that's not why I'm here."

Dickstein's face screwed into an even angrier scowl. "Get out, damn you! I will not stand here and—"

"Then sit," Max ordered, pushing the little man back into the secretary's empty seat. Dickstein's wingtips whooshed upward as he plopped down. Despite his humiliation, the Congressman kept his mouth shut, responding only with a truculent glare.

"Listen, we have a common enemy."

Dickstein shuffled in the chair and smoothed his tie before asking, "Who?"

"Richard Osborn and the National Crusaders."

The tight face relaxed a little. "That playboy? He's just in it for the dough. Besides, the Khaki Shirts are nothing but a glorified strikebreaking outfit."

"Look a little deeper and you'll see that strikebreaking was just basic training for them. The National Crusaders are planning a March on Washington to seize power."

Dickstein sneered. "Ridiculous. There are only ten thousand Khaki Shirts in the entire country."

"That may be, but they have some powerful backers now."

"Yes, yes, I know Elias Haskell funds them."

"Not just Haskell, but a lot of other Liberty Leaguers."

"The Liberty League?"

"Just a few members. Irénée Du Pont, John Raskob, Grayson Murphy, Sterling Clark, and Al Smith."

Dickstein leaned back, smirking. "Anyone else you want to throw in there? Maybe Mayor La Guardia? Hell, I'm surprised I'm not on this little list."

"They've also enlisted General MacArthur. He's the one who'll let them into the henhouse."

Another laugh, harsher than before. "You're accusing some of the most powerful men in America of plotting a coup d'état?"

Max gave a shrug. "It happens in Europe and Japan often enough. Why not here?"

The sneering skepticism returned. "Any proof of this?"

"I just heard them discussing it at the Union Club. Lovely reception. The cream puffs were delightful."

"You expect me to believe you? The same snooper who tried to blackmail me?"

There was a deep-seated contempt in Dickstein's gaze, ready to shoot bullets. This was the look of a man who'd almost had his fun spoiled by exposure. Max had seen that same look painted on respectable dry politicians he'd caught at speakeasies before they coughed up bribes.

"Don't take my word for it. You have a committee to investigate this stuff, don't you? Or is that another one of your grafts?"

The Congressman bolted up, blood-red. "How dare you—"

"Shut up," Max barked, pushing him back down. "We don't have much time. The March on Washington is scheduled for November 11th."

"Armistice Day?"

"Poetic, isn't it? Look, you have contacts, Dickstein. Ring up Roosevelt and—"

"This entire plot sounds like something straight out of the funnies."

Max sighed. "Don't you remember what happened in Italy?"

"Even if you are telling the truth, the National Crusaders aren't even the most dangerous Fascist party in America."

Tell that to Yago Garcia, Max thought. "What makes you say that?"

"Compared to other colored-shirt lunatics, like the Silver Legion, their Jew-baiting is mild. Like I said, the Khaki Shirts are nothing more than Elias Haskell's private militia to rough up strikers."

"Well, you haven't met their newest member."

"Who?"

"Major-General Nathaniel Norris."

"Him?" Alarm cracked Dickstein's smug face. "That Jew-baiter had the gall to pass out copies of *The Protocols of the Elders of Zion* to West Point graduates. Disgraceful!"

"Surprised he wasn't kicked out for that."

"There are lots of anti-Semites in high places, Dietrich. But I'm more concerned with the enemy abroad."

"The enemy abroad?"

"Adolf Hitler." Dickstein's face tightened again into a snarl, a dog ready to bite. "He's already set up a Nazi group in New York, the Friends of the New Germany. They're a bigger threat than anything America's lunatic fringe has produced."

That Walt Disney picture – *The Three Little Pigs* – along with its irritating jingle, popped into Max's head. Except in this cartoon, Congressman Piggy claimed that only the Big

Bad Wolf *outside* was dangerous. The wolf sitting inside his own house of straw, he insisted, was a vegetarian.

"Look, it's America's homegrown Apple Pie Fascists who are preparing a putsch. If we act now, then we can—"

"Dietrich…" The Congressman pursed his mouth in thought. "That's a German name, right?"

"Very astute, Dickstein. I didn't even wear my lederhosen today."

"Yes, I understand now." Dickstein slapped a palm against the desk. "The Friends of the New Germany must have hired you!"

"What?"

"A German-American like you must harbor sympathies for the Nazis."

Max plopped the umbrella on the desk, stooped over, and glowered down at the little Congressman.

"Me, a Nazi? Christ, I'd rather vote for *you*, Dickstein."

"I see what's happening! You're trying to divert my attention away from the Friends of the New Germany, send me on some wild goose chase. Hell, if I went knocking on the doors of Du Pont and the others, I'd make a complete ass out of myself!"

"More than usual?"

Dickstein bolted to his feet. "I should investigate you, see what Nazi skeletons you have rotting in your closet!"

"Call me a Nazi one more time…"

"You Nazi bastard, I'll—"

Grabbing the umbrella, Max thrust the metal tip into Dickstein's soft gut, sending the little Congressman flailing backward. He hit the wall with a heavy grunt, sending the Roosevelt portrait crashing to the floor. Rubbing his head, Dickstein heaved himself up, eyes blazing with a seething hatred.

"Get out, now. Or your license won't be worth more than a Cracker Jack badge!"

There was no point in continuing. Max turned and stormed out. This son of a bitch had made up his mind, and someone as disreputable as Max Dietrich wasn't going to change it. Over the years, he'd become accustomed to lying down in the dirt, but now its stench was almost unbearable.

CHAPTER FIFTY-TWO

Max returned to his office, drenched and defeated. Even this fancy umbrella couldn't withstand a sudden torrent of rain, turning his suit into a sodden heap. His mind blank, he tromped upstairs with squishing footsteps. Opening the door, he noticed a lamp blazing in his inner office. Dropping the umbrella, his hand flew to the revolver, but through the door's pane glass, a feminine silhouette was visible – Cornelia Osborn.

He entered and found the Haskell heiress puffing away on a cigarette, a tremulous look marring her pretty face. Her tweed coat, decorated with buttons as big as doorknobs, was freckled with rain drops. Brown leather gloves held a cigarette to her full lips, while a jaunty felt hat covered waved brown hair. Compared to her crispness, Max felt like something that crawled out of the Hudson River.

"What are you doing here?" he asked, stripping off his wet overcoat.

"Waiting around the penthouse was killing me. I had to get out, so I came to see you."

Max cranked the electric heater up, savoring its warmth. "Won't Richard and Daddy Warbucks get suspicious?"

"No, the three of them went out to Long Island," Cornelia said, in between drags.

"Last minute preparations probably, since the March on Washington is set for November 11th." He unbuttoned his shirt, halted, asked, "Mind if I change?"

"Go ahead. What did Dickstein say?"

"Before or after he spat in my face?"

Tossing the sopping jacket into the closet, Max peeled off his shirt, then threw on a long, belted brown robe. Not suitable attire in the presence of a lady, but these weren't suitable times. Only then did he look back at Cornelia, puffing away with a forlorn look. Outside, rain pelted against the window with an irritating 'tap-tap-tap,' like Chinese water torture.

"So…he won't help us?" she asked, a quaver distorting her voice.

"Lady, I'll be lucky to keep my license."

She took another deep drag, sending cigarette smoke wafting throughout the office. But even through the bluish veil, he could see her eyes were rimmed with tears. Few things bothered Max Dietrich more than a weeping woman.

"I have a pal in the Police Department," Max offered, plopping down behind his desk. "But it's a longshot."

She took another drag, banishing her tears and hardening her soft features.

"Do you think they'll succeed?"

"I'd give it a fifty-fifty shot. But it doesn't matter what I think," Max said, shrugging. "The important thing is that *they* think it will. It worked in Italy, why not here?"

Through the smoke, her eyes narrowed. "America wouldn't allow it. We're too independent to accept a Fascist dictatorship."

Max let out a laugh. "Lady, Americans consider themselves free-minded individualists, but in reality, we're nothing but a country of joiners. As long as our Yankee Doodle Fascists wear bald eagles on their uniforms instead of fasces or swastikas, well then, your average Yank will march right along, still thinking he's a 'free man.' Remember how easy it was to whip us into a war frenzy? Just give us a uniform to wear and an enemy to kill, and off we go."

"You sound like a Red yourself…"

"Even broken clocks are right twice a day…"

"Not all Americans are as cynical as you," Cornelia spat back through clouds of smoke. "The democratic tradition is too strong here."

"Maybe, but they'll wind up like my father. Bleeding in the gutter with a cracked skull. His crime was speaking English with a Bavarian accent. If radio and newspapers give the go ahead, this country will turn Fascist overnight, providing it's not called Fascism, but Americanism. And your husband has taken care of that detail."

Max shook his head but couldn't dismiss an admiration for Richard Osborn. A true leader of men, that man was. He'd seen it in 1918, and now, in 1934, the whole country would too. And what would Max Dietrich's role be in this new America? Secret policeman for the new regime? Ridiculous. Even he had some scruples. It still wasn't too late to make tracks for Canada.

Cornelia took a final drag, held it for a moment, then released a smoke ring, drifting to the ceiling. Max pulled out a guest ashtray from his desk and slid it toward her. She mashed the cigarette out, then fixed him with an icy glare.

"You have to kill them. My husband and Norris."

Max searched her face for any hint of humor, but found only a chilling sincerity.

"Lady, you're looking for a torpedo, not a PI."

Her gray eyes widened, misting again. Christ, she really could turn it on and off. "Don't do it for me, do it for your country."

"Mickey Mouse means more to me than Uncle Sam does, sweetheart."

"Isn't there anything you believe in?"

"The almighty dollar." Max grinned. "How much are you willing to pay?"

Her face flushed. "Well, I…I don't have any money right now."

"Just ask for an advance on your allowance."

"Allowance? Oh yes, well, you see, money is tight right now—"

Max held up a hand. "Relax, I was just joking. Listen, I've been paid for some dirty jobs, but murder takes the cake. But why don't you do it?"

"M-me?"

"Play the jealous wife angle. The courts will go easy on you. It's more common than you'd think."

"And my father would have me committed to an insane asylum. Maybe I can share a cell with Francis?"

That shattered face invaded his mind again, scraping about on all fours like a mutilated dog. How many more would end up like that if Osborn and Norris got their war? Husks of men more grotesque than any freak show. Senator Nye and rags like *New Masses* claimed that diabolical Merchants of Death tricked people in war, but they only reaped the profits. The truth was that humanity was a wild beast, and with the slightest provocation, it'd gorge itself on blood.

"Richard loves you, you know," Cornelia said. "Not in that way, but like a little brother. He wants to mold you into a junior version of himself."

"Saving a man's life does that, I suppose."

She leaned forward, her gloved hands flat against the desk. "Exactly! I'm not his wife, just a beautiful decoration, like a Ming vase. But he trusts you enough to let his guard down."

"So, I can plug him in the back? Lady, I'm not a hired gun."

Backing away, Cornelia fixed him with a skeptical glower. "I can tell a killer when I see one."

He figured she wasn't referring to the war. Perhaps he didn't hide his past as well as he thought. Max turned the chair and stared out the window. Streaks of rain reduced the Paramount Theatre's neon lights to a glittering smear, reminding him of the glowing nickelodeons Papa Dietrich had taken him to as a child. He never forgot the anger he'd felt upon learning his father's fate, nor the despair that filled him when the perpetrator – an angry drunk with a grudge against Germans – was let off with a reduced sentence. After all, his "patriotism" made the crime more forgivable.

But Max didn't forgive. His father passed soon after, but it drove his mother to an early grave, though the Spanish flu helped too. His sister wept and wept until finding religion through one of those "tent revivals" upstate. Max was left all alone with his anger. One of his first cases was for himself, tracking down the "patriotic" thug to a speakeasy in the Bowery. Calling in a few favors from the underworld, a gunman took care of him with a bullet to his skull. Papa Dietrich had been avenged, but a deep resentment toward America rooted itself inside Max, blooming ever since.

None of his old Mob contacts would touch someone like Richard Osborn or Nathaniel Norris. But an ideologue might.

"There is one candidate," he said, facing her again. "Mike Rafferty."

She shot back a smirk, then, "He won't get within ten feet of Richard before the Khaki Shirts gun him down."

A good point. But maybe Max could lead Osborn and Norris into an ambush. Or perhaps force needed to be met with force, one paramilitary against another. He remembered the drubbing Partridge and her comrades received in Union Square.

"The Communists might be willing," Max offered. "I'll contact them tomorrow. But right now, I need some sleep. Your husband is coming by bright and early tomorrow."

"Why?"

"To fit me for a khaki shirt of my own."

She smiled. "See? He's already turning you into his protégé." Cornelia withdrew to the door, then said, "Good night, Max. America is counting on you." She left, her clacking heels merging with the pattering rain. Max heaved himself over to the couch and spread out, letting sleep overwhelm him, the words replaying in his mind – '*America is counting on you.*'

America must be desperate.

CHAPTER FIFTY-THREE

Max scraped the last bit of Burma-Shave off his face and yawned. Gazing into the mirror, his eyes looked like blue marbles crammed into dark, puffy bags of skin. He'd slept like hell the past few nights, but he'd need to be wide awake today. An electric percolator on his desk bubbled and popped, belching out spurts of coffee. Snug in his robe, Max poured a cup and choked it down. It didn't hold a candle to Horn & Hardart, but at least this muck was caffeinated.

Max peered out the window and into the misty dawn. New York lurched itself awake as traces of morning sun stabbed through a gray sky. No rain though. Days like these needed a downpour, a true reflection of the times.

A sudden knock sounded at the outer door's glass pane, and Max called them in. Osborn, followed by Norris and another Khaki Shirt – carrying two suitcases in each arm – entered with rigid poise. Crisp in their uniforms and polished boots, these boys looked ready to lead a parade down Broadway, straight into the White House.

"Morning, gentlemen. Want some joe?"

Osborn scowled at the percolator. "Artificial stimulation, Maxie. A National Crusader is invigorated by life itself."

Max took a final swig, set the mug aside, and gestured to the suitcases. "Are those for me?"

"Crusader First Class Williams is our regional quartermaster," Osborn said, summoning the Khaki Shirt closer. "He'll outfit you."

"The Chief told me you were tall – six foot, I believe," Williams said, unlocking a suitcase on the floor. He pulled out three different tunics and held them against Max's spindly frame. The Khaki Shirt selected one tunic, set it aside, and measured Max's legs and feet. Rifling through the first suitcase, he withdrew the other items and handed them over.

"Give me a minute, boys," Max said, walking to the bathroom. Inside, he stuffed himself into the getup, almost smashing his feet into the tight boots. He clicked the Sam Browne cross belt into place, donned the side cap over his blond widow's peak, then straightened up for a closer inspection. Gazing into the mirror banished his cynicism, inflaming something he hadn't felt since 1917 – pride. The uniform, with its blue Crusader eagle armband, and twinkling squad leader insignia, was more intoxicating than any drug.

But the chatter of machine guns, the scream of heavy artillery, and the noxious smell of mustard gas ignited again in his memory, freeing him of such thoughts. A deep cynicism had hardened Max Dietrich into an aloof snob, but most Americans weren't hindered by it. For thousands, a uniform and a purpose were all they needed from life. He stepped out of the bathroom and greeted the three Khaki Shirts with a straight-armed Fascist salute. Heels clicked and the salute was returned, before Osborn offered a genuine smile.

"That uniform fits you, Maxie. I decided that a man with your leadership experience should be commissioned a squad leader."

"Chief Osborn told me about your gallantry during the war. Thank you, for that," Norris said, a sentimental gleam in his eyes. After all, Max had saved the love of his life. "I certainly don't approve of your past sins, but the Bible tells us that all men can find redemption."

Such religious sentimentality made Max squirm. However, if Cornelia Osborn could put on a Fascist facade, so could he. But another straight-armed salute was all he could muster.

Osborn checked his wristwatch. "Time to go."

"Go? Where?"

"A Hooverville down in the Village. A sort of last-minute recruiting drive before—" Osborn paused, glanced over to

Williams, packing up the suitcase "—Crusader Williams, please excuse us."

Williams saluted, then tromped out, lugging the suitcases behind him. So, even the rank-and-file Khaki Shirts were in the dark about the putsch.

"Don't we have enough men?" Max asked. "I thought the bulk would come from CCC camps."

"Hoovervilles too, but this is merely a warmup exercise," Norris said. "I'm a bit rusty, and need some practice before speechifying to larger crowds."

Max nodded, but a question still plagued him. "I've been meaning to ask, Richard. What will your role be in the new government?"

A bright smile flashed as Osborn held his head high. "In Italy, Mussolini reorganized the Black Shirts as the Fascist Militia. I envision a similar role like that for my Khaki Shirts...until the war begins."

"And...then?"

"The United States Army is a shell of its former self. Truncated by budget cuts, sapped of spirit by incompetent leadership. The National Crusaders are young, vigorous, and bursting with patriotic energy. When war comes, General Affairs Secretary Norris will place the Army under the National Crusader umbrella, merging the two into a new American force."

Max let out a whistle. So that was Osborn's angle – a new American Army under his sole command. Not bad for a former captain.

"But what about...General MacArthur?"

The name clenched Osborn's face into a stony mask. "He will answer for his crimes against the Bonus Marchers. And be punished accordingly."

Which meant a noose or a firing squad. Max suddenly felt like a driver whose brakes had failed. The plot was rushing forward, with or without him. He moved around the desk and unplugged the percolator, his mind reaching out for some plan.

Max's eyes gravitated toward the soggy overcoat, hanging in the closet like clumps of rags. The snubnosed revolver was nestled inside, and it would be all too easy to saunter over, scoop it up, and pump Osborn and Norris full of bullets. But without the pretense of self-defense, he couldn't go through with coldblooded murder, much less avoid a trip to the electric chair.

Just like with Papa Dietrich, a surrogate would make murder more palatable and provide plausible deniability. Mike Rafferty was only one man, and as Cornelia Osborn said, couldn't get near the Khaki Shirt Chief. The only match for Osborn's bully boys was Comrade Partridge and her bruisers. But how to contact them without arousing too much suspicion? He'd have to think of that later.

For now, he followed Chief Osborn and Troop Leader Norris out of the office, the first steps in the March on Washington.

CHAPTER FIFTY-FOUR

Max surveyed the last remaining Hooverville in New York City, crawling with over a hundred men – destitute, dirty, and forgotten. Spanning two blocks on West Houston Street and nestled behind a row of buildings, it was a far cry from the sprawling slum that had sprung up in Central Park. Somehow this one had survived the crackdowns, an open sore on a canvas of scarred skin.

Men with unshaven faces and threadbare clothes milled around ramshackle huts slapped together from scrap metal and wood. A few bundled up against the November chill, wrapping themselves in spare newspapers. A bloated garbage can stood at the Hooverville's center, squirming with vermin. But even in this squalor, there was some dignity in the form of coffee pots, campfires, and even a small library.

These weren't bums and tramps, but the bastard children of bank runs, factory layoffs, and home foreclosures. As in most Hoovervilles, there were no women or children to witness this sad state of American manhood. Here was living proof that despite all of Roosevelt's trite slogans, the country's best days were behind it.

The only glimmer of hope was a makeshift soup kitchen, run by a small squad of Khaki Shirts. The Forgotten Men lined up for a steaming bowl, crust of bread, and cigarettes. Kilmer and his squad formed a perimeter as Norris strode to the center of the Hooverville. Osborn and Max stood beside the makeshift soup kitchen, arms stretched out in Fascist salutes.

The Forgotten Men eyed Norris with suspicious glares. After all, the General might look respectable in that crisp tunic and side cap, but these men had been betrayed before. Ashen features suggested a bitterness that wouldn't be placated with mere words.

"You may not know me," Norris announced, hands set on his Sam Browne belt, a commander's pose. "But I know you. The soldiers who fought with me in France. The workers who built this country into a land of prosperity. The Forgotten Men of America."

That set a few heads nodding, but the others just stared in grim silence, slurping their soup.

"You've been forgotten by the country you bled for, the women you protected, and the politicians who you believed in."

A Forgotten Man shambled forth and spluttered out, "Hey, you're General Norris! I saw you in Washington!"

Norris shifted his frame and asked, "You were with the BEF?"

"Yeah, the speech you gave—" the man's voice throbbed "—meant a lot."

Norris clapped him on the shoulder with a paternal smile. "Who else here marched for their bonus?"

Well over half the crowd's hands flew up.

"And who here served in the Army?"

Almost all the hands rose now, but even those who hadn't served looked like they'd survived a war. A few jeers erupted toward the back.

"Take a hike, ya two-bit Nazi! Roosevelt took away your stars, didn't he?"

With a flash of anger, Norris turned to the heckler but kept a steady poise. "I resigned my commission of my own volition. I could not continue to serve a president who had no intention of giving you men the bonuses you were rightfully owed. My career doesn't matter when honor is at stake. Like I said to the BEF on that hot July day, 'If a government cannot care for its veterans, then it loses the right to govern!'"

That kindled the Hooverville, but a blaze hadn't yet ignited. Still, such sentiment from an active duty general had been so inflammatory, it was a wonder President Hoover hadn't dismissed Norris then and there. But so far, there hadn't been any mention of Jews. Norris must be biting his tongue.

"Roosevelt is no better than Hoover. Instead of a bonus with cold, hard cash, he creates his alphabet soup agencies that do nothing but suck the taxpayers dry. What has the New Deal done for any of you? It's a confidence trick, cooked up by the money changers at the top. And as Christ Almighty said—" Norris spread his shoulders wide, chest ballooning, "—'*My temple shall be called a house of prayer. But you have turned it into a den of thieves*!'"

A smattering of applause rippled through the Hooverville, their bitterness aroused.

"And who are these money changers? The thieves who ruined the country and reduced you to this miserable state?"

"Yeah? Who?" the crowd called out, practically snarling.

Norris's eyes gleamed, a predator closing in for the kill.

"The capitalists on Wall Street! The politicians in Congress! Republicans and Democrats are the same grafters under different aliases. And alien foreigners, swarming into our nation like contaminants infecting the bloodstream! Why pay a red-blooded American man to work, when the bosses can throw a few pennies at low-skilled coolies?"

Jews were left out, but the euphemism got the point across. Rubes and boobs blamed everything but themselves, but these men had a right to be angry. They'd worked hard, played by the rules, and look at them now – Uncle Sam's dregs.

"What this country needs now is action, not talk! The National Crusaders, under Chief Richard Osborn, stand for 100% Americanism. We need soldiers for a new war. A war against graft. A war against decadence. A war against this depression!" Norris strutted back and forth through the crowd, the spurs on his jackboots clinking with every footstep. "The Khaki Shirts offer you a shave, a uniform, and self-respect. How many of you will join us when we march straight down to Washington and make our voices heard?"

Some nodded, throwing their hands in Fascist salutes, but the majority responded with lukewarm stares. Murmurs spread through the Hooverville, soft mutterings of debate. After all, they'd been taken in by pretty words before.

"And what? Get tear gassed?" someone cried. "I ain't going through that again!"

Norris planted his feet firmly, thrust his chin up, and said, "This will not be a repeat of the Bonus March. 1934 will mark the dawning of a new America! I led many of you men to victory once. So, help me God, I shall do so again!"

The promise swayed a few more, but others continued hushed debates. The dynamite was planted, but the fuse still needed a spark.

Down the street, a throng marched toward them, enveloped in a reddish glow. Red flags whipped in the misty air, red armbands were fastened to several marchers, and red placards – showcasing Vladimir Lenin, Joseph Stalin, and Earl Browder – were held high. Max gawked at the oncoming Communist horde, counting as many as he could. There were well over a hundred Reds, and at the snake's head was Susan Partridge, coming for her revenge.

CHAPTER FIFTY-FIVE

The Reds spread out, taking positions around the Hooverville. The dull sunlight, revealed a hodgepodge of weapons – brass knuckles, pocketknives, baseball bats, blackjacks, and the occasional gleaming pistol. Squad Leader Kilmer and his men retreated to the inner part of the Hooverville for a final stand. Max found himself next to Osborn and Norris, their backs to the bloated trash can.

Max did some quick math – twenty-five Khaki Shirts against a hundred Reds – four to one odds. More than enough muscle to pay the Khaki Shirts back for humiliation at Union Square. Although quite a few were women and bespectacled dilettantes, the men surrounding Susan Partridge were bruisers with meaty fists. Common street thugs she'd sweet talked into joining the Revolution.

A hopeless battle, yes, but an opportunity presented itself. After all, what better way to rid the world of Osborn and Norris than having their hated enemies do them in? The Bolshies showed up on their own accord, and Max didn't even have to waste five cents on a phone call.

"Fellow workers," Partridge began, adjusting her glasses like a schoolteacher before students. "Do not believe these Fascist lies. The National Crusaders are funded by the Merchants of Death, greedy war profiteers. They want to send you to fight and die in a 'crusade' against Russia! They fear the triumph of socialism and a new imperialist war is the only way capitalism can lift itself out of this depression! Comrades, the only justified war is class war!"

Rumblings percolated throughout the Forgotten Men, pulled between the Left and the Right. Well, this Bolshie shrew was right about a new war, but it'd be much closer to home. Osborn stepped forward and sank an angry glower into Partridge. Was it because she was a Communist or a woman?

"Funny words coming from a Moscow stooge. But whether they're Bolsheviks from Russia or Bolsheviks from New York, the National Crusaders will protect America from this Red scum!"

Sneering laughter poured from the crowd, before Partridge quieted them.

"Fellow workers, you are being misled by this Fascist playboy. He and his Khaki Shirts are nothing but wind-up toys for big business and—" she stopped, eyes screwing into slits behind her glasses. Her stare was so sharp, Max almost felt impaled. Then a flash of recognition. "Dietrich! I always knew you were a Fascist at heart!"

Attention shifted onto Max, the Forgotten Men eyeing him with curiosity. Even Norris gave him a suspicious glare. If Partridge started squawking, the Khaki Shirts would learn all about his past dealing with the Communist Party. Even worse, wearing this uniform was a bullseye for these bloodthirsty Bolsheviks.

The mass of Communists began chanting "Death to Fascism! Death to Fascism!" their chorus crashing out like war gongs. Max brushed against the bulging trash can, the perfect way to stop Partridge from spilling too many secrets. Summoning all his strength, Max hoisted it up and flung it straight toward the screaming horde.

A storm of garbage rained down, pelting the bruisers with filth, but showering Partridge completely. Muck and grime clung to her clothes, ran down her mussed hair, and poured from her mouth. The chanting stopped, replaced by angry cries and humiliated gasps.

No more chants, no more speeches, just a roar for blood. The Communists surged forth, smashing against the khaki wall. Max and the others held firm, but blows from brass knuckles and blackjacks slammed into their ribs, cut their cheeks, and cracked against bone. Max threw punches wherever he could, connecting with one bruisers' nose with a sickening crunch.

One of the dilettantes – a scarecrow with bookish features – slid out a pistol, fumbling to aim. It was only a matter of time before the heavy artillery was brought out. But Norris stuck his head up and boomed, "There are no more bystanders! The choice is clear! Do you stand with us and Americanism, or with godless Bolshevism?"

The words electrified the Forgotten Men who joined the fight, their hemming and hawing discarded. And why not? In their khaki tunics, the National Crusaders looked like US Army Doughboys, the same men they'd been in 1917. Foreign creatures like Lenin and Stalin were no match for the Crusader bald eagle. Somehow, Max doubted that swastikas would have the same effect on these men.

Even against an armed enemy, these Forgotten Men fought like wildcats, eager to unleash the anger that had simmered for years, beating back the Communists with everything they had. The pistol-wielding dilettante was knocked to the ground and pummeled, turning his bookish face into a bloody smear. Bleating whistles signaled the advance of police officers – only five in total – but their mere sight split this Red sea. Half broke and ran, while the others collected the wounded and shambled away, another inglorious retreat for American Communism.

Her boots slipping on slimy garbage, Susan Partridge limped after them, humiliated, defeated, and utterly pathetic. The cops didn't give chase, but surveyed what remained of the Hooverville, now littered with puddles of blood, broken teeth, and a few discarded weapons.

"What happened here?" the lead copper, a grizzled sergeant, demanded.

"What happened?" Osborn thrust his shoulders back and addressed the crowd, "Why, we beat back the Red Terror, didn't we men?"

A cry of "Hurrah!" swelled from the Forgotten Men and Khaki Shirts, so contagious even Max joined in.

The Sergeant nodded. After all, there was an understanding between Khaki Shirts and cops in this town. The cops took a brief statement from Osborn, and requested his presence tomorrow afternoon, just to review certain details. How silly would they feel when Osborn and Norris marched on Washington instead? After the cops left, Norris assembled the crowd again.

"You see that the National Crusaders stand for action, not empty slogans. I ask you again. Will you march with us and take your country back?"

Another shout rang out, along with straight-armed salutes, men eager to be led. A few stayed behind, but the vast majority poured out of the Hooverville and into Crusader trucks that had arrived from Long Island. If this practice run was any indication, Nathaniel Norris would have an easy time convincing Americans to storm the White House.

Osborn drew up beside Max, concern etched into his chiseled face. "You're wounded."

Only then did the pain strike him, buzzing across his face. He tasted blood leaking from inside his cheek, and felt cuts crisscrossing his chin. At least nothing felt broken. But Osborn examined Max with such tenderness, as if caring for a bullied little brother.

"It's nothing," Max said, ignoring the sting. Up above, the gray skies growled like the roar of an angry dragon. "Bad timing."

"Didn't you read the papers, Maxie? The forecast is cloudy, but no more rain. We will march to Washington unhindered."

Norris drew a breath. "Ah, truly a sign from the Almighty himself!"

God and his damn jokes. Who else would sic Susan Partridge and her Reds against Richard Osborn, only to have them lose at the last minute? The only hope of stopping this putsch was the snubnosed revolver back in his office…or Mike Rafferty.

"I'll meet up with you after I patch myself up."

Osborn pursed his lips and nodded. "Be quick about it. Afterward, come back to the penthouse. Mr. Haskell wants a few words with us before we depart for the staging area."

"Staging area? Where's that?"

Osborn and Norris shared a laugh. "Always with the questions, Maxie."

"Well, I am a detective."

"You are also a National Crusader now," Osborn snapped. "And your first and foremost duty is to obey."

Max couldn't argue. Without thinking, he clicked his heels and pumped out a salute, as if puppeteered by an invisible force.

CHAPTER FIFTY-SIX

Mike Rafferty savored each bite of doughnut, one of life's only remaining pleasures. For the past few days, he and Eddie Gardner had survived off a diet of soup, doughnuts, and coffee, courtesy of the Bowery's Salvation Army kitchen. Religion might be the opiate of the masses, but it had *some* benefits.

Washing the last crumbs down with coffee, Rafferty noticed a lingering stare from across the communal table. The man's eyes, set deep above a ratty beard, bored straight into Rafferty's broken face with abject disgust. Most of these Bowery Bums learned to avert their gaze when Rafferty removed his scarf, but this dumb son of a bitch sat gawking as if he were watching *Frankenstein*.

Death was looking better each day. He would be a wanted man for the rest of his life – if not by the Police, by Richard Osborn and his Khaki Fascists, and Susan Partridge and her Red Fascists. G-Men had tracked down Dillinger, even after plastic surgery. What hope was there for Mike Rafferty?

Gardner – sitting next to him – choked down his doughnut. Even swallowing was a daily torture for poor Eddie. But there was still one last thing they could live for – revenge.

A shrill ring cut through the kitchen, and one of the Salvation Army officers – a shriveled little grandma – answered.

"Yes?" he heard her say. "Who? Well, this isn't a hotel, sir, but I'll ask anyway..." cupping the receiver, the woman called, "Rafferty? Is there a Michael Rafferty here?"

On instinct, Rafferty tucked his head, anything to avoid detection. But then again, it could be Dietrich with a lead. He rose and traipsed over to the phone. The Salvation Army officer didn't blanch and even offered a motherly smile as she handed the receiver over. A woman of her age had seen many *gueules cassées* over the years.

"Yeah?" Rafferty said, after she was out of earshot.

"Hello again, handsome."

"I'm impressed, Dietrich. How'd you find me?"

"Easy. Those duds you and Eddie were wearing at my office weren't from Brooks Brothers. I figured you got them free from a Salvation Army outpost. And criminals tend to stay in places they're familiar with, so that narrowed it down to the Bowery. And it's about suppertime, which meant there was a good chance of you dropping by for a free meal."

"A regular Sherlock Holmes, you are. But I'm not a criminal."

"Of course not. You're a revolutionary. A genuine American Trotsky."

"What do you want?"

"Isn't it obvious, my dear Watson? I want to help you fulfill the dream we discussed. If you want your shot at Osborn, then make tracks up to my office, pronto."

"This better not be a trick, Dietrich."

"If it is, feel free to shoot me."

The line went dead and a surge of energy pumped through Rafferty. Until this moment, his body had been a numb husk. Now, a fuse was lit, the explosives packed, and the target set. He slammed the receiver down and yanked his scarf from the coat rack. Gardner looked up, an eagerness shining on his gaunt face.

"It's time, Eddie."

Gardner grinned and stood, ready to follow his lieutenant back to war. Rafferty wound the scarf around his shattered face, but paused and glared back at the gawking Bowery Bum.

"Show's over, pal."

The disgusted gaze shifted down to the soup bowl and settled there.

*****

"You're outta your mind, Dietrich." Burks said between fits of laughter. "A coup?"

Max sighed into the receiver. After returning to his office, he doused his cuts and slashes with iodine then called Sergeant Burks. Police assistance was a longshot, he knew that. Haskell and his conspirators practically owned New York City, but he at least had to sound the alarm.

"Yes, Burksy, I heard it with my own ears from the mouths of the Liberty League."

"The Liberty League? You mean all them rich Republicans?"

"They accept all types of Roosevelt haters. Al Smith, for instance."

Barking laughter poured from the receiver. "You just want me to go arrest the former governor?"

"Not you, blockhead. But I'm sure the commissioner might be interested."

"You don't know this new guy, Valentine. He's one of La Guardia's cronies. He's been on a rampage lately, purging anything that smells of Tammany Hall. I'm on thin ice as it is."

Max sighed, unhooked the stiff collar on his National Crusader tunic. They were smart uniforms, but it was understandable why the Army ditched them. These damn collars would chaffe until your throat was raw.

"Look, Burksy, just a few words that would persuade Valentine to pay a visit to Elias Haskell. A beat cop might not matter much, but if the police commissioner showed up at Haskell's door, it might spook him just enough to call off the coup."

"I'd need evidence, Dietrich. Not just your words, which we both know ain't worth much to men like Commissioner Valentine."

Max couldn't argue with the latter half. "Look, his proof is marching and drilling out in Long Island. An entire Fascist training camp!"

Burks laughed again, derisively this time. "You've been reading too many pulps, Dietrich."

Max sighed. He knew it'd be a hard sell, but Burks was implacable. Not that he blamed him. If the shoe was on the other foot, Max would laugh off such a ridiculous story too. Only idiots fought doomed battles.

"Thanks anyway, Burksy," he said and hung up.

After what he'd done to Susan Partridge, and with his only lead in the Police Department a dead end, Mike Rafferty was his – and America's – last hope. The outer door creaked open and through the window pane, a pair of silhouettes moved closer. Gardner entered, followed by Rafferty, face bundled up with a scarf.

"How've you been, comrades?"

"Comrades?" Rafferty puffed into the scarf, muffling the anger in his voice. "Looks like you joined the enemy, Dietrich."

Max gave the uniform a once over. "These duds opened a lot of doors.'"

Rafferty unwrapped the scarf, fully revealing his flesh-and-blood fright mask, twisted further with a grin.

"Details, Dietrich…"

"The Khaki Shirts march tomorrow. They'll hit every Hooverville and CCC camp between here and Washington, recruiting men into their 'superorganization.' And Haskell has enough guns for them all to hold the country for ransom."

"And the Army?"

"They're blackmailing General MacArthur into supporting their putsch. We can't count on him."

Rafferty and Gardner brooded in silence.

"What about Dickstein and Nye?"

Max shrugged as the lies poured out. "They believe me, but you know how bureaucracies work. They have to wait until Monday to even open a formal investigation. It could be weeks before G-Men are on the case."

The shattered face was ice cold. "What do you suggest?"

"We settle this ourselves. I'll lead Osborn and Norris to you, and you two take care of the rest. Once the snake is beheaded, this entire plot will collapse. Norris is under Osborn's sway, and without the General, the Khaki Shirts won't have the manpower to march on Washington. Point is, if you only hit one, hit Norris."

"Don't worry, I'll kill them both. But how do we know you're not really in league with Osborn? After all, you might lead us into a trap."

"After all this? Christ, I could have set you up the moment you walked through that door, Rafferty." Max leaned forward, voice sharpening to a razor point. "The fact of the matter is, you've failed at everything so far. I'm giving you one last chance to go out like a true revolutionary, to strike a real blow against Fascism. Take it or leave it."

Rafferty and Gardner shared a tense look. Rafferty's shredded features twitched with anxiety, and what remained of Gardner's Adam's apple bobbed up and down. It was a suicide mission, to be sure, but these two broken men were ideal candidates. Finally, a wheezing hiss came from Gardner, filling Rafferty's shallow eyes with a predatory gleam.

"All right, Dietrich. We'll do it."

Max sighed, savoring the small victory. "Your country thanks—"

"I don't give a damn about this country."

"Of course. I have to meet with Osborn in half an hour. From there, we're to rendezvous at a staging area."

"Where's that?"

"Not sure yet, but I'll let you know once we get there. When I find out the details, what roads they'll take, the exact time it'll begin, I'll slip away and telephone you. You simply cut them off and—"

Max shot the air with his fingers. Rafferty nodded along, turning the plan over in his mind.

"That could work. But why don't we just tag along with you—" Rafferty and Gardner slid Colt automatics from their coat pockets. "—and plug them both? No fuss, no muss."

"The putsch is tomorrow, and Osborn's not taking any more chances. He's got an entire squad acting as his bodyguard. I doubt you'll get close with those heaters. But at the head of a march, he and Norris will make easy targets, even with gats like that."

A cruel grin curled Rafferty's twisted face. "Perhaps heavier artillery would work better?"

"Like a Tommy gun?"

The grin dropped, replaced by stunned surprise. "How'd you guess?"

"Figured you skimmed a few guns off the top. Let me guess, they're stashed down in the Bowery?"

"Quit showing off, Dietrich," Rafferty said with a half grin. "Where will you ring us? Tommy guns and soup kitchens don't mix."

Max shrugged. "Why not here? You've already shown yourself in. After you grab your choppers, come back and make yourselves at home. I'll call you as soon as I can."

"All right, Dietrich. Don't make me regret this."

"I was about to say the same thing."

CHAPTER FIFTY-SEVEN

Walking up to Haskell's penthouse, Max's jackboots pounded the pavement, sounds that would soon be amplified a thousandfold. Gray, soupy clouds swirled above Manhattan, but not a drop of rain fell. More mockery from the Almighty.

Max took the elevator to the top floor and found Squad Leader Grant Kilmer, along with a dozen Khaki Shirts, waiting inside the lounge. They snapped to attention and thrust out stiff salutes as Max entered. Funny what a change of clothes could do for a man. But then again, they were saluting the Crusader uniform, not the man.

Nevertheless, he clicked his heels and returned the gesture, his form poor, judging by Kilmer's disapproving grimace. One Crusader in particular – Bill Compton – scowled with particular distaste. But perhaps his anger came from the bright scar that ran down his cheek, like a pink, puffy caterpillar. Lash marks, compliments of Osborn's riding crop. Well, the Chief had promised to discipline Compton for all his loose talk.

Thankfully, Cornelia Osborn approached them with mincing steps and a radiant smile that matched her shimmering, sequined evening dress.

"Maximillian! Or should I say, Squad Leader Dietrich?"

"As long as it's not Maxie…"

She gave a purring laugh. "So glad you joined up. My husband can pull the last ounce of patriotism from even the most hardened cynic."

They stepped away from Kilmer's squad, toward Elias Haskell's private office. For now, they'd have to play along until the final curtain. A strange dame, this one. Was she always acting? Up until now, he'd bought her motives for revenge, but those queer mannerisms last night hinted at something buried beneath her masquerade. Who was the real Cornelia Osborn, or rather, what was she? An embittered daughter? A grieving sister? A jealous wife? Or something more callous?

"Do you have a plan?" she whispered.

Max nodded. "Rafferty will be our torpedo. Tomorrow morning."

"Can you trust him?" Her voice was tight with skepticism.

Of course he couldn't. Like all ideologues, Mike Rafferty was unstable, unhinged, and unprofessional. There were millions like him, ready to shoot, stab, and bomb for political fairy tales. A lunatic like Rafferty would gun down everything in his path, Max included. No, he'd take a powder long before the shooting started.

"Don't worry," Max whispered back. "I'll ring you after. Then we can deal with—" He glanced at Haskell's door.

"How?"

"I'll figure it out later," he said.

"Wait…" Her eyes went cold. "Leave everything to me. Just come back here afterward…"

Max nodded, then glanced over to Kilmer and the others, still unconcerned. They knew better than to eavesdrop on the Chief's wife. Cornelia gave a Fascist salute and Max entered the office. At the far end of the room, Haskell, Osborn and Norris sat opposite, stiff in their seats, but wearing gleeful expressions.

"Ah, Mr. Dietrich," the Merchant of Death said. "Richard here was just telling me about your actions today."

"Splendid job there, Maxie. Fighting trash with trash! That Red bitch finally shut her mouth."

Laughter rose up and even Max joined in. It *was* a little funny, he had to admit.

"You've proved your worth, Mr. Dietrich. And your talents will be put to good use…very soon."

Max could almost picture his new life as a secret policeman.

"Time to go," Osborn said, checking his watch.

Max fought down a litany of questions. Where was this staging area? Long Island? If so, why not just say it? But no, National Crusaders obeyed, never questioned. Norris and Osborn jumped to their feet and saluted. Haskell grinned back, but then hobbled over to the liquor cart. His spindly fingers poured four glasses of Scotch and divvied them out.

Leaning on his cane, the Merchant of Death raised his glass and toasted, "To a new America!"

"A new America!" Osborn and Norris chorused, before downing their glasses.

Max swirled his Scotch with a grimace. How many years had it been since his last drink? With the day he was having, he'd likely vomit.

"Drink up, Maxie. That's an order."

On command, he tossed back the Scotch, burning every inch on the way down. Just as disgusting as he remembered.

*****

Rafferty sat atop Gardner's shoulders, grasping at the fire escape. After a few yanks, he gripped the ladder and heaved himself up, ascending to firm ground. The metal was biting cold, but at least it wasn't raining tonight. Down below, Gardner tossed up a burlap sack – pilfered from the Salvation Army kitchen. A crude, but effective, way to hide Tommy guns from suspicious eyes.

He made his way up to the third floor to their old room, the shattered window now covered by a paltry sheet. That cheap old bitch. Whoever now occupied the room would have to be dealt with quickly and quietly. Rafferty drew the Colt automatic and smacked the remaining cracked glass away with its butt. A few sharp blows crumpled the window into shards. Pulling himself through, he found a middle-aged man – unshaven, half-naked, and reeking of alcohol – passed out on that filthy mattress.

The dipso stirred with a groan, but then lapsed into a deep snore. If only Forgotten Men like this could rise, turn their anger at the bosses and…

No time for bitterness. Dreams of a world revolution smacked of childish fantasy now. Mike Rafferty had always been on the search for a new cause, a new belief, a new purpose. A shrieking shell killed both God and his patriotism in a blinding flash. He'd found a new religion in the Soviet Union, the workers' paradise. But then Stalin had been revealed to be more devil than prophet. And, although it pained him, even Leon Trotsky seemed more like Santa Claus now.

But there was still one thing he could believe in, something that wasn't a childish dream. He knelt down, tossed away the ratty rag, then cracked open the floorboards, revealing two Tommy guns and five drums. Modern day Excaliburs waiting to be claimed. Shoving one chopper into the burlap sack, he removed the other and stared at it, hypnotized. It was a weighty beast, yet hauntingly beautiful – death itself molded into metal.

It was more than a weapon. It was Mike Rafferty's last chance to become the revolutionary he'd always known he was.

CHAPTER FIFTY-EIGHT

Long before they reached the outskirts of Brooklyn, Max realized the staging area was the warehouse in Canarsie. An odd choice, given how many Khaki Shirts he'd seen out in the Long Island camp. But he kept such probing questions to himself and obeyed like a good Fascist. The entourage of sedans parked across the street, and, after Kilmer's squad secured the area, Max followed Osborn and Norris into the warehouse.

A round of salutes greeted them, along with the chant, "Hail the Chief!" Osborn returned the gesture, and the Khaki Shirts – five of them – returned to duty. Ten green Mack trucks sat crammed inside the loading area, their beds wide open, being filled with an endless supply of crates. Although some were labeled "Canned Food," a majority were unmarked, but a metallic rattling betrayed the guns hidden inside.

Kilmer's squad assembled before the catwalk that stretched across the warehouse, now bedecked with the Stars and Stripes, hanging alongside the blue National Crusader flag, emblazoned with the bald eagle, its talons grasping a rifle and sword.

Max remained below as Norris and Osborn ascended the stairs, their jackboots banging out hollow thuds against the metal. They took a lofty position on the catwalk, high above their dreamy-eyed followers. A small crowd, but even Mussolini started out with a few local hoods. Besides, these weren't cynical Hooverville bums, but zealots in a new political religion. Osborn drew himself up, hands behind his back, and head tilted high.

"Men, patriots, Crusaders," he began, voice booming throughout the warehouse. "When I founded this organization, it was with one purpose in mind. The National

Crusaders is not a glorified fraternity, interested in endless debate and blather. Only by direct action, not talk, can we defeat our enemies that are slowly strangling America."

Kilmer and his squad stood there blank-faced, awaiting orders. After all, "direct action" could mean anything. Again, Chief Osborn had the answers.

"There have been rumors in your ranks about what we're planning. Some speak of assassinations, while some talk of seizing cities through armed insurrection. Others whisper of a second civil war." Osborn swept the air with a hand, dismissing such fantasies. "A good officer never sends soldiers into a doomed battle. I value each and every Crusader life too much to waste it in some harebrained scheme."

A valid point, but the Merchants of Death wanted this fodder alive and healthy when the real war erupted.

"No mere insurrection will bring us to power. Instead, tomorrow morning, we will march on Washington and make our voices heard throughout the entire nation, throughout the entire world!"

Concerned murmurs spread among the Khaki Shirts. Many had already gone through this song and dance during the sweltering summer of 1932. Leaning against the catwalk's railing, Osborn seemed to sense the tension.

"I know that some of you may mask your fears, but rest assured. This will not be a repeat of the Bonus March. We have taken precautions to ensure that there shall be no inglorious retreat." Osborn gestured to the four parked trucks, still being packed with crates. "At dawn tomorrow morning, five thousand National Crusaders will march out of the Long Island camp and rendezvous with us here. Then, the March on Washington will begin!"

Kilmer jerked up a rigid salute and every Khaki Shirt followed with a thunderous, "Hail the Chief!" Osborn returned the gesture, then continued.

"But you men have an important mission to fulfill. An armed column of men might alarm local authorities, killing our National Revolution before it can begin. That is why Squad Leader Kilmer and his detachment will drive our entire cache of weapons—" Osborn flashed an almost gracious look down at the Mack trucks "—collected over the months from our dear friend Elias Haskell, out of New York before we begin our march."

Max swallowed his guilt. After all, if he hadn't found those stolen guns, this putsch would have been dead in the water.

Kilmer clicked his heels. "As you command, Chief!"

National Crusaders obeyed orders, but someone as megalomaniacal as Richard Osborn needed others to marvel at his plot.

"As I lead the column down to Washington, we'll augment our numbers with Khaki Shirts from Philadelphia and Baltimore until our ranks swell to ten thousand. But our final stop will be Elkridge, Maryland. That is where you, Squad Leader Kilmer, will park these munitions trucks, away from prying eyes." Osborn gestured to Norris, standing beside him, rigid as a statue. "Troop Leader Norris will persuade thousands of men from Hoovervilles and CCC camps to join our cause, and then, the final strike on Washington will begin! The arms inside the trucks you men have driven will arm and equip a superorganization of a hundred thousand patriots, that will devour this corrupt system in one fell swoop."

So that's why Osborn and Norris had come here instead of the Long Island camp. Most Khaki Shirts were in the dark about this putsch, and if they got a whiff of its machinations, word might get back to Roosevelt ahead of schedule. G-Men or loyal troops might quash the coup before it even began. Better for Osborn to deliver instructions in secret to his most loyal squad.

Kilmer led another salute, but no cheers this time. A silent dread lingered, one that had crushed their dreams back in 1932.

"This time, you have nothing to fear from General MacArthur or any other Washington guard dog. We have friends in the Army now." Osborn's eyes slid over to Norris, arms clasped behind his back. "I assure you men, 1934 will be the year of victory. We shall enter the White House, not as conquerors, but as liberators!"

The words had a hypnotic effect, banishing any remaining fears. A cheer swelled through the warehouse, accompanied by Fascist salutes and a deep-throated, "Hail the Chief!"

Max found his own arm outstretched, his voice blended with the rising shouts toward Chief Richard Osborn, gazing down like a god upon mere mortals.

CHAPTER FIFTY-NINE

Gathered in a circle, the Khaki Shirts ate a dinner of canned beef and vegetables, the standard meal in store for the March on Washington. Osborn went on to clarify that Kilmer and his men would intermittently drop off crates of canned food by the road, an easy way to sustain the marchers. Well, it beat foraging off the land.

Max slurped down his canned beef, stealing glances at the overhead office. Inside, he remembered, was a rotary telephone, the perfect way to ring Mike Rafferty. Hopefully, that lunatic Red was camped out in his office, waiting for the signal to move. But how to get up there without being seen? Under the cover of darkness, when everyone was passed out, that's how. Max returned to his food, but noticed an intense glower fixated on him. Bill Compton glared across the warehouse with murderous intensity. Somehow, that scar on his cheek looked even more grotesque.

Better retreat to the protection of the Chief.

"Just like chow time during the war," Max said to Osborn and Norris. Chewing on their canned gruel, they nodded in somber silence. They could easily morph from rabble-rousing demagogues to soldier's soldiers, accustomed to hard campaigning alongside their men. That sort of "aw, shucks" humility would play well when recruiting men to their cause.

"But no mud," Kilmer piped up.

"No rats, either," Max said. That got a little laughter from the Khaki Shirts.

"And no rain, either," another Crusader said.

Max grinned. "Well, not according to the Chief."

Osborn set aside his canned slop, then drew himself up. "That's enough talking for tonight. You men need rest if you're going to drive all day tomorrow."

Kilmer and his men gave silent, submissive nods. After all, reminiscing about the war's miseries might make them hesitant to fight another one. Osborn summoned two Khaki Shirts.

"Crusaders Compton and Jones – you two will be on guard duty tonight. Jones, you first, then Compton. This is a chance to redeem yourselves."

The two Crusaders saluted, eagerness mingling with gratitude on their weary faces. Compton shot Max another glare before returning to a stoic poise. Osborn, hands clasped behind his back, barked out a final order.

"The rest of you, turn in now. The March on Washington begins at sunrise."

*****

Snug in his sleeping bag, Max closed his eyes and waited. He fought to stay awake until legions of Khaki Shirts marched through his mind. The procession continued into no man's land, pockmarked with shell craters, while the endless crack of rifles echoed into infinity. A towering wave of poison gas, larger than any black blizzard from the Dust Bowl, swept across the shattered landscape, choking it into oblivion.

His eyes shot open, adjusting to the darkness around him. Moonlight filtered in through the overhead skylights. Osborn, Norris, Compton, and the rest were passed out in their sleeping bags. Resting with minimum amenities was a good skill to have on a road march. But Max had marched across enough muddy roads to last himself a lifetime. Hopefully, he'd spare this generation that torture.

Still, the rest of these Khaki Shirts would have to be sacrificed, but it was for the greater good. Christ, he was sounding like a Bolshevik himself now. Some of these men were probably halfway decent folks underneath those khaki tunics, just like a lot of decent guys wore German *feldgrau*. No time to ponder that now. Max squirmed out of the sleeping bag and crept up the staircase, toward the catwalk. The American flag and the National Crusader banner hung still in the darkness, like two nooses from an enormous gallows.

Each footstep rang out like a grenade blast, but nobody stirred. Crusader Jones was likely outside on patrol, allowing Max to cross the catwalk unmolested. In his tunic pocket, the snubnosed revolver rustled back and forth, smacking against his hip. The small office was straight ahead, and after a final glance down to ensure he wasn't followed, Max eased the door open and entered. Inside, the moon shone through the cracked window – evidence of Rafferty's earlier entrance – casting evil, twisting shadows.

The poster, resplendent with a gallant Khaki Shirt and stamped with the slogan, "*The National Crusaders Stand For 100% Americanism!*" took on a far more sinister appearance in the gloom. Hopefully, those two idiots were lounging in his office, choppers ready. Max gripped the telephone receiver and dialed his office. Moments later, Rafferty's voice answered.

"That you, Dietrich?"

"Yeah. Listen, Osborn and Norris are at the Canarsie warehouse. Same place you raided. Everyone is asleep and there's only one guard on duty."

"How many Fascists?"

"About a dozen. But you two can take them by surprise if you make tracks here quick."

"All right, Dietrich. We'll meet you there."

The line clicked and went dead. Max hung up and took a gulp of chilly air. Like hell he'd stay here. A nut like Rafferty wouldn't distinguish between friend and foe, gunning down anything in a khaki uniform. Besides, the sooner he could leave this Fascist nest, the better. Out the window and down the fire escape, then take a powder back to Manhattan and Cornelia Osborn. He hung up the receiver, when a metallic click shattered the silence.

"Well, well," a sneering hiss poured into the office. Max turned and found Crusader Compton in the doorframe, aiming a Colt automatic straight at him. "Looks like I caught a spy. And we can shoot spies, can't we, Chief?"

Compton stepped inside, allowing Osborn and Norris to crowd in behind him. Osborn gave Max a glare, burning with anger and betrayal.

"Yes, Crusader Compton. Spies deserve no mercy."

*****

Rafferty hung up the phone, adrenaline pumping through his fatigued body. It was the same surge that came just before battle, a strange dance between elation and terror. He looked back at Eddie Gardner, sitting on Dietrich's couch, Tommy gun sprawled across his lap.

"Ready to go over the top again, Eddie?"

A firm nod and hissing rasp was Gardner's answer. Rafferty looked down on Dietrich's desk, where his own chopper sat, a metallic monster ready to awake. He checked his wristwatch – half past two. By car, they could get over to Canarsie in about thirty minutes with no traffic.

Bundling the Tommy guns into the burlap sack, they tromped down the stairs. The Paramount Theatre still glowed but was outshone by the brilliant glare of Times Square, a few blocks away. They made their way down to the sea of neon lights, a flickering temple of capitalism. Few people were out this late, but Times Square still flashed gaudy advertisements – Camel cigarettes and Chevrolet signs buzzed alongside Coca-Cola and Squibb Dental Cream logos.

Underneath were dozens of Forgotten Men, bundled up in tattered, threadbare coats, trying to soak up every ounce of neon warmth. Forget the Statue of Liberty, this was the perfect symbol of America in all its shameless hypocrisy! Rafferty's only regret was that he wouldn't live long enough to see this detestable system smashed into rubble. Even in this depression, taxi cabs still prowled Times Square for customers, and within seconds, Rafferty flagged one. The cabbie pulled to the side and flicked on his meter.

"Where to, bub?" he asked as Rafferty approached from the driver's side.

Gardner whipped out a chopper and jabbed its muzzle into the cabbie's soft neck.

"Nowhere, with you," Rafferty said. "Get out."

Trembling, the cabbie wormed out of the driver's seat. Rafferty hopped into the passenger side while Gardner took the wheel. The cabbie gawked in mute terror as they sped off, past the dancing lights and shaggy bums, toward Canarsie and their final battle.

CHAPTER SIXTY

A good soldier knew when to take cover, when to advance, and when to surrender. It was hopeless now, Max could see that. The pistol in Compton's hand would bark twice before he could even reach the fire escape. His only chance now was to stall until Rafferty and Gardner showed up, Tommy guns blazing.

"Sorry, Richard, I was just following up on another case. Some clients are real nighthawks, you know."

Osborn stepped forward, patted him down, then yanked out the snubnosed revolver from his tunic. Several moments ticked by, until Osborn lashed out like a striking snake, cracking Max against the cheek with the butt of the pistol. Pain throbbed from his face down to his spine, collapsing him into a twisted heap on the floor. Running fingers across his skin revealed no blood, and working his jaw proved it wasn't broken. Osborn placed the revolver atop the desk. Apparently, they weren't going to shoot him just yet. But that riding crop still dangled from the Chief's fingers, ready to whip Max into bloody chunks.

"A client, you say? Who?" Osborn sneered.

He needed to stall until Rafferty arrived, Tommy guns glazing. Few options remained, except one. The truth.

"Your wife."

The crop almost dropped out of Osborn's hand. "Cornelia?"

Norris snarled a harsh laugh. "Preposterous. The female brain isn't capable of such intrigue."

"That just proves you know nothing about women," Max said, then turned to Osborn. "You either…'Dick.'"

Osborn's eyes flared and his lips compressed into a tight, thin slash. The riding crop shook in his hand, wobbling a little as he gestured Compton out the door.

"Leave us, Crusader Compton."

After saluting, Compton marched out the door, leaving Dick, Nate, and Max alone.

*****

Gardner pressed the accelerator harder, speeding across the Brooklyn Bridge. Manhattan blurred into Brooklyn as the taxicab shot eastward, toward Canarsie on the fringes of New York. Though the engine thumped and gears groaned under the strain, they were making good time, thanks to only a trickle of traffic out tonight.

Threading through the empty streets, Prospect Park – Brooklyn's answer to Central Park – spread out on their right. They were getting closer, and Rafferty felt sweat bead along his forehead, oozing down and sinking into his cavernous scars. He gripped the Tommy gun, resting on his lap, steadying himself.

There was still a possibility that Dietrich was leading him into a trap, but it didn't matter now. As long as he struck down the Fascist beast, his life would mean something. And what of Dietrich? He might be working for Dickstein and Nye, but that wouldn't spare him. He was the epitome of a bourgeois liberal, a cog in this detestable capitalist system. Those two Fascist demagogues would remain his target, but any remaining bullets would be reserved for Max Dietrich.

*****

Max readjusted himself to a kneeling position and looked up. Norris and Osborn loomed above, both tense and rigid. Fear permeated the small office, two men scared that all their dirty secrets were being dragged out into the light.

"How much do you know?" Osborn asked.

"That you boys are in love. Cornelia knows too."

Norris stepped closer, fists balled. "How dare you accuse us of such sinful perversion!"

Osborn whipped the crop up with a loud whoosh, silencing him. "Perhaps she isn't such a vapid fool. Serves me right for being duped by an actress, albeit a rank amateur. So, she hired you in a fit of female jealousy?"

"Being used for your family money would make anyone a little angry."

A flinty glaze swept over Osborn's face, cold and inscrutable.

"She can blame her old man for that. Haskell knew all about Nate and I, but our connections to the US Army were more important than his own daughter."

"You made out pretty well in this deal…"

"What choice did I have? My Army career was ruined by jealous rivals. You don't know what it's like to have your manhood mocked by smug puritans and sanctimonious hypocrites." Osborn glanced at Norris, his rocky face soft with emotion. "We fought for this country, only to be dismissed and hated as pansies, fairies, sissies. I am a warrior, Dietrich. And as head of a new American Army, I will prove it to the entire world."

No more *Maxie*, just *Dietrich*? If he wasn't up to his neck in trouble before, he was drowning in it now.

"Looks like the Liberty League is going to get their money's worth," Max said.

A flash of rage, then the riding crops cracked down, slicing Max's other cheek.

"We are nobody's puppets. The Liberty League will get its gold standard and Haskell will drown himself in blood money, so long as they play by *our* rules."

"You're really going to start another war?" Max's voice cracked with anger. "After everything we saw over there?"

Osborn was implacable. "It is the only way to save America from decadent weakness."

Max gripped his cheek, spurting out small trickles of blood. "Then there will be many more Francis Haskells."

Osborn's harshness relaxed into momentary confusion.

"That's right, Haskell's son is alive. Or rather, he isn't dead."

But there was no great shock, only a calm understanding. "I know. He's locked away at Kings Park."

"What kind of father would do that to his only son? Throw him away like a broken toy? For someone of Haskell's wealth, there are treatments, plastic surgeries…"

Osborn and Norris shared a knowing look, then a deep laughter. Max sat there in stunned silence, blood squirming between his fingers, the odd man out.

"Is that what that scheming bitch told you?" Osborn sneered. "Well, looks like she fooled us both, Dietrich."

"What…what do you mean?"

Osborn flicked the blood from his crop, before answering. "When they brought Francis home, his mother and father wanted to spare no expense. The old man was ready to spend every penny he had on experimental treatments, plastic surgery, the works. But then Cornelia started whispering into his ear. She convinced him that Francis was already gone, even if his body hadn't died yet. 'Why put a mask on a madman?' she argued."

Max almost laughed. "Sounds familiar."

"According to her, it would be better to honor his memory as a hero who died in France, rather than the disfigured freak they shipped back."

"And…Haskell locked him away?"

Osborn nodded. "Cornelia's forked tongue was very persuasive, and she became Haskell's sole beneficiary. It devastated her mother though, knowing her son had become some hideous creature, scurrying about in a dark cell. Quite understandable she poisoned herself, don't you agree?"

"How do you know about this, Richard?"

"Cornelia told me. Cold-hearted bitch is proud of swindling her own brother out of his inheritance. She even bragged that she was able to squeeze money out of that old buzzard as if he were a lemon. But then…"

"Then you came along."

A broad smile creased Osborn's lips. "Good guess, detective. I was his new son, full of vigor and vitality. I would continue the family business. But using Cornelia's persuasive charm, I was able to convince him to fund the National Crusaders, although it took Roosevelt going off the gold standard to convince the other big shots. Those stuffed shirts are terrified of anything that might dent their fortunes."

Suddenly, Max felt he owed an apology to every client who'd been cuckolded and conned. To be taken in by an amateur actress filled him with a burning humiliation. There had always been something amiss with Cornelia Osborn, like having a piece left over after completing the jigsaw puzzle.

"Answer me one thing, Richard."

"Yes?"

"Does Cornelia still get an allowance?"

Another deep laugh, almost keeling Osborn and Norris over.

"We cut her off long ago. She's a parasite, Dietrich. Accustomed to spending men's money on frilly dresses and jewelry." Osborn's handsome face contorted into a grotesque grimace. "In many ways, she is everything wrong with this country. Soft, vain, greedy…all weaknesses that must be burnt away with fire. But enough about her. I want to talk about you, Dietrich."

"You already know everything about me, Richard."

"No, I don't. I overlooked your obvious flaws since you'd saved my life. I thought I could reform you, mold you into a selfless patriot. But it's now apparent that you've been corrupted beyond redemption."

Max turned to Norris. "Didn't Jesus speak of forgiveness?"

The General's eyes burned like hot coals. "Only after the sinner is given proper punishment."

The riding crop swished through the air again as Osborn stepped closer.

"I don't think you're being truthful about that call, Dietrich. That wasn't Cornelia you were speaking to."

"Okay, okay, I'll be square with you, Richard."

"No, you won't. You're an irredeemable liar, Dietrich. I understand that now." The crop strained in Osborn's hands. "But after a few hundred lashes…you'll spill everything and more."

CHAPTER SIXTY-ONE

The taxi's headlights stabbed through the darkness that enveloped Canarsie. Haskell's warehouse loomed before them and Gardner parked the cab down the street, then cut the lights. Rafferty squinted out the front window, gazing up and down the building. Minutes passed without any movement around the premises, no sentries, no patrols, no signs of life. Dietrich had mentioned the building was lightly guarded, but he couldn't shake the dread of running straight into a trap.

But then why was he here?

He searched and found the answer quickly -- he was tired of running. It was the end of the road for Mike Rafferty and Eddie Gardner. Their fates were tied to this derelict building, looking more and more like some enormous tombstone. Rafferty gripped the Tommy gun and tried to speak, but his mouth was tight with tension. Gardner gurgled a quick statement, a poetic testament to their final stand. They stepped out of the cab and crept toward the warehouse. A damp chill hung in the air, just like that dreary day in France.

The loading dock was shuttered tight. A full blast from their choppers would only raise the alarm. There must be another way in. They slid into the alleyway, where the fire escape still stood and, for a moment, Rafferty considered using it again. But a dim light twinkled in the top floor window, quashing that idea. The guard was probably camped out there, ready for them. Instead, they crept past it toward the alley's mouth. There was a door on the immediate left, the front entrance.

"Stop right there," a voice boomed from above.

Rafferty jerked the Tommy gun up and opened fire, spurting a lethal spray at a silhouette, looming over them. A twisted wail howled as the figure contorted and tumbled off the roof, splattering to the street with a hideous crunch. Even in the darkness, the face of Crusader Jones was recognizable, albeit smeared with blood. His khaki uniform was a mass of tattered shreds and lifeless hands loosened from a Springfield rifle. A few nights ago, he'd shown pity to these Khaki Shirts, brother workers duped into Fascism. Tonight was different. Mike Rafferty's mission, no, his destiny, was to strike down the American Hitler like a true revolutionary, no matter how many National Crusaders he had to blast his way through.

Rafferty spun around and tried the doorknob, but it didn't budge. There was no time to strategize or bother with stealth. That volley would raise the alarm, so the only course of action was a frontal assault. He raised the Tommy gun and let out another burst, pulverizing the wooden door into splinters. Pushing through, he and Gardner charged headlong into the warehouse's expanse.

Two flags – one American, one Crusader – dangled from a catwalk above. Few crates from the other night remained, as if the insides of the warehouse had been scooped out. A row of Mack trucks, parked in the loading bay, explained why.

Commotion stirred near the trucks, silhouettes snapping upright, their wobbly stances showing just how groggy they were. Mercy melted away and Mike Rafferty hardened himself into a steel blade, the sword of the people. These weren't men, not like the brother workers he'd killed in France for wearing different uniforms. No, these Fascists *were* their uniforms.

Gardner ambled beside him as they unleashed rapid shots from their Tommy guns, piercing the darkened warehouse with flaring light. The Khaki Shirts fumbled and lurched about in confused panic – dazed and helpless. Each belching blast revealed another face, warped by grotesque terror, as a storm of bullets ripped through their bodies.

They kept firing, streams of lead blazing up and down, left and right, slicing through Fascist after Fascist, like wheat in a thresher. Rafferty glanced over to Gardner, his Tommy gun cackling like a witch, flame spurting out like hellfire. A new stream of bullets mingled with the carnage, cutting into Gardner with loud, wet slaps. Blood spurted out of Gardner's chest and throat, dousing his old scars in a geyser of fresh gore. Eddie Gardner staggered back, his chopper still blasting in short, stuttering burps.

Rafferty swung his own Tommy gun around and opened fire. Flashing volleys revealed a Khaki Shirt officer with gold insignia on his collar, cap, and shoulders – one of their so-called squad leaders – firing a Colt automatic from the open bed of one of the trucks. But as Rafferty advanced, blazing away, the uniform faded from khaki to field gray, the side cap morphed into a German steel helmet, and the warehouse melted into the desolate mud and waste of the trenches.

*****

Osborn stepped closer, the leather crop creaking in his fists. Max's cheek had stopped bleeding, but still buzzed with pain. The wound was intentionally shallow, a mere appetizer for the gory feast Osborn had planned. Norris drew up behind him, his thick, solid hands gripping Max's shoulders like a vise. There was no reason to struggle anymore. Despite his age, this old timer was harder than steel. Hoisting Max up to his feet, Norris steadied him for Osborn's blows. But the Khaki Shirt Chief hesitated, reluctance etched deep into his handsome face. What was it Cornelia had said?

'*Richard loves you, you know.*'

Perhaps there was still a chance of talking his way out of this but it'd take all the delicacy of disabling a time bomb.

"Richard, I—"

Gunfire rattled outside the office, illuminating the warehouse like lightning strikes. The door swung open as Compton shoved his terror-stricken face inside.

"Chief, we're under attack! Two intruders with submachine guns!"

The riding crop fell to the floor, and Chief Osborn moved over to the desk in one lengthy stride. Norris released his grip from Max's shoulders, taking a place beside his lover. Two Colt automatics were withdrawn, one for Osborn, one for Norris, and clips were snapped into place, ready for battle.

"Crusader Compton, execute this man," Osborn ordered, his voice harsher than the gunshots outside. "Then join us."

Norris was the first to leave, with Osborn close behind, but not before casting a final wounded glance back, like a man in mourning.

"Farewell, Maxie."

CHAPTER SIXTY-TWO

Hopping out of the muddy trench, Rafferty squeezed the trigger, pumping out an endless stream of bullets. The onslaught hurled the Kraut backward, his *feldgrau* uniform exploding with splattering gore, before slumping to the ground. Blood pooled underneath him as his tunic faded from gray to khaki, the mud reverting back to wood and steel.

But the bodies remained, grotesque monuments to his final mission. A dozen or so Khaki Shirts lay in twisted heaps, wide-eyed in frozen terror, their crisp tunics blotted with blood. No matter how hard he tried, he could never escape the war, nor the shameful role he'd played in it as a hired mercenary for capitalism. He shook his head clear of the past, focused back on the present. Rafferty stooped over each corpse, but Osborn and Norris weren't among the dead. Poor Eddie Gardner lay there too, silenced forever.

He choked back a sob of pity, for his comrade, and for himself. Had Dietrich set him up? Or was this yet another cosmic joke on fate's favorite clown, Mike Rafferty?

Gunfire split the silence. Rafferty whirled around and looked up. A silhouetted figure stood on the catwalk, flame spitting from the pistol in his hands. Muzzle flashes illuminated the stodgy face of Nathaniel Norris, fixed into a hard grimace. Bullets rained down, chipping the floor, splintering wooden crates, far away from Rafferty. For a former general, the old man was a lousy shot.

Rafferty thundered out a renewed volley, bullets sawing through Norris's frame, jerking him every which way. The pistol clanked to the floor, and a gurgling scream echoed throughout the warehouse. Norris stumbled forward, toppling off the catwalk, hands grasping the empty air for help, tearing the Crusader flag off its hook, and plummeting to the harsh cement below.

Norris hit the floor with a crunching splat, his body twitching in little jerks, blood oozing beneath him. Glazed, vacuous eyes glared back at Rafferty as he approached, the chopper's hideous cackle now quiet. One down, one to go. But where was Osborn?

A burst of gunfire answered. Pain stabbed through Rafferty's torso, but he glanced up. Osborn dashed across the catwalk and bounded down the steel stairs, firing his automatic in a whirling melee. Rafferty heaved the Tommy gun up and released another staccato blast, hammering volleys in every direction. The chopper flew out of control, spitting bullets round and round, arching through the air, pinging off the catwalk, the office windows, and tearing the hanging American flag asunder.

A hollow click echoed. The Tommy gun's drum was empty, but it didn't matter. Richard Osborn lurched down the stairs, gripping his stomach with an agonized scowl. The pistol clattered beside him, as he almost doubled over, but still trudged closer. Pain and nausea seized Rafferty, pulling him facefirst to the floor with a loud smack. He could feel blood gushing from three different wounds, all near his heart. It didn't matter though. Through the maelstrom, Osborn had been fatally hit.

Osborn staggered past Rafferty, toward the bullet-ridden corpse of Norris, but they were soon submerged by the muddy fields of France. Rafferty could feel the cold slime on his face, whole again, no longer a freakish deformity. But he couldn't move, as if pasted to the muck itself. Shrill rings reverberated in his ears, signs that he was fading fast. No, that sound, that evil wail—he'd heard it before.

The shell! It had returned to finish him off!

A monstrous shriek grew louder and louder until his skull almost burst. His eyes crawled around for help, for someone – Eddie Gardner, Peter O'Hare, his mother, or anyone else – to save him. But there was only blackness, an empty void of nothingness before a bright light burst forth, swallowing everything in its path.

*****

Crusader Compton raised the pistol like a one-man firing squad. Max looked about for some escape, settling on his snubnosed revolver, sitting mockingly on the desk, just out of reach. Instead, he traipsed backward, his jackboots scraping against Osborn's riding crop, discarded on the wooden floor. A longshot, but the only weapon he had, aside from his tongue.

"Compton, wait, I know you're sore at me, but we can work something out."

The scarred face sneered. "You ratted me out to the Chief and now my kisser looks like raw beef."

"I know things about Osborn and Norris. You can have them eating out of your hand with this information."

The gun drooped slightly, as Compton considered the offer. A faithful dog abused by his master had its breaking point, but in the end, Compton was still an animal to be led.

"I won't betray the Chief. He's the only hope for America."

The pistol locked back into position, Compton's finger tight on the trigger. Gunshots exploded into the office, not from the Colt automatic, but from outside. Glass shattered into gleaming jagged shards, spiraling outward. Compton ducked, shielding his face, but leaving himself exposed. With one motion, Max grabbed the crop and lashed out, striking Compton's face, tearing another gruesome gash across his flesh.

Compton howled in pain, bringing a hand to his bloodied face, the automatic stabbing about in blind, probing thrusts. Max spun around toward the desk, the snubnosed revolver within reach. Grasping it, he whirled about and fired once, twice, three times, the blasts blending with the firefight outside.

CHAPTER SIXTY-THREE

Compton struggled to raise the automatic, but his body sagged, blood dribbling over his lips. The automatic fell from loosened fingers and he slammed to the floor with a loud crunch against the splintered glass. Then, everything went quiet, except for the sound of Max's breathing, pumping in and out with nervous, noisy gasps.

The silence was all encompassing, spreading throughout the warehouse like some invisible, suffocating gas. Haunting memories of another tortuous silence resurfaced, on November 11th, 1918, when the guns stopped on the Western Front. Leftover adrenaline shook Max's body in trembling jerks, but he managed to pocket the revolver inside his tunic and take slow, plodding steps outside the office and across the catwalk.

The morning sun seeped through the skylight, illuminating the warehouse little by little. A grisly spectacle revealed itself by the loading bay, the tortured bodies of Squad Leader Kilmer and his men lay strewn about like khaki rags, next to Eddie Gardner, caked in his own gore. This bloodbath made the Saint Valentine's Day Massacre look like a light drizzle.

Max descended the stairs and found Mike Rafferty, bloodied and dead, his mangled face contorted even further in mute horror. Whatever he saw in his last moments wasn't pretty. Above the catwalk dangled the shredded remains of the Stars and Stripes, while the Crusader flag lay wrapped and twisted around the mutilated corpse of Nathaniel Norris like a death shroud. And there, cradling the General in his arms, was Richard Osborn.

The Chief lolled his head up and Max could see his face was smeared with a mixture of blood and tears. The dark splotches on his khaki tunic grew steadily, draining what color remained in his face. He was fading fast.

"Why, Maxie? Was it for money? Senator Nye? Or—" a tearing rasp of blood spewed up, splattering across Norris's prostrate body. "—the Reds?"

Max stepped closer, gazing down. The Fascist dictator of America was dead and his grand vizier reduced to a whimpering heap. Sympathy welled inside Max's soul, but he quashed it.

"For the future," Max answered, then responded with a question of his own. "Why didn't you kill me, Richard?"

A ghoulish smile crept across Osborn, though his eyes rimmed with a new flood of tears. "Because I'm weak, Maxie. Thank..." he took a labored gasp, "Thank you, Maxie."

"For what?"

"For punishing my weakness. The weak are...unworthy. Only the strong deserve to live." Osborn sucked in another rasping breath as blood bubbled from his lips in a grotesque foam, a mad dog ready to be put down. "The future...belongs to the strong..."

A death rattle echoed off the warehouse walls, the end of an era. This horror show should have filled Max with revulsion, but the same numbness that accompanied him in the trenches returned. It kept him clear-headed and alive then, and took control of his instincts now, banishing any lingering sentimentality. It was morning now, and the main force of the National Crusaders would arrive soon.

Max bounded across the warehouse and out the back door, now a mass of broken wood clinging to its hinges. Outside, he doubled back around the alleyway, ran underneath the fire escape, coming around to the rear area with its loading bay. Above, gray clouds blanketed the sun, but hazy light shone through. Peering into the distance, he saw a khaki mass, columns of Crusaders marching in rank to their staging ground. Max looked around for some escape, but few subways ran to this neighborhood.

Then how had Rafferty and Gardner gotten here? He searched the street for some sort of getaway car, and zeroed in on a parked yellow cab. Taxis were rare in Canarsie, especially this early. Its doors were unlocked, and even if Rafferty had stolen it, there were no other options. Not unless he wanted to explain to the entire Khaki Shirt army how their beloved Chief had kicked the bucket.

Max hit the starter and the engine rumbled to life. Life as a Prohi had taught him basic driving skills, and he knew outer boroughs well enough to get back to Elias Haskell's penthouse. Cornelia said she had a plan how to handle the old buzzard. Her place in this sordid affair was a nagging mystery, but now, after what Osborn had said, he knew where she fit in.

He threw the taxi into first gear and turned left, speeding toward Manhattan. In his rearview mirror, the columns of oncoming Khaki Shirts shrank as they marched toward nowhere.

*****

Cornelia Osborn was waiting for Max as he entered the penthouse. Wearing a high-necked black blouse, she already looked attired for Osborn's funeral. But her charcoal gray pants, with deep, wide pockets, gave the impression of a modern woman ready for action. Max gave the sitting room a once over, hand inside the lower pocket near the snubnosed, just in case he'd walked into a trap.

"Where's Jeeves?" he asked.

"I sent him off on busywork. It's just the three of us."

"And Daddy Warbucks?"

"In his office." Cornelia paused, then asked, "Is it…done?"

"You're a widow now, if that's what you mean."

A wispy smile bloomed across her lips, laced with cruelty, before quickly vanishing. "Do you have a gun on you?"

"Right here." He motioned inside his tunic pocket. "What's your plan?"

"Just follow my lead."

"Lady, I'm through taking orders. Either you tell me what's cooking or I walk."

Cornelia glowered, then said, "Suicide is the only option left for him. Follow me or you'll miss the show."

She turned and walked toward Haskell's door, her wide-legged trousers swishing with every stride. A strange sound followed her, like the clinking of glass. Jewelry? Or was something inside her pockets? Either way, Max had a few secrets to share himself and followed her into the office.

CHAPTER SIXTY-FOUR

The door shut behind them, booming out like a gunshot. Leaning on his cane, Elias Haskell stood near the stock ticker, belching out the latest numbers from Wall Street. He glowered back at them, shrewd and guarded.

"Dietrich? What are you doing here?"

"It's over, Father," Cornelia answered for him. "Richard and Norris are dead."

Shock swept across Haskell's face, leaving it slack and drawn. Stumbling on his cane, he collapsed into his chair, face buried inside his withered palms. Little sobs leaked out, mournful wails for his son-in-law, or were they for his business empire? Even the Merchants of Death could weep.

"You two," Haskell sneered, lifting his face up, "were in cahoots from the beginning."

Well, not from the *very* beginning, but why complicate things?

"That doesn't matter now, Father. All you need to know is that your plot has failed. Dietrich has gathered enough evidence to expose you and the entire Liberty League. We'll present the evidence to Gerald Nye."

Mention of Nye ignited a passionate rage within Haskell, his own daughter collaborating with his worst enemy. He tore open a desk drawer and held up that small Baby Browning again, bony fingers curling around the trigger in an unsteady, jerking grip. Cornelia squealed and moved aside as Max whipped out his revolver, aiming it back at the old vulture. Like something out of *Little Caesar*, this Merchant of Death wouldn't be taken alive.

"What are you waiting for?" Cornelia hissed.

Max grinned back at her. "Are you talking to me or him?"

Cornelia swallowed hard but kept quiet.

"Haskell, you might want to check your magazine. I have a hunch that some little mouse was rooting around your desk when you weren't looking."

The Baby Browning rattled in the old man's fingers, but suspicion got the better of him. He slid the magazine out, then slammed it on the desk. "Empty!" He glared at Cornelia, a thunderstorm swirling in his gray eyes. "Why?"

"Isn't it obvious?" Max said, lowering the snubnosed. "You pull an empty pistol on me, I shoot you in self-defense, case closed. A plan worthy of the pulps." He looked back at Cornelia. "You Haskells really are a family of schemers. But you're not as clever as you think you are, lady. You were a little too eager to know if I had a rod on me. Besides, it took me a moment, but I figured that jingle-jangle inside your pockets came from the bullets you swiped from Daddy Warbucks's gun."

Cornelia slid her hands over her pockets, staying silent.

"What's your angle in all this, Dietrich?" Haskell asked from behind his desk.

"Dough, at first. I don't give a hoot about Roosevelt and our song-and-dance democracy, but you profiting off the blood of a new generation doesn't sit right with me."

Haskell scoffed. "Hypocrite. You didn't have any issue finding guns destined for South America."

"That may be, but I can't stop Bolivia and Paraguay from killing their own kids. However, I have a thing or two to say about Yanks going into the meat grinder. Even if your putsch failed, there's a good chance it'd result in a civil war. A man's life is his own and shouldn't be thrown away over some mindless slogan or a stupid flag. The world doesn't need any more Francis Haskells."

"That's right, father," Cornelia said, her voice sharper than a knife. "What you did to poor Francis—"

Max cut her off with a laugh. "Drop the act, lady."

"Act?" She almost pouted. "What do you mean?"

A haunting shame lowered Haskell's head, a man confronting his past sins. His daughter, however, exuded a frustrated irritation, a petulant child whose plans had been spoiled.

"Snakes and spiders have more warmth than you Haskells," Max said. "The only thing you two love is money. Not that I don't sympathize, but even my greed has limits. But Little Orphan Annie here puts us both to shame, Haskell."

"What do you mean?" he asked.

"Just that, like most crimes, cash was at the heart of all this. Let me back up."

Max took a few steps around the office, relocating himself underneath the Civil War painting, just in case Jeeves appeared with a gun in his back. A longshot, but he'd read enough pulps to never underestimate the butler. Haskell ran bony hands through his silver hair, a man on the brink, while Cornelia looked ready to throw a hissy fit. But up above, Lucius Haskell's portrait gazed down, a captive audience.

"Pardon me, Mr. Haskell, but you raised a spoiled brat for a daughter. Preening, deceitful, and above all, greedy. A woman accustomed to the finer things in life. Sure, she has a few passions, acting for one, but I have a hunch you put a stop to her budding career."

"He said Broadway was 'beneath a Haskell,'" Cornelia sneered.

Max shrugged. "What else did she have in life, except money? Or rather, men's money. She might be a bird in a gold cage, but as long as it was 14 karat, it didn't bother her too much. But then, Francis Haskell shows up, a mass of shredded flesh, and her good life was threatened. After all, you and your wife were going to spend every penny you had to try and restore Francis to something resembling a human."

Behind his desk, Haskell slumped in his seat, but didn't reply.

"Cornelia didn't want the family fortune to be spent on someone else, especially someone who might take half her inheritance, so she whispered evil thoughts into daddy's ears.

After all, 'why put a mask on a madman?' Well, you allowed yourself to be persuaded, and locked your own son away, alone and forgotten. Didn't sit well with your wife, who killed herself to escape this family. Can't say I blame her."

Haskell stooped a little more.

"So, all was hotsy-totsy for a while. Cornelia Haskell settled into her role as a society woman, but then you introduced her to Richard Osborn. Of course, you knew Osborn was a fairy, but it didn't bother you, did it Mr. Haskell? He was the perfect son-in-law. Not only was he connected with the Army brass, he was a more fitting heir than Francis ever was."

Elbows on the desk now, Haskell rested his forehead against tented fingers.

"But then Richard goes to Europe and returns with dreams of becoming the American Mussolini. You balk at such fantasies until Roosevelt goes off the gold standard and the New Deal gets workers chattering about unions and higher wagers. Your rich friends panic. Now, a private Fascist militia sounds like a good way to keep labor disciplined. And that's all it was at first, Strikebreakers Inc. Your son-in-law though, he's got big plans for a Fascist America. But you dismiss them all as crackpot fantasies. However, Roosevelt's New Deal soon gall your rich friends more and more. Congress passes an arms embargo. And Senator Nye declares war on the Merchants of Death. You realize, Mr. Haskell, that something drastic needs to be done. And lucky for you, Richard Osborn has a plan to seize power, just like his idol in Italy. Sound about right?"

Haskell's scrawny frame sagged, like a puppet whose strings were being cut.

"At first, Al Smith and the others just want to win big in the midterms, so they create the Liberty League. But you start planning your contingency putsch, secretly financed by the Liberty League big shots. However, when it becomes clear the election is going to be a Democratic rout, Du Pont and the others give you the go ahead for a coup. Providing General MacArthur agrees to it, that is."

Across the room, Cornelia glared back with cruel amusement, her earlier tantrum squelched.

"Of course, this all doesn't sit well with your daughter, who knows your company is on thin ice. For years now, Haskell Munitions has been losing money. Sure, the contracts with Bolivia helped stave off the bleeding, along with the shares purchased by Du Pont. However, Cornelia was worried that you were spending all your money, *her inheritance*, on her husband's Fascist boy's club, especially since it has no shot of winning any election. They didn't even run in the midterms, after all. Of course, she didn't realize you and the Liberty League were planning a putsch."

Haskell buried himself into his palms as Max continued.

"So, what does she do? Sabotage you from the inside, of course."

Mocking laughter pealed from Cornelia. "And wind up in a Hooverville? Why would I do that, Dietrich?"

"Unless she's working on behalf of someone else," Haskell suggested. "Like Senator Nye?"

"No, she's just trying to rile you," Max said. "She's not working for Nye, Dickstein, or any other politician."

"Then who?" he demanded.

"Isn't it obvious?" Max allowed himself a grin. "Mr. Haskell, you've been so fixated on Nye, that you ignored the wolf right outside your door. Vickers-Armstrongs."

Haskell's lips compressed to a thin line, but a single, strained word squeaked out. "Vickers?"

"Richard suspected them too, but for the wrong reasons. Only just now did I put the pieces together. Think about it, Haskell. Didn't they try and buy you out, right after your factory closed? They've always wanted you out of business."

Haskell looked ready to melt in his chair.

"So, the way I figure it," Max went on, "a few months ago, Cornelia approached Vickers and told them all about your secret contract with Bolivia. Your daughter told me that the arms industry is incestuous, but only when you whet appetites for the big boys. Instead, you went behind their backs. According to Teagle, they're mighty sore at you for undercutting them with cheap, second hand junk.

"But here's where shrewd little Cornelia offered Vickers a deal. In exchange for a tidy sum, she'd sabotage your entire organization from the inside. She knew that if just one sale was disrupted, your shaky business would collapse like a house of straw. So, she sniffs around Broadway, hires a second-rate Cuban actor to masquerade as a Paraguayan officer and a go between with that bugsy Red, Mike Rafferty. Only a devotee of Shakespeare could concoct a plot this melodramatic.

"But then I uncovered your plans for a putsch, so Cornelia hired me to stop it. Not that she gave a hoot about democracy or America, but she knew that you invested everything in this last roll of the dice. And if it came up snake eyes, you and your company would be sunk. A win-win for her and Vickers. Much simpler than hiring trigger-happy Communists to swipe guns."

Silence filled the room like poison gas, punctured by an occasional belch of the stock ticker.

"Is this true, Cornelia?" Haskell asked, voice frail.

She didn't respond, instead sliding a delicate hand inside her side pocket, withdrawing a single, gleaming bullet. Striding across the office, Cornelia stood erect before her father, as if in a boardroom meeting.

"You might have married me off to that pansy, but I draw the line at the poorhouse." She set the bullet next to the desk globe. "This is one way out, father. The other is through Senator Nye and his committee. Through swarms of reporters. Through complete and total disgrace of the Haskell name. And the Liberty League will sip champagne while the wolves rip you apart. Make your choice."

She spun around and marched out. Haskell stared at the bullet, his gray eyes, now hollow and washed out, slid back and forth between it, and the automatic. A lifetime of schemes, double-dealing, and intrigue had all come down to a single bullet. The wheels were turning. A desperate man was capable of anything, and Max didn't want to see what he chose.

He turned and followed Cornelia out into the sitting room, closing the door behind him. Sucking on a cigarette, she greeted him with a wry smile.

"I'm impressed, Dietrich. Guess I'm not as good an actress as I thought."

"Quite a cynical move. Playing Francis like your ace."

She shrugged. "I figured as a veteran, you'd be sympathetic to his condition. You'd backed me into a corner with your accusations, but I'm quite adaptable."

"You fooled me for a while, but I still had doubts where all your money came from. Once Osborn said he'd cut off your allowance, Vickers was the prime candidate, thanks to what Teagle said to your father." He grinned. "Pretty sneaky, trying to get me to kill Daddy Warbucks. I go to jail and you take your inheritance and run?"

"We could have framed it as self-defense," she said through a cloud of smoke. "I'd have told the cops it was over a business dispute. But suicide was a contingency I prepared for."

"Not a bad haul. How much did Vickers pay you for all this?"

She blew out a long smoke ring. "Enough. But I wanted something more valuable from them."

"Oh?"

"A job." Her lips curled into a malevolent grin. "I'll never depend on a man, any man, ever again for money. I'll be their first armaments saleswoman, the true American Zaharoff. So long as men rule the world there will be war, whether they're Fascists, Democrats, or Communists. Why can't a girl make a little money off you boys and your insatiable bloodlust?"

Max nodded along, taking it all in. Forget Francis, Richard, Norris – this ice queen was Haskell's true heir and legacy. A new generation of death merchants was blooming, far more ruthless than their forefathers. And their new line of products? Why, they'd make rifles, high explosives, and machine guns look like Tinkertoys.

A deafening gunshot blared out of the office, like concentrated thunder. Max and Cornelia raced inside, where Elias Haskell slumped over his desk, a skeletal hand wrapped around the smoking Browning. Trails of gore oozed off the chirping stock ticker. Blood leaked from his temple in slow, gushing pumps. At least this Merchant of Death could have an open-casket funeral, unlike his son.

Cornelia steadied herself with a deep drag, then crushed the cigarette beneath her high heel. Her hand slid down into her other pocket and – for a moment – Max reached for his revolver, but relaxed when she pulled out an envelope stuffed with bills.

"Five hundred in total," she said, handing it over. "You were never here."

Max couldn't argue with that. He pocketed the cash and headed toward the door, but called out, "Just curious, once you collect your inheritance, do you plan on staying in New York, or relocating?"

"I'll go wherever Vickers sends me. War is an international sport, after all."

"Too true. But if I were you, I'd ask for a permanent assignment overseas."

"Why?"

"Don't stay too close to the Liberty League. After all, you were the one who ruined their putsch. You'd better hope they don't find out who hired me to spy on them."

She snorted a laugh. "*You* killed Richard and Norris—"

"Wrong. Rafferty's corpse is still there. Even the slowest New York bull can piece that one together."

"But, they'll…they'll blame you…"

"And I'll spill the beans. About everything. So you'd better hope they don't get wise."

Fear rippled across her lip, as if this poor little rich girl had finally realized the weight of her actions. "But…but…you—"

"Me? I was never here," Max said, closing the door behind him.

CHAPTER SIXTY-FIVE

Mickey Mouse loomed over New York City, floating like a wraith down Broadway. The Three Little Pigs followed, trailed close behind by the Big Bad Wolf until a damp gust of wind blew him back a little. Macy's Thanksgiving Day parade and its giant balloons always drew crowds, but half of New York City thronged Broadway this morning. Max couldn't blame them, since it was free entertainment. But the route blocked Horn & Hardart, and his chance at a hot Thanksgiving meal and a slice of pumpkin pie.

But then again, with the cash he'd netted, he could afford something a little ritzier. Katz's Deli? Port Arthur? Maybe even Delmonico's for a steak dinner. Gray clouds hung above the city, but no rain fell, allowing the parade to march on unencumbered. Children squealed and cheered as Mickey passed them, then booed and hissed as the Big Bad Wolf floated by. Adorable, but insufferable. It was too early for this noise.

Max spun around and traipsed back toward his office, eyeing a sewer grate across the street. A few weeks ago, he'd stuffed the snubnosed Detective Special down there, just in case the Police Department traced the bullet lodged in Compton back to him. A shame, since it was an ideal pistol. But with the money leftover, he could buy himself a brand new one as an early Christmas present.

He paused in front of the magazine kiosk, admiring the row of pulp magazines – *G-8 and His Battle Aces*, *The Spider*, *Weird Tales*, and *Operator #5* all looked enticing, but an issue of *The Phantom Detective – The Tomb of Death* – with a sinister Chinaman, caught his attention. A quarter bought him the pulp and the morning edition of *The New York Times*, with a nickel left over.

Entering his office building, Max checked his mail. For the first time in months, overdue bills had stopped as if it were like old times. Who knew when his next case would be, but for now, he'd enjoy the good life for a little while longer. Sitting down at his desk, he plugged in the percolator, and dove into all the news that was fit to print.

Buried toward the back was an article dedicated to the so-called "Business Plot." After discovering the massacred bodies of Richard Osborn, Nathaniel Norris, and their men, the New York Police Department had issued a statement that two radicals – Michael Rafferty and Edward Gardner – were responsible. Thousands of weapons were confiscated, but since the warehouse belonged to the late Elias Haskell, notorious arms merchant, it was to be excepted. An open and shut case. Without their beloved chief and funding from Haskell, the National Crusaders had disbanded, their revolution ending like a wet firecracker.

But, the article went on, rumors that the Khaki Shirts had been planning a coup d'état refused to disappear. Max had secretly leaked choice information about this Business Plot to key members of the press, kicking up such a firestorm of controversy, that even Congressman Samuel Dickstein promised his committee would look into it. A lofty goal, Max admitted, but any accountability from the Liberty League was doubtful. Roosevelt needed these modern Robber Barons to rejuvenate the economy and end the depression, regardless of whether they attempted to overthrow him.

The New York Times dismissed rumors of a coup as a "cocktail putsch," fanciful slander against the late Elias Haskell. General MacArthur denied it completely, probably secretly relieved it had failed, despite his reputation as a Roosevelt hater. The article wrapped up by saying that after Cornelia Osborn had collected her father's inheritance, she'd sold off the remaining assets of Haskell Munitions to Vickers-Armstrongs. Du Pont followed suit, liquidating its shares of the defunct company, leaving hundreds unemployed. Mrs. Osborn, the article elaborated, now a grieving widow, had relocated to Britain, coincidentally the headquarters of Vickers.

Senator Gerald Nye crowed about Haskell's demise, declaring that "those who live by the sword, die by the sword." But, he added, the end of Haskell Munitions was only brought about by the leviathan of Vickers swallowing a minnow. Nye blustered that his "crusade against the Merchants of Death will continue until the entire arms industry accounts for its sins!"

Fat chance but it made for great publicity. Max flipped back to the front page. Baby Face Nelson's recent death by Federal agents dominated the headline, but an article beneath the fold caught his eye. "*President Ousted by Coup in Bolivia.*" Apparently, two days earlier, Bolivian President Daniel Salamanca had been deposed by in his own generals in a bloodless putsch, replaced by Vice-President Tejada Sorzano. The generals blamed Salamanca's weakness on their recent defeats, but now they hoped to bring the Chaco War to a victorious conclusion.

"But then again," the article concluded, "these coups are a staple of South American politics. We should be grateful that such intrigue doesn't happen in the United States."

Max folded the newspaper and tossed it aside. He poured himself a cup of coffee, cracked open *The Phantom Detective*, and escaped the world for a few hours.

Afterword

An American Putsch has many inspirations, both in historical fact and the pulp detective genre of the 1920s and 1930s, which are some of my favorite books to this day. Max Dietrich is my own take on the private detectives of American pulp fiction, from Sam Spade to Mike Hammer, fused with the wry cynicism of the 1930s. Most characters in the book are entirely fictional, but there was a forgotten chapter in American history which formed the main story.

This novel was inspired by the so-called Business Plot, also called the Wall Street Putsch, an alleged conspiracy to install a Fascist dictatorship in America. A concise account of this coup is as follows. In 1933, retired US Marine Corps general Smedley Butler was visited by a bond salesman, Gerald MacGuire who urged him to run for leadership of the American Legion, a veterans organization. MacGuire provided Butler with a speech, urging the reinstatement of the gold standard, which President Roosevelt had abandoned earlier that year.

Butler refused but met with MacGuire again in August 1934, with a new proposal – to lead an army of half a million veterans to use as a "bluff" against the government into installing a dictatorship. The plan was roughly similar to how it's presented in *An American Putsch.* It would have seen Butler leading a "superorganization" of five hundred thousand veterans, modeled after France's Croix-de-Feu and Italy's Black Shirts. How exactly this superorganization was to be raised wasn't made clear. Although, there is strong speculation that the American Legion was to be its nucleus. In my novel, the National Crusaders serves as a stand-in, albeit much more overtly Fascist.

Neither was the details for the putsch itself specified, though some speculate that Butler was to march this superorganization into Washington DC and bluff President Roosevelt into appointing him as the first secretary of general affairs. Thus, General Smeldey Butler would become de facto dictator of America and Roosevelt would be reduced to a ceremonial figurehead.

This was parodied in a Time magazine article from December 1934 titled *Plot Without Plotters* in which Butler leads a march on Washington on a white horse, followed by the superorganization and wealthy backers like John P. Morgan and General MacArthur. The article is very tongue-in-cheek, illustrating how dismissive the press was of the Business Plot. When crafting my novel, I imagined how the plotters would build this superorganization, with CCC camps and Hoovervilles being the likeliest candidates.

The key difference between Smedley Butler and the fictional Nathaniel Norris, is that Butler was no Fascist (he didn't hate Jews either) and had no intention of following through with the plot. He was only chosen due to his popularity among veterans, in part for his fiery support of the 1932 Bonus March. In fact, Butler was highly critical of big business and the arms industry in particular.

Correctly assuming that MacGuire was an intermediary for a larger group, Butler strung him along until he was able to glean as much information as possible. In November 1934, Butler went public and exposed the alleged plot.

The main intriguers were the American Liberty League, a conservative organization formed in August 1934 to defeat President Roosevelt. It was comprised of some of the wealthiest men in the country who were to finance the plot. Some of the alleged plotters included Irénée Du Pont, Robert Sterling Clark, and Al Smith. According to Butler, they wanted America to go back on the gold standard, and to dismantle the New Deal, which they felt was leading to Communism. Only Fascism, they believed, could rescue America from the Great Depression and discipline the workforce.

Strange as it is to believe, even General Douglas MacArthur was named as plotter. Some wanted him to lead the March on Washington, but he was deeply unpopular with large parts of the American people, given his harsh handling of the Bonus March. Roosevelt even called him one of the two most "dangerous men in America," the other being Huey Long. MacArthur seemed destined for obscurity but was reborn as an American hero during World War II.

Many newspapers dismissed Butler's story, but the McCormick-Dickstein Committee did launch an investigation, taking multiple testimonies – including Butler's and MacGuire's – and concluded that Butler was telling the truth. However, the financers of the plot were never called to testify, likely because of the scant evidence Butler provided. While Butler's allegations made a stir at the time, they soon faded into obscurity and were forgotten about. Even today, there is still debate as to how serious the plot was. Some allege it was on the verge of success, foiled only by Butler's selfless patriotism, whereas others insist it was a mere "cocktail putsch" which was nothing more than empty talk. The lack of details about the "superorganization" and how the coup would play out, suggest that, even if it was serious, the plot was in its infancy.

Smedley Butler would later go on to speak out against the arms industry in his 1935 book *War is a Racket* in which he described himself as "gangster for capitalism" due to the US Marine Corps involvement in the Banana Wars and interventions in China. Butler became a strong proponent of isolationism until his death in 1940.

Rather than rehash these events, I created a new fictional story, based on what would have happened if more overt Fascists were involved, along with the so-called Merchants of Death, and all wrapped up in a hardboiled mystery. For authoritative nonfiction accounts of the Business Plot, I recommend *The Plot to Seize the White House* by Jules Archer and *The Plots Against the President* by Sally Denton.

Like Nathaniel Norris, Richard Osborn and the National Crusaders are fictional, but America had a plethora of Fascist parties and would-be dictators in the 1930s. One in particular that's been forgotten about was the Sentinels of the Republic, which was funded by the American Liberty League and opposed the New Deal as "Jewish Communism." There was an actual Khaki Shirt group, led by Art J. Smith, a con artist and huckster, who planned his own March on Washington in 1933. This attempted coup ended in a dismal failure as only forty-four Khaki Shirts showed up. Needless to say, Smith's group and my fictional National Crusaders don't share many similarities other than the name "Khaki Shirts." There were many other Fascist parties such as the Silver Legion, Friends of the New Germany (forerunner to the German-American Bund), the Black Legion, and many smaller groups too numerous to count.

Added to that were the popular demagogues, such as Father Coughlin and Huey Long, a Fascist or a Communist, depending on whom you asked. Sinclair Lewis so feared encroaching Fascism that he wrote *It Can't Happen Here* in 1935, where a Huey Long-inspired strongman is elected dictator of America. Richard Osborn's fictional National Crusaders represents a unique form of American Fascism, one bearing bald eagles instead of swastikas, and although small, is more seductive to the American psyche.

Elias Haskell is entirely fictional, but he represents the Merchants of Death, which were widely despised in the Interwar Era, thanks in part to the March 1934 *Fortune* magazine article "Arms and the Men." The contents of the article were expressed accurately, although I swapped the Remington Arms Company out with Haskell Munitions. Indeed, Remington was suggested as the arms dealer that would supply Butler's superorganization with weapons for the coup.

"Arms and the Men" inspired Senator Gerald Nye to launch the Special Committee on Investigation of the Munitions Industry, which aimed to expose the conspiracies of arms dealers who allegedly started wars for profit. Most notably, it tried to draw a connection between the munitions industry and America's entry into the First World War, but ultimately failed.

The *Fortune* article unleashed a wave of hatred against the munitions industry, such as the 1934 nonfiction book *The Merchants of Death* by H. C. Engelbrecht. Added to that were numerous fictional accounts where arms dealers were portrayed as villains, instigating wars for profits. The Nye Committee helped birth the four Neutrality Acts of the 1930s, along with a deep sense of isolationism in the American public. Indeed, on the day of the Pearl Harbor attack, Senator Nye was delivering a speech in Pittsburgh, demanding America stay out of the war.

The Business Plot was a propaganda godsend for the Communist Party USA, which published lurid exposes in their magazine *New Masses*. The threat of Fascism, coupled with the hardships of the Great Depression, ballooned their membership in the 1930s, the zenith of Communist popularity in America. Susan Partridge is fictional, but the other Communists like Earl Browder were real figures and fixtures in New York City's fringe political scene.

The Chaco War (1932-1935) was another historical event that's been forgotten in the decades since. Paraguay and Bolivia fought a brutal three-year conflict over the Gran Chaco region, each side financed by oil companies – Shell backed Paraguay, while Standard Oil supported Bolivia. Paraguay won most of the battles, but a negotiated peace occurred in 1935. In the end, the Gran Chaco had no oil reserves, and the war was for naught, costing some 200,000 dead on both sides.

Thank You

Thank you for reading *An American Putsch*. If you would like to see more Max Dietrich novels, please let me know!

Also, if you enjoyed this book, please leave a review on Amazon! Positive reviews from readers like you are absolutely essential for authors to survive in today's marketplace.

Travel back to 1930s Japan with the Reiko Watanabe/Inspector Aizawa series in *Shadows of Tokyo*, *Smoke Over Tokyo*, and *Treason in Tokyo*. Also, sign up to my mailing list and receive the free prequel, *Conspiracy in Tokyo*!

Also check out *Shanghai Twilight*, Book 1 of the Tom Lai series, set in 1932 Shanghai as war looms between Japan and China.

Thanks!

About the Author

Matthew Legare has always loved reading, writing, and history. He's combined his passions to tell stories set during little-known, but fascinating, events of the past. His style is a smooth blend of old pulp magazines and contemporary thrillers, which makes for a pulsating read.

Matthew would love to hear from his readers! Please contact him at:

Website: www.matthewlegare.com

Twitter: @mlegareauthor

Printed in Great Britain
by Amazon

52767646R00182